The Animals at Lockwood Manor

Jane Healey studied English Literature at Warwick University. She has been shortlisted for the Bristol Short Story Prize 2013, the Costa Short Story Award 2014, the Commonwealth Short Story Prize 2016 and the Penguin Random House WriteNow mentoring programme 2017. *The Animals at Lockwood Manor* is her first novel. She lives in Edinburgh.

The Animals *at* Lockwood Manor

JANE HEALEY

MANTLE

First published 2020 by Mantle
an imprint of Pan Macmillan
The Smithson, 6 Briset Street, London EC1M 5NR
Associated companies throughout the world
www.panmacmillan.com

ISBN 978-1-5290-1418-1

1 3 5 7 9 8 6 4 2

A CIP catalogue record for this book is available from the British Library.

Typeset by Palimpsest Book Production Ltd, Falkirk, Stirlingshire
Printed and bound by CPI Group (UK) Ltd, Croydon, CR0 4YY

Visit **www.panmacmillan.com** to read more about all our books
and to buy them. You will also find features, author interviews and
news of any author events, and you can sign up for e-newsletters
so that you're always first to hear about our new releases.

She herself is a haunted house.

Angela Carter, 'The Lady of the House of Love'

Prologue

Large houses are difficult to keep an eye on, to control, my mother used to tell me, looking fraught and harried, before bustling out of the room to find the housekeeper or the butler or the tweeny maid to demand a full reckoning of what was happening in the far corners of the house. Lockwood Manor had four floors, six sets of stairs, and ninety-two rooms, and she wanted to know what was happening in each of them, at all times.

It was the not knowing that seemed to concern her most, but she had a long list of specific fears too: mould that squatted behind large pieces of furniture; rotten window frames that let in an unwholesome breeze; mice that had gnawed a home in a sofa; loose floorboards whose nails had pricked their way free in the heat or the cold; wires that sparked and spat; birds that had nested in a wardrobe in some forgotten servant's room, scratching the walls with their claws; damp that had bled through a gap in the roof tiling; a carpet that was being feasted upon by hungry moths; pipes that rattled their way to bursting; and a silt flood that slithered ever closer to the basement.

For my grandmother, who had grown up in the time when every task had a servant assigned to it, when calling for tea necessitated the manoeuvring of a veritable regiment, it was the servants she suspected. They were lazy, slapdash in their work, *prone to stealing; they spent their time idling and daydreaming and making mischief. She wore a vast selection of pale gloves, neatly pressed by her own personal maid, ever ready to sweep a pointed finger along a mantelpiece or a shelf, and if she found the merest whisper of dust she would summon the housekeeper. Because my grandmother was also of an age where the lady of the house did not deign to speak to any servants but the house-keeper, the poor woman was forever being called away from her tasks to rush through the back corridors of the house and appear in front of Lady Lockwood as if from the ether.*

There was thus relief felt amongst the servants when my mother and grandmother died a few months back in a single awful motor car accident, and I did not begrudge them it; I knew what harsh taskmasters these two women had been, and besides, I had seen the servants weep dearly at their funeral, so I knew they also cared. I swore that I would not share my relatives' habit of making impossible demands on the servants, and yet my mother and grandmother's role – that of keeping an eye on the house, that of keeping it in mind – was one that I reluctantly took on my own shoulders, like the fur coats I was also left; scratchy, heavy things that bristled with the claws and teeth of the beasts that had been skinned to make them, and swamped my form completely.

Ever since I was a young child, I had suffered from attacks of nerves and a wild imagination that made sleep hard to come by. It was my favourite governess, the one who used to sing lullabies to me when I was a few years too old for them, who taught me a way of tricking my mind into sleep: I should picture myself walking through Lockwood Manor, she said, gliding through the rooms one by one, and count them as if I was counting sheep – and before I could finish even one floor, I would be asleep. It was a method that worked just as she said, although it did not succeed in removing the monstrous nightmares I suffered once I had fallen asleep – dreams of a beast hunting me and, sometimes, of a desperate search through the corridors of my home for a blue room in which I knew some horrible creature was trapped and scratching at the walls, a search which baffled me when I woke up, knowing that there was no such room at Lockwood.

But after my mother and grandmother passed away, it no longer felt like a simple counting game, a trick to help my mind ease into sleep; it took on a new and frantic urgency. I could not sleep until my mind had completed a full tour of the house, and if I made a mistake – if I forgot the buttery, or the bathroom on the second floor with its sink ripped out, or the housekeeper's bedroom with the narrow eaves – then everything was ruined and I was compelled to start again from the very beginning, my heart rabbiting in my chest, my back prickling with sweat.

Sometimes, though it was mad to think so, I felt that if I did not concentrate, if I did not count all the rooms and hold them all in my mind, everything that my mother had feared would occur, and more; that the very edges of the house would spin apart, that the walls would crack and crumble, that something truly terrible, something I could not even fathom, would happen.

Lockwood had too many empty rooms. They sat there, hushed and gaping, waiting for my mind to fill them with horrors – spectres and shadows and strange creeping creatures. And sometimes what was already there was frightening enough: empty chairs; the hulk of a hollow wardrobe; a painting that slid off the wall of its own accord and shattered on the floor; the billowing of a curtain in a stray gust of wind; a light bulb that flickered like a message from the beyond. Empty rooms hold the possibility of people lurking inside them – truants, intruders, spirits. And when there is enough space for one's mind to wander, one can imagine that loved ones are not dead, but only waiting in a room out of the way, a room you forgot you had, and the urge to search for them, to haunt the corridors and the rooms of your house until you find them, becomes overwhelming.

But there was respite on the horizon, because the house would not be empty for long, and myself and my father and the servants – not that we had many by this stage, for we seemed to find them hard to keep – would soon have company. For it was August, and trucks were on their way from London, evacuees from the coming war looking for shelter within the walls of Lockwood. A population feathered, furred, beaked, hooved, ruffed, clawed and taloned would soon lodge here, and when the rooms were occupied again, when they had a purpose, and were full to bursting, my mind would settle again, and the house would settle again. No more empty, echoing rooms; no more bad nerves; no more ghosts. I was sure of it.

Chapter One

The mammals were being evacuated. The foxes went first, in their cabinet with dust underneath so thick it was almost fur; next the jaguar with his toothy snarl; the collection of stoats, their bodies lovingly twisted into rictus shapes by the original taxidermist; the platypus in his box, who was first believed a hoax because of the strangeness of his features; the mastodon skull with the nasal hollow that once caused it to be mistaken for the Cyclops; and then the inky black panther, the melanistic Javan leopard, that had been my favourite since I first saw him as a child visiting the museum. I had taken great care tying him up in sacking and rope so that he would not be disturbed on the trip north, stroked his broad nose as if to reassure us both.

The animals and the fossils, the specimens of this fine natural history museum, were being dispersed across the country, each department bound for a different location, to save them from the threat of German bombs in London. The mammals were being evacuated to Lockwood Manor and I was accompanying them as assistant keeper, a position I had reached after a rapid series of promotions due to two senior male members of staff enlisting. I would be in charge there, the de facto director of my own small museum.

It was a position I might have thought forever beyond me only a year ago, when I had made one of those stupid human mistakes that threaten to undo everything you have ever worked towards in one fell swoop. I had been in one of the workrooms under the museum galleries late one afternoon, copying some faded labels for a collection of rodents that had been amassed during the journeys of an eminent evolutionary theorist and which thus had historical as well as scientific importance. I also had the only fossil of an extinct horse species out next to them, ready to clean after I had finished the labels. I had skipped lunch that day, but then that was not out of the ordinary – I was often so fixated on my work that I forgot to eat the sandwiches I brought with me – and I was wearing an older, tired pair of shoes because my usual pair was being reheeled.

I had slipped as I returned from retrieving more ink, my leg buckling and my shoe skidding on a wooden floor polished by many years of footsteps, and I had knocked both the fossil and the two trays of rodents onto the floor and bashed my forehead on the table edge. But I cared not a jot for any injury I might have sustained as I stared in utter horror at the mess of specimens and labels – I had unpinned the latter from the box so that I could look more closely at them, and now that they were separated from their specimens, the collection had been rendered almost useless. And then there was the shattered fossil. The other occupant of the room, a fellow mammal worker named John Vaughan who was the very last person I would wish as an audience for such an embarrassment because he was forever fond of making snide comments with prurient undertones about my being female, watched with a dark kind of smirk on his face.

What made my accident worse, as I was reminded during

my interview the next day – and the particular tone used by Dr Farthing, the head of the department, when he said *accident* made it seem anything but – was that an American visitor was due to arrive any day to study the very fossil I had broken, a scientist who was as rich as those gentlemanly Victorian scientists of old and who the museum had been hoping to woo as a donor.

I had escaped with a reprimand that day – it would have been hard to fire me from my position since the museum was part of the civil service – but despite my exemplary work on every occasion bar that one disastrous afternoon, I knew that any slim chance of promotion had vanished. It was only the arrival of the war, the enlistment of Dr Farthing, and the anticipated conscription of the majority of the male members of staff (added to the fact that my wages as a woman were lower than a man's, and the civil service was keener than ever on penny-pinching) that found me in the position of assistant keeper of the evacuated collection. But as Mr Vaughan had personally reminded me, before he left to join the Navy as his forebears had done during the last war, once this war was over things would be very different: *They'll have you back with the volunteers in no time, just you wait,* were his exact words, by which he meant, *back with the other women.* There were only a handful of women on the permanent staff, and myself and Helen Winters were the only two who were not junior members. The rest of the women who worked for the museum – who prepared and assisted the mounting of specimens, who catalogued and copied and studied, who travelled and collected and made countless new small discoveries – were either 'unofficial workers' paid a measly one shilling an hour, or unpaid volunteers.

My directorship of the collection that was to be housed at

Lockwood Manor was thus not only the chance of a lifetime as a member of my sex, but also a vital opportunity to prove myself for what came after the war, when all the men came flooding back to their old positions.

Plans for the evacuation of the mammal collection had been in place from the first murmurs of war, even before I had first joined the museum years ago, and we had spent weeks packing everything up for the workmen to carry into the trucks. But the museum was too large to evacuate in its entirety, and we had had to decide which animals, dried plants, rocks, birds, and insects would be transported and which would be left to their fate. We played God all the time at the museum; we named and classified and put the natural world into an order of our own making – family, species, genus – now we would decide which of our specimens were precious enough to be saved.

Although the collection at Lockwood Manor was only supposed to include mammals, other creatures soon sneaked their way into the plans and onto the trucks. The telephone rang with calls from geologists and ornithologists already evacuated: could we please take the cabinet in room 204, could we fit in the box of nests from the Americas and the collection of ostrich eggs, the chunk of meteorite that was forgotten in the move, or the parrot stuffed by the venerable (and generous) Lady so-and-so? In the final week, items were still being found in corridors and misplaced rooms, their species hastily penned in handwritten addenda to the neatly typed lists we had previously prepared. And then at the last minute we had realized that we had one more truck to fill, and thus the workers carried out specimens from the entrance hall that were not at all rare in a hurried rush – the foxes, weasels, two tigers, a polar bear, a wolf, a lion, and even a plain brown rat.

*

How quickly the rooms emptied of their inhabitants. I had thought that the sight of their contents being whisked out of the museum would make me frightened of things to come, that the empty rooms would look like tombs ransacked by opportunist robbers, but truthfully I was so thankful to be heading away with the animals, to be employed still with the museum and part of the only happy family I had ever known, that I only felt excited at the change.

No one outside the museum knew that I was going away, for I did not have anyone to tell – apart from my landlady at the boarding house who did not care where I was off to, only that she needed to find someone to replace my rent.

I had a family once. My parents adopted me when I was very young and they were the only parents I had known. They were relatively wealthy, and old; their three sons had been killed in the Boer War and I was brought in as a kind of replacement, I suppose. But I was a disappointment to them; a disappointment to my mother.

After all I've done for her, she would say to her closer friends over tea or on the telephone. *Such a sulky child, her head always in a book, an ungrateful child.*

How was a child meant to be, how was a mother? These were not questions I thought of until much later and they still seem odd thoughts to ponder. My mother was strict with me, unhappy with me, and I received many punishments during my childhood. But surely children need to be punished to improve themselves, to learn how to behave, especially orphans like I was? *We do not know anything about your true parents,* one nurse had told me (for, like other children of the well-to-do, I was looked after by various nurses; some kind, some not), *so we must take great care to remove any possible influence.* That was the same nurse who used to make me sleep on the floor because my bed was, in her opinion, far too soft, who did not believe that children needed luncheon as it would make them too indulgent as adults, who made me write out Bible verses until my hand cramped.

The nurses who looked after me did so in separate rooms of the house, and thus it seemed that my mother occasionally forgot that I was there – although perhaps she did not, perhaps that is just a child's fairy-tale thought, for how could you forget you had adopted a daughter?

Once, when my nurse was sick, my mother had forgotten that I needed meals and shouted at me when I stole a couple of apples after feeling dizzy with hunger. When she did notice me, she often said that my face was *glum* and *peaky* and *ugly* – when in fact it was only a pale face that has never smiled very easily – and she beat me on the legs with the fire poker for it. She compared me often to her natural sons. *I could have left you there, I didn't have to adopt you*, she would say, and I could hear it in my mind even decades later, *so buck up*.

I remembered a telephone call from my mother when I was at Oxford studying zoology, and how excited she was at first. *I hear that Professor Lyle has taken a particular interest in you*, she said. *Yes, he's been encouraging my work on mammalian locomotion*, I replied innocently. *Oh, you stupid girl*, she had said after a gaping silence. *When your father and I allowed you to remain at university it was with the understanding that you at least find yourself a husband, however meagre his standing might be. I shall hear nothing more of this nonsense. Call me when you are engaged*, she had said, then hung up the telephone.

When my father died of old age, I came home to see her. She told me after the funeral, and after I had told her about my interest in someday working for a museum, that I was a spiteful girl. I was not allowed to use my full double-barrelled surname any more, she decided, I was renounced. *I do not want to be connected to you. You shall be Miss Cartwright from now on*, she said, hissing the 'Miss' aggressively. So I had been Miss Cartwright ever since, and though I might have wished to be *Professor* Cartwright, I had still achieved more than I had dared dream.

I became an adult with a strong sense of fairness, of right and wrong, and I was not cowed by my childhood despite it being as unhappy as I thought it might have been in comparison to others. Even if I had not yet found love, and often felt lonely or sometimes had to go to the bathroom and cry after a difficult encounter with a superior or a co-worker like Mr Vaughan, being dismissed by others only made me work harder to prove them wrong. I was prouder than anything of my work with the museum – at least I had been until my accident – and it was my dearest hope that my time at Lockwood would help restore that confidence.

I would not let one stupid mistake spoil everything, I swore, as I checked my office for anything I had forgotten before the next day's journey and folded my coat over an arm; I would not be the useless girl my mother had believed I was, and my time in the country would be my making.

When I had first heard the name Lockwood Manor I had imagined something out of Brontë – wide, rugged moors and a dark house full of secrets and barely restrained passion. But there were no moors in the Home Counties, and the house was owned by a major who had, according to the precise letters from his secretary, *spared no expense with the modernization of the manor*. I knew that if I had told my mother where I was going she would have looked up Major Lord Lockwood in *Who's Who* and then, finding out from her friends that he was

a recent widower, get desperately excited that I might catch
his eye. I had seen a photograph of him in a newspaper after
I asked a librarian if she could find me anything on the history
of the manor: he looked tanned and fit for his age and had a
crowd of lean hunting dogs at his feet. The article was about
his investments and imports from the Empire, his munitions
factories. But all that mattered to me was that he had promised
us space for the museum; lodgings for myself for the duration
of the war, and temporary accommodation for two other workers
from the museum – Helen Winters and David Brennan, who
expected to be conscripted soon – who would both be accompanying me initially and staying briefly to help make sure the
animals were settled; free range of the entire house; the assistance of his staff should we need it; and retired members of
his former regiment, who were too elderly to enlist, for guards.
The lovely grounds the house was situated in, the *estate*, would
only be a bonus.

The proctor turned off the lights in the museum with a chorus
of clicks and pings but it did not scare me; I had never been
frightened of the dark. The windows had been boarded up but
it seemed there was still light sneaking into the building somewhere, it was not quite pitch black. I stared at the great shape
of the mammoth skeleton, which in the darkness seemed to
be made of something darker and heavier than air, a silhouette
cut out of the afternoon. It was too large to evacuate and would
be surrounded by sandbags in the hope that it would remain
unscathed when the war was over.

When the war was over. Would I be much changed then, I
wondered, and what would the museum be like? How many
walls would still be standing?

Chapter Two

I arrived at Lockwood Manor with the kind of headache that came from sitting in a truck with poor suspension for many hours, while worrying about the cargo of the other trucks in our convoy, the animals muffled and blinded by sacking and rope, juddering and swaying and knocking against one another. It was a warm sunny day, but as we drove along the curving driveway around the front lawn, I could not say that the weather made the house look any more welcoming. Lockwood Manor had stood on this spot for many centuries but most of the house as it was had been built in the Jacobethan style in the nineteenth century. The stone used had dulled to a grey; narrow windows were set in a long, squat, uniform front bracketed by two round turrets, and a pierced parapet with pinnacles bristled against the sky.

I knew from the plans that I had studied that this front hid a more untidy rear, a newer extension to the kitchen on the ground floor of the east wing and, most importantly of all for the museum, the long gallery. This was a single-storeyed building that jutted out from the back of the west wing next to a private courtyard, and was Tudor in origin – once part of another building since lost to one of those catastrophic acts of destruction that seemingly happened to very old estates in this country. The long gallery had not been occupied for many years and would have enough room to house many of the museum's crates and cabinets without furniture needing to be moved or people displaced. Other museum pieces, especially the mounted animals that needed a closer watch for potential damage from atmosphere or pests, would be housed inside the main building, leaving only a few rooms solely for the Major and his daughter to live in. This was their chosen war sacrifice: where other owners of country houses would be preparing for evacuated children and babies, the Lockwoods would receive a quiet menagerie who would not race around or run their sticky fingers along the walls and wake the house with their cries.

I got out of the truck, dropping to the gravel driveway, the four storeys of the house looming high above me as if taking my measure. Major Lord Lockwood arrived at the main door with his crowd of dogs, as if he had appeared straight from the photograph that I had seen in the newspaper. The dogs swarmed down the stairs towards me and nudged at my legs. One of them started to growl before the Major called them off me, hitting the offending beast over its back with his stick. Another man with a pinched, folded face like a bulldog rushed down the stairs in a tweed jacket and led the dogs away. I straightened my suit.

The Major welcomed me to Lockwood Manor with an unenthusiastic handshake. 'We were expecting a Dr Farthing,' he said, 'but I hear he's left his post.'

'He's enlisted, yes,' I replied.

'Well.' He clapped his hands together and we sized each

other up. 'I'm sure you'll do just fine. Come along into the house now, they've started unpacking already.'

'They really should have waited for me,' I said, under my breath, as I followed him; this was not an auspicious start to my directorship.

Our path was blocked by a woman with white-blonde hair and a fur-ruffed cardigan. She was clearly leaving, carrying a rather large suitcase for her slim size, but it was not the suit-case that made me stare – it was the tear tracks down her anguished face and the dark patches on her scarf which implied earlier crying. Her breath hitched as she moved to the side for us to pass and, though she looked at the Major beseechingly, when she turned to regard me it was with such loathing that I felt a wash of shame, as if I had done something terrible to her, this woman I had never met before. She sniffed, her top lip curling, and wiped at her tears with a pale glove as I took a step back, and then she turned away with a furious puff of breath and continued down the front steps, struggling with her load.

'Come along now,' the Major admonished from the gloom of the hallway, clearing his throat impatiently.

I tried to brush off the lingering image of the woman's tears, of her hatred, as he led me through room after room of the house, which felt dark and close compared to the late summer's day outside. We started with the parlour and sitting room to the left of the entrance hall, which looked out across the front lawn and would house the Chiroptera and Insectivora that other keepers had begged us to take; then we crossed the hall to the smoking room next to the dining room, where the Marsupialia would live; next we turned right past the ballroom, with its walls of gilded mirrors in which I caught my harried reflection as I passed, and which would be kept empty of museum specimens because the Major wanted to host gatherings for the nearby regiment.

Next, we moved along the west corridor, which held the billiards room, the library, the morning room, the music room and the Major's mother's old sitting room, as well as the summer room, the writing room, which would hold bones related to the Cetacea; and then my office, which had been another parlour and which shared a wall with the Major's office and his own connected private library, both of which he declined to show me and which would be off limits.

Next to the Major's office there was a doorway that led to a corridor through which one could access the long gallery itself. This, as its name suggested, consisted of a long, wide corridor with teak walls and a low coffered ceiling, with a row of half a dozen rooms to either side that were linked together so that the corridor itself only had four doorways cut into its walls. The workmen were carrying boxes and crates along the corridor, and as we made our way through the rooms I was pleased by how full they looked, how many specimens we had been able to pre-emptively save.

We left the long gallery and went back into the main house and through to the entrance hall.

'Dr Farthing wanted to see the *other* rooms, so that he could know the architecture of the house and the evacuation routes, I think it was. The parlourmaid will show you those,' the Major said, waving me towards a young woman in starched grey and white.

Dr Farthing was renowned for being nosy, and had probably made this up in order to have a look round. We had a plan of the house back in London after all, made only a few years ago, so there were unlikely to be surprises. But I was quite thrilled at the chance to see the great backbone of a country house,

the engine taking up one ground-floor wing: the kitchen, scullery, flower room, brushing room, the stillrooms, three pantries,
the butler's room, the lamp rooms, the endless doors and
shelves and little anterooms, most of them with no window to
the outside; and the servants scuttling about carrying buckets
and cloths and trays and boxes. At some point in the tour, I
lost my sense of direction and could not tell whether I faced
south or north or was even in the same wing. The parlourmaid
brought me out into the grand entrance hall again by the same
door I had entered, even though I swore it was another, and
there the Major was talking to the man who had taken the
dogs away.

'Ah, tour went well?' the Major asked me.

'Fascinating,' I said, although by the slight creasing of his
face that was not quite the right word. Perhaps it gave away
too much my desire to snoop – which was clearly acceptable
from Dr Farthing, but less so from me.

'Shall we move to the drawing room?' he asked.

Once there, alongside the shrouded animals that had been
newly unloaded from the truck and awaited unwrapping, he
turned to me with hands on his hips.

'This is still a working estate, Mrs Cartwright – I hope that
won't be a problem, and that the museum and the house can
work harmoniously side by side.'

Obviously he had been put out by my interest in the servants'
quarters. Or perhaps he was hiding something. Was this a
veiled warning?

'It's Miss Cartwright,' I corrected, 'and I am confident there
shall be no problems at all. The museum is immensely thankful
for your generous offer to temporarily house the nation's most
valuable mammal collection while London is under threat, and
as the correspondence between Lockwood and the museum

has shown these past few years, I do believe our collaborative work will be exemplary.' I intended to bamboozle him with long words and flattery.

'Excellent,' he said, his hands stuffed into his pockets and his eyes already skimming to the door to get away from me. 'If you'll excuse me now, the housekeeper will find you shortly.' He spoke with the louche arrogance of the landed gentry.

Left alone in the drawing room, my eye was drawn to a glimmer of silver, and when I moved past the brocaded sofa, I found a strange sight. A worn kitchen knife had been stabbed an inch deep into the delicate veneer surface of a side table. The incongruity of the weathered knife in a room full of gilt and fine fabrics, and its upright position, as if it was even now being held by some ghostly hand, unnerved me and, without thinking, I tugged it from the table and then dropped it on its side with a clatter, the wood of its handle so worn it had felt soft in my palm. I moved back around the sofa and rubbed at my arms, where the hair had stood up.

'Hullo there,' a pleasant voice said from the door. 'Are you Miss Cartwright?'

'I am, yes.'

'Lady Lockwood, but you can call me Lucy,' the woman entering the room said, and I stuck my hand out only for her to move to kiss my cheek instead. She smelled of a perfume so light I knew it was expensive, and had remarkably short black hair, only a few inches long. It was shorter than a boy's but brushed and pinned carefully as if to hide its length. A *fever haircut*, I thought to myself, *like something out of Austen*. Or perhaps she had had an accident with curlers? Rich people were allowed to be eccentric and have silly haircuts, I supposed. She had dark eyes with tired bruises underneath that could be seen through the pale powder she was using, freckles across both cheeks, a square jaw and perfectly applied red lipstick. She was one of those beautiful women made all the more lovely by her flaws – the little nick of a scar on her chin, the left ear that jutted out slightly more than the right – and something about seeing her here in the sedate surroundings of the house surprised me, as if I had not expected to meet her, but one does not know who one is to encounter for the first time on any given day, so I did not know why I felt this strange resonation.

'Now, here's a sheet with mealtimes and other information like laundry,' she said as I gathered my wits again, 'and keys to the museum's rooms and to the long gallery. This is a key to the main door of the house; I wanted you to have one on the very odd occasion when no one is manning it, or if there's an emergency or something.' She handed me a great big heavy thing and I slipped it and the other keys into the pocket of my jacket, feeling their weight against my side.

In the correspondence from the Major and his secretary, he had mentioned that his daughter might be able to help while we were at Lockwood, but in what capacity had been left vague. I had gathered the impression that she was either very young or some society beauty being whisked to and fro by a driver, so would have little time for the museum. I could see now that she was about my age, and seemed very enthusiastic. I wondered if Lord Lockwood was simply one of those men who did not want his own daughter to work.

She looked up from her list and paused, the polite smile fading into seriousness.

'Forgive me,' she said, 'but you looked shaken for a moment when I walked in; are you all right?' she asked, lightly touching my arm.

'Oh, it's nothing.' I shook my head but she was watching

me so intently that I felt I should say something. 'I was walking around the room and I put my hand out for balance and almost cut myself on the knife on the side table over there,' I said. 'I can be a bit clumsy sometimes, I'm afraid,' I added hurriedly, thinking that this was not the kind of pulled-together first impression I wanted to make.

'Oh, goodness me, what on earth is that doing in here?' she said, peering over at it with a puzzled frown. 'But are you all right?' she asked, taking my hand and turning it over, looking for a wound.

The slide of her fingers across my palm startled me and the earnestness of her search made me feel a sudden wave of tenderness towards her.

'Oh no, I didn't get hurt, I caught myself just in time.' It was silly to come up with a lie like that, but then it had been silly of me to tug the knife out too.

'Thank god,' she said and let my hand go. 'I can't think how someone misplaced that here; I'll let the housekeeper know. I hope it hasn't soured your arrival.'

'Oh, of course not,' I insisted. 'It's my own fault for not looking where I was going. You'd think someone that worked around so many sharp-toothed beasts would take more care.' It was an ineffectual joke but she laughed all the same, revealing dimples in her cheeks.

'Well,' she said, 'I do hope that you shall be very happy here at Lockwood Manor. It's such an honour to offer a home to the museum's mammal collection.'

'It's a truly magnificent house,' I said.

'It looks even more splendid with your animals inside, Miss Cartwright,' she said, touching my arm quickly. 'Now, we've put you in the east wing, in the red bedroom as it's called. I hope that's all right. It's a lovely cosy room with views over the front gardens. I used it myself a few times while convalescing as a child because it was closer to my nurse's room and, truthfully, I've never slept better.' She smiled tremulously at me.

I wanted to tell her that even a cupboard would do for me, that there was no need for such concern for the quality of my sleep. I was not used to being catered to in this manner; I was used to landladies who pursed their lips and sighed wearily if I asked for a leaking tap to be fixed and complained that I was too loud when I came in from work late.

'Please, call me Hetty,' I said.

'Lucy!' the Major called then, striding into the room. 'Ah, there you are, my dove,' he said. 'Cook wants your advice on the menus.'

'Father—'

'Come along,' he said, and swept his arm towards the door. 'The rooms are quite filling up with beasts,' he added, looking around with satisfaction as I watched Lucy leave. She smiled at me and the skin at the corners of her eyes crinkled.

'Are you getting Lucy excited?' the Major said, turning to me once she had gone. I could not quite grasp his tone. His enthusiasm had fallen away in a flash to reveal something hard and intelligent.

'I was just talking about the museum—'

'Because she is very delicate, Lucy. She is not to be troubled with too many difficulties or dramas. And with the loss of both her mother and grandmother a few months ago . . .' He paused. 'She's sensitive, you know. If there are any true problems you must come to me or to the housekeeper, or to my man, Jenkins.'

I guessed the latter was the bulldog-faced man in the hall earlier. 'Of course,' I replied.

We had foreseen awkward politics with the collection being here, with many of our discussions hinging around that

all-encompassing word 'diplomacy', but I was not expecting it to present itself in a manner quite like this. When we heard that the late Lady Lockwood and her mother-in-law had both passed away recently, there were questions about whether we should choose a different location, but after we sent a carefully worded letter to the Major saying thus, he had insisted that the museum still be housed at Lockwood Manor. The two women had died tragically in an evening car crash on a country road, quite horrible. I remembered that at one of our meetings, David – one of those brutish-looking rugger types who surprise with their hidden bookishness and encyclopaedic knowledge of detective stories – said he had asked a journalist friend about the crash and whether there were any suspects, and been told that the police had thought it an accident. I remembered it because the whole room had paused after he said it, none of us having assumed it was anything other than an accident originally. I hadn't given it much thought after that, my mind busy with the practicalities of the move, with my animals, but now that I was here, I found myself wondering about the late Lady Lockwood, Lucy's mother, and just what had happened that night.

A worker passing the door with his arms braced around a large frame called out for instructions, and I returned to the task at hand.

'That's a butterfly case; it goes with the others in the summer room. Just as we talked about,' I said, shortly, because I had pegged this particular worker for a troublemaker back in London. It was a motley crew anyway, with so many men having already enlisted.

When I turned again to the Major, the lightness was back in his eyes. 'I can see that you are eminently reasonable, Miss Cartwright, and I apologize for belabouring my point earlier.

Young women can be so flighty, you know, but I can tell you are of sensible stock. You'll be a good companion for Lucy, I think – she has been lonely these past few months with only me and the servants for company.'

'I shall do my best,' I replied, after a moment while I thought of what to say. Flighty women? Sensible stock? I sincerely hoped that things would indeed go smoothly here, and that he would not be one of those old bores who would not listen to a woman if his hair were on fire. Would he be paying me to be his daughter's companion, I wondered, a little absurdly, or would that be covered by my wages from the museum?

It was no matter. I was intrigued by Lucy in a way I could not quite explain and had felt welcomed by her far more heartily than any landlady previous. It would be rather nice to share a house with her and my animals and cabinets from London, instead of the drab loneliness of the lodging house in Kensington with its sour-faced inhabitants.

When I was a child, I had the frankly nonsensical habit of trying to classify those around me as animals, being generally more fond of them than people and, embarrassingly, it was not a habit I had been able to shake. I had only told someone about this occupation once before – a girl at my school called Constance who I said reminded me of a mongoose, and who told all the other girls that I was trying to insult her, when I really was not, and I was unable to claw my way back from that pariahdom. Lucy had been called a dove by her father but, as a mammal lover, I thought that she rather reminded me of a cat somehow, in her glamour and warm smiles – even though of course I knew that neither of these attributes had anything to do with a real *Felis catus*. Lord Lockwood though,

I had him pegged as a Bengal tiger, wearing his authority coolly, or perhaps a Eurasian wolf. And as for myself, sometimes I was a European badger, blundering around in the dark, and other times a golden mole: pale, solitary, industrious, and rather unenchanting.

As I walked along the long upstairs hall behind the young maid who was showing me to my assigned bedroom, I felt the rich carpet pull at my feet, a little like the way thick snow makes it hard to walk. My eyes could barely see to the end of the corridor, and I kept expecting a sudden mirrored wall to appear, and almost wanted to keep my hands out in front of me. The museum occupied the ground floors but no higher. On the floors above, there lived a handful of people and many empty rooms. We had already passed five empty bedrooms; three had their doors closed but I peeked in curiously at the other two as the maid named them – the first was the yellow room, dominated by a massive four-poster bed which had its curtains firmly pulled shut, and opposite that was the purple room, with a dizzying wallpaper and a mirror set just opposite the doorway that startled me when I thought my watery reflection was another unexpected guest.

There were rumours, the maid had said, nervously shifting away from the door, that this room was cursed, that guests who slept there had heard strange sounds at night.

'I should get back to the kitchens, ma'am,' she continued quickly. 'We're rushed off our feet at the moment. You can't miss your room; it's the only one in this wing with red wallpaper.' She bobbed and hurried away, disappearing into the alcove where a mammoth vase and giant spray of dried flowers disguised the doorway that led to the service stairs, put in place so that the servants could enter and leave the corridor without a trace of a footstep on the grand staircase.

The next pair of rooms I passed had their blackout curtains already closed and in the gloom I could see that each piece of furniture, chandeliers included, was shrouded with dustsheets, turning their recognizable shapes into strange, hulking objects. The room opposite mine had twin beds either side of the window, whose outside was crowded with ivy, and a loud clock sitting on the windowsill whose ticking I had heard from several rooms away. Beyond my room was a bathroom and two more empty – I assumed – bedrooms with their doors closed, and the shut-up turret rooms. I was the only one staying in the east wing – David and Helen would be in the west wing, and the Major's suite of rooms was in the round turret at the end of that long corridor.

I was not a superstitious person, not someone prone to whimsy aside from my classification game, and I liked facts far more than fiction, but there was undeniably something unsettling about a row of unoccupied rooms, like being the only guest in a hotel, or those moments when one is a child and one's house is so quiet one has the irrational thought that everyone has gone and left you behind.

As I reached my assigned room, the thought was banished when I saw a flicker of movement in the corner of my eye – this house was truly far from empty with its busy servants scurrying about.

I turned. There was a figure at the other end of the corridor. As many sconces as there were, the space was too large to light completely, and the figure was so far away I could not see their face or even tell their sex. Yet I knew that they were staring at me, and that there was something unfriendly about their posture, furious even. The corridor seemed to swell and stretch as I stood and stared back, and then they moved to the left and disappeared, a door slamming so loudly behind them that it made my shoulders jerk.

An angry figure, a weeping woman who hated me, a lord of the manor who warned me against exciting his fragile daughter, and talk of a cursed room. What kind of place was this? I stepped into my room and shut the door behind me. Every home, and every workplace, had its own human current simmering underneath, histories and grudges and idiosyncrasies; it was only that this was a rather grander setting for them, that's all. I would concentrate on my work, on the animals, as I had always done, and let the living occupants of Lockwood do as they may.

Chapter Three

In her last years, my mother grew unwell, the strange fits that she had suffered through all my life multiplying. She became suspicious of everyone, seeing enemies everywhere, and kept various sets of binoculars stationed around the house to use to peer out of windows and spy on the gardeners or any visitors, or else she hurried up and down the corridors of the house, whipping open doors as if she expected to find people lurking behind them. My grandmother was frail by then and ignored any suggestion that her daughter-in-law was unwell. There was only room for one mad occupant of Lockwood, according to her, and that was me – despite the fact that by that time I only had the occasional nightmare, and I was doing so well that I was thinking of leaving the manor for a life in London. A life all of my own away from the watchful eyes of my mother.

It was only in retrospect that I thought of how my mother seemed to get worse as I grew better, but when she was alive her concern for me was so smothering, her madness so frightening, that I was desperate to leave her behind, that I did not want there to be any connection between us beyond the fact of my birth.

Children can be cruel, my father bemoaned when he first heard of my plans. You give them everything and then they leave you with nothing. *He said it with a dramatic swoon, with a joking manner, but I knew that he hated the thought of me leaving, that I was precious to him.*

He had been the one to tell me that they had died, coming into the parlour where I sat listening to the wireless, jotting down some half-formed thoughts about my plans for the future, and I had not believed him. They were taking a trip to a friend's house for tea and they would be back later, I told him stubbornly as my pen fell from my grip and my notebook slid to the floor. They would be back soon, he shouldn't worry, I said, and he said, Oh, Lucy, it's only us left now, and the tears in his eyes brought a keen to my throat.

My plans were set aside, a curtain drawn over my vision of my future. My father needed me, the servants needed me, the house needed me. And besides, with my mother's and grand-mother's deaths, any improvement in my nerves had also been cruelly snatched away.

One day, about a week after the joint funeral, after the horror of seeing her coffin so small and narrow and thinking about her there inside, locked away from the world, I had looked in the mirror while I brushed my hair, with tears rolling down my cheeks, remembering my mother brushing it sometimes when I was a child and how back then, when I was small, she had more good days than bad; how, as I grew older, those happy days dwindled to rare afternoons and the rest of the time another mother took her place, a nervous, frightened creature. I had looked at my reflection, my dark eyes and dark hair, the particular bump on the bridge of my nose, and thought that I looked too much like my mother, that every time I saw my reflection again, I would think of her – how I loved her and tried to leave her, how I feared I would one day become her. And so I picked up a pair of scissors and sheared my hair off, close to the skull, ringlets and curls dropping around me like I was shedding a winter coat of fur.

My father had looked horrified when I emerged from my room newly shorn. He did not like my bad nerves, perhaps because they reminded him of my mother's, and, when he could, he pretended that my nightmares never happened. We all have bad dreams, *he would say*, there's no need to make more of them than that. *Still, that day when I emerged from my bedroom with my grief and madness plainly visible, he telephoned the Harley Street doctor he used to call out for my mother, because he did not trust local doctors not to gossip, and I was soon sedated and put to bed, with a pile of blankets over me so thick and heavy I felt as if my body was being pushed down towards the earth, as if I was halfway buried.*

But don't other cultures cut their hair in mourning? *I remembered thinking, as I lay there and the room spun around me, as my eyes burned from lack of sleep and my heart jumped in my chest as if it were trying to run away.* Wasn't this a normal response?

It was not the first time I had taken scissors to my own hair – for I had cut off a chunk of it on a dare when I was young, during the summer when my mother was on bedrest after what I later learned was a miscarriage, when I roamed the gardens half-feral with children from the village. It was Mary, the niece of Lockwood's cook, and her brother who were the wildest, along with another girl who dressed like a boy and begged her mother for a haircut like one too. In the summer months, our days were endless. We made dens in the woods and in the hedges, gorged on stolen unripe apples that made us sick, stripped off our clothes and swam in the lake, climbed trees and roofs, made up complicated sports with ever-expanding rules and took part in giggling kissing games. I did not always take part in the dares – to run for a hundred yards with one's eyes closed, to climb the rickety hut with its loose tiles, to jump from the topmost branch of the beech tree, to grip rose thorns in one's hands, to try and steal eggs from the chickens without the farmer noticing – but I did that day we used gardening shears to cut off pieces of our hair, because I had had enough of Mary jeering at me for being pretty and vain.

I hadn't known what to do with the thick lock of hair once I had cut it. The others threw theirs at each other, or into the bushes, but I felt anxious about letting it go, as if it was still a part of me, even though it had been separated. If I threw it away there in the gardens, the birds would pick it up and use it for their nests, and the idea of that, of naked, wrinkly hatchlings curled up in my hair, disturbed me. Instead, I kept it clutched in my fist until it became damp with perspiration and, when the day's excitement finished, I took it back inside and hid it in the drawer of my childhood dressing table.

My mother had found it after summer was over, my forgotten curl of hair, when she had come into my room to wake me from a nap for dinner.

I woke to her asking for my hairbrush and the sound of the drawer opening and then she let out a fearful gasp that had me sitting up in bed, clutching the blankets.

'What is this?' she asked, holding the hair up as if it was dangerous. 'Is this yours? What are you doing with it? You know you have to be careful,' she said, her voice cracking. 'She can make a spell with this; she can use it against you. Haven't I told you to be careful of her, of la diablesse, of the woman in white and her beasts?'

It wasn't the first I had heard of her, the devil woman, the *ghost, the spirit that my mother said was haunting her, haunting us. When she had first told me about her, we had been playing a game of hide and seek – for as much as my mother could be distant when her nerves were bad, when she was well she could also be light-hearted, eager to see the world through a child's eyes again, as if we were playmates and not mother and daughter. She had hidden while I covered my eyes and counted and when I came searching and opened the last door in the corridor, that of the purple bedroom, expecting to find her waiting on the other side of the door, for her to smile delightedly and take me in her arms as if she had found me and not the other way round –* There she is, *she would always say.* My very own girl, my looking-glass girl *– I found her glancing around at the room as if in a trance.*

'It was here,' she said. 'This was where I first saw her.'

'Saw who?'

'The woman in white,' she said, her voice thin. 'I had dreamed of her as a child, out there in the forest beyond our home, waiting for me, hunting me with her beasts.' She'd folded her arms in front of her chest as if trying to protect herself. 'She was haunting me,' she said, 'and I was desperate to leave, to get away from her, and your father was my escape, he saved me and brought me here.'

I had been spellbound by the look on my mother's face, the tender joy, the happiness. I could picture even then how she must have been as a bride, young and hopeful, arriving in a foreign land arm in arm with a handsome lord.

'On my wedding day my husband gave me a tour of my new home, of Lockwood,' she had continued dazedly. 'Room after room after room, all his, all mine, with no thick jungle outside, only a neat lawn and woodland beyond. Room after room, and then we came into this one, the purple room, he called it, with this sloping floor and the window that rattles in the wind, and I turned to my left and there she was, waiting for me. I saw her.'

She'd turned towards me, her face a mask of horror, her hands now flitting like trapped birds in the air before her.

'I hadn't escaped at all; she was here, she had followed me, she's here,' she had said, and then our game of hide and seek was at an end and my mother took to her bed for the week and each night I heard her cry out in her sleep, shrieking and whimpering.

That day when she discovered my lock of hair she came and kneeled beside me, took my face in her warm hands. 'All I want to do is protect you,' she said, desperately. 'I want to keep you safe.'

Then she fled from my room and retreated to her bed again, cocooning herself like some animal who wished to sleep away a season and wake to find the world changed and new again. She did not come down to dinner and I stared at her seat as I swung my legs back and forth over the edge of mine.

'Your mother has a headache,' my father had said, looking up from some papers he was reading in between courses, and noticing my gaze. 'She won't be joining us. But since she isn't here, we might just help ourselves to some ice cream,' he added, motioning to the maid.

My father was often busy – with his businesses and with my mother and their turbulent relationship – but he had far more time for me than many other fathers of his ilk and could be kind and indulgent, calling me his little doll, tweaking a curl and smiling as I narrated some childish concern of great importance – the new barn kittens or the dress I was going to wear to Sunday dinner or the paper cut on my finger. He was also the one who insisted later that I be taught at home by a tutor instead of going to the local school, saying what was the point in having a child if she spent all day with other people, that he would miss me if he could not drop into the schoolroom and say hello, and furthermore, that I would surely be spoiled by mixing with the grubby local children.

My mother always said that ice cream would give me a stomach ache, and my grandmother said it would make me fat, but she wasn't there that dinner either; it was just my father and I, and two crystal bowls of strawberry ice cream being set down before us. He smiled at me and winked, but before either of us could pick up our spoons to take a bite, there was a telephone call and he left the table without a backward glance. I could hear his voice barking down the telephone as I sat alone at the long dinner table, eating small slivers of the ice cream and trying to enjoy it, watching as his serving melted into soup, thinking about my mother all alone in bed, her hair tangled and wild on the pillow, and then my stomach really did start to ache and I put down my spoon, my teeth chattering at the chill.

I did not know what happened to the hair I cut off after my mother's death, the armfuls of it. I had been too hazy with grief to notice, and I was trying my best not to think of it, to worry, remembering the nonsense my mother had said long ago. If any creature had stolen it, it was more likely to be the mice, dragging it through a crack in a floorboard and piling it in some hidden hoard, or the pigeons or house martins carrying it off for their nests. Besides, the servants would have surely swept it outside, I thought, picturing each separate curl dancing in the wind, strands floating across the gardens, pieces of me littering the estate, tangled up with the plants and trees, invisible to anyone searching.

Chapter Four

I woke the next morning before dawn to the noise of strange crying, fraught and wild, an animal I assumed, yet it seemed to be coming from inside the house. By the time I had my faculties about me, all was quiet again and I had decided that it was a fox, having heard them screeching often in the garden of my old lodging house.

The weight of the specimens lurking below would not allow me to go back to sleep, so I dressed quickly, pinning a braid across my crown because I had not put my hair in rags before bed – even when I did use rags or pins my flat hair stubbornly refused to hold a curl anyway – and picked up my notebook and pen.

But when I tried to leave my room, the doorknob stuck in my hand. It was one of those old well-polished brass knobs that slipped underneath my palm as I tried to wrench it round. It simply would not budge. A memory came to me then, of the time several girls at school had tried to trick me by holding the schoolroom door closed from the inside, and I had the unbidden thought that there was someone outside this door too, someone with a strong grip who wished to scare me just the same.

I stepped back and puffed out my hot cheeks. If I was stuck

in there, I thought, a planner as ever, how long would it take for someone to notice I had not appeared at breakfast, or for them to come and find me? Were David and Helen's rooms close enough that they would hear my shouts? It would be evening at the latest, I decided. Or perhaps I could see if there was someone at the front of the house and call out of the window to them.

I looked at my door warily.

This was ridiculous. There was no one outside of it, the gears of the lock were just sticking, it had worked perfectly fine yesterday. I pulled my shoulders back and then reached for the doorknob, which suddenly turned like butter in my hand, and I swung the door open, feeling flustered and silly.

As I closed my door I heard that same cry, at least I thought I did, but it might well have been the squeak of the door hinges, or something else. The sconces had yet to be switched on but ambient light leaked up from the grand staircase, and as I walked towards it, I did so slowly, listening carefully.

There! Another sound, coming from the west wing.

When one lives long enough in a house one builds a map in one's mind and can match the sounds to different locations, but this house was so large, the sounds echoing strangely, and though I had seen plans it felt very different inside, almost as if it were not the same house at all.

I passed two doors which were shut and as I neared the third, a figure walked out and screamed at the sight of me, dropping the sheets they had been carrying, which fell in a pale hump on the floor.

'Sorry, sorry, I thought I heard a sound,' I said, feeling very foolish indeed.

'You frightened the life out of me,' the servant said quietly, with a shaking voice, for I could now see the white of her collar and apron. She bent to pick up the sheets. 'It's not good to wander about in the dark, miss, not in this house – our nerves are tired enough with all this talk of ghosts.' She tucked her sheets closer to her chest.

'Shall I turn on the hall lights?' I said, after a baffled pause.

'Oh no, Lord Lockwood is particular about lights being off before dawn,' she replied, and then hurried away.

Downstairs, I dodged around another maid who was washing the entrance hall with a mop and bucket, feeling like I was getting in the way of the natural rhythms of the house, and breathed a little easier as I entered my museum rooms.

I had checked the animals and cabinets, the drawers and boxes and other miscellaneous containers – jars, bottles, cases and stands – against my list the previous afternoon after settling in to my room, and had found everything as it should be, yet out of my worry and desire for everything to go well under my directorship, I decided to check again while much of the house slept. It was only when I had neared the end of my list, when I had just the last few rooms of the lower west wing to walk through, that I found that the jaguar was missing from its designated place in the billiards room.

Since it was still too early to wake Helen and David without appearing as if our move here had turned me into some kind of tyrant supervisor overnight, it was up to me to dash through the other rooms again, admonishing myself for my earlier hurry and slapdash work. I was sure that I would turn the corner and find the low skulking shape of the jaguar gazing at me censoriously with its glass eyes, its patterned coat unmistakable. But as thoroughly as I looked, and looked again – even in the rooms that were not allotted to the museum in case it had been misplaced there by one of the workmen – I could find neither hide nor hair of it, and my heart kicked frantically in my chest.

I stopped in the drawing room and studied its occupants as if they might have the answers. The hulking Sumatran tiger, its rich fur a little faded now from when we had first received its skin during my first few months at the museum; the rare okapi in its large glass case, which had only been discovered by the Western world this century, and which was sometimes called a forest or zebra giraffe because of the white stripes on its legs that contrasted with its reddish-brown coat; the cabinet of foxes, arranged as a family even though the skins had been gathered from different parts of the West Country; the massive polar bear; my black panther; and the grey wolf with its right foreleg that a child had injured by kicking it a few months before, as if the animal had personally aggrieved them.

I knew all the stories of the collection; I knew exactly where these animals would sit in the museum in London. I knew what the faces of visitors would look like when they saw each particular animal, the furrowed brows, the open-mouthed delight, the look of dismay or horror, the awe and disappointment. And I knew that I had seen the jaguar placed in the billiards room only yesterday.

A missing jaguar is not like a smashed fossil, I reassured myself as I felt perspiration seep into my blouse. *It can still be found; all is not lost.*

I had yet to find the housekeeper on my search, so I ducked into the dimly lit servants' quarters and hesitantly tried to make my way to the kitchens, following the fug of hot linens and the echo of voices. I passed two closed doors and then paused at an unexpected sight: a dark, cramped room, bristling with a thick spray of flowers hanging upside down, so thick you could not see the ceiling or indeed the furthest wall, as if they were growing here in some subterranean forest, the air thick with their hazy perfume. Looking closer I saw that the various blooms were pale, their colour bled to whites and pastels, and there was a carpet of dropped petals on the floor like thick flakes of snow or ash.

'The funeral flowers,' a voice said from my elbow, startling me. 'I'm Dorothy,' the middle-aged servant said, introducing herself with sleepy eyes and a keen smile, and then waving at the room. 'Young Lady Lockwood wants them dried, preserved, and displayed about the house. Poor thing, she was so heart-broken.' Dorothy clucked her tongue. 'Most of them are orchids, exotic flowers for the Lord's exotic wife. His mother certainly wouldn't have approved, she would have chosen good English flowers, but then, god rest her soul, she was no longer here to make her preferences plain.' Dorothy reached out to pick up a bundle of flowers tied like a wedding bouquet, their colours leeched from weeks in the dark, their long petals like ghostly dried tongues. 'I think the house misses her – Heloise, I mean; Lady Lockwood – just as much as she does. It has that feel about it, you know? Woeful and difficult.' I was coming to realize that Dorothy was one of those women who seem to take every person into their intimate confidence, and had already catalogued her as an African civet for the elongated way she held her neck. 'The lights in the hall blew out twice last week and I swear every door seems to be sticking. We'll need them all rehung soon enough. You've met Lord Lockwood,' she said then, leaning closer so that I could smell the bitterness of tea on her breath. 'Tell me, does he seem heartbroken to you? Because I just don't see it. Grief can be a funny thing but I swear he was back to his tricks only a few days after she was cold in the earth—'

'Dorothy, please refrain from idle chatter with the guests,' a crisp voice admonished. We turned to see the housekeeper (who I had earlier distractedly classified as a Rüppell's fox for the narrowness of her face), who was weighing a large ring of keys in her hand and looking at the both of us distastefully.

'Excuse me,' I said, remembering my initial task, 'one of my specimens has been misplaced and I was wondering if you could help me.'

'The servants' quarters are a maze, Miss Cartwright, and a busy one at that with boiling water being ferried along the corridor. Next time, please ask another member of staff to fetch me.'

'Of course,' I said. 'It's just that I was worried about the missing jaguar.'

She smiled thinly. 'I shall ask the staff if they have seen it,' she said, and then motioned as if to push me out of the servants' quarters.

Throughout the morning, I heard her tell the servants as they passed that they should look out for a jaguar – although sometimes she called it a panther instead, or a large cat, in a tone of voice that seemed to imply that not only did she think that *I* was foolish but the whole feline species was – and the servants mostly responded with bemusement or declarations of innocence.

I wanted to ask Lucy, or the Major, but he was away for the day and his daughter had last been seen walking in the gardens. At one point I left the house by the back door to see if I could spot her returning, but there was another figure walking towards the house instead – the Major's man, Jenkins, with a shotgun across his shoulder.

'Excuse me,' I said, and then repeated myself when he did not look up even though he was only a few yards away.

'Can I help you?' he replied in his guttural voice, a note of irritation unmistakable.

My eyes were drawn to the two rabbit carcasses he was holding in one fist, their blood dripping to the dry grass below.

'One of my specimens is missing, a jaguar,' I said, looking back to his face.

He stared at me blankly.

'I don't suppose that you've seen it anywhere in the house? It was supposed to be in the billiards room.' I felt like a child who has lost their skipping rope.

'Aye,' he said after another pause.

'You have seen it?' I prompted.

'No, it's a big house,' he replied shortly, as if I was unaware of that very simple fact. Shifting the gun on his shoulder, he made for the kitchens with his quarry.

David and Helen helped as best they could once they had woken up and I had told them the news, but three pairs of eyes were no better than one at finding something that simply was not there, and I felt the shortness of breath that came before frustrated tears.

Eventually, because as worried as I was about my own position, I was also by nature quite dutiful, I put a call through to London to check that we had not left it behind, despite being sure that I had seen it with my very eyes yesterday. The harried secretary who answered said they would get back to me in a few days' time, because they were rushed off their feet – problems with the country house where the ornithology department was lodged, she said. When I set the receiver down I hoped that she would forget to mention the missing jaguar, or, uncharitably, that problems with another department might overshadow my failure.

'You mustn't fret,' Helen told me kindly as we took our lunch in the dining room. Her small face and red hair, her neat mannerisms had always put me in mind of a nervous red squirrel. Being one of the only other women employed by the museum, it was supposed by all that she and I should be good friends – but Helen herself seemed mostly startled when I tried to start conversations with her, as well she might, for I have never had the gift of polite everyday conversation.

'I imagine all the departments are the same,' Helen continued. 'That there have been half a dozen things missing. We're not a military outfit; we can only do our best and that is all.'

'Yes, but a *jaguar*,' I said. 'A mounted animal about as long as a person. How on earth can that simply go missing? It's not a loose button or a sheaf of papers.'

'I don't know, but it has,' Helen said, and then reached a hand out as if she was thinking of patting me on the arm, before retracting it – to the relief of both of us, I think.

'It's a funny thing,' David said, as he dabbed at his mouth with a napkin. David (a brown bear, or perhaps a walrus) was the taxidermy specialist amongst the three of us, and although we were all competent enough to do repairs if need be, he had the lightest touch despite his large hands and meaty fingers. 'Lord Lockwood might know more about where it is, or his daughter.'

Yes, I thought, but if it is not in any of the rooms of the house then how can they know any more than we do? But I did not say this, because they were only trying to console me.

Added to our missing feline, the other problem that the museum's temporary lodgings had thrown up was the condition of our collection, for we were quite literally seeing the animals in a new light. In the museum, they were displayed in dusty cabinets with painted backdrops, but many of the specimens had been liberated for the evacuation because they were easier and smaller to transport and rehome individually than in their monstrously heavy glass cases. Now the myriad windows and lamps of Lockwood Manor had revealed faults and shabbiness, even in the dim long gallery – places where fur had worn away, thread or glue had loosened, eyes become scratched or dull, cabinets bashed or rotten.

It was as if, I thought, pausing at the end of the gallery, the animals had already been waiting here for some time, neglected and alone, mute and fading; as if the war had already raged for years outside these walls and they, and the sparse human occupants of Lockwood Manor, were the only things that remained of the living world. I could not suppress a small shiver at the thought.

Chapter Five

That afternoon, I tried to put the missing jaguar at the back of my mind and busied myself with making a very long list of repairs needed, as if the length and thoroughness of the list might prove my competency. Then I met with the six retired men from the Major's old regiment who would be serving as the museum's night guards on alternating nights, and who seemed a bit bemused by my forcefulness in emphasizing how important the collection was and how much care should be taken guarding it, with one of them using the phrase 'how they do things in London', as if to suggest that the Home Counties were a locale free of all crime unlike the horrors of the Big Smoke – a notion I was not feeling too charitable about after the loss of one of our animals.

Later, as I worked at my desk under the watchful glass eyes of the dik-dik perched on the shelf above me, I heard several of the servants congregate by the back door.

'Goodness me, have you seen the strange beasts they've brought here?' one was saying, her voice muffled as if she had put a hairpin between her teeth while she fixed a curl.

'However odd they are, I'll take them over evacuees. At least stuffed animals don't need fresh linen and feeding three times a day.'

'It gives me the willies, the way the eyes glint at you when you walk in a room,' the first said with a huff, as I set my pen down. I was used to all manner of reactions to the museum's animals, some startling in their vehemence.

'I wonder what Lockwood's ghost will make of the new guests,' the second woman – whose voice I now recognized as Dorothy's – mused, her tone conspiratorial.

'Oh, Dorothy, I wish you'd shut up with all that, really.'

'You're saying you've never seen anything funny working here, never walked out of a room and seen a figure gliding down the corridor out of sight?'

'All old houses have ghosts,' a third woman said, tsking, 'but they're harmless.'

'Like the ghost that her late ladyship swore she saw? The woman in white she thought was out to get her?' Dorothy asked.

'I don't blame a *ghost* for her accident,' the other woman replied.

'Ah, but you do blame someone . . .' Dorothy said, before the clinking of keys heralded the housekeeper's arrival and the servants quickly dispersed.

That night, after an interminably long day, I tried to wash my tiredness from my face, still not used to the particular distortion of the mirror in my bedroom, nor the snaking twists of the densely patterned red wallpaper behind me. The window of my room was larger than that of any room in a lodging house but the red of the wallpaper, the dark walnut of the desk and chair, the dizzying oriental carpet, and the high bed with its thick mattress made the room feel heavy and sepulchral.

When I settled down to sleep, hand reaching to turn off my lamp, I noticed a trail of pale petals, like the dregs of confetti left after a parade, leading from my door. I must have tracked them into my room, I thought, and when the room plunged into darkness I strained my eyes to see them there, ghostly white in the gloom.

The next morning, when I heard Lucy's voice in the hall speaking to the housekeeper, I came out of my office to meet her.

'I heard that we've lost your jaguar,' she said to me, frowning worriedly. I was pleased that she had said 'we', because I had felt as if the housekeeper in particular judged the museum as an unwelcome, nuisance guest.

'Yes, it's a baffling thing,' I said, and then the Major strode past. 'Lord Lockwood—' I began.

'Yes, I've heard already,' he said, cutting me off. 'It's a damned shame you've lost an animal. A big cat, was it? Still, I'm sure it will turn up soon, there's a lot of nooks and crannies in a house like this, you'll get used to it in time.'

'The museum in London is a veritable warren,' I said pointedly, and the corner of his mouth tightened.

He smiled thinly. 'Well, best get on, I imagine we both have lots of work to do now. Miss Cartwright,' he said, and nodded curtly before walking away.

'Lucy, how many servants does Lockwood have?' I said, partly as something to say – I had never been much good at small talk – and partly because a maid swept a broom past the door, and I realized that the Major had given us a thorough accounting of the house and its rooms before the museum arrived, but not the servants, as if they were merely static furniture.

Lucy tilted her head and considered my question. 'Every time I count them recently, there seems to be one less with so many leaving us: we've always had difficulty keeping servants – rumours of ghosts, you know – but the war has made it worse, with lots of men enlisting, and women signing up for other war work. There's the housekeeper, of course; then my father's old batman, but he's ill at home at the moment and not expected to return; there's the cook; my lady's maid; the scullery maid; the kitchen maid; the new laundress; four, no, three housemaids now, one girl has just joined up; and Paul who's just started as a footman. And there's the tweeny as well, and Jenkins, although he's my father's man rather than a servant technically . . . I'm sure I'm missing people out.'

'Goodness, a full house,' I said, thinking that I had surely only seen three or four of them – or perhaps I had not looked close enough, perhaps my eye had glided over them just as the Major had in his accounting of the house. If the missing specimen had been small enough to carry, and not a feline as large as a man, I might have been worried that the culprit could have been a servant. Instead, I wondered which of them had been the figure standing at the other end of the corridor my first day here.

'Cook said you didn't have breakfast,' Lucy said then. 'Shall we have some tea and scones?'

'That would be lovely,' I said, feeling my shoulders relax as she led me out onto the terrace into the September sun.

'How are you settling in, aside from the dreadful business with the jaguar?' she asked after we were seated, with tea in front of us in the finest of china, a bowl of sugar cubes with polished tongs to use, and a spread of savoury scones and biscuits. She was wearing a summer dress of a green floral print with delicate ruffles around the neck and in the outside light I feared that my plain blouse and workable trousers looked even more drab in comparison.

'Oh, very well. It's certainly very comfortable here,' I said, and she smiled above the rim of her cup and then set it down.

'You know where my room is if you need anything, don't you? One floor up from you and right to the end of the west wing in the turret,' she said. 'I have to admit it's lovely to have the house busy again after the quiet of the last few months,' she added a little haltingly, nudging a cube of sugar with one of the silver tongs before it fell in a clatter and she apologized.

'The museum and I are so terribly sorry about your mother and grandmother,' I told her, thinking that it was impolite to mention her loss so baldly, but doing it anyway because I felt I would rather risk overfamiliarity than say nothing about the pain she must be suffering.

'Thank you. Thank you, Hetty,' she said. I thought about taking her hand but I worried that I would knock over some of the delicate crockery. 'I feel I'm used to it now,' she said, touching trembling fingers to her collarbone. 'It's only very rarely that I'll think of calling for my mother or believe that my grandmother will be sitting there at breakfast time – but I still feel so very sad. I confess that the war starting so soon after, and the blackout curtains on every window, as if the house has been shut up in mourning with us inside of it, hasn't helped matters, and the doctor still has me on tonics to sleep.' I could see her chin trembling and I leaned awkwardly around the table to touch her arm. She held her hand on top of mine for a moment and closed her eyes.

I had never been the sort of person who was first to offer sympathy, a handkerchief, a listening ear, to an acquaintance who looked distressed, but something about Lucy made me wish to be. I wanted to help her; I wanted to make her smile.

She squeezed my fingers and then reached for her teacup again. 'I went quite mad when we got the call from the police, quite mad. Grief does strange things to one, makes one believe all sorts of things.' She seemed to consider saying more, but then smiled a little too brightly. 'What about you?' she asked eagerly. 'Do you have a large family?'

'No, I don't. Just my mother now but I'm adopted,' I admitted, as I had not admitted even to many of the people I knew at the museum. There was something raw about Lucy that made me want to share my own hidden hurts, if only so that we were on the same footing and it did not feel like I was simply a voyeur. '. . . and our relationship has always been – strained. I view the museum and its animals, all its workers, as my family.'

'Oh, I'm so sorry to hear about your relationship with your mother. But I love the way you speak of the museum,' she said. 'And to be in charge of this collection at your age, it's marvellous. I wonder –' she broke a biscuit in half and then, shrugging, decided to take both halves anyway – 'do you have a favourite piece?'

'I have several favourites. I can show you them, if you want?' I offered, surprising myself, since I was never the type who enjoyed giving tours, preferring to ensconce myself at my desk and get on with my work.

'Would you mind awfully? I'm not stopping you from doing something important?'

'No, there's so much to do that an hour or so won't make a difference. Besides, it'll be nice to show someone what we do have, rather than racing around the rooms looking for what we don't,' I said, as if I could convince myself as well as her that the matter of the missing jaguar might be easily brushed off.

'Wonderful. Then lead the way,' she said, holding up the biscuit halves, 'I have sustenance for our safari.'

I smiled, already utterly charmed by her.

We started in the long gallery, working from the south to the north, and as I guided her around, naming and classifying specimens, I felt my usual calm return: everything was in its appropriate place, fixed and knowable, the only mysteries here were of the intellectual sort – the evolution of a particular foot or the mating habits of a reclusive species.

I showed Lucy the drawers containing delicate bat skeletons, the two-headed lamb foetus in its spirit jar, the armadillo skins, and the baby Brazilian tapir, eagerly studying her reactions to each new sight. I showed her the wide Victorian hummingbird case set in one of the furthest rooms in the long gallery, which from a distance seemed to hold a small shrub, before you got closer and realized that every cluster of leaves on the bare branches was in fact a single hummingbird, faded by time, and that the case held hundreds of them, so many that it became something horrifying and cruel. I explained how our methods of collecting and curating had changed since the Victorian era and its voracious love of excess; and she seemed as unsettled as I still was by the tableau. Then I led her back to the main house to see the lynx, the polar bear, and the Sumatran tiger, and finally the black panther in the drawing room.

'I am a cat lover myself so I approve,' she said. 'It's funny that we used to have its twin.' Her hand was hovering over the soft fur of his head.

'You can touch it if you like, gently,' I said, without telling her that this was a very rare offer for me to make.

She stroked towards his nose with the tips of her fingers; the pink of her nail varnish standing out against the midnight black of his fur.

'What did you mean, its twin?' I asked.

'My father owned a panther just like this one; he used to keep it in his office. I spent many hours as a child sneaking in there and watching for the pattern on its fur to appear when the sunlight was strong enough. I even tried to ride it once until he found me and spanked me for it. It got eaten up by moths, I think, and had to go.'

'Does he have other taxidermy in his office?'

'He did have a stag and a wolf but they aren't there any more. I don't really remember what became of them, but I assume they came to the same fate.'

'Fur is hard to keep well,' I said.

'I know,' she nodded. 'The women in my family have had a dreadful time keeping our furs from harm. I have inherited quite the collection.' She stroked a finger across the panther's ear. 'My father used to love coming back from a trip into London with a fur for my mother, or for me when I was old enough – ones to wear I mean, not to stuff.' She laughed lightly. 'Some of them are a little too extravagant, the ones with all the claws attached and the clasps made out of jaws, you know, but others are quite gorgeous, soft and so very warm, although I don't have the opportunity to get much use out of them living here.' She tapped the hardened nose of the panther.

'My dove,' the voice of the Major called from another room.

'Sorry,' Lucy said, standing up and brushing her hands on her dress. 'I should see what he needs.' She stopped with her hand on the frame of the door. 'Thank you for joining me for tea and giving me such a wonderful tour,' she said, smiling at me.

'It was my pleasure,' I replied. 'I should like to do it again some time; there is still lots you have yet to see.'

'I should like that very much,' she said ardently.

I had the same feeling I'd had at our first meeting, that she was keen for us to be friends but seemed to fear I might reject her offer of friendship, when she need not have worried at all, for I was surely the more eager party. I could not imagine that a woman like Lucy – who was both kind and glamorous – could want for friends. Nor that, if she got to know me, she would continue to want *me* for a friend, with all my awkwardness and shy conversation.

She gave a wave, and as she left to meet with her father, she used the same hand to gingerly press her short curls back into place on the side of her head. I turned back to the panther. There was a small, darker, patch of fur where she had brushed against the direction of the hair. I smoothed it back and was oddly sad to remove the only evidence of our time spent together.

Chapter Six

The rooms were full again, crowded with all manner of beasts and wonders, with creatures gathered from every land. The museum workers strode up and down the corridors with clip-boards held in their industrious hands and with eager eyes, checking lists and putting everything into order. I felt more settled during their working hours, soothed by the hum of new noise, by the weight of the new inhabitants of Lockwood.

But at night, my nightmares had returned and they took the same form every time.

I would find myself standing in one of the rooms of Lockwood, a different room each time, with no memory of how I had got there. I would be searching for something, something small – a young hare, a leveret, orphaned and shivering, that had been brought inside for safety – but it was nowhere to be seen.

I knew where this dream had come from but not why it was repeated each night, why I felt so deathly afraid.

When I was a child, perhaps six years old, I had found an abandoned leveret in the gardens – though later, when I knew more about animals, I wondered if it had really been abandoned, and not just waiting in the long grass for its mother to return from foraging – and brought it inside in a cardboard box, declaring that I would care for it and raise it.

My mother, who looked at the world through kinder eyes back then and was indulgent of my childhood games, swiftly fetched a plate of carrots to feed it and a bunch of straw from the farm to help line the drawer she pulled out of my chest, and cooed over it with me as I stroked my fingertip over its back and tried to comfort it.

'What shall we call it?' she asked, chin resting on the heel of her palm, legs crossed in the air behind her.

I didn't remember if I had answered her, or if I had ever named it, but I remembered my father arriving at the nursery and how I had chattered to him excitedly about my new pet before he had sighed and said, 'It's not worth it, darling, it won't survive for long inside the house. Your mother is cruel to get you so excited.'

'I am the one who is cruel?' my mother had replied with a strange laugh. 'And why shouldn't it survive, if we're careful?'

She set out to prove him wrong and slept on the couch in my nursery so that she could help tend to the leveret at all hours, gathered all sorts of foliage from the gardens and quizzed the gardeners and the farmer and the cook for advice, spending hours next to me watching it, trying to play with it as we let it loose in the room and it cautiously hopped about.

When I thought of that week now, I felt such a tenderness towards her, the lady of the manor marshalling all her resources to keep an orphaned animal alive, at how dedicated she was at trying to make my wishes come true. But my memories were also coloured by knowing that she failed, that my father was right.

The leveret had been too young to be parted from its mother and Lockwood Manor was no home for a wild animal. One morning, we had woken to find it listless and poorly and not even my returning it to the patch of grass where I had found it – in some childish repentance for bringing it inside, for trapping it within the walls of our house – could save it.

Now, years later, I was searching for the same leveret in my dreams, my chest tight with panic as I raced down the corridors of my home, darting in and out of every doorway, desperately following the quiet scrabble of claws, the soft hush of fur brushing against a doorway, the thump of feet on hardwood floor. But Lockwood was a maze, even more so when I was asleep, and each night, as I continued my panicked search, I became convinced that the leveret had returned to one of the rooms I had already searched, that something terrible was happening to it there, behind me, where I could not see, or far at the corner of the house, in the shadows.

And in the very worst of these dreams, I would run after it and find myself in a strange room, with blue wallpaper crawling with horrible shapes, with a cobwebbed chandelier swaying violently as if the whole house was shaking apart, but when I tried to leave and scrabbled at the door, it was locked, and the leveret was gone, and terrible eyes were staring out at me from the fireplace and I was trapped there, alone with some horrible creature—

And then I would wake with a cry caught in my throat, hands grasping for a doorknob, for the soft silk of the leveret or its warm, trembling sides, finding only the cold, still sheen of my bedclothes in their place, and weep.

The next day, I would find myself leaving doors ajar, nervously double checking their handles and locks, or scurrying outside to spend my morning under the open sky with the grounds and the hills unfolding before me. Later, when I returned inside, I would see a dropped scarf that I supposed was the leveret and leap towards it excitedly before I remembered that there was no leveret, or pass a book on a table in the parlour and think it an animal crouching and waiting for me.

It was such a silly nonsense dream to cry over, to let affect me, and yet the notion that I should be searching for something in the house, that there was something that I was not paying attention to, something that I could not see, could not be swept away like the grains of sleep from my eyes. It was only that the museum had just arrived, I told myself. Once its occupation had become more commonplace, my nerves would soothe, and I might begin to dream of other things again. The blue room I found myself trapped inside did not exist, after all, and that hare that I had rescued as a child was long gone, there was nothing I could do to save it now, nor any way I could turn back the clock to happier times when my mother had still been here with me.

Chapter Seven

Each morning at Lockwood, I would wake from strange nightmares that set me on edge for the rest of the day. In London, my usual nightmares were of a logical fashion – that I had dropped a specimen and it had shattered on the floor; that the mount I had made for a new specimen had unfathomably collapsed and the animal had sagged pitifully like a too-large coat; that I had tripped on the stairs and a cloud of fluttering labels had spilled out into the air while the director of the mammal collection stood waiting for me at the bottom, hands on hips, and I knew that the next words out of his mouth would be the termination of my employment – but the ones I experienced at Lockwood were not. In my dreams, there was a beast hunting me through the corridors on padded feet as I fled, dressing gown flapping behind me like the useless wings of a flightless bird. The beast was larger than a hound, too large for any mammal without hooves native to this island, and sometimes it was not a beast at all, but a woman with the claws of an animal and crazed eyes smeared with soot, who crawled out of a mirror dressed in white and trailed pale petals in her wake.

I woke often to the sound of a cry – my own? Or someone else's? The hazy boundaries of sleep made it difficult to tell

– and with the rumble of a growl that seemed to shake my bed. I had twice jerked in horror when I opened my eyes and thought my desk chair was something crouched and lurking.

'I've slept so well here,' Helen remarked on her last morning – for she and David were to return to London that very day, having successfully seen the specimens settled into their new home (if, indeed, losing one of those specimens could count as successful) – as she carefully sliced a green apple. 'I'll be sad to leave.'

'I will too,' David said, his smile exaggerated by the smear of marmalade at its corner.

'It's the quiet here, I think, and the lovely thick beds. I've been quite happy to be tucked away here in the countryside and not in London worrying about when the war will finally begin for true.' David made a noise of agreement. 'What about you, Hetty? Will you miss us when we're gone?' Helen asked after a pause.

'Oh yes,' I said, not wishing to start off a conversation about dreams. 'It's lovely and quiet here though, as you say.'

Too quiet, I thought as we left the breakfast table and I returned to the first floor and my empty wing of the house. Was that why my sleep was disturbed, why I did not feel at ease in any of the rooms here? Was I only missing the comforting hum of London outside the window, the sounds and smells of every other human in my boarding house, the crush of people on the underground and the crowds of visitors in the museum? I had never thought of myself as someone that needed the company of others, but I found myself disconcerted to see Helen and David leave, for without them I would have to face Lord Lockwood's imperiousness alone. Without them, I would be solely responsible for the museum's precious collection's safety – and was I really up to the task, I thought later, feeling a wash of prickling anxiety when my colleagues brought their suitcases down to the hall and waited for the car to be brought round.

'You won't run yourself ragged on museum business, will you, Hetty?' Helen said outside, pausing at the top of the steps with a kind smile that hurt me for what it seemed to say – that she questioned my ability to do my job.

'I'll be fine,' I said firmly, as if trying to make myself believe it too. 'You look after yourself too.'

'And good luck with Lockwood's ghost!' David added mirthfully before he carried both their suitcases down the steps, and my mood soured further.

I did not believe in ghosts, but neither did I enjoy these jokes and hints, the overheard conversations of the servants, that spoke to something irregular happening here, to nightly wanderings, to a house so large that its remaining occupants could not be certain what might be occurring elsewhere in the building.

'I wondered if I might ask you something, Hetty,' Lucy said that afternoon as she sipped on her tea, leaving a red lip print on the rim of the pale china cup.

'Of course.'

'I've been feeling at a loose end, you see. I had thought about volunteering to help the WI or the WVS but I'm not sure I have that much to offer besides providing a meeting place here. I had wondered though whether I might help out with the museum. I overheard one of the maids complaining about dusting and cleaning the taxidermy, that it was unnerving her, that she didn't like them watching her as she did it,' Lucy related with a wry smile.

'You don't have to clean the animals, that's the museum's responsibility,' I said. I might have called Lucy and me friends, although there was still some barrier of politeness, of things not said, between us. I liked the idea of her helping with the museum very much, of being able to share more of my world with her, although I did not wish her to feel pressured.

'I want to, I want to help,' she pressed. 'Especially with David and Helen gone. Let me help, Hetty. Besides, this gives me a chance to get closer to the animals, which I confess is something I've been dying to do.'

'If you're sure,' I said, and she nodded firmly.

I showed Lucy how to dust and clean the mounts that were open to the air, with vacuum cleaner and duster and spirit and cloth. And when we met every other day for tea she would report back and ask questions about the taxidermy, about the seams she had found on the animals and the delicate glass eyes that were hand-painted for each beast, the frames made of clay or of plaster and wire and all manner of stuffing hidden beneath the skins. She liked to work with her hands, she said, to concentrate on a task, and feel that she was doing something useful, and I was thrilled to have someone who shared my zoological interests.

She found the type specimens particularly interesting, though most of these were carefully hidden away in drawers. I had explained that the collection here at Lockwood was unusual in that we had a mixture of the animals and curiosities we normally had on show, and those that were kept in storage, like the type specimens. These were the whole skins, skeletons, or even parts of an animal that were used to identify a new species and which became, after the species classification, *the* example of that species – the type – that researchers would compare with new finds. This was why the evacuation of our animals was particularly important, for we held some of the only examples of certain species and very many of the type specimens.

'So it's a little like Noah's ark, the collection,' Lucy said one morning over breakfast.

I had it perfectly timed now – I would wake early and do some work in my office, before eating a late breakfast with Lucy, thus avoiding Lord Lockwood, who always ate as early as possible, and in whose company my small talk felt even more graceless than usual.

'Yes, I suppose so,' I said uncertainly, 'although they cannot actually repopulate the earth, and we only have one each, not a pair.'

'Yes, it's not a metaphor that works if one looks at it too closely, is it,' she said, laughing deprecatingly.

I admired Lucy's good humour, and her laugh, which was deep and almost mannish.

'It's still a thrill to enter a room I thought I knew well and find it full of exotic animals. They seem so out of place here,' she said as she passed me the milk before I had the chance to ask for it.

On the contrary, what I found most discomforting about the museum's new home was that the animals did not look *out of place* in here at all. There used to be many more private collections of taxidermy in stately homes such as this one. The Victorians had gorged themselves on collecting treasures from across the Empire and it seemed to me, oddly, as if the collection had come home to roost here. No longer pretending to be about education and scientific research, the collection had now become trophies in a manor house, jewels in the crown of a single aristocratic man; a notion that disturbed me.

But I did not say that, for it would not endear me to Lucy

to obliquely insult her father. He had not won me over during the brief time I spent in his company – at meals or in passing in the house – and I still smarted from his dismissive response to the lost jaguar. It was a particular annoyance that my office was so close to his across the narrow hall that led to the long gallery, for it meant that I was a party to his occasional telephone conversations, the majority of which appeared to be to various women he often called darling, as if he had forgotten their individual names, with a good number of conversations being composed of him soothing their understandably hurt prides.

'Things were getting too serious, too quickly, you know that, darling,' he said that afternoon, his voice close to a croon through the wall. 'It's only been several months, I can't be seen to have a girlfriend just yet, and there are too many eyes about the house with that blasted woman and her menagerie, too many visitors poking into things.'

A pause and then a laugh. 'Nonsense,' he continued breezily, 'don't be silly, you know I get invited to events, you know I need to socialize for business. I can hardly bring the same woman along to each one, can I? Think of what that would look like so soon after my wife died. And besides, don't think I haven't heard about you,' he said, voice becoming sly and harsh, 'and your own visitors, your dalliances.'

Another pause and then the sound of his door opening.

'Can a man get a decent cup of tea?' he called into the hall, genial and long-suffering, and then returned to his call. 'You're working yourself up into a state. Of course you'll still be invited to the soldiers' ball, I'm not a monster, I just think you need to get some perspective, there were never any promises made, my angel.'

I could feel the grimace on my face as I got up and left for another room, not wishing to hear more of his easy cruelty, or more ridiculous blame placed on the museum for his own actions. I had been right to imagine him as a Bengal tiger, I thought, picturing his callous grin and those lazy piercing eyes.

In contrast to her father's irritation with the museum, Lucy continued to embrace its presence, although there was an awkward element to her assistance. Occasionally I would walk through the rooms and find some of the smaller animals out of place – not that there was any particular reason they needed to stay where I had first arranged them, I supposed. There was no visiting public here to educate with careful groupings of different species or pleasing contrasts; the only need was for the specimens to stay safe and undamaged – but when I brought this up with Lucy she said that she was extremely careful to make sure that nothing was moved. It must have been the maids being absent-minded in their cleaning, so I left it as a quirk of the museum's new home and endured that odd discombobulating feeling of entering a room that looked ever so slightly different to when you had seen it last – the glint of eyes from a different corner, a snout sneaking out from behind a cabinet, the curling tail of an animal whose back had been turned.

On my third Saturday at Lockwood, after waking from another horrible nightmare and being further panicked when I blundered across my bedroom and saw a reflection in the dresser-top mirror and thought it some ghostly spectre, I decided that I had simply been cooped up in the house too long. I therefore took a walk to the village, hoping to work my frustrations and worries out on the brambled path that led away from Lockwood. The village was similar to ones I had seen on day trips as a child, the villagers unremarkable, but as an adult I noticed elements I would not have before: the shops shuttered by the Depression, the shabbiness of the houses – flaking paint and shoddy slate repair – and the heavily darned clothes of some of the people I passed.

The seam on my watch strap was coming loose and as I hunted for a jeweller's or a cobbler's to fix it, I found myself almost knocked over by a woman hurrying out of the newsagent's. It was the same woman I had encountered on my first day at Lockwood, the one with pale blonde hair and tears down her cheeks, and once again my appearance seemed to turn her face sour with loathing.

'I'm sorry,' I offered awkwardly – for getting in her way and perhaps for whatever I had done to displease her.

'What are you doing here?' she asked, peering at my clothes with such distaste that I glanced down to see if I had picked up stains on my walk over.

'I'm trying to get my watch strap fixed,' I said, and then yelped as she snatched out a hand to clutch my wrist.

'Was it a present?' she demanded, twisting my wrist to see.

'No,' I said, tugging my hand from hers with a huff. 'It's old.'

'I can see that,' she said, rudely.

'Do you know where I might get it fixed?' I asked, as I held the offending watch behind me, trying to find some polite way of ending this conversation.

'I suppose you could try the cobbler,' she said curtly with a wave of her hand towards the lane opposite us. She was staring at my hair now and my scalp was prickling.

'Thank you,' I said, then, 'I'm sorry, I don't think I caught your name.'

'Mary.'

'Well, thank you, Mary,' I said breezily, and turned away, doing my best not to look back because I feared she might still be there watching me. 'What an odd woman,' I muttered under my breath.

'Ah, the lady from the museum,' the cobbler said when I entered his cramped hut. Was there something obvious about me that marked me out as not from around here, I thought, or was it only that the village was small and that everyone knew everyone's business? 'It's quite the coup for us, having you here,' he said as I handed over my watch, 'and for Himself,' he added. 'How is our lordship?' he asked as he drew out his tools and got to work.

'He seems well,' I replied tentatively, unsure what else to say.

The cobbler sniffed and tipped the cap on his head further up his forehead. 'I bet he is. No mourning clothes for him. I knew his wife well, I did, she used to come and get her shoes fixed, even though she could have had them sent over. A lovely thing, she was, bright as a button when she arrived here; she loved this place and we loved her. All those garden parties she hosted, the fairs for the children, the money she gave to the church. It was his fault what happened to her, how troubled she became; he shut her away, trapped her there. My niece used to work at the big house, she said that Lady Lockwood became quite ill, that she felt like something was after her, poor thing.' He gave a troubled frown. 'It's not a happy house you've come to, I'm afraid, miss,' he remarked.

When I emerged from the gloom of the hut, buckling my watch around my wrist, I saw that Mary was standing with two other women by the entrance to the lane, and as I passed they laughed and I knew by their looks that they were probably laughing at me.

Smarting from my encounter, I made my way back to Lockwood, descending into the shallow valley, the thick grass of the verge whipping against my ankles. The gates to the house gleamed dark in the hot day and I shielded my eyes from the glare of a window that had become a fiery mirror of the sun. As I slipped past the gatehouse, my feet crunching on the gravel of the driveway, a sudden thud against the fence made me jump. The wood shook again, as if something was trying to break its way through to me, and then there was a growling bark, then several thuds and barks. My heart hammered and I let out a yelp, reminded unwittingly of my dreams. My eyes lifted to one of the shadowed gatehouse windows and I saw a man's face – Jenkins, I presumed – and then the curtains were pulled smartly across. I eyed the fence, hoping that it was strong enough to hold back the dogs, wishing I could ask the Major to have them sent to some other estate somewhere where they could not bother me, and then I turned back to look at the manor house. The sun had shifted, and the lit window was dark again, indistinguishable from the rest.

The tinny sound of starched, officious voices came drifting out from the wireless in the drawing room before I even stepped across the threshold. The housekeeper had recently bowed to pressure and the wireless was now turned on for the different daily news reports which, even if one did not crowd around to hear like the others, still floated through the house and set one on edge. We had also had our first trial run of the manor's air-raid siren a few days ago and though we had all been prepared in advance, the sound was utterly alien, turning the stately rooms of the house into the setting for unimaginable horrors.

If an attack on the manor was imminent, we would not have time to evacuate the museum's collection only to gather what we could carry by hand and take down to the damp cellars with us. My mind kept conjuring up images of the collection in ruins – every single egg, nest, shell, and bone shattered; the glass from the windows embedded in the furry sides of the mammals; the cabinets collapsed and the few spirit jars we had brought exploded so that the floor would be tiled with oozing, rotting matter. The dust in the air would be thick with hair and skin and feather fragments; fossils crumbled, as humans and their bombs managed what thousands of years of geological forces had not. So many years' work, so many patient hands and long nights, our best attempt at gathering the great and the good, the vicious and the venomous, the tiny and the large of the animal world in one place; all gone. From a selfish point of view, a direct hit on the manor would mean the end of my job, and what was my life without it?

That evening, I could not find my blasted watch. I was sure that I had taken it off and put it on the shelf of my desk while I wrote a letter, but it was not there and nor was it on the floor or in a drawer. I had dragged the sheets off my bed to check inside them and gone through all the papers piled up on my desk downstairs, passed through the museum's rooms to check tables and surfaces even though I knew I had been wearing it when I came upstairs.

Frustrated, I sat on my bed to pull out my earrings, but my hand fumbled and dropped one, which fell with a plink. And of course, it had to be the pair that was false jade and impossible to find in the dim light of the room. I sighed, kneeled down, and peered first at the floor and then beneath the grand wooden base of the bed, smoothing my hands back and forth to try to feel the earring or possibly the errant watch. Nothing. I leaned in further and stretched my arms as far as they would go under my bed, and felt something against my fingertips that made me jolt up in alarm and bash my head on the underside of the bed. It felt soft, furred, like matted hair. I reached for it again and dragged it towards me.

A doll made of straw and linen, about the size of my hand, dangled from the pale yellow wool of its hair, with brown beads for eyes, and a dress made out of scraps of white lace. But what was most disturbing about it were the three large pins that had been poked into the doll, one in the forehead, one in the heart, and the third in the belly.

Chapter Eight

The doll was dusty, so I knew that it had not been put here recently, purposefully, to scare me, and I did not think it was one of Lucy's old toys: it was too rough-hewn, too hurriedly made and from packing and straw, not the velvets and satins that would be available to a child living in a house such as this. The white dress – the woman in white – was beside the point, I told myself; anyone might be unnerved to find such a thing stabbed with pins under their bed.

I checked the clock in the hall, and finding it was only nine o'clock, I made up my mind to go and knock on Lucy's door straight away, and ask her about the doll before I lost my nerve. As I pulled my door to behind me, I felt a brief lift in my spirits at the thought of seeing her. I was curious about her, and her situation at Lockwood. It was out of the ordinary, perhaps, that she still lived at home unwed at her age but she had not offered many personal details after our first few more intimate conversations, and neither had I, beyond some superficial talk of our families, so I had no idea if she had any gentlemen callers, or why she had yet to marry. I was strangely relieved that she had not enquired about my own romantic life, or lack thereof. Were anyone else to ask, I would always make some joke about being a happy spinster, brandishing that word before it could be used against me, but if I were truthful I might say that beyond any formless disappointment at being without a spouse, what I felt more than anything was a yawning, and sometimes unbearable, loneliness. But one could not state that one was lonely, could one? It seemed to be the very height of gaucheness and would only make the other person desperately uncomfortable.

I padded down the hall in my stockings, clutching the doll in my hand and hoping I would not run into anyone needing an explanation. The gilt-edged frames of the paintings and prints lining the walls – family portraits and inoffensive landscapes, including one odd painting of the Major and his dogs whose artist had used the wrong paints, oxidizing parts of the canvas, turning it into a sludgy gloom and giving Lord Lockwood a black spot on his chin – glimmered under the hall lights, and as I entered the west wing I felt a twinge of unease that I did my best to ignore. It is funny the irrational connotations one's mind invents, I thought; how my dreams of being chased along that patch of corridor had bled into my waking life – and I reminded myself that that was all they were: dreams.

I followed the spiral staircase to Lucy's suite and rapped on the door before I could think twice. She swung it open, looking a little startled. She was wearing a slightly faded navy housecoat and had taken off her make-up. I could see her freckles spilling freely over her nose and cheeks and forehead, with one or two flecks on her chin and even her lips, and her hair was sticking up like she had just been sleeping.

'Oh hello,' she said, smiling and clutching the edge of the door. 'Are you all right?'

'Yes. No,' I corrected. 'I found something under my bed.' I thrust out the doll before I could flee with embarrassment.

I could have asked her tomorrow; it was tremendously silly to intrude on her rest.

She took the doll with a frown, seeming to recognize it.

'This was in your bedroom?' she checked.

'Yes.'

'My mother made this,' she said softly, fingering the lace. 'She wasn't well and she thought I needed protecting.' She paused, seeming to consider something, and then continued. 'She made several of these to put under the beds I slept in, or to hide in my room. There's a folk tale from the West Indies, where she grew up, about *la diablesse*, a devil woman who wears white and can command a horde of beasts – at least that's the tale she told me, I never knew if she had only made it up herself. She was so frightened of her, of the woman in white . . .' She trailed off before rousing herself with a little shake. 'I'm sorry if it unnerved you, finding this, Hetty.'

'Oh, no, I was just curious. It could have kept to the morning, I'm sorry to disturb you—'

'I wasn't busy, just idling away my time,' she said, with a wry laugh, and then pulled the door wider, ushering me into the room. 'Come in, I'll get you something to drink.'

Her bedroom was a portrait of every typical girl's fantasy, and I did my best not to look gormless with awe. The pale pink carpet was thick enough to lose your toes in and the walls were papered with exquisite floral pinks and pale reds. For light, there was a large electric chandelier, golden wall sconces, and lamps shaded with pretty pink tulles and bright ribbons. Dried flowers were arranged in vases on little tables and on the mantelpiece, which was painted white and topped by an elaborate etched mirror. The mattress on the four-poster bed was almost at my waist it was so high, and there were gauzy red curtains hanging between each post. She had a pink velvet pouffe to sit on, and a pale gold one as well, a large make-up table with a glass top and silk skirt, laden with make-up and brushes and perfumes, and a padded stool with gold tassels. The curtains were thick velvet, like theatre curtains. I liked the metal spiral staircase best – it was so modish, and I wondered what the room upstairs in the eaves looked like.

'It's a little bit extravagant, isn't it?' she said, noticing my admiring gaze. 'I have rather been cooped up in this house the last few years, so I've had a lot of time to spend decorating.'

'It's lovely,' I said. 'Like something out of a film.'

'Crème de menthe?' she asked, setting down the doll on a table and moving towards her drinks trolley. 'That's what I like in the evenings.'

'I've never had that before.'

'Never?'

'I don't really frequent bars and it's not the kind of drink one keeps in a lodging house with a strict landlady.'

'Well, I hope you like mint,' she said, pouring the green liquor into two delicate glasses.

'Thankfully, yes.'

She handed me a glass and I hunted for somewhere to sit. She tugged the gold pouffe over next to her bed where she sat with hers.

'Cheers!' I said and we clinked glasses softly. I could feel a giggle bubbling up inside of me. The drink was so sweet it made my teeth ache and then it warmed my throat nicely. 'Lovely,' I said, and took another sip.

'I like to think the mint makes it good for you, like a fresh broth,' she said, with a wry smile.

'Or toothpaste?'

'Quite,' she said, and I let go of my laugh, sniggering between sips as she laughed too.

'Forgive me,' I said, 'but sitting here with you feels like a dream, all this pink and softness compared to my boarding-house room, it's like I conjured it up from childhood fantasies of a princess tower or something.'

'It's nice to have someone to show it off to. No one's had the chance to visit my room since we used to have lots of parties years ago. The girls used to sleep off their hangovers in here; it was gloriously cosy.'

I suppose that answered the question of whether or not she had a beau, although even if she had, he would hardly have seen the inside of her bedroom: however modern she looked with her short hair, I knew from first-hand experience how protective her father was of her, and I could not envisage her conspiring behind his back to slip upstairs with a gentleman friend.

'I can imagine,' I said, leaning back and pressing the soles of my feet into the plush carpet. 'Are you excited about the dance?' I asked, fumbling around for conversation appropriate to a room such as this. The house had been full of chatter about the ball soon to be held at Lockwood to support the Major's old regiment.

'Oh, I suppose.' She shrugged one shoulder. 'There is that sadness that it's only occurring because of the blasted war. It's difficult to dance with the soldiers knowing that they shall soon be off to fight in Europe. But my grandmother always said it was the job of us women to show men what they are fighting for, civilization and all that.' She gulped down the rest of her drink and leaned past me to put the glass on one of the little occasional tables.

'I'm not a very good dancer,' I admitted.

'Oh, but then you must have a good dress,' she said, resting her hand on my shoulder. 'A dress can hide all manner of bad dancing.' She was so close I could smell the mint on her breath.

'I have to admit, I don't believe I have one smart enough.'

'Well, we shall have to find one for you.' She leaped up and swung open the long curtains of her wardrobe. 'I tend to wear the same things now but I have mounds of dresses from the last few years that will fit you, and some of my mother's too.' She brought out a long silk number. 'Stand up a minute,' she said and held it against me.

The touch of the back of her hands against my hips almost made me jump. I could not remember the last time I had been touched by someone else – there were not a lot of hugs at the museum and I had not really had a proper friend since school. And even when I did meet people who were affectionate with those around them, at the odd party or event, it seemed that I wore an invisible 'don't touch me' sign that kept them away from me.

'Too old-fashioned,' she said, and grabbed another, holding it against my shoulders this time. 'Hmm, maybe.'

She let the blue dress fall to my feet and I had to resist the urge to pick it up, not wanting it to crease. She gathered about a dozen different dresses, holding them in her arms and dropping them in front of me. 'Try them on,' she implored, pouring us more liqueur.

And so, in between sips of endless crème de menthe, I tried on a dozen different dresses, at first awkwardly with my back to her and then not bothering to hide my underwear at all, while she helped me with the ties and buttons, tugging down bodices and hems, twisting me to and fro. I was quite dizzy with the attention, with the slide of silks over my skin, the ruffle of tulles over my knees, and her nimble lacing fingers.

Finally, we settled on a blue silk number with a wide netted neck and a bow at my waist. I twisted back and forth in front of her long mirror, standing on tiptoes to mimic heels as she held the too-large hips of the dress behind me to see what it would look like once it was taken in. It felt like we were dancing.

'Can you see it properly? Sit down at my mirror,' she said.

She adjusted the neckline as I sat looking at my reflection, feeling like a theatre star in her dressing room. I could almost imagine that the perfumes and potions and silver brushes on the table belonged to me, that my life was this rich and fanciful.

'This is a lovely watch,' I said, fingering the delicate silver band of a neat timepiece abandoned on the table. 'Mine has gone missing from my room and I have searched everywhere.'

'It is a big house and things *do* go missing,' she said, moving the straps of the dress around my décolletage with hands so light they tickled my skin, 'but you should think of locking your room when you're not there, just in case.' We shared a glance through the mirror.

'I shall do that,' I said, nodding, and then she was lifting me up from the chair again and ordering me to stand on the pink pouffe in the middle of the room so she could pin the dress.

She did the hem first, folding it neatly in between more sips from her glass, holding pins in her mouth so that her words were mumbled. Then she straightened up to pin the material around my hips.

I stood as still as a slightly swaying statue as she circled me and touched and measured and tugged, and it was as if her fingers were little suns: wherever they lay my skin grew warm. Or perhaps that was the drink.

'I'll be honest with you, Hetty,' she said, 'I do believe I may be a little *tight* to have altered it correctly just now. We shall have to do another fitting sometime, and with my seamstress, who will help me with sewing the fiddly bits.'

'Of course,' I said, and took her hand to help me down from the pouffe, stumbling as I did so, a little tight myself. She held me by the waist until I had found my feet, and then I peeled myself out of the dress, only realizing how close she was when my arms knocked against her. She shifted me back a step with her hands on my bare waist, and I turned round and redressed quickly, feeling hot and embarrassed.

'Shall I take the doll with me?' I said, spotting it on my way to the door as I almost collided with a side table. 'I wouldn't want it to upset you.'

'Oh, no, it's fine.' She waved me off. 'This house has more than enough reminders of my mother – she lingers in every room.'

'Well, thank you for the drink, and the company,' I said softly as I saw her mouth twist.

'No, I should thank you,' she said, putting her hands on my shoulders, 'for taking my mind off things. We shall have to have another drink sometime.'

'I'd love that,' I said, and she hugged me tightly.

I made my leave, and tripped back down the stairs, feeling warm, and perhaps a little bit drunk with crème de menthe and female confidences. It was only when I reached the door to my bedroom that I remembered Lucy's warning about locking my room. My heart raced as I checked through my belongings, but nothing else was missing, except for that blasted earring I had dropped, which I hoped would be revealed in the daylight tomorrow, and the watch, which was probably in the upstairs bathroom, now that I thought about it. The jaguar was still missing of course, but it was not supposed to live in my room, I thought hazily.

I locked my door from the inside and got dressed for bed, only stumbling slightly when I bent down to change socks.

Before I slid beneath the blankets, I allowed myself the truly illogical act of checking under my bed – but not for the jewellery I had lost. And if I tucked the sheets carefully under my feet so they would not poke out into the night air, then so what? It was September and might yet get cold. And if I took a little longer to get to sleep, listening to creaks in the hall and staring at the shadow of the great wardrobe in my room, then it was only the crème de menthe swirling its macabre green pictures in my mind.

Chapter Nine

I should never have come to this house, *my mother used to say, and it was always this* house, *not this country, even though she complained enough about how the weather compared to her childhood home – the endless days of drudging grey, the bare trees in winter, the frozen drizzle, the narrow hours of weak winter light. She used to describe the grand estate where she grew up to me as I sat and watched her do her toilette – the afternoon thundery showers, the heat of the jungle that made your limbs so hot they pulsed, her favourite swimming pond and the raucous birds that swooped down from the hills and swept past her veranda.* The green, *she used to say, with a voice full of longing,* they call this a green land but they lied to me; it's a poor cousin to it, dry and pale, with every leaf so small and mean. Your father promised to build me an orangery, *she would say gloomily,* and fill it with my plants, but he lied too, for there is no orangery, there are only these grey stone walls, these endless rooms and all the things hidden away in them. *And then her voice might trail off and she might turn to look at me as if she did not know who I was.*

I've had enough of this house, *she would say in various tones – bitterly, fearfully, angrily, despairingly, and sometimes she would shout the words so loudly you could hear them the floor below or above, and then she would throw something – a china figurine, a book, a side table – which the servants would have to tidy up and, if possible, mend.*

Why did you bring me here? I heard her sob to my father once, as I lingered outside their bedroom, frightened after seeing a shadow in the hall outside my own bedroom and thinking it someone lurking, but equally too frightened of my mother's distress to knock on their door.

It was Martha, a maid who had worked at the house since before I was born, who had found me that day, and taken me by the hand down to the kitchens for hot milk and then set me to work helping her to fill the vases crowding the cramped flower room, showing me how to remove the leaves that would sit under the water line. Martha had long been my favourite servant because she was plump and motherly in a way that my mother wasn't, with no invisible tripwires where something you did might unwittingly set her off, but also because she was the only person who could manage my mother and deal with her fits of madness.

'It's like you cast a spell on her,' I told Martha once, I who had been raised by a woman who spoke often of spells and charms and curses.

'It's not a spell,' Martha had replied with a laugh. 'My father trained horses and I learned how to soothe skittish animals from him. More likely it's that something about me – my voice or my face – reminds her of someone from her past, like a childhood nurse.'

Martha was wise, no nonsense, and she always had an answer for me when I was frightened about something, a rationalization.

That scraping noise you hear is ivy scratching the windows in the breeze, *she would say when I cried and told her my fears.* The scrabbling sound is mice in the wall, hurrying home to their family. *When I became scared of the large beast from my* nightmares – with four legs or six, with a great furred side and teeth sharp enough to slice through my fingers – she would say, Your father's hounds will hunt down anything larger than a rat that dares enter the house. Ghosts do not exist, she would say when I told her my fear of the woman in white, the dead are slumbering peacefully in heaven, and it is only the wind or a shadow or a servant ducking out of sight into the back stairs.

Yet she could not be with me all the time, for comforting me was not her job, and she could only spare an hour here or there. I tried to cling to what she said, to the way the house did not seem to affect her as it did everyone else, but the nights were dark and long, and my imagination was boundless.

A few years ago, Martha had grown too old to walk easily up and down the stairs, to do the fiddly polishing and cleaning that was the work of many of the maids, so she became Lockwood's laundress, and I used to like spending time with her in that boiling cauldron of a room, my hair curling tight to my head, my face flushing damp, as she listened to me speak of my wishes and dreams and I listened to her speak of what her nieces and nephews were doing, how her father's old stables fared.

When a maid would bring me my laundered clothes, I would know that Martha had worked them with her tough hands, had tended to them as she'd once tended to me, and folded them carefully, slipping in the odd linen bag stuffed with dried lavender now and then. She might not have believed in charms, but I did, and she was mine.

But now she was gone. Not because she wished to leave, but because my father had wished it so.

'She upset you,' he said when I argued against it, 'and made your nightmares worse; this is your home and I won't have someone *living here who upsets you, my dove. Servants come and go but I only have one child.'*

'But it wasn't her fault,' I said.

'I've made my decision,' he said firmly, laying a hand on my shoulder. 'And besides, she's getting old, losing her wits. People like that, liars, can be dangerous.'

Martha was the furthest thing from dangerous, or a liar, and all this mess was because of one particular afternoon two months after my mother's death, when she had been found wandering the house feverish and out of sorts.

She's only caught a chill, I had said to one of the newer servants who gawped to see Martha scrambling along the corridor of the second floor, searching in the servants' rooms, and then hurrying down to the floor below to search those rooms too, eyes wild and manner frantic.

'You need to rest,' I told Martha, as the servant ran to get the housekeeper.

But Martha tugged her arm from my grip and continued her search, grasping at each doorframe in turn and pulling herself inside as if she were on a boat and had lost her footing, whipping her head from side to side.

'What are you looking for?' I asked, trying to soothe her as she had once soothed my mother.

'The blue room,' she replied. 'Where has she put it?'

'The blue room,' I repeated, feeling my stomach hollow and a rush of blood to my head. 'Do you mean the morning room?' I said. 'That has duck-egg-blue walls. Or the room where the tweeny sleeps?'

'No, the blue room,' she had said crossly, dashing into the next bedroom, shaking her head, cursing words under her breath that I had never before heard her say.

'What's in the blue room?' I asked, thinking of my nightmares, of the walls with their pattern of blue swirls, of an eye staring at me from the fireplace as I tried to find my way out . . .

'Her daughter.'

My knees buckled as I followed her into one of the unused rooms that had been shrouded in dustsheets. 'Whose daughter?'

'Heloise; her little daughter.' Even as she spoke, her hands scrabbled at the wall.

Me, she meant, I was the daughter, and Heloise my mother. 'You have a fever, Martha, you need rest,' I said.

She scoffed and then, as if she had only just realized that I was standing there, she turned round, her mouth white. 'Where have you put it?' she asked me.

'I don't know what you mean. Please, Martha.'

She had dug her fingers into my arm so tightly it hurt. 'Heloise,' she said, and I knew then that she thought I was my mother, the both of us dark, our faces so alike. 'Where is the blue room, where is it?'

'I don't know. I'm not her. Please, Martha,' I begged.

'Lucy?' she asked then, finally.

'Yes, you're ill, Martha, you need to rest.'

'You need to help her, you need to help Heloise, she's in danger—' she said and then she groaned, clutching her hot head, the frenzy leaching from her.

I dragged over a chair for her to sit in and she drooped forward.

'Why is she in danger?' I asked quickly, as I heard other footsteps run down the hall towards us, but she didn't reply.

The housekeeper arrived at the door, bringing with her two maids, and Jenkins as well, as if the old laundress was a wild animal that needed rounding up.

Martha was duly led back to bed on the top floor, where the doctor gave her something to sleep off her fever. She was lucid the next day and remembered nothing of her frantic search, nor *her words of warning, the ones I excused as confusion – perhaps wilfully, not wanting a reminder of my mother's fears, of her infamous woman in white – and which had in any case come too late.*

My father said that Martha disturbed me, and it is true that I had some of my worst nightmares for a week after her episode – but they could be triggered by anything; they were always in the crucible of my mind, ready to boil, and was it not only a few months since my mother had died, was that not the reason why my cries woke the house?

And even if it were not the reason, it was wrong of my father to make Martha leave after just one afternoon of madness, when my mother and I had been mad in our own ways for many more afternoons than that.

I thought of her that evening, as I picked up the evening gowns Hetty and I had left in a pile on my floor – my mother's dresses that were now mine. I thought of how careful Martha was when she cleaned them, each sequin and ruffle and silver thread immaculate.

I thought of how she had kept back the darkness for precious hours, of how she had protected me.

I thought of her looking at me as if I was someone else, her face creased in anguish, clutching my arms and crying, Where have you put her, Heloise, where is your daughter? *and I saw that blue pattern swimming again before my eyes, felt the prickle of unease scramble up my spine.*

Chapter Ten

It was the night of the ball and Lockwood had come alive. The floors of the corridors and ballroom had been buffed with beeswax polish until they gleamed, and the house itself was groaning under the weight of fresh flowers in monstrously large vases, while tables covered with thickly starched linen sported a dazzling array of delicate canapés – pastries, cakes, tiny sandwiches, fruits – and servants held silver trays crowded with crystal glasses of champagne. A butler and footman had been hired to give the impression that Lockwood still had a full complement of staff, and some extra help from the village had been pressed into service that night, along with two of the more presentable groundskeepers, wearing white gloves to make their hardened hands suitable for indoor work. The only element missing from the age-old scene was lights along the drive, an impossibility under blackout.

The officers at the dance were tall, and also well-polished, their uniforms neat and manners confident; they walked through a room with the easy arrogance of the well-bred, and chattered away during dances, occasionally remembering that they were supposed to ask questions, *Oh, I don't suppose you like riding, do you?* (it was surely not a coincidence that many of them reminded me of thoroughbred horses) or *Didn't*

I meet you at Malcolm's do a few months ago? They made me
nervous and I was cross with myself for that. I was not
hunting for a husband here and I knew who I was and who
I was not; I should not let them intimidate me. Perhaps it
was the dress, which had felt so comfortable when I tried
it on with Lucy but now felt like a costume that did not
quite fit.

Lucy outshone all the women in attendance of course, in
her wine-red silk dress whose hem was slightly longer than
fashionable, and with her neat white fox fur cape, and the
diamond pins in her hair, which had grown out just enough
to no longer look odd. Even the way it seemed like she had
simply thrown on her outfit, as if she might say, *this old thing*
with a shrug and really mean it, only added to her charm. She
was certainly the most popular dance partner, whisked off her
feet before she could even catch her breath, passed from officer
to officer to local dignitary, with a polite smile and the occasional charming laugh as she circled the floor, skirts flowing
around her legs like liquid. I was jealous of her, I could admit
that, and it was not just the wealth, for I had grown up in
comfortable surroundings too, nor was it her beauty; it was
her ease that I envied the most, the way the ballroom looked
like a backdrop in the play of her life.

Her father paused from his own busy dance card to cut in
on a youth with curly blond hair, and as father and daughter
circled the room, he murmuring to her with a smile, his hand
light on her waist as her skirts spun out, you could tell he was
proud of her, and feel the warmth of those watching such a
happy scene.

'His mother and his wife in one blow,' a woman nearby
murmured to her companion with a cluck of her tongue, 'and
on a Sunday drive on empty roads – it beggars belief. Thank

goodness his daughter wasn't in the car that day. What a comfort she must be to him now, and looking so much like Heloise.'

'Yes, but his mistresses are always blonde, haven't you noticed?' the companion answered archly as the woman told him to hush.

As I sipped my champagne and felt the fizz in my gullet, I felt a rising uneasiness at the scene before me. The military band was playing a very old song and the scene in the ballroom – men in uniform or tails and women in formal gowns – seemed little changed since the turn of the century (at least if one did not look closely enough to realize that the women were not wearing heavy corsets and silly hair, that there was slightly more flesh being flashed: a back, a smooth shoulder, a firm calf). There was no hint of war here – the uniforms seemed only a smart costume, there were no missing limbs or injured faces, no blood or destruction. It was the same everywhere in the country, I knew – we were waiting for war to start even though it had been declared more than a month ago, waiting for the bombs to fall. But the scene here felt too much as if we would always be waiting, that we were frozen in some kind of opulent tableau.

I made my way around the edge of the ballroom and out into the hall, stopping near the smoking room when I heard my name spoken in conversation.

'– I don't know,' a man was saying, before pausing to inhale on his cigarette. 'If that's the best the museum has to offer, the best the government can muster . . .' He laughed.

'Yes,' the man speaking with him agreed, 'she's an odd duck, terribly gauche. I asked her a polite question and she took it as an invitation to lecture me on the finer points of mammal classification.'

A lie, I thought, my face flushing with shame and embarrassment, lurking in the hollow behind a tall plant. That bore of a man had asked me himself what made a mammal a mammal, and I had answered him in three sentences at most.

'Yes, she certainly seems very *intense*. But these women in male professions are, aren't they?'

More laughter, and I turned away swiftly, my cheeks hot and my throat tight, only to knock into someone striding past.

'Steady on there,' a man in tails said, putting out a hand to stop me from falling into him.

'Excuse me,' I said, mortified, and then when I got a better look at him, my breath hitched and a little shocked noise escaped my mouth. He was older than me by about ten years, solidly built, with dark hair and a reddish sheen to his five o'clock shadow, and I was utterly horrified to recognize him.

Then he looked up from readjusting his bow tie and the features of his face rearranged themselves into someone unfamiliar.

'I say, are you all right?' he asked.

'I'm quite fine, thank you,' I said, my voice high and strange, and hurried away along the corridor, ducking into the small bathroom and bolting the door firmly behind me. My hands slid against the mahogany door as I leaned against it and tried to get my breath back, my heart shivering with the after-effects of a fight-or-flight response.

About six months before I came to Lockwood Manor, I had visited a private fossil collection near the coast as a representative of the museum, staying in a little hotel which I was ferried to and from by a local bus. It was at the hotel that I had met a man who had called himself Jeffrey, and who I had just mistaken the man in the hallway for.

Jeffrey and I had made polite conversation over breakfast, dinner, and tea in the lounge, and on our first meeting I had – oddly, and for a reason I could not have clearly articulated to myself – chosen to introduce myself by a different name, as Elizabeth Treadway, a name conjured unthinkingly from the ether. He was not wearing a wedding ring and his cheeks were rough with stubble at all hours as if his razor was not quite sharp enough. He smelt of good cologne and cigar smoke, and his clothes were of a fine quality. I did not recall his personality, beyond the fact that he reminded me rather of a cocker spaniel; the only important thing to me then was that he was inoffensive and quite clearly attracted to me.

I think I only decided on my last night that I was going to sleep with him. It was a strange decision that had bubbled up in me sitting there in the parlour without apparent forethought – and yet by giving the false name, was I thinking of it in some way from the very start? I would never see him again and I was tired of being a spinster and resentful that other women had experienced something that I still had not, since I was untouched in every pitiful sense of the word.

Decision made, I had sat too close to him in the parlour, acted awfully interested in whatever he was saying, and laid my hand on his arm a couple of times. When he had asked me why I was staying there, I made up an aunt I was visiting or some such. He said he was leaving tomorrow afternoon, and I expressed appropriate sadness.

I was telling him one of my favourite facts about male giraffes, and he was pretending to be interested, when he remarked that the drinks in the cabinet in the parlour were stale.

I brought some better whisky with me and it seems a shame to keep it all to myself, he had said.

Oh, really? I said, leaning closer.

It's upstairs, in my room, he said and paused.

I did not know how forthright I was supposed to be.

Would you like a drink upstairs? he asked.

All right then, I replied, relieved that the parlour had stayed empty for our conversation.

He got up from the seat and I followed him out into the hall, where the grandfather clock was chiming the hour.

He put his hand on the small of my back as we came to the stairs.

After you, he said, and I felt the sensation of his eyes on my backside as I walked up. I felt powerful all of a sudden, and desirable. I was a film noir siren, I decided, trying to slip into a role. I would sleep with him once and then break his heart. In my mind's eye my nails were long red talons, my heels were higher and my skirt tighter; my wit devastating.

It was awkward in the hall as he shuffled around me to lead us to his room, the both of us trying our best not to glance around like bad spies. He invited me in and I strolled forward as if I had done this a hundred times before. Inside myself, though, I felt a shiver of nerves.

He poured us two slim measures of whisky and drank his in one quick gulp. I sipped at mine and then he took the glass and with his hand on my chin, turned my face towards him. He kissed me, his stubble rasping over my skin. He clutched me to him, his arms squeezing my body against his, his desire for me strangely thrilling.

Shall we move to the bed? he whispered, as he fingered the buttons of my blouse.

Do you have a prophylactic? I asked, thinking it best to be direct: I might have been inexperienced but I was not naive and I wanted no unexpected repercussions.

Oh, right, yes, he replied, and moved away to fumble in his suitcase.

While his back was turned I licked away the last of my lipstick, because I knew that it looked terrible half-done, and wiped the back of my hand across my damp upper lip. Should I remove my clothes or let him do it? I started to unbutton my blouse and he groaned at the sight and raced over to help me with it.

But all that power, that image of some arch villainess from the pictures, vanished with my clothes off, and I simply felt like a body. There were my breasts and there were his hands; here were my thighs, my hip bones digging into his sides, his breath panting by my ear; here was my head shifting up and down on the pillow as he thrust into me. It did not hurt, because I was not a prude who had reached the age of thirty without touching herself or finding her own pleasure. But he did not touch me where I wanted to be touched, and I did not move his hand for fear of seeming too enthusiastic. My arms rested loosely on his back, which was clammy and cold, like a slab of meat, and I had to remind myself to smooth a hand up and down it at intervals.

Was this what all the fuss was about? I thought resentfully about five minutes into the act. Then he squeezed my right hip tightly with his hand and I felt a fluttering in my belly and a rush of blood. He squeezed again and I caught my breath, thinking that I was approaching something close to the very start of pleasure. But then he finished with a groan, and lay on me, panting. I had the urge to brush his hair back from his forehead, like he was a boy. He pulled out and shuffled over to lie beside me.

How would another woman act now? Was I supposed to share a cigarette, or say something about his performance? *I should get back to my room*, I said, suddenly desperate to be alone.

I put on my skirt and blouse hurriedly with my back to him, scrunching up my stockings in my hand because I did not want to waste time putting them on.

I did not remember what I said at the door, but probably something breezy and very unlike myself. Then I left, rushing down to my own room and locking the door behind me, leaning against it and breathing heavily. I had gone into it with eyes wide open, but now I could not help but feel cheap and used. I felt my eyes pool with tears, but ran a hand across my forehead until the urge to cry had passed. Then I ran a bath and washed myself briskly.

I felt a little calmer once the smell of his skin was gone and the warmth of the water had soaked into my limbs. I got out and dried myself with the thin hotel towel and then hung it back over the rail. As I did so, I caught a glimpse of my naked body in the bathroom mirror, and moved to regard myself more closely, twisting my torso to clutch at my hip with the opposite hand, squeezing it just as he had done, but feeling nothing. I felt the weight of a breast in my palm and then the softness of the skin underneath my arm. I went to get the chair from the other room and, standing on it under the light in front of the sink, I looked in the mirror at my hips and the curling hair between. I turned round and looked over my shoulder at my backside, at the mole that decorated the right cheek. I remembered discovering the mole during a particularly boring afternoon spent with a hand mirror while I tried to set my hair in curls that would stay; I remembered thinking that my future lover would press their finger on the mole, that it would excite them. But it had been too dark in his room to see it.

I stepped down from the chair and moved it back into the other room. It felt ridiculous to be naked while carrying a chair. Would this excite a man, to see me doing this, I wondered. I had learned from years of overhearing half-conversations in streets and bars that men were attracted to very odd things, not just breasts and backsides, but feet and noses and thick underarm hair and sneezes, the way a woman's perfume reminded them of their childhood nurse, or the shade of downy upper lip hair.

I sat down on the chair, but it felt like I was waiting for someone so I got into bed. I had always worn pyjamas but that night I did not want to put them on. I slid my legs back and forth under the sheets and curled and uncurled my toes.

I had woken the next morning with a start while it was still dark and, with a churn of shame in my stomach, dressed and packed in record time. Once finished, I took a seat again on that rotten chair, this time fully clothed and with neatly pinned hair and a thick layer of powder covering any possible blushes. Thank god I had given a false name, I kept thinking as I smoothed my hands down my skirt and picked up my watch at intervals to check the time. I would leave the moment it got light – any earlier and I would look suspicious. I would have to walk past his room to get to the stairs, and I prayed that I would not run into him. How embarrassing to be seen in the light of day with my coat and suitcase, I thought, how unbearable to have his eyes watching me, have him knowing what I looked like underneath.

I could walk straight from the hotel to the station and be on a train in no time at all. I pictured myself sitting in a carriage, reading the book I had saved for the journey, the countryside rushing past, thinking that soon enough I would be back in London, slipping into the crowd outside Euston and descending into the crush of anonymous bodies on the underground. And then back to my little room and my flat bed and the noise of Beth in the room to the right of me and Shirley to the left and the traffic outside my window, the fiddler who lived opposite playing on Sunday mornings, the smog of London, the damp rain and fluorescent lights, the honk of car horns and heels tripping down the pavement.

I remembered it all now in the bathroom at Lockwood Manor, standing in my borrowed ball gown, and was embarrassed anew.

A knock on the bathroom door made me jolt. 'Just a moment,' I called, and splashed some water on my wrists, pressing them against my clammy neck and smoothing errant strands of hair back into place as I stared into the mottled mirror. My curls had dropped as they always did, and my face was ghostlike.

How ridiculous to think that he would have said anything if it had been him; he was probably married anyway, for god's sake. I hated that I felt ashamed by the whole thing when it was hardly out of the ordinary, but it was the utter failure of it, the way that sex with him had felt like an awkward inconvenience, nothing more – a quasi-medical event – that bruised me the most. I think I had convinced myself that once I found out what I was missing, I would approach my romantic life with more enthusiasm, and instead I was more reluctant than ever to make a match – not that there was a great crowd of men clamouring at my door to take me out.

I could spend the rest of my life alone, I thought, as I used the mirror to reorder my expression into a polite smile and left the bathroom, apologizing to the two women waiting outside.

I could be happy alone, I could survive; I had done so all my adult life, what was thirty more years? I reasoned, as I headed towards the comforting familiarity of my animals, wanting their placid gaze to help me forget the trials of the evening.

Chapter Eleven

The long gallery had been locked before the ball, but the other rooms were left open so that guests could wander freely through them, sipping champagne and perusing their private show. I had been a little nervous about mixing a party with the museum but when I had said so, the Major scoffed and said that the kind of guests he invited would hardly be the type to take liberties and besides – and here he had tapped his nose in an almost mocking motion – two of the museum's own guards would be also on duty.

Yet apparently I had been right to be nervous, because when I entered the drawing room, I found a group of soldiers standing close to the okapi, who was secure in his cabinet, and the polar bear, who was not. They were rowdy with alcohol and one of the soldiers, a man with a nose that looked broken, was pressing his hand on the polar bear's back as if it were a horse and he was about to jump on it, while another man with red hair slapped his hands forcefully on the okapi's cabinet, making the whole box rattle.

'Can I help you, gentlemen?' I called across the room. By the time I reached them they were all staring at me, like a pack of hyenas interrupted in their jape, apart from another of their number – whose small eyes resembled those of a capybara – who was holding his fist against the polar bear's head and miming a soft punch.

'I can think of lots of ways you can help,' the cabinet basher said, and two of the men jeered.

I put my hand on my hip as if I was a schoolmistress, and these my delinquent pupils. 'I'm the director of the museum which has been evacuated here. Are you looking for a zoology lecture to go with your champagne?'

'No thanks,' said the potential rider. 'But if you give me a hoist you can get me up on this thing.' He pressed down with both hands again. It was a wonder the preserved bear had not yet buckled under his weight.

'Get your hands off the polar bear,' I said, and the men, sensing a fight, cheered.

'We've got a firecracker here, men,' one said.

'It's a party. We're taking advantage of the entertainment,' the aspiring rider said, patting the bear.

'If you'd like to spend three hundred pounds to fix the polar bear once you've broken it, that's fine. What's your address so I can make sure the insurance offices know who to contact?'

'This shoddy stuffed bear?' he said. 'Like hell it's worth that much.'

'Of course, the museum is part of the civil service, so there'll be a government investigation too, and they'll be eager to recoup the costs and punish the man responsible.'

'What a bore you are, miss,' he said as he finally stepped away.

They filed slowly out of the room, giving me dark looks for spoiling their fun, while I stood there sternly with my arms crossed. Once they were gone, I let myself relax and gave a long sigh. I walked over to the bear and checked its back carefully to see if there was a rupture or a sunken patch. All seemed well, thank god. Not that the polar bear was really worth an awful lot; it had been one of those last-minute additions to the spare truck during the evacuation, and we had three others of its kind down in London.

My animals not having proved the sanctuary I had hoped, I asked one of the guards to make the rounds of the rooms, stressing that no one should be touching any of the animals – or trying to climb them.

I wanted the party to be over. I wanted all these guests who had infringed on the museum's space gone. I wanted to go up to my room, get out of this ridiculous dress, and have a good cry and then sleep off my bad mood. Instead – fearing it would be rude to just disappear – I made my way through the busy crowd of the ballroom again, pushing past the heavy blackout curtains to get to the terrace and the fresh air outside, pausing for one moment on the threshold when I saw a flash of white ahead of me before the light of the full moon revealed the shape leaning against the balustrade to be Lucy.

I felt my spirits lift for the first time that evening and walked over to join her.

Lucy kissed me on the cheek in greeting and I caught a wave of her rich perfume. I settled next to her, pleased to be in her company.

'Cigarette?' she offered.

'Please,' I said. She slid one from a silver case inside her beautiful beaded bag. Her fingers were cold against mine when she handed it over. She had lost her fur somewhere and her collarbone gleamed as if she had applied powder to it – perhaps she had, was that not what the movie stars did?

'Are you having fun tonight, Hetty?'

I leaned against the balustrade to take the weight off my bruised feet. 'Well, I just had to shoo a pack of men out of the drawing room; one of them wanted to ride the polar bear.' I thought about telling her about the man I had knocked into, and what I had overheard the guests say about me, but since neither anecdote painted me in the best light, I decided not to.

'Silly boys,' she said, twisting her body to stub the last of her cigarette out on the stone, 'but at least there hasn't been a fight yet. There tends to be when there's enough young men about. They get their prides bruised.'

'That sounds a bit ghastly,' I said. The crowds of soldiers inside had taken on a more hostile tone in my mind now, their shiny brass buttons like eyes glinting. 'As to your question, would it be terribly ungrateful of me to say, not really?' I admitted. 'It's so busy and loud, and the little dancing that I did has made my feet ache. This is not my natural habitat, I'm afraid.' I sighed. 'I suppose you're used to it, that it must be small fare after the season in London.'

'You've got an eyelash on your cheek,' Lucy remarked softly, brushing it off with a feather-light hand. My eyelids fluttered. 'And I've never been to the season. I wasn't well enough to be a debutante,' she said.

'I'm sorry, I just assumed.'

'My grandmother was apoplectic about it,' she said, arms around her own shoulders. 'She said in her day you would attend every party even if you had scarlet fever, that my attack of nerves was deplorable. Maybe if I'd come out properly I would have a nice husband by now.' She gave a short laugh and lit another cigarette and I thought it was good that she was not married to one of those bores inside, the ones who saw their pretty wives as trophies more than anything else.

What exactly her attack of nerves referred to, I did not quite understand, but I assumed it was part of what her father meant when he said that she was 'delicate', and it would hardly be polite to ask, although I dearly wished to. I wanted to know her better, for us to be the kind of good friends I had only ever heard about, the ones who told each other everything – and we could be, I felt oddly sure of that. Perhaps I only needed to be bold enough to tell her more of my past, or of my worries for the future. Perhaps if I made the first overture – but that had never worked with other potential friendships before.

'That dress suits you,' she said, adjusting the neckline, and blowing smoke from the corner of her mouth, the red of her lips matching her own dress perfectly.

'Thank you,' I said. I should tell her how wonderful she looked tonight, but surely that went without saying.

I looked at the blacked-out windows of the house that loomed above us, cutting out half the sky, and said, 'It's strange, the house tonight, with the crowds and the music, feels so different from usual, as if I could turn a corner and see a woman in a corset and bustle, as if time is playing tricks.'

'Yes,' Lucy said, also staring up at the house. She paused and licked her lips as if she was about to speak, and then shivered. She rubbed her hands against her chilled arms. 'This is the first party we've had for years, you know. Back when my mother was well, there would be at least one a month. And when I was a child, I would be brought downstairs by my nurse, wearing muslin and petticoats, and with my hair in ribboned ringlets.' She patted the short curls of her hair, eyes soft with remembering. 'I must have looked like a little doll being paraded about, and sometimes my father would carry me on his hip and introduce me to some of the dignitaries – the lords and ladies, the princes,' she said, with a smile and a sidelong look at me as I pictured the wondrous grandeur of her childhood. 'And I would shake their hands very solemnly, or curtsey very prettily.' She bobbed her knees as she gently mocked her childhood self. 'One evening, my father let me stay longer, and I stood on his feet as we danced in the middle of the ballroom. I was ever so jealous when I was whisked back upstairs, I used to cry about it and my nurses would cluck and my mother would kiss me on the cheek and say, *It's all right, darling, It's quite boring down here with the grown-ups, really.* But when I glanced back, I used to see my parents standing there looking so glamorous, with a crowd of fawning admirers around them, my father's arm tight around my mother, her gazing up at him with such adoration, and know that a part of them was always hidden from me, that they had some secret adult accord, and feel sour with envy.' She frowned and twisted a foot before her. 'I was a strange child.'

'Children are envious creatures,' I mused. 'We're supposed to be such angels but I was the crossest little madam as a child, stubborn and sullen.'

'Really?' she said delightedly, and studied me. 'I can't imagine that.'

'You can't imagine me as stubborn, as serious?' I jested.

She laughed and tapped her thumb against her tooth before taking another drag from her cigarette. 'By the time I was old enough to join the parties, to stay downstairs all night, they were infrequent and had lost their allure. When my parents were drunk they could both be such flirts, and cruel with it,' she confessed. 'My mother would dance with a dashing young man and then be furious when my father danced with a woman younger, prettier, than her. There always seemed to be some spectacle or other, some shouting match, and my father herding my mother upstairs and apologizing to the guests.' She shook her head and her voice grew small. 'And then, at the very last party, maybe seven years ago now, my mother attacked a woman dressed in white, thinking she was her ghost, and tore at her face with her fingernails.'

'Oh, god,' I said, putting an ineffectual hand on her shoulder as she brushed her fingers across her forehead as if to brush away the memory. 'I'm so sorry.'

'It's all right.' She shrugged, and then coughed. 'I should head inside, find my fur stole.'

'I think I shall stay out here for a little longer, it's quite warm in there,' I said, noting that she had not invited me to join her and thinking that she might want to leave the memories exhumed by our conversation behind.

'All right,' she said, and kissed me on the cheek in farewell.

I watched the liquid sway of her walk and the glint of the pins in her hair. She was taller than me by a few inches and had proper woman's hips compared to my shapeless figure. I was not totally objectionable in looks – I liked to think of myself as forgettable more than anything else – but I hoped out of some strange vanity that we did not appear too much of an odd twosome when standing beside one another.

I looked out across the grounds, the light wind brushing my dress against my legs; a dress so expensive I could never hope to buy it on a museum salary. My stomach was warm with champagne, the hairs on my arms standing up in the cool of the night. Life had performed a strange trick to wash me up here in exactly the kind of place my mother had always wished I would find myself – though without the necessary husband of course – but the longer I lived at Lockwood, the less I envied its inhabitants and their gilded lives, and the more all the talk of curses seemed to make some kind of sense.

I stepped down into the gardens, away from the house, and circled the fragrant knot garden, running my fingers over the prickly box hedge, when I saw movement by a tree. There, half hidden by the night, were two figures embracing, the moon casting a stripe of light on their Brylcreemed hair. It was two men, kissing like lovers. I was no ingénue – I knew of the Greeks, of Oscar Wilde and his ilk, that there were men who loved other men – but to see two men like this now, here, was shocking.

And who were they? I was too far away to see if either or both were wearing uniform. I turned round in case one of them saw me watching – and besides, I did not want to be a voyeur, to intrude on a private moment – and made my way quickly back to the terrace and then inside. I could not tame my thoughts though; I kept looking at the men I passed and thinking, *you too?* Wondering what the scrape of stubble against stubble would feel like. What they would *do* together. Suddenly every gesture became suspicious, every friendly slap on the back, every arm slung over the shoulder. Would a man like that know another on sight? Was there a tell, a secret signal?

I left the ballroom again, thinking about heading for my office – the key for which I had placed in my purse, foreseeing my need for an escape route – but when I came to it I found the door next to it, the door to the narrow corridor that led to the long gallery, ajar.

I pushed through it and walked along the corridor and through the other open door. The lights in the long gallery were on and I could hear the murmur of a voice and the shuffle of feet coming from one of the rooms. My heels clicked on the wooden floorboards as I strode down the gallery to find out who had wandered in here, and just how they had made it past a locked door in the first place.

Chapter Twelve

As the men at the ball danced with me, they complimented my dress (praise which I palmed off on the tailor), my elegance, my 'radiance' (a term I always suspected referred to the perspiration that bloomed on one's face as an evening of dancing progressed), and my nimble feet, but inevitably their conversation soon turned to the house itself. Such a gorgeous house, they would say, as they held me in their arms; what a grand estate, what a glorious ballroom, they would remark as the hand on my back nudged me in the direction they wished; and I knew that in their eyes I was a part of the house they coveted, that when they looked at me, when they clutched me close, they thought of my inheritance and wondered whether they might seduce me into giving them Lockwood itself.

If I told them about my bad nerves, if I called it madness, would that only make them want me more? I thought darkly; would they think that they could shut me up somewhere and have free rein of the house for themselves?

It was easier when I was younger, when the men my age had not yet turned their thoughts to property and legacy and women as parcels of land or crumbling estates that needed only their expert financial guidance to recover, when attraction was what mattered, the frisson of a hoped-for dalliance later that night.

No doubt there would be quite a few illicit dalliances taking place that night, couples roaming out into the gardens looking for a private corner or tiptoeing upstairs to take advantage of the many empty rooms. It was something I had done myself a few times at parties at other houses, in those handful of years after my nerves had improved enough that I considered myself almost well, and before my mother and grandmother died; met young men and danced and later slept with them, though I always woke up regretful and cross in the morning, feeling that it was not worth it for an unsatisfactory fumble. But I had only once tried to take a man to my bed here at Lockwood, in an aborted first attempt at intimacy.

My parents had thrown a twenty-first birthday party for me and my mother had made sure to invite many eligible men, nonchalantly dropping their names into conversation in the weeks before, while my father, who said I was surely too young for all that, glowered and mocked the calibre of the young men available, their weak chins and schoolboy moustaches. I heard them fighting about it, my parents, over breakfast.

'You've only given me one child,' my father said in answer to my mother's shriek of frustration at his jeering, 'and now you want to rush her to grow up and leave us. Or are you living vicariously through her, hmm? You think you could have done better than me, better than Lockwood, from where I plucked you from?' I was sure worse followed, but I scurried away because I couldn't bear to hear them be so cruel to one another.

I had been in no hurry to marry – the idea of tying myself permanently to a man was unfathomable, almost frightening – but like all other girls I wanted to be admired, to have my fun. And so, after descending from my rooms after some champagne with a friend, the both of us swathed in silks and furs, diamonds glinting in our ears, I duly danced with every boy and man that asked, flirted back with the ones who were the least objectionable, and later found myself standing on the terrace at the rear of the house with one boy a year or so younger than me by the name of Charles. Lanterns lit the gardens in front of us as couples walked amongst its greenery, searching for somewhere quiet, and I was listening to Charles speak of a holiday he had taken on the south coast and watching, in an almost detached manner, the way he looked at me, his gaze lingering on my mouth before flicking down to my chest; the way he kept swiping a tongue across his dry lips when he listened to me speak; his face a picture of yearning, of youthful sincerity.

I asked him if he wanted to see the view from the roof outside my rooms up in the west turret and he nodded enthusiastically. We made our way through the house, his hand hot on my back, and then took the stairs to the first floor and walked down the long corridor to the west wing, our footsteps quiet on the thick carpet, nervous excitement (I assumed) making his movements a little stilted, before he stopped a few steps away from the spiral stone staircase that would bring him to my room.

He said that he would just be one moment, that he needed to use the facilities, and seemed so embarrassed that I did not offer him the use of my own bathroom. I sat on my stairs, tucked away from the hall as I waited for him and pictured what was about to happen in my bedroom, how his hands would fumble on the buttons of my dress, how he would be eager and appreciative, how the act itself would be uncomfortable and strange but that I would get my first time over with.

But when he had yet to return after fifteen minutes, I left to find him. He had got lost, surely; the house could be confusing to a new visitor. I knocked on the door of the nearest bathroom and pushed it open but it was empty, and then I crossed to the east wing and tried the bathrooms there too – the first was *empty, the second occupied by two girls who had giggled at my knock.*

I stood at the top of the stairs, feeling suddenly ridiculous in the dress that I had adored at the start of the evening, with half-thoughts that maybe he had fallen asleep somewhere or perhaps he had found another girl and changed his mind – but that was rather unlikely, when he had been so keen: he had danced with me for half an hour and looked as if he might die on the spot when I invited him to my room.

I waited there for five minutes, twisting on my heels, listening to the hum of the party, and there he was, finally, climbing the stairs. But his cheeks were red and he looked, I couldn't help but think, absolutely terrified.

'Everything all right?' I had asked.

'I'm sorry,' he had said, voice trailing off. He was trembling slightly and he wiped a sleeve across his forehead. 'I don't think this is such a good idea.'

'What's happened? Please tell me.'

'It's nothing. You're a great girl, I just – can't.' He grimaced a smile. 'I can't stay here—' he said, biting off the rest of his words and scurrying back down the stairs as I felt my own cheeks heat with embarrassment.

I stood there wondering what on earth had happened – a crisis of confidence? It didn't seem like it – and then two other figures climbed the stairs towards me.

My mother in her black dress and pearls, white fox fur draped over her elbow, hair mussed as if a hand had run through it, and lipstick faded and smudged; and my father, his bow tie loose around his neck.

'Hello, darling,' my mother said with a bright but tremulous smile. 'What are you doing on your own up here; you aren't waiting for someone, are you?'

'There was a boy, Charles, he wanted to see the family portraits,' I said as my father frowned. Charles had been one of the boys he mocked; a toothless runt, he had called him when my mother pointed out his pedigree to me, the grand estate he would inherit. 'He was frightened of something . . .' I trailed off, unable to explain.

'Maybe he saw her,' my mother said with a confidence that could only come from madness, 'the woman in white.' Her mascara had bled beneath her eyes, drawing out the dark hollows we both shared.

Maybe it was you, I thought spitefully, clenching my jaw. Maybe you scared him off.

'I think they're bringing the cake out soon; you should head on downstairs,' my father said kindly. 'Your mother needs some rest.' And I watched them leave, his hand tight on her arm, the white fur like a tail against the liquid black silk of her dress, hating her, feeling utterly rotten.

After that, I never tried to bring another partygoer back to my room, feeling bruised and embarrassed, fearing that my mother would make a scene or that they too would be spooked.

Maybe I should find myself a husband with an even grander house, I thought wryly as I smoked another cigarette and watched the crowds in the ballroom, and leave Lockwood altogether. Perhaps it was the house that was at fault – and I thought of the young maid who had left a few months ago, the one I had over-heard muttering to Dorothy that even with my mother and her fits gone, she could not bear to stay at Lockwood any longer, that there was something here, a lingering malevolence. Maybe if I left too, my nightmares would not follow. But maybe they would. Maybe it wasn't the house at all; maybe it was me, and had been all along.

And besides, although I had mocked my suitors for confusing

me with the estate itself, it was true that I was tied here, that I felt a responsibility to Lockwood as if it was woven into my very bones; that it was unlikely now that I would ever be compelled to leave, and that I would no doubt join my mother one day in the graveyard just up the lane with all the other Lady Lockwoods – locked up in our coffins, dry hair spilling across our shoulders, nails like claws reaching out towards the packed earth above.

Chapter Thirteen

It was the Major's voice echoing down the long gallery, I realized before I even reached him, and he was talking about the museum.

'I've seen larger butterflies on my travels, of course, I imagine you have too,' he was saying to someone. By the noise of feet shifting on the creaking floor, I pictured a crowd of about half a dozen with him. The long gallery only had four doorways inside of it, one pair at either end of the corridor, with two sets of six rooms linked together. The Major was in one of these middle rooms, hidden from my view.

'Oh, we have everything here, all the mammals.' The Major was now replying to someone else's muffled question. 'Every beastie you could want,' he said, and then did something that caused the guests to laugh.

I took the door on the opposite side of the corridor and walked through the rooms, checking that everything was still in place, my nerves on edge.

All was well until I came to the last room and the humming-bird cabinet.

The glass of the cabinet had been smashed open in the middle, as if a fist had punched right through it, and in the centre of the jagged hole I could see a bare branch and the empty spaces where a handful of hummingbirds had sat only this morning.

I marched across the hall and through the opposite doorway to find the Major and the crowd, and the thief that was likely amongst them.

'A marvellous example of plumage,' the Major was saying as I entered the room, a finger stroking one of the tail feathers of a bird of paradise, and then he took the same hand and tweaked a red curl of the woman standing next to him whose cheeks were pink with wine. 'What do you think, darling?' he asked her.

There were two men in officer's uniform with him and one in a tailcoat, plus four women, three of them at least half the age of the Major.

'Excuse me, Lord Lockwood,' I said, clearing my throat.

'Ah, Miss Cartwright!' he said, smiling at me with a touch of condescension. 'I've just been telling people about the museum.'

About my *museum*, I thought, *not* yours; hating the way he acted so proprietorially, as if he were responsible for the museum's careful collection of specimens, the curatorial work, the cataloguing and mounting of the animals, the building of the cabinets and the preparation of accurate labels and records.

'Did you take people through the rooms on the other side?' I asked. 'I've just found some damage there—'

'Back to the party now, everyone,' the Major said, clapping his hands together. 'I need to deal with some museum business. Work never ends,' he sighed jovially, and the women took the elbows of the men and left the room.

'Now,' he said, turning to me with a face free of humour, 'what's this about damage?'

'Come with me,' I said, not caring to be polite, and led him to the broken cabinet.

'You see,' I said, holding out a hand towards it. 'And there are some hummingbirds missing too. Do you know what happened? Was the door to the long gallery locked when you arrived?'

'Yes, it was locked,' he said and then he peered closer at the cabinet. 'Hmm, they *are* quite faded, aren't they, I thought that was just the distortion of the glass. Do they keep better away from the light?'

'This is a historical piece,' I stated, as if I needed to defend the poor hummingbirds and their discoloured feathers. 'Some of these specimens are very rare, and the display hasn't been touched for fifty years. You didn't hear a smash when you were in here, or a muffled crash? You're *sure* the door was locked?'

'It was,' he nodded vaguely, still staring at the birds.

'This was not here this morning; one of the guests has done this,' I stressed. 'One of the guests has taken the birds.'

'Taken the birds?' he scoffed. 'I can't think why.'

'*Why* doesn't matter, Lord Lockwood. Something must be done.'

'Quite,' he said, straightening himself up and pressing his fingers lightly against his bow tie to check it was still in place.

'So you'll make an announcement?' I pressed. 'And ask the culprit to come forward?'

'An announcement?' he said distractedly. 'Of course.'

'We won't prosecute, naturally,' I said, as he left the gallery.

'Of course not, Miss Cartwright.' His words were thrown over one shoulder as he strode down the corridor towards the main house, and I almost had to break into a run to keep up with him.

I turned off the bank of light switches and then called out to him, 'Your key!'

He paused in the second doorway and then turned round. 'Here you are,' he said, holding it towards me and then waiting while I locked the door so that I had no choice but to give it back to him. If it were up to me he would not have any keys to the museum's rooms, he would not have such free rein, but of course, it was his manor, so there was nothing to be done about it.

I squeezed past the guests lingering in lazy circles in the hall, entering the ballroom as the Major was calling everyone's attention by hitting a knife against his crystal glass.

He started with thanking us for joining him tonight, for our good humour and excellent dancing feet, for draining his cellars dry (there was much jocular laughter at this remark). He informed us that the party was drawing to its close now, that there would be a collection at the door for the regiment, and to let the housekeeper know if any of us were without transport, for they would gladly be put up in one of the available rooms. Lastly he asked, in an offhand way, if anyone had seen any stuffed birds – a question that resulted in more laughter which plucked at my already tight nerves. He quietened the crowd and explained that one of the cabinets had been knocked by an errant elbow and a few of the hummingbirds had fallen out of it and been mislaid – making it sound as if they had tumbled to the ground right in front of the cabinet and that I was the idiot who could not find them where they lay.

'All jokes aside,' he then said, 'please do check your pockets, just in case one of our guests has played a schoolboy joke and stashed a little feathered fellow there.'

A few people half-heartedly patted their pockets and then

the crowd made their slow exits, leaving glasses and crumbs and bags and stray gloves in their wake.

I strode up to the Major, who was hobnobbing by the door with the officers. 'Excuse me,' I said quietly.

'Yes, Miss Cartwright?' he asked, turning away from his group, his irritation at being interrupted again obvious yet replaced by a blank expression that was somehow all the more threatening for its blankness.

'Shouldn't the guests be searched as they leave?' I asked.

'No, they should not,' he said, moving us a little way away from the others. 'If someone really wanted to steal those birds, faded though they are, they would have already removed them from the house or slipped them inside their shoe, or something.' He leaned a little closer, voice dropping, and added, 'Should you like my guests to be patted down like miscreants? A handful of birds does not call for a hysterical reaction like this. I will gladly pay the cost of replacement but I will hear nothing more of this tonight. These men,' and with this, he pointed behind him, 'are off to fight for us soon and you want me to accuse them of being thieves? Get some perspective, *Miss* Cartwright, this country is at war.'

I stood there under his onslaught and bit my tongue, feeling angry and the kind of righteous frustration that would lead to later bitter tears. I would not let him know that I felt cowed so I tilted my chin up and listened to him as if he was saying something reasonable. Would he treat me like this if I were a man?

'Do you understand?' he said.

'Perfectly,' I answered, and he nodded and walked away, calling to Mary, whose pale dress gleamed in the light from the decorative candles. When she saw me over the Major's shoulder, she gave me a dirty look – just as she had every time she had met me – before she turned to beam at him, and I did my best not to give in to the childish impulse to stick my tongue out at her, to stick my tongue out at the both of them.

I retreated to the long gallery to the sounds of maids clearing away the party – the sweep of brooms, the clink of bottles and glasses, the scrape of cutlery against trays and plates – and the murmurs of a handful of guests moving upstairs to use the promised empty rooms to sleep off their revelries. I looked for the birds for the next half an hour, but came up empty-handed. I searched the rest of the museum rooms too, before locking the doors myself and checking in with the night guard, who was slumped in his chair by the door but still awake, his tie askew, looking like a reveller who had not had the energy to leave with the others, or perhaps a pale-throated sloth.

'I had a feeling something was going to happen tonight, but I thought it would be a scuffle outside rather than a theft,' he said, and I was pleased that someone else had been just as unsure about the ball as I was. 'It's high spirits, that's all,' he added quickly, though, dimming my good opinion of him. 'I remember when we were about to be shipped off, the mischief we got up to. Half those lads didn't come back, you know . . . I should be out there now, but for my leg.' As he spoke, he patted the offending limb forcefully.

'We appreciate what you do for the museum,' I said. 'This collection is of international importance; the specimens we have are incredibly rare, and valuable to all sorts of scientific research and discoveries.' He nodded politely, and I realized that I was making my case for the museum to him because I had failed to do so to the Major, to some of the other guests tonight who I had heard making wry comments. It was as if, if I could only get this weary man to understand, to agree with me, the night could be salvaged.

I left him there with his torch, feeling annoyed at myself for that impulse, that justification. If this house continued to cause problems, if other items went missing, I would call London and tell them another home for the museum would have to be found, even though it would cause all manner of fuss and would no doubt lose me my job and have me shuffled down the career ladder to a simple assistant again. But it would be worth it, to save the museum. It would be worth it too to see the Major have to put Lockwood to use for other war efforts – perhaps the army could use his lawns to practise throwing grenades, or his rooms could be filled with evacuated children with eager, sticky hands. I smiled at the thought.

I unlocked my room with the key from my purse, relieved that this had become a habit since Lucy's words of warning after my missing watch. But where was Lucy? I had not seen her in the ballroom when the Major was giving his announcement, nor afterwards. Perhaps she had been wisely hiding away in her tower room, tired by the noisy crowd who had invaded her home.

As I shucked my fine dress, feeling a little like a child who has borrowed her mother's glamorous but ill-fitting clothes, I stared at my reflection in the mirror, my wan face. There was a handprint smudged on the glass, its fingers splayed. It must have been left by an absent-minded maid, for it was not my hand, with the crooked joint in my little finger, and yet I did not remember seeing it before I left for the ball. But maybe the light was different now, or maybe it was because I stood at a different angle.

That night as I slept, with the full moon hidden by the

blackout curtains, my dreams were filled with scenes from the ball, with faces and bodies whirling around, with mirrors cracked and cabinets smashed open and mute animals standing vigil.

It was not a restful night's sleep.

Chapter Fourteen

I had escaped the party before it ended and curled myself into *a ball under my bedclothes. I had a headache, and the kind of jangling nerves that come from being on show, from being surrounded by a heaving mass of people who seemed to expand to fit inside every room so there was no place left to think, to breathe.*

How did my mother do it? She was the host of so many social occasions here at Lockwood: summer soirées, spring celebrations, Christmas, Halloween, Harvest; birthday parties and anniversary gatherings; extravagant dinners and weekend get-togethers; hunt balls and debutante comings-out. She liked children's parties best of all, for there had always been something childlike about her, a love of games and play pretending. She would hire entertainers – clowns and magicians and men with docile ponies to ride – and invite children from the village to bolster the crowd of family friends and servants' children. The house would be decorated in various fanciful themes and she would order the servants to create a veritable feast of sandwiches, cakes and ice cream, and would organize games that she often took part in too – ribbon races in the garden, sporting tournaments and musical chairs, charades, simple card games, and even a maypole on one occasion. But it was my eighth birthday – eight being the age I was when my nightmares first began – when she was unwell that I remembered most of all, and found myself recalling as I sheltered under the heavy weight of my quilts.

It had fallen on my new nurse to take charge of the children's games and after Mary, the cook's niece, had made two other girls cry, my nurse announced that we would play hide and seek. But unlike my mother, who was wise enough to confine such a game to a corridor or a single floor, the nurse told us to use the whole house, perhaps hoping that the game would last long enough that she could sit down and rest her feet. She made Mary be the seeker and as we set off from the entrance hall, giggling and racing, I glanced back to see her standing there looking sullen even with the nurse's hands held over her eyes so that she could not peek, counting to thirty in a petulant voice.

The children of the servants, who visited the house now and then and heard the stories of their parents, knew good hiding places, but I who had spent all my life here knew the best ones. That day, I chose one of the servants' bathrooms on the top floor, the one that was slightly concealed by a large cupboard. Once inside, with the door closed, I climbed into the bath. It still had a shallow puddle of water in it from the last bather, which seeped slowly into my dress the longer I waited.

I was giddy to begin with, from the excitement of hiding and the sharp sugar of the cake we had gorged on, but as time went on, as the light that leaked through the small window dimmed with the arrival of afternoon clouds, as the silence of the house grew around me like something I could touch, like a smothering blanket, I became frightened.

Soon, I was too frightened to even think about leaving and abandoning the game, for my mind had decided that something – someone – was steadily climbing the stairs to my floor, that they had made their silent way along the corridor, eyes *unblinking, and lurked just outside the door, that their hand was reaching right now for the door handle that I stared at with utter terror, my teeth chattering, my fingers cold with fear. In my mind, the party guests had gone home hours ago and the other members of the house had all vanished too. It was only me, and them – the person outside – remaining, and there was only an unlocked door between us.*

And when that door did finally open – when one of the servants who had been sent to find me opened it – I was hysterical with fear, screaming and fighting as they lifted me out of the bath and carried me down to my nurse, and even though they kept telling me all the while that everything was all right, that I was safe and found, they were indistinguishable to me from the monster who had been stalking me, and I knew I was lost, and could not be persuaded otherwise.

The party ended abruptly, the other children all having returned from their hiding places of their own accord after growing bored waiting to be found. A doctor was called for me as I lay on the floor of my nursery inconsolable, fending off arms trying to pick me up, while my mother, who had emerged from her sickbed after the guests left, with a scarf around her ears, upbraided the nurse for letting us wander the whole house. But it was only when the servants were halfway through clearing up the detritus that Mary herself, the missing seeker, returned, dangling one of my dolls in her fist. She had not found a single hiding child because she had fallen asleep, she said, looking flushed and chastened, dropping the doll in a heap of limbs on the floor and running outside swiftly before her aunt could spank her.

My father, once he emerged from where he had taken sanctuary in his office, decided it had been the game that had frightened me and told my mother that she should not play such a game with me again, an order that she did not keep. But perhaps she should have; perhaps he knew that there was something fright-ening about the games of children – all those blindfolds and chases and hunts, the make-believe and play-pretend. Perhaps a child like myself with a wild imagination should have stuck to books and wholesome walks in the gardens, or studious needle-work, and never raced down the long corridors of Lockwood while my mother laughed and chased me until we were both winded and silly, giggling in a heap on some faded Turkish rug, gazing up at the dust motes dancing in the air above us.

My mother should still be here, keeping her beady eyes on the house, being beautiful and glittering and difficult. Now all that was left were her clothes, her shoes, the painting of her on my father's bedroom wall, and the memory of her lingering in each room just as her funeral flowers did. It wasn't fair; she had been so careful, so worried that something, someone, was out to get her, that her death was somehow foretold, that she had lived her last years crazed with terror.

And if she was right, a sly voice inside me said, if she was right about her death, then might she not be right about all her other fears, about the ghost haunting Lockwood?

It was only the ball, I told myself, as I turned over and pushed my face into the pillow – only the guests reminiscing about my mother, the women in their furs.

In my dreams, the fur coats in our wardrobes kept coming alive, the mice gnawed at my bedposts and the leveret skittered away from my fingers; in my dreams I was always searching, always weeping, as blue walls crept closer and enclosed me tight. The bathroom where I had hidden so many years ago did not have blue walls and the bath itself was a faded cream, so that was not where those particular nightmares began, and though I had searched for it in the daylight, that room I dreamed of was nowhere to be found.

And when I didn't sleep, when I lay awake in the quiet of the early morning hours, I couldn't help but notice that if I listened hard enough, the shush and thrum of my blood sounded like soft footsteps, like a dress dragging across the floor outside my room.

Chapter Fifteen

The morning after the ball, I went straight to the long gallery and the hummingbird cabinet. A silly part of me had hoped that it had only been a dream, but there was the jagged hole, there the shards of glass on the floor, glittering like sharp snow, and there were the bare branches where half a dozen humming-birds had once been fixed in place, their dry wings paused in motion, their eyes dark beads of glass. It did not make me feel any better that it was an old exhibit which had never been of much use to scientists, that they were faded and often poorly mounted.

The jaguar, the handful of hummingbirds – surely the third incident would mean the end of my tenure here. I felt angry and hopeless, as if I too were being toyed with by someone, that it was personal, when I knew that rationally it had nothing to do with me, that it was the museum that was being targeted. Evacuation was supposed to mean safety and yet we had suffered more loss and damage than London by this point, and without needing the assistance of the Luftwaffe, who were still biding their time on the Continent.

As I patched the hole in the glass with board, hiding half of the remaining hummingbirds from view, I thought of the ball last night, of the crowds wandering hither and thither, spirited with champagne and dance. I had searched the museum rooms for the birds, but I had not searched on any other floor. Perhaps the person who had stolen them had discarded them in a different part of the house? Perhaps it had been some poorly thought out drunken jape forgotten the moment the attacker returned to the party.

I decided I would check myself rather than asking the housekeeper for assistance, because although she could be cold with the other servants, she was positively glacial when I asked for help, taking any request as a monstrous imposition, and I had no intention of humbling myself further before her by explaining how personal this was to me, how my future might just rely on a handful of dried birds.

That evening, I started with the rooms on my floor, but discovered two problems – the first being that the servants were forever striding up and down the corridor and I was quite conspicuous with my torch, and the second that to search a room for a greying object the size of a thumb would take far longer than I had first supposed.

I only managed to search one room, the twin opposite mine, whose bed linens I had to remove and the bed remake, for fear I would squash the fragile birds if I patted down the covers to discover if they had been tucked under the blankets. I worked to the sounds of the loud ticking of the clock on the windowsill, the disquieting scrape of ivy against the blacked-out window, and frequent footsteps along the hall, none of which were exactly conducive to a calm atmos-phere for my search. I looked under the beds, behind the heavy drape of the curtains, in the whitewashed wardrobe with its loudly squeaking door, inside the nightstand (whose drawer required a three minute jiggle of its handle to pull out), and underneath the heavy rug, in case I found the flattened bird skins there. For my troubles, my clothes were now coated with dust and it was an hour beyond my usual bedtime.

One room down, dozens more to go, I thought as I fell asleep to that same sound of the clock, drifting its way through the crack underneath my door, as if it was a metronome, and the rooms of the house were pipes of some giant organ waiting to be played.

It was not until couple of days later that I saw Lucy for the first time since the ball. A group of us – including servants and the lady of the house – were in the drawing room crowded around the wireless, listening to the news of the bombing of Scapa Flow, of the losses to our naval fleet.

'How many men do you think can fit in the *Royal Oak*?' Lucy asked, face creased with pain.

'More than a thousand,' one of the maids said. 'My uncle is in the navy,' she explained.

'A thousand,' Lucy repeated, her voice shaking, and when someone asked about the lifeboats, about air pockets, I left, unable to bear such gruesome talk.

Lucy followed me to the summer room, which had become one of my favourite places to linger because it was as quiet as my office but did not have a stack of work there to upbraid me for being idle. She sat down on a sofa that was situated next to the looming antelope and the cabinet of Tapiridae skulls, in front of the wall of pinned butterflies, wrapping her arms around her shoulders.

'It's so dreadful what happened to the sailors,' she said. 'I can't imagine the terror of being sunk, of struggling in the water.' Her hands fumbled at her lighter.

'Here, let me,' I said, cupping the flame and lighting her cigarette.

'There's a particular nightmare I've had since I was young, of being trapped, of being smothered, and I can't help thinking of it when I think of the sailors,' she said. 'Do you ever feel like the anxieties of your nightmares follow you into the next day?' She tapped out ash as she asked the question, and I nodded. 'It's all this waiting around, isn't it? This agonizing wait for the war to begin in earnest, beyond these dreadful few attacks. I should be mourning them, not hurrying forth more tragedies.'

'We knew the war was coming,' I said. She was wearing a well-loved pair of navy trousers today and their knees were slightly faded. 'It's understandable that everyone wants it to begin, wants to know what we're up against. We want our fear to have form, to know how we should face it.'

'Thank you, Hetty,' she said, smiling a little sadly and rubbing a hand across her collarbone. 'You know just what to say to comfort me.'

I do? I wanted to ask.

'I heard about the poor hummingbirds at the ball,' she continued. 'I'm so sorry about that; what an awful thing for someone to do. You still haven't found the birds?'

'No,' I sighed. 'Perhaps they are wherever the blasted jaguar is,' I added drolly.

Her mouth twitched in a smile and then she shifted her legs to cross her ankles. 'I also wanted to apologize for my father,' she said gingerly. 'I know he can be quite brusque in his manner.'

Only if brusqueness is a politer way of saying that he is a bully, I thought. 'I had assumed that he would be quite busy with his businesses. He had implied that he took regular trips elsewhere, and I wonder if it is not just that he feels the museum is very underfoot, you know,' I said diplomatically.

'Then I should definitely be the one to apologize. Because it's true, he isn't keen on being cooped up here all the time, but I think he's worried about me, after losing Mother and Grandmother, and the funny turn I had.'

'Oh goodness, I didn't mean to suggest—'

'Of course you didn't,' she said, picking up my hand and squeezing it. 'I am perfectly well now; he is overprotective to a fault, my father, especially now that my mother and grandmother are no longer around. I'm sure he'll be off soon and leave you to it.'

'The museum has found a wonderful home here,' I said, glancing down at our hands. I had been so busy getting irritated at the Major, as if he was trespassing here, that I had forgotten that this was Lucy's home too.

'I just enjoy the house being full again, especially knowing that we're likely to lose more of the servants to the war, even if Father rants and raves to the War Office about them being *absolutely essential*. As if losing them to rumours of ghosts wasn't bad enough.' She stubbed out her cigarette and sat back to regard the room. 'It's so diverting having your animals here, Hetty. Even when I'm not helping with the cleaning, I love to wander through the museum rooms; it's like my own private exhibition, and every time I walk around I spot new things in the cabinets, as if they've been shuffled around by stagehands behind the scenes.'

'Yes, quite,' I said, slightly discomforted by her words – for was I not still noticing that the animals and the smaller cabinets looked out of place when I opened up the rooms in the morning, as if they had shifted in the night, mad as that sounded?

*

I did not tell Lucy about my new quest for the hummingbirds. I was not sure why, only that I did not want her to feel troubled. Evening after evening, I continued my search through the unoccupied rooms of the first floor, but there was another hurdle to overcome, for the day after the news about Scapa Flow, it started to rain heavily and, as the news came in about further bombing raids on the Scottish coasts and attacks on our merchant fleet, it became apparent that Lockwood Manor leaked. And so the servants and I were to be found hurrying about with pots and pans and dishes, looking for puddles and damp patches, ears pricked as if we were listening for Morse code and not drips and splashes of water. I wanted to blame the Major for the poor condition of Lockwood's roof but I knew that rain like that – great, thick sheets that drummed on every surface with a loud roar – caused the same kind of leaks back at the museum building in London.

I could not blame him for the mice either, who had retreated from the floods outside into the warmth of Lockwood, with its large kitchen and stores, with its mounted animals waiting for the little rodents to gnaw on, and who remained even after the rain had cleared, delighting in the exotic wonders of their new home. We set endless traps and took it in turns between us to unlock the museum doors in the morning, breath held to wonder how many dead mice we would find, and then ferry them at arm's length out of the back door. When I would lock up the museum rooms each night, I could not help but feel I was only locking *in* the mice, that I was condoning their feast somehow, saying *here, have at 'em*. The mice liked the cabinets as well, god knows why, maybe it was just the lingering smells and scents of animals and human visitors, or perhaps something in the varnish. They chewed on the corners, a horrible scratching sound that echoed, so that you thought you might turn the corner and find a whole crowd of them and not just one industrious fellow who fled quick as a shot when he saw your foot.

And of course, mice could be of a similar size to humming-birds, the birds' feathers a grey like the rodents' hides, so now when I searched for my missing birds in the last of the rooms on the first floor; as I lifted rugs, threw back dustsheets that clouded the air with their catch, opened drawers, swung back heavy wardrobe doors and billowed curtains away from windows; as I discovered the lesser secrets of Lockwood, the furniture that covered up patches of mould and peeling paint, the scribbles of ink in various hands inside wardrobes and underneath beds, the spots of damp that chilled a wall, the slight depressions where old doors or windows had been bricked up; as I tried to be as quiet as possible for fear of being discovered myself, I had in the back of my mind the thought that if I did find a little grey hump, it was just as likely to be a mouse, alive or dead.

I had tried to search during the day, thinking that it would be easier with the natural light from outside, but in the first room I tried, I had glanced out of the window to see Jenkins standing near the back of the house, rifle across his shoulder, the smudge of a fox in his fist, staring right at where I stood, as if he had noticed the curtain was out of place, and I ducked out of sight, nonsensically afraid of – what? Being found in one of the spare guest rooms? Still, I took it as a sign that I should restrict my search to the evenings and light my way with my torch.

The barn cats from the farm had been brought into the house for the mice and lolled in awkward spots during the day, staring slit-eyed as we tried not to trip over their fat bellies. They spent their nights on a parallel hunt to mine, and yet they had evolved for such a task, stalking the halls and the rooms of the manor house noiselessly, squeezing their way through hidden passages and holes after their quarry. In the dark of the blackout they would have an advantage over the mice, and myself, with our comparatively poor vision.

I told myself that I had not got where I was by being half-hearted about my endeavours, and that my reputation – my very future – was staked on the welfare of the specimens; and thus it was that I started tentatively searching the second floor, where a handful of servants lodged in the east wing, in rooms that had been refurbished in the last decade and were markedly more spacious than the poky rooms in the west wing that had been barely touched since the turn of the century. I tried to choose days and times when the servants would be busy or asleep, hurrying up and down the stairs and along corridors with my torch in my hand and my heart in my throat, expecting every groan of the floorboards and creak of doors shifting in the creeping draughts to herald my discovery.

It was while I was searching one of these darkened rooms late one afternoon, lying on the hard mattress of the narrow bed while the spiderwebs in the eaves above me trembled, with my head jammed painfully between floor and bedframe, shining my light under the bed, that the door to the room opened with a loud rasp.

'What on earth is going on in here?' the housekeeper demanded as I bashed my head on the bedframe in my hurry to turn my torch off and sit up.

I stared at her, feeling a flush of shame spread down my chest, unwittingly reminded of my mother's reprimands.

'Miss Cartwright, may I be of assistance?' she asked scathingly.

'I was looking for the hummingbirds, the ones that went

missing at the ball,' I admitted, unable to come up with a better excuse.

'But we found those a week ago! Did Dorothy not give them to you?'

'What?' I asked.

'Yes, in one of the guest rooms.'

'But I searched the guest rooms!' She looked at me with something that was almost loathing, but I could not stop myself from asking another question. 'Where exactly were they found?'

'Oh, on top of the bedside table in the purple bedroom, in plain sight apparently. I'm sure we'd have found them even sooner, but it is hard for us to manage the whole house with so many maids leaving us,' she said pointedly, almost as if I was somehow responsible for that. Her words, if not her manner, were reasonable, and yet what she was saying could not possibly be right because I had searched that very room top to toe. Or was she right, and I had missed the birds completely?

'If you have concerns about the house,' she continued now, 'please come to me; this is the servants' floor, and neither this nor the other guest rooms are part of the museum.'

You have no right to be here, I heard – and she was right, which was why I was so embarrassed. It was a fault of mine to get obsessive about my work, to be so single-minded as to ignore constraints and niceties – my habit of skipping lunch, the brusque way I had been known to treat people who were preventing me from hurrying back to my desk, my assumption that others were just as focused as I was – but this was something else.

What has this house done to me? I found myself thinking as I returned to my room and stared at the pile of unread books

I had brought with me, listening to the tinny sounds of the wireless and laughter from the parlour below.

There was something about Lockwood, about the potential of all its empty rooms. The sheer scale of them made one think that things one had lost, things one desired to find, could be hiding in them, waiting for one to come upon them. The house seemed to encourage wandering, hunting – the long corridor of its first floor, with the wall sconces leading you forwards, the tall windows, the neat condition of each room that a dozen servants tended to; the hidden service stairs waiting to be found; the narrow warren of the servants' floor; and above all the vacuum of life, the absence of people in the rooms that had been so lovingly prepared for them.

Had it been her all along? I thought, when I woke from a nightmare that night, the remnants of my dream – of a woman dressed in white gliding through the corridors of Lockwood after me – lingering and making my heart race. Was the housekeeper playing a trick on me? Had she hidden the hummingbirds, which now sat on my desk ready to be mended and placed back in their home? Or was it me, was I going mad?

Chapter Sixteen

*T*here was a world outside of Lockwood, I reminded myself
in the small hours of the night when I woke from nightmares
and could not get back to sleep, when the dark shapes of my
bedroom pulsed around me and my mouth felt dry and hot, when
I felt sorry for myself. I would try to listen to the wireless, thinking
that at least I might use the lost hours to keep myself better
informed, that my own meagre misfortunes wouldn't stand up
against those of others.

But when I fiddled with the dial of the machine trying to find
a signal, the hissing sound, the voices in different languages
sliding and burbling in and out of range across Europe, made
me frightened. As if, were I to turn the dial to the right position,
a ghostly voice might speak to me and call me by my name.

I should keep my hands busy, I thought next, distract my
mind by putting myself to industry. But I had never been good
at knitting, and my shaking fingers were forever dropping
stitches, and what use would my hats and scarves be to the
sailors who needed them if they were full of holes to let in the
icy winds of the North Sea? And when I occupied myself with
looking through the attic or the shut-up rooms for goods I could
give to the drives or to auctions in aid of war efforts, I would
only find myself unnerved, partly because old and faded things,

broken things, have a tendency to make one feel melancholic, and partly because, as I scrabbled through boxes and cases and under dustsheets by the bright spotlight of the lantern and torches I brought with me, it didn't feel like I was searching for iron or fabric or whatever else was needed, but something else, something nebulous and shifting, as if I was almost tempting the house to reveal something terrible to me, as if I wanted to hasten whatever horrors it felt like my dreams were foretelling.

But a brisk walk around the gardens – there could be nothing sinister, nothing frightening about that, surely? Every nurse of mine had espoused the wonders of a walk, as had my grandmother, whose walking stick and sturdy boots were kept polished and ready by the door for her twice-daily constitutions.

'She's surveying,' my mother used to say when we caught sight of her through the windows, arm resting on the crook of her stick as she stood on the lawn and peered back at the house. 'She's checking that everything she owns is still there, still up to snuff; she's striding the boundaries of her little kingdom.'

'The old servants say that Lockwood was a wreck when her husband arrived, that she married him only for his money,' my mother said one morning when we were taking tea on the terrace and watching my grandmother parading around the garden with the help of a long-suffering servant at her elbow. 'The east wing had been shut up completely, with birds nesting there and wood rot and damp and all manner of mess, and his money filled it with servants again, a whole host of them to do her ladyship's calling. She should have been happy, and perhaps she was, but in later life, she has never been able to get over the fact that your father didn't marry for money as she had done – because he met me and my family didn't have any left,' she said with a laugh. 'He married me for love, and saved me.'

Saved you from what? I *thought later, when her nerves were at their worst, when she blamed my father for ever bringing her here.*

They argued about money sometimes, my parents, about the cost of all her parties, even though I knew that my father relished each one, that there was nothing he liked better than sweeping across the ballroom or a crowded drawing room greeting all and sundry and showing off Lockwood at its best.

'Old houses bleed money,' he used to say, especially when we had been visited by the men he had to hire from outside, the craftsmen, the blacksmiths, the plasterers and builders, 'they're an endless pit of gold.' That was why, I surmised – because my father had stopped talking to me of money long ago, fearing perhaps that it would only worry me – he had set up his businesses and built his factories, to raise funds for the upkeep of Lockwood.

'Even walls can crumble, remember that, my dove,' he told me once, and I remembered his words as I circled the house on my walks, pausing in the orchard where the arms of gnarled apple trees had been pinned to the worn brick wall, the mortar wet and crumbling beneath my searching fingers.

If I concentrated on the gardens, on my memories of a child-hood running through the grass and down the paths and weaving in between the trees, laughing with the other children as we shone buttercups beneath our chins, made daisy chains and gathered colourful leaves, then I would not be tempted to look up at Lockwood, to let my eyes run across its walls, its windows, its turrets and its towers. Because there was another motive to my walks, one that I was trying to ignore – for, having searched the interior of Lockwood from top to toe for a room with blue wallpaper, a room with an old candle chandelier and bare floor-boards, a room that came to life only in my nightmares, and having found no such room, I was now searching from the outside, counting the windows and the spaces between and mapping out a ghostly floorplan. As if my tired eyes might be able to peel back brick and wood and plaster and find it there, my lost room, and whatever terrible secrets it held.

Chapter Seventeen

A fortnight after the hummingbirds had been returned to me and I had placed them back in their cabinet, hidden behind the wooden board that was a temporary stopgap until a new glass front could be fitted, I was working in one of the museum's rooms, answering letters on a mahogany writing desk I had moved by a chair, when one of the maids, Joyce – who I had catalogued as a Sclater's lemur for her startling pale blue eyes – came in to dust and clean.

I had arranged my letters in various piles around me and stood up, offering to leave, but she said, 'Don't leave on my account, miss, I can easily work around you,' and the tone of her voice, her exhausted stare, made me feel that if I did get up and leave it would be some kind of insult to her work.

So instead I sat there, while the clock ticked loudly and my pen scratched louder still, as Joyce circled the room, sighing when she shifted the vases of dried flowers and petals crinkled to the floor.

I found myself following the careful, practised movements of her hands as she wiped the bases of the taxidermied animals with a cloth and polish, and then brushed her duster along the curved horns of the lechwe, the cabinet holding the

Japanese marten, and the back of the snarling honey badger with its white cap of hair and beady eyes.

When I had entered this room an hour ago I had idly noticed the honey badger there on the mantelpiece in front of the gilt-edged mirror, its tail almost curling around the base of the vase of flowers, but now I remembered that it was usually housed in the billiards room on a side table.

'Did you move that in here?' I asked suddenly. 'The badger?'

'Pardon?' Joyce said, looking put out. 'This creature? No, of course not, I'm very careful with my cleaning, miss, and besides, I wouldn't like to pick it up and touch it.' She grimaced. 'I'm sure it's important from a scientific point of view, but you'll forgive me if I find it a bit horrid.'

I was sure that I had seen it in the billiards room only the previous evening, when I made my final check of the specimens before locking them up, not here in the sitting room. And the large-spotted genet that I had idly walked past in the music room when I opened up this morning, had that not been in the library on top of the squat cabinet by the door previously?

I gathered my papers, thanked Joyce and left the room, trailing through the museum's collection, ducking around tails and outstretched wings, circling the hulk of larger mammals, peering along rows of smaller animals, species who would never have a chance to meet in the wild now squashed next to one another on the fine marble mantelpiece of an English lord, their fur dry, their eyes unblinking glass baubles.

The pine marten, with its orange neck and small snout, had it been turned to face the wall or had it just been knocked out of place by a stray elbow or someone dusting?

I had not been here long enough to form a map in my mind of each animal and its rightful location; I must simply be remembering wrong, I thought, reaching out to touch the raised paw of the black bear in the drawing room, an animal that I knew for certain was still in its correct place, for I had gazed at it a week ago while pondering how to politely refuse the request of a researcher asking to study a particular set of bones that were shut up in crates in the long gallery of Lockwood.

It must just be my mind playing tricks on me, or one of the maids cleaning. As long as no other exhibit followed the jaguar's example and disappeared, there was nothing truly amiss.

Still, that afternoon, I put aside my pressing work and made another inventory of the museum's collection – finishing well into the evening, my legs sore from kneeling and squatting before each specimen, my back from twisting and bending around cabinets and looking inside chests – but found no other animal besides the jaguar missing.

It was nothing, I told myself as the weeks went by, and I had far more important things to be doing – a mountain of letters to answer and forms to fill out, the Ministry of Works and Buildings to coordinate with, the upkeep of the mounted animals themselves – than checking if the specimens had been moved ever so slightly.

It was nothing, and yet each night in my restless dreams I was forever walking through the museum rooms and seeing the shift of movement from the corners of my eyes, turning round to find the entire space rearranged, or a marauding beast charging after me, and waking with a panicked snort.

It was nothing, and yet I was confining myself inside the house even though the autumn weather had turned the gardens glorious with colour; crisp with bright, clear days that were always my favourite for a tramp across London's parks.

I had forgotten what a small relief it was to take a train home from my place of work, to have no responsibilities beyond my lodging room and never to worry that the museum's exhibits might be tampered with in the night, trusting the guards and the soaring museum building to keep its inhabitants safe. Living amongst and above the specimens made it hard to escape from them; I felt them there underneath me at night when I felt too nervous to fall back to sleep, a great crowd, a silent hum, so many eyes in the dark waiting. How many more autumns would I spend here, I thought in the loneliest hours before dawn, how many more years of broken sleep and worry?

One day in early November, desperate for a respite from the house and its walls that seemed to press in ever closer, I caught Lucy leaving by the front door and asked her if she wanted company on her errands.

'I was going to cycle up to the village today,' she said, 'get there and back before it rains. Can you ride? I'll get someone to bring out my mother's old bicycle.'

'I can ride but please, you needn't go to all that fuss, I can join you another day.'

'It's not a fuss,' she said with a smile, as a second bike was wheeled out to join the first.

'All right then,' I said, feeling warmed by her easy inclusion, and as we rode away from the house, I made a point not to look back, not to allow myself a moment of worry.

Lucy was wearing a coat with fur neck and trim that made her look impossibly elegant, her cheeks flushed with health once we had made the rise of the hill out of the valley and puffed our way up to the village.

As we entered the tobacconist's and rounded past the huddle of children peering at the jars of sweets, I was still trying to catch my breath, having spent far too much time in the past few months secluded inside. The man behind the counter greeted Lucy warmly, just as others we had passed in the village had done, with varying levels of deference, as she asked them how their families were, their sons who were off to war. It must be strange to have everyone know who you are, I thought, as Lucy's polite smile became increasingly strained, to know that they were all watching you and would report back their observations, gossip about your family.

'Cigarette?' Lucy offered when we left the shop, lighting one for herself. 'I know it's terribly uncouth to smoke in public,' she added as a matronly woman looked over in disapproval. 'My grandmother would have had a fit. Perhaps that's why I haven't caught myself a husband yet,' she joked, and I was trying to think of a way to ask why she *didn't* have a husband, when I noticed a familiar figure at the end of the street, her pale hair like a beacon.

'Oh god,' I muttered.

'What's wrong?'

'That woman over there,' I nodded. 'Mary, I think her name is. I had a terrible encounter with her the first time I came to the village. She seems to loathe me and I haven't the faintest idea what I've done. Do you know her?'

'I do, yes,' Lucy said, 'and I'm not sure I have the strength for an encounter with her today either. Come on,' she said, taking me by the elbow and pulling me down an alleyway, leading me on a different route out of the village as we walked alongside our bicycles. 'We used to play together as children,' Lucy explained. 'But I'm not sure we were ever that fond of each other; she was such a cross little girl, and could be a bit of a bully. She stole my doll once and didn't give it back to me until my father gave her another as a replacement.' Lucy clicked her tongue in mock anger. 'I think I might have been jealous of her too; she had blue eyes and lovely blonde ringlets, like an angel.

She married some rich fellow young and I hadn't seen her for years before he passed away and then, not long after the accident, she became my father's girlfriend of sorts.' Lucy winced.

'Gosh,' I said, and then Lucy's bike got tangled up with a bush at the front of someone's garden and clattered to the ground.

'Oh dash it, the chain's come off,' she said, hands fluttering above it.

'I can fix it,' I said, crouching down, pleased I hadn't thought to change out of my workwear for our trip, eager to help her in this small way at least. 'That must have been awkward for you, Mary and your father,' I said, to nudge her back to our previous conversation, while I rocked the bike forward and back and eased the greased chain into place.

'Awkward is the right word,' she said with a snort, resting a hand on my shoulder. 'She practically moved into the house, but I was in such a state then that I couldn't muster the words to complain to my father. He was only grieving in his own way, I think; he's not a man that does well alone. But luckily, the arrival of your museum seemed to give my father the impetus to put an end to things. So I must thank you for that, Hetty,' she said with a pat of her hand and a laugh, 'and for fixing my bicycle,' she declared, when I had stood up and was wiping my hands on the leaves of the unruly bush and then on my single handkerchief, which was quickly ruined.

'Here,' Lucy said, 'you've got some on your cheek.' She rubbed at my cheek with her own embroidered handkerchief, her fingertips tilting my chin up to the waning light.

'It's going to rain,' I said, because I feared that we might be here for quite some time if she sought to remove all the grease from my person.

'Oh, it is, drat,' she said with a tsk and a glance at the

darkening clouds. 'Race you to the house?' she dared, with a jaunty cock of her eyebrow, and then we were off, the cold air whipping past our faces, our legs furiously pedalling, as I thought about what she had said about Mary and the reason for her hatred of me. She must have thought that I had some personal hand in her being turfed out of Lockwood, and I was irritated anew with the Major for not correcting her assumption.

Thinking of Mary distracted me at least from the black clouds above us, the rising winds, from the way it seemed as if we were making some descent into a forbidding landscape. The brooding bulk of the house loomed out of the valley, widening to fill the entire vista before me, the gravelled path kicking up stones like little needles on my calves, my greased hands slick and uncomfortable when I clutched the handlebars to stop myself from skidding.

We returned to a house in uproar – a burst pipe that had only been noticed when water had bled through the ceiling of one of the empty bedrooms. Lucy dashed off to find the source of the leak and I left Dorothy in the museum rooms, scouring ceilings for signs of water, and raced upstairs to the servants' floor and then, following the noise of voices, up to the attic.

'Have you turned the stopcock?' I asked, out of breath, the dust of the space making me cough.

'Of course we have,' the housekeeper said. She was speaking to Paul, Lockwood's youngest servant (who I had named an old world otter for his easy grin) who was studying the wall in front of him, with Lucy by his side.

'It's an old house,' Lucy said, 'the pipes are higgledy-piggledy. The water hasn't reached the museum yet, has it?' she asked me, a hand on my shoulder.

'No, it's fine.' *For now*, I thought.

'They think it's something to do with my bathroom. It's the

other side of this wall,' she said, knocking the wood in front of her with her knuckles.

Paul had a crowbar in a gap between two panels of the wall. 'What colour is your bathroom, my lady?' he asked Lucy.

'Pink.'

'Not blue?' he said.

'Blue?' she repeated, her voice gone strange.

I glanced at her just as Paul pulled two wooden panels free with a loud crack and saw an expression of absolute terror bloom on her face at the sight of what he had revealed.

I turned to look through the gap in the wood, to see what had so horrified her.

A small room, with faded blue chinoiserie wallpaper and bare floorboards, a narrow black fireplace that gleamed in the light spilling from some crack in the roof, a bricked-up doorway opposite us, and an old cobwebbed chandelier swaying gently in the breeze.

Chapter Eighteen

As if the panic of the leak, which had been hastily fixed, and the stormy winds outside, which were currently plucking tiles off the roof of Lockwood, were not enough, and the house was desperate to make the most of the season, that same night, around one o'clock in the morning, its occupants were woken up by screams, blood-curdling and savage, the kind that had you leaping up with an answering noise trapped in your own throat.

I wrapped myself in my dressing gown and came blundering out of my room. There were figures at the west end of the hall, the same direction the noise was coming from.

'What's happening?' I asked Joyce, who was standing there with her hair in rags.

'It's nothing, miss. You should wait downstairs.'

'But what – who – is it?' I said, even though I had a terrible idea of who might be in distress.

'It's Lady Lucy, she's had a funny turn.'

'Is she all right?' I asked, aware that this was a useless question, that from the sound of her cries she was obviously not *all right*.

'Her father is with her – he returned a few hours ago – and the housekeeper too, and I imagine the doctor has already been called.'

The night guard came labouring upstairs to investigate the noise and I turned and told him that all was well, and that he should go back to his post. I was about to reluctantly return to my room when the screams hit a new pitch, and I was rooted to the spot.

'Stop talking nonsense and pull yourself together, girl!' I heard the Major exclaim.

I told myself that if I heard him slap her, I would go up there and stop him, and my legs tensed in anticipation. But the screams only turned into sobbing, interspersed with high keening notes. I wanted to help her, to comfort her, but what use would I be compared to a doctor and a father and a housekeeper who had known her for many years? I could feel sympathetic tears prick at my own eyes.

'If you go and wait in the drawing room, I shall come and bring you some tea,' Dorothy said to me, having also emerged from the dark behind our group.

'Oh no, please, there's no need,' I said, coughing to hide the thickness of my voice.

'Nonsense, miss, it'll give me something to do too. I got quite the fright when I woke up to the screaming,' she said, looking towards the end of the corridor distractedly.

I sat awkwardly in the drawing room surrounded by my looming animals; although they normally gave me comfort, tonight I felt particularly lonely, and pictured the servants who had been woken huddled together in the warmth of the kitchens. In London there was always a siren or the sound of motor cars passing on the street, feet tripping their way along the pavement, and voices calling no matter what hour it was, and I missed the city suddenly with a great ache.

After an interminably long amount of time, Dorothy arrived at the door to collect my cold tea.

'Poor thing,' she said, motioning her head towards the thin, reedy cry that could still be heard – for the hum of the wind did little to camouflage the sounds coming from upstairs – and which plucked at my heart. 'It was terrible what happened to her. She was such a happy little thing until she turned eight or so. The troubled year, us servants called it; sometimes children have those difficult times, don't they, but hers stuck with her. There was the incident on her birthday of course, the game of hide and seek that went on too long and frightened her, but if you ask me, it was the bird that decided things, that traumatized her.'

She paused and looked sideways at me. She did not often have the opportunity to tell this story and was obviously savouring the occasion.

'What happened?' I asked, because I was curious and desperate to know more about Lucy, for an explanation for her anguish, even though I knew that what I should have done was to respect her privacy and not listen eagerly to gossip.

'Her parents were hosting a late summer party in the gardens, tea on the lawn and croquet and a brass band,' Dorothy said, 'and she was dressed like a little angel, all lace and froth and a necklace of pearls given to her by her daddy. She came tripping along the path –' she pointed towards where the garden was, out in the dark of the night – 'and we had the dovecote still then, of course. So she comes skipping down there and turns the corner at a hedge, and *crunch*.' She sucked the breath in through her teeth. 'She had stepped on a little bird, feathers and wings and all! And she had bare feet. Can you imagine?'

'The bird died?'

'Of course, though we tried to tell her it was going to die anyway, lying there on the path; its wing was probably already broken,' she added, twisting one shoulder up to illustrate her point. The lights in the drawing room flickered for a minute and we stopped and stared at them, as if remembering that there was a war and a threat of planes out there, outside. But the electricity settled and she continued, 'She was inconsolable. She shrieked and cried and fair tried to claw her own eyes out. She had marks across her face for a month after that. They had to call for a doctor and drug her that week, she wouldn't stop crying. That's why she walks the way she does, I reckon.' She lifted a foot.

Had I noticed that Lucy had a half-limp, a cautious footstep? At that moment, Dorothy could have convinced me that she did.

'They say the body remembers what the mind doesn't,' she continued. 'The feel of that little dove under the sole of her foot.' She shivered and the teacup rattled on its saucer in her hand. 'And after that . . . poor thing. Would have given anyone a fright, I bet.'

I thought about the little girl and the bird as I listened to the wind shake the window frames and whisper through gaps in the floorboards, chilling my toes. And then, just as Dorothy left and shut the door behind her, I stopped with a start. *But, my dove*, I thought. *He calls her 'my dove'.*

I went back up to bed, but even when the noise, which now had the soft timbre of a hurt animal and wrenched the soul, finally faded away, I could not sleep. I had felt a sudden burst of shame after sliding into bed, like biting into a sour raspberry and feeling the wash of juice prickle the back of your tongue. What was I doing talking about Lucy to Dorothy like that; what was I doing betraying her trust? Had I been so long an observer of other people's friendships that I did not know how to behave inside of one? I vowed that I would tell her what had been told to me, even if she chose not to be friends with me in return.

I was losing my professional distance living here, the focus that had won me the directorship despite my mistake, listening to stories of ghosts and making a mad hunt for lost humming-birds. Lockwood was a claustrophobic world in miniature, with old hierarchies still in place, with its maze of rooms, and sometimes it felt like those of us who lived in the manor were the only people alive and that the war was but a dream. The 'phoney war' they called it, since the promised bombing of London had yet to start, but even London itself sometimes seemed phoney to me, a city I had imagined, full of an anony-mous crowd of people and streets stretching endless to the horizon. The atmosphere here was so stifled and close, no wonder Lucy was ill at ease.

The Major had strong words for me at breakfast, his eyes sunken and tired, his manner terse. I kept hoping that someone else would come in and disrupt him but no one obliged.

'The housekeeper said that you've put Lucy to work with a vacuum cleaner, dusting your animals,' he said as he cut up his cooked tomato. 'Need I remind you that you are a guest here, in my home?' He set his knife and fork to either side of the plate and leaned forward on his elbows.

'I haven't put her to work; she kindly offered to help for a few hours here and there,' I said.

'You should have turned her down; she was only being polite. I told you on your first day here that my daughter was sensitive, that she was not to be troubled. Encouraging her to spend her days combing the coats of dead animals is beyond the pale, and you will stop this, right now.'

'It's up to Lucy,' I insisted. 'I can't physically drag her away.'

However troubled he – and she – felt she was, she was not a child to be ordered around, and I would not treat her like one.

'Don't make me regret inviting the museum here, Miss Cartwright,' he said, and picked up his knife and fork to attack the rest of his breakfast.

Chapter Nineteen

I thought I knew all the rooms of the house, I who spent my evening mapping them, walking through them in my mind. I thought I knew what was real, a memory, and what wasn't, what was just a dream.

There were stories from my childhood that I thought only nightmares, things I thought I had only imagined, and others that had left behind only a feeling, a fear, an echo. But I remembered now; as if the room had held the memories for me, like an egg, and when the wooden panels of its wall had been cracked open, they had oozed out.

My mother used to lock me in that room, when I was nine years old, I remembered now.

Had it started like one of our hide and seek games? It must have, for I remembered the first few times, of waiting in there with the short candle she left me, of peering around the room as the wallpaper shifted and whirled with the flicker of the flame, and of seeing the blue tiles set into the fireplace, the blue tiles with their painted hares, their eyes dark blobs of midnight. I remembered waiting for her to open the door and find me and, when too much time had passed, trying the door myself, only to discover it locked. I remembered when the usual sour, fizzing thrill of waiting to be found curdled into terror. I remembered when the candle went out . . .

You tricked me, *I cried to my mother when she finally let me out and hugged me to her,* I thought it was a game.

It was a game, *she said with a bright smile and nervous eyes.*

It wasn't, it was mean, *I sobbed.*

But she didn't stop doing it, didn't stop locking me in there even as I battered my hands against the door trying to open it and calling for her to let me out.

I'm trying to protect you, *she said desperately when she brought me in there, even as her voice shook.* I'm trying to keep you safe, to stop your nightmares.

You're lying, *I screamed, and then called for the servants to help me, for anyone, my voice dying down when I got no response. Maybe no one could hear me, would ever hear me, maybe I would stay here forever in the dark alone, I had thought, weeping silently.*

I'm here, *I started saying to the room whose walls disappeared in the gloom, as if trying to convince myself I existed and had not melted into the darkness.* I'm here, *I said.* Please, *I whispered as I cowered by the fireplace, feeling the thin breath of air fall from the bricked-up chimney, my fingers slipping over the cold tiles, as if the hares painted on them could come to life and comfort me.*

And then when the door was finally opened and the rush of light swept inside and my mother brought me out, saying here she is, my very own girl, *I would weep like a wounded animal, sickened by her soft touches, by what felt like a parody of love.*

I'm trying to protect you from her, *my mother said in a small voice a few weeks into this horrifying routine. I had asked my grandmother for help and she had said that if my mother was punishing me it was only because I was a rotten girl. My father had barely been in the house at the time, he was working such long hours for his businesses, and though Martha and several other servants tried to whisk me away to different floors and rooms, my mother always found me.*

She was sitting on the floor, her arms around her knees as if she was the girl and I was the poorly mother.

She didn't have to tell me who 'her' was, for she had already talked of the ghost she feared had followed her from her childhood home.

Her mad confession only added to my fears, for now when I was locked in the room and my candle went out, I worried that I was not the only one there in the dark, that at any moment I would hear the shift of a dress on the bare floorboards, feel the sigh of someone's breath brushing across the back of my neck, or a sharp hand grabbing me from the gloom.

I no longer tried to talk to myself in there, for fear of my voice sounding like someone else's, but instead tried to keep as still as possible, tried to breathe quietly even as my heart raced like it was trapped too; I shut my eyes and wished I could disappear, wished I could be so small and quiet that she would never find me.

It was my father who saved me, after what must have been only a month or so of my mother putting me inside that room – but it had felt like years.

One day, I had emerged from my terrified trance to hear him shouting outside the blue room at my mother. Where is the key, you witch! *he was shouting.* What the hell have you done to my daughter? Give me the fucking key. *My mother screamed back about how she was protecting me, how I was safe in there.*

He broke down the door in the end and I cried so violently I was sick, trying to cover my eyes because the light hurt like daggers after hours of dark.

I've got you, my father said, and I turned my face to hide in his chest as he shouted at my mother to get away from me.

I wished then that he had married another woman; I wished I had a normal mother who did not see spirits, who was not mad.

My father had the room bricked up and my nightmares, which had begun after that other fated game of hide and seek during my birthday a year previously, worsened. I had to take spoonfuls of sedatives most evenings and would tearfully demand not only that two lamps be left burning in my bedroom but also that the curtains were open to let the moonlight in so I was never shut up in the dark again. My mother was sent away for a month and then returned looking pale and sad, telling me she was sorry she scared me, that she was only trying to keep me safe, but I never played a game with her again – no hide and seek, no blind man's bluff, no chasing down the halls, no spinning on the spot until I turned dizzy, no games of pretending.

I had forgotten that time, or thought it only a nightmare, a dream. As if my mind made its own brick wall and shut away my memories of it. I knew now why I was frightened of the dark, frightened of being trapped and smothered. Was this why I was dreaming of the hare too, was it the creatures scampering out from the tiles of that room, was I chasing a lost memory?

If I opened the other locked rooms, the ones that had been shut up waiting to have the plaster of their walls fixed and their warped floorboards replaced, their furniture shrouded by dust-sheets like mourners; if I turned the key in their locks, would other memories come spilling out?

If a house could hide a missing room for more than a decade, a room from a nightmare, only one wall away from my rooms, what else could it hide? If I, who spent my evenings roaming the house in my mind, mapping all ninety-two rooms, had not known that there was a ninety-third, did I know anything at all?

I was too frightened to close my eyes, fearing the press of the dark, fearing the things that might hide in the gloom – the brush of fur, the pinch of cold fingers, or something unknown, something worse . . .

And when I did fall asleep, I would wake inside my dreams to find that I had never left that room after all, never grown up, never been rescued, that I was still there, locked away from the world and frozen still with terror.

Chapter Twenty

'It looks like the red pandas are breathing, in their cabinet, I mean,' a voice said as I entered the library one day in early December.

'Pardon?' I said and turned to see one of the newer servants reapplying her red lipstick using the reflection of the glass of the cabinet as her mirror. Her shirt collar was tucked down at the back and her apron straps were twisted.

'The condensation,' she said.

I joined her in front of the glass. There was, as she said, a patch of condensation in front of the two little faces of the red pandas. I sighed, and my own breath created a cloud in front of me in the chilly air.

'They're not alive then?' she asked, eyes twinkling.

'No,' I said, and tapped on the glass, 'but something else is, something small and hungry, hiding inside from the cold.'

'I don't blame them, this house is freezing,' she said, rubbing her arms distractedly, her eyes flicking towards the door and – I surmised, after walking past the lord of the manor flirting with her in the billiards room – the Major's office.

Had she come from there just now? Was that why her clothes were out of place, or did the lipstick mean that she was hoping to catch his eye? I could not think of the Major as anything other than brutish, could not imagine wanting his hands on me.

Lockwood was losing a steady stream of servants, far too many to blame on the war effort alone, but far too many to blame solely on broken hearts and bruised pride either. Lucy had told me that newer staff sometimes struggled with the demands of such a grand house and left soon after being hired but now things were exacerbated by the demands of the war, and the housekeeper was increasingly harried – such that I had started to physically hide from her if I heard her nearby, to close doors and hurry through to other rooms, because she always found some way of mentioning the work that was needed to keep the museum rooms clean, work that the museum paid for by way of government funds, although I never said that, not wishing to spark her to some new height of hatred.

'I better get back to work,' the maid standing next to me said, and I heard her footsteps pause in the hallway for several long moments as I stared at the pandas with their pretty white faces and luxurious brush of red hair.

When I removed the red pandas from their cabinet, I found the remnants of a shrew's nest inside one of their torsos and set to work repairing both the animal and the hole in the cabinet where the shrews had squeezed their way through, thinking of how I would narrate this tale for Lucy if we were still meeting for tea like we used to, and thinking, too, of all the many other things I wanted to talk to her about.

Since she had suffered her night terror, she had retreated to her tower room. She did not have any more dreams that woke the house, nor did I see the doctor come to visit her, but she was clearly still shaken or at the least ill at ease with company. She hardly ever came down for breakfast, and only occasionally joined us for dinner. She was quiet, she avoided eye contact, and ate very carefully, looking down at her plate as if she could find something there to ground herself.

I felt for her dearly, and I tried to think of light and breezy things to mention when she did join us for dinner; like the day the cow from the farm got loose and trampled the new cabbage patch; or the afternoon a starling had got trapped in the long gallery and how I got into an argument with myself over whether the primal human fear of winged creatures close to one's head was a callback to some giant avian of the past that hunted our ancestors or not – but then I had never had the gift for casual conversation and these topics were politely rebuffed by silences and short answers. I knew that I had to trust her to approach me when she was ready for company, and I tried my best to show that I would greatly welcome the return of our friendship. In the meantime, I was lonely and I missed her.

Lucy was of a similar age to me but she had spent nearly all of her life here. I could not imagine staying with my parents, even if they had wanted me, but then again what did I have to show for my adult life having flown the nest? No home, no family or children, only my work. I had mounted a few animals for the museum and repaired others, classified specimens and catalogued acquisitions, written notes and organized storage, helped researchers and compiled papers of my own, studied bones and flesh and fur, and written mountains of correspond-ence. The bulk of the museum was there when I arrived and would still be there when I left. The only mark I would leave on the world would be some lines of ink soon discarded when they faded or when better theories of natural history were proposed, anonymous stitches concealed by fur, and perhaps a fingerprint or two pressed into a moulded skeleton underneath the skin of a long-dead animal.

I wished that I had someone to talk to about my own silly fears, about how I held my breath each time I opened the locks of the museum rooms in the morning, waiting to see what animals seemed out of place. Just this morning I had found the juvenile giant otter shrew, a tawny animal about a foot long, not in the morning room where I had believed its home to be, but in the music room instead, placidly waiting for me on a bookcase.

I could draw separate diagrams for each room, of course, to check which specimens were definitely out of place, but what would be the point when there were other people who worked in these rooms and at least four other sets of keys besides mine – with one belonging to the housekeeper, another to the Major, a spare for the other servants, and another shared between the night guards. Instead, all I could do was to remind the keyholders, and the servants who passed through the rooms, that the specimens were not to be disturbed or touched, while cursing Lockwood itself as the museum's chosen location for evacuation. At least in London, people understood that things should stay where they were, that everything had its proper place.

The servants had definitely cooled in any warmth towards me and started neglecting the cleaning of the museum's rooms, which certainly did not help matters, and it was maddening being seen as some kind of tyrant, yet all the while wondering who it was who was playing with me in this way – for by this stage, I had convinced myself that this was hardly simple carelessness and must surely be a trick aimed at me personally, a joke at my expense, and nothing to do with the museum at all.

Could it be someone from outside the house, I thought wildly as I tried to sleep one night, having noticed the spotted cuscus in the billiards room that afternoon and not the summer room where it should have been. Was it the housekeeper, who I still suspected was behind the abduction of the humming-birds; or Dorothy, with her enjoyment of tales of ghosts and horrors? Or someone else, whose motivations I could not fathom?

'Miss Cartwright,' Joyce said to me early the next morning as she caught me frozen in my bedroom doorway.

I had attempted to leave for breakfast as usual, after a night of horrible dreams of giant hands plucking animals from shelves, of the animals coming back to life and sauntering off where they wished as I scrambled feebly after them, but had been stopped short by the sight before me.

The squirrel monkey was there in the corridor, barely six feet away, in front of the open door to the purple bedroom, its tail posed in the air and dark eyes glinting, its head tilted enquiringly to the side, its cap of dark hair and face of pale flesh making it look unnervingly human.

Joyce stopped next to the monkey and leaned the heavy vacuum cleaner against the wall. 'It makes my job that much harder if you're bringing the animals up here to the corridor, I have to clean around them,' she said wearily.

'I didn't bring it up here,' I said, feeling the smarting of tears in my eyes now that the shock had passed. 'I swear it.'

She did not look convinced.

Late that night, at half past two, and unable to sleep after a day of feeling hurt and ashamed, embarrassed by what others might be thinking and saying, I decided to head down to the museum rooms to see if I could find any traces of the person who might be playing these tricks. What was I hoping to find, I thought, cross with myself as I pulled a jumper over my head – Dorothy sitting in a chair waiting for me like some grand villain?

As I locked the door to my bedroom, torch in my pocket, I heard a noise, only just audible, but a noise all the same – like a piece of paper being drawn out of an envelope, or a hand brushing against a thick fur coat – and I turned round to look down the long corridor towards the west wing.

There was something there, someone in the dark.

I felt a quiver in my legs, and my breath caught as I clutched my keys tightly in my hands.

The figure walked closer, solidified out of the darkness, as the hairs on my arms stood up.

They were dressed in white and moving calmly and evenly. As they came closer still, I could see that they were wearing a nightgown and dressing gown a little like mine, the sweep of it creating a soft dragging sound on the carpet as they moved.

It was Lucy.

I took in a breath to call to her, but then let it out again. Something was not right. As she drew nearer, her face was oddly blank; her eyes were not peering into the darkness like mine, but wide open instead.

She was sleepwalking. And now I could see that clutched in her hands, camouflaged by the pale fabric of her dressing gown, was one of my animals, the pygmy anteater, about a foot and a half in length, with its thick white fur and long silken tail that disguised it from predators as a hanging silk cotton seed pod.

I moved towards her, catching the clinking sound of something heavy in her dressing gown pocket; keys?

'You're sleepwalking, Lucy,' I whispered, hovering by her elbow. She was warm and smelt like lavender and I felt my fear wash away.

She did not reply and continued staring ahead. I stopped her tentatively with a hand on her shoulder.

'What are you doing with this, you silly thing?' I said, touching the animal in her arms.

I knew that you were not supposed to wake sleepwalkers, and if I did wake her and she found herself in the dark corridor clutching a dead creature it would surely only upset her greatly.

'Up to bed with you,' I said, and took her by the arm, gently guiding her in the other direction, unnerved at the way she easily followed my lead as if she had no mind of her own.

I walked us slowly along the hall and even slower up the stairs to her floor. Her bedroom door was wide open, the inside brightly lit. Carefully, I tugged the anteater out of Lucy's arms and set it down on the pink pouffe at the bottom of her bed.

I decided to help her out of her dressing gown, fearing that it would tangle about her legs and startle her into waking. It was made of a pale pink silk that slipped easily from her shoulders aided by the weight in her pocket. I draped it over the back of a chair and helped Lucy into her plush bed, relieved that she seemed amenable, because I would not have been able to lift her up that high. I pulled the covers up to her chin and stepped back.

'Goodnight,' she whispered suddenly, her eyes still open and staring. But it was reflexive, she was not yet awake.

'Goodnight,' I said, feeling an urge to kiss her on her forehead, but patting the bedding over her shoulder instead.

I picked up her dressing gown, felt around for its pocket and brought out a large, heavy ring of keys.

This was how she opened the locked doors and wandered

through the museum rooms then, her sleeping mind coaxing her to pick up specimens and set them down somewhere new. I opened a drawer of her chest, careful not to do it so sharply it would make a noise, and stuffed the keys inside a pile of unidentified silks, the fabric startlingly soft on my fingers. I would tell her where I put her keys tomorrow, but I did not want her going off on another expedition with them tonight. I slipped out of the door and closed it quietly behind me, making my way down through the house in order to return the anteater to its rightful place.

Was Lucy, then, Lockwood's sole mischief-maker; was she gliding down the stairs every night to move the exhibits with sleeping hands and unseeing eyes? How did her mind know to keep her body safe; what if she missed a step on the stairs or lost her way and walked through a window? And how could we – she or I or both of us together – stop her nocturnal expeditions? Even if she – or I – were to hide her keys from now on, what would happen to her sleepwalking after that; where would she go with no doors open to her?

As I passed the night guard, who woke up with a startled snort – I had been working late on fixing a loose seam, I told him, when he saw the anteater in my arms, and he nodded slowly as if he did not know enough about taxidermy to know whether to believe me or not – I wondered if it was possible for Lucy to be responsible for every animal moved, but never once be spotted by the guards. They could not sleep all the time, surely? She was certainly not strong enough to ferry the jaguar upstairs, I thought, stopping to stare at the dark patch of the room where the beast had stood for only a day before disappearing, as the glint of a dozen pairs of glass eyes stared at me from the gloom.

*

I woke up early the next morning and knocked on Lucy's door, announcing myself before she even answered because I did not want the embarrassment of being mistaken for a maid, of my coming into her room while she was expecting someone else.

She was surprised to see me, propping herself up on her elbows, hair tangled and face creased by her pillow. That she looked beautiful even at this hour was surely unfair.

'Hullo,' she said, wiping sleep away from her eyes with her fingertips. 'Is everything all right?'

'Yes,' I said, closing her door softly behind me, 'it's only—' I paused, unsure what to say. 'Lucy, have you ever sleepwalked?'

'I know that I used to as a child,' she said, responding to my question without looking at me as if I was silly to ask it. 'My nurses were always finding me in the oddest spots of the house, carrying on with things like I was awake, taking books down from the shelves of the library or drawing in the dark, getting dressed, you know. It used to frighten them something rotten but I never remembered anything about it. Why?'

'Well, you see, I found you sleepwalking last night in the corridor near my room, carrying the pygmy anteater in your arms and with a ring of keys in your pocket,' I said in one breath.

She inhaled sharply. 'Goodness, that must have been quite a sight. Oh, Hetty, I'm so embarrassed,' she said. 'Is he all right, the anteater?'

'Oh, he's fine, none the worse for wear for his night-time excursion.'

'What the hell was I doing with it? I can't imagine what was going through my head.'

I moved closer to the bed, leaned against its post. 'The thing is, this has been happening for a while now. Specimens being moved from room to room, animals picked up and put down, with none of us the wiser as to who might be doing it.'

'Oh, Hetty, *no*,' she said, aghast. 'Oh god. I've been so busy with my own troubles, shutting myself away up here, I had no idea. What must you think of me, barging into your rooms at night? I'm so sorry.' She bit her lip, her eyes were filling with tears.

'Please don't be sorry,' I said, coming to stand by her side as she reached out to take my hand. 'You didn't know, you were sleepwalking. If I had told you earlier, it might have twigged for you and this would have all been sorted out.'

She squeezed my hand. The bright morning light that sneaked through the seam between her blackout curtains and the window had revealed the little lines by her mouth, the creases at the corner of her eyes.

'I understand if you feel you have to move the museum elsewhere,' she said evenly.

I shook my head quickly. 'Don't be silly; it was nothing, I was making a mountain out of a molehill, every specimen is quite all right. We're quite safe here.'

'If you're sure,' she said.

'I am.'

She squeezed my hand again and then took hers back. 'You didn't tell me about the intruder because you didn't want to worry me, you didn't want me to have another funny turn, did you?' she said, without blame.

I nodded, although there was another reason of course: I had not wanted her to think that *I* was mad, to have her judge me just like the rest of the house had. It had not been entirely altruistic, I thought, with a small measure of shame.

'Thank you for trying to protect me, it's sweet of you, but you don't need to do that. The museum is important and I'm not a fragile flower, not completely anyway,' she said with a dry little laugh. 'Promise me you'll tell me if something like this happens again, if you're concerned about something.'

'I promise,' I said, meaning it. It had been a long time since I had promised someone something. I had the silly thought that we might swear on our pinkie fingers now, or shake on it, but she reached for her water glass instead.

'I'll leave you now, and see you down at breakfast,' I said, stepping back from the bed. 'Oh –' I suddenly remembered – 'I hid your keys in a drawer last night, in case you went for another walk.'

'Which one?' she asked, swinging her legs to the side of the bed and standing up.

I motioned towards the chest of drawers and then tugged the right one open, reaching inside the pile of what I now saw were silk camisoles and knickers to pull the keys to the surface. She moved to stand beside me and we both stared at the keys, and the underthings, and suddenly I felt terribly embarrassed, as if I had chosen this drawer specifically, even though I had not.

'Good,' she said, and I turned away without looking at her, saying a cheery goodbye and closing the door of her room behind me.

Had there been an inflection on that word, that *good*, or was I just imagining things? I paused and then smoothed my hands down my blouse and headed for breakfast.

Chapter Twenty-One

If there was a spirit in this house, it was me; if there was a haunting, it was my own.

Am I awake? I murmured to my reflection the morning after Hetty had told me of my nightly wandering, watching the slow way my mouth moved, the swallow of my throat.

Am I dreaming? I thought as I sat on the lip of the bath in my tower bathroom, staring down at my body, my limbs, the pool of water beneath my chilled feet.

Am I real? I said out loud as I buttoned up my slip and settled a necklace my father had given me for my last birthday around my neck, the empty locket a spark of cold on my breastbone that made me shiver.

Maybe my mother had been right to lock me in, I thought, as I ran a hairbrush through my wayward curls, as I patted powder over the freckles on my cheeks, and then I screwed my eyes shut so I did not ruin everything and cry.

Chapter Twenty-Two

As January arrived, so did the coldest winter in living memory – not that one would know we had even a wisp of a cold breeze if one read the newspapers, which were censored to avoid giving out valuable weather information to our enemies – and no matter what Lord Lockwood had promised about modernizing the house, no matter how many radiators there were or special deliveries of coal arranged for the hulking new boiler, it could not mask the fact that Lockwood was an old manor house, and houses like that were always cold in winter. Colder, it sometimes seemed, than outside. Cold enough, one sometimes thought, to have been purposefully built that way, to have the draughts and the chilled stone walls carefully penned in on the plan by the original architect: strange frozen spots in the house, windows that always rattled no matter how much one plugged gaps with rags, and water from the tap so icy one risked frostbite each time one washed one's hands. A house like that was used to being served by a battalion of servants lighting and tending fires in every single room, black-leading fireplaces, breaking their backs ferrying wood and coal up and down the stairs, shovelling endless bucketfuls from the great mountain in the coal cellar, singeing their fingers with sparks, cleaning rooms of smoke that had blackened its corners. As winter deepened, I started to think that the house was a kind of temple and that without the appropriate worship of enough servants, several of whom had now left for war occupations, it would refuse to heat up fully, even if the physics of radiators meant that it should; that it demanded we tend to it personally.

And then a blizzard arrived, and as the snow and freezing rain fell, in quantities no one had seen before this far south, the world outside the manor house became impassable. We could only stare out blindly at the whirling gusts, as half the servants who took rooms in the village were stuck there and the other half were trapped in the house, unable to make it through snow drifts that were over five foot deep in places. A delivery of coal had been due and the hungry boiler that fed the radiators of the house could not run on the wood the groundskeepers had cut while clearing land at the edge of the forest last autumn. The Major was said to have a new electric heater in his room, but the rest of us had to make do with log fires in ours, which did little to keep away the cold. The housekeeper brought out musty blankets from Lockwood's stores, moth-nibbled and furred with unidentifiable hairs and dust, which I dutifully piled on top of my bed and shivered underneath at night, struggling to sleep, chilled to the bone.

After three nights without coal, I woke to a dark house, as if the snow drifts had been pushed so tightly against the house that they had swallowed it from ground to roof. My breath made a silvery cloud in the air as I scrabbled out from my blankets, emerging from a dream of being smothered by some great creature, of being buried alive in ice.

It was the electricity, Dorothy told me when I came down for breakfast in the dining room, layered with two jumpers and a scarf. The ice had frozen the cables and brought them down, plunging Lockwood into the past, where the only lights were candles and gas lamps that the servants brought out from the attic, the air smelling of beeswax and oil, flames flickering and casting shadows onto the walls.

That evening, by some unspoken agreement, the inhabitants of Lockwood – except the Major, who had seemingly barricaded himself in the safety of his room – slowly congregated in the kitchen, where the large wood-fed range was belching out warmth as we sat or stood around the table, cups of tea in hand.

I stared at the pockmarked wood of the table, trying not to notice if anyone was looking at me strangely, knowing that the servants had no doubt complained heartily about me and my unreasonable demands these last few months. I had never felt comfortable in groups, not after being bullied at school, and it was one of the joys of working at the museum that we very rarely gathered together for meetings or were expected to socialize with one another.

Lucy was the last to arrive in the kitchens, carrying a great mound of fur in her arms that had me out of my seat with confusion before she dropped it to the floor with a grimace and a little laugh and the heap slid apart to reveal flashes of rich silk innards, in reds and purples and blacks.

'My mother's and grandmother's furs,' she said, lifting a coat up by its collar. 'I had the thought that we might as well get some use out of them.' She smiled and I noticed the kitchen maid opposite me looking at the coat with naked longing. 'I think there's enough to go round.'

'I'm fine, thank you, my lady,' the housekeeper said firmly when she was offered a capelet of mink, but every other servant – Joyce, Dorothy, the kitchen maid, the new laundress, the cook and the tweeny, even Paul – took a coat and pulled it around their shoulders.

'Well, this is an adventure,' Dorothy said, as she pushed her arms through a large fox fur that swamped her form. 'It's like we're in the Arctic or something; what a lark.' The room laughed but I could not join them in their merry mood; I felt unsettled, and the white mink coat I wore was scratching at my neck and wrists.

'I'm worried about the animals,' I blurted out. I had shut the museum rooms up that day, with the assistance of several of the servants, shrouding the exhibits in the sacking they had been transported inside, for fear of the damage the cold would do, and borrowing some of the blankets for some of the more fragile specimens, swaddling them to save them from winter's icy grasp. But with no night guards making it through the storm, there was no one there now to watch them.

'You think some hardy thief will be burrowing through the snows to steal a giraffe in this weather, miss?' Paul said, and the housekeeper snorted as others grinned at the image he painted.

I felt my cheeks blush hot.

'I'm sure they'll be just fine, dear,' the cook said, but her wide smile at Paul's joke undermined the consoling tone of her words, the word *dear* sounding condescending.

The fire in the range cracked and a piece of wood inside fell with a thump. The floorboards behind me creaked. I felt penned in and anxious. I stood up and my chair screeched, which had the laundress flinching.

'I'm going to check on them, on the specimens,' I said, flustered as I grasped at my torch on the floor.

'Do you want help?' Lucy asked.

'No, I'm quite all right, thank you,' I said, not wishing for her to be put out.

It was only once I had emerged from the servants' quarters into the pitch black of the house that I realized I was still wearing the fur coat.

The quiet of the empty house felt visceral, absolute, but as I moved forward, I could hear the scurrying of mice, the soft shush of snow against the windows, and each of my steps brought forth an answering crack from floorboards that had shrunk with the cold. The walls felt narrow as I swung my torch across them; the corridors of the west wing where the exhibits were kept seemed to have changed dimensions, and when I moved the light to illuminate the ground, the carpet seemed to be manifesting out of nothingness before me, as the bristling pelt of my coat prickled at my neck and nose.

The keys for the museum rooms were icy cold in my hand as I turned the lock and entered. *What am I hoping, or fearing, to find?* I asked myself as my torch beam glanced off glass eyes that glinted strangely, the sheen of cabinets, the soft shadows of fur and hide. The furniture looked like strange angular beasts, the rugs had become pools of dark water, and the darkness seemed to come alive and shuffle around behind me, while my breath formed a cloud in front of me. Every time I saw myself in a gilt-edged mirror, or the glass of the exhibits, I was surprised anew by the hulk of my white coat, and, once or twice, there would be a flare of light from the reflection of my torch beam, and I would flinch and see an after-image behind my closed eyelids, a pale creature with hair as white as my fur.

I had never been afraid of the dark and I was not now; just apprehensive, watchful, I told myself as I toured through the drawing room, billiards room, library, morning room, music room, summer room, sitting room, and writing room, pressing my hand to cabinets and over the sacking and blankets, peering at each animal snout, each tail and pelted side that emerged from the gloom. Everything was in its place, frozen still.

I made my way through the short corridor, unlocking the door to the long gallery, where it felt even darker and colder, as if the walls had absorbed the very last glimmers of light and warmth, each scuff of my foot sounding louder, and when I raised the torch I saw that my breath was creating great billows of condensation. I worked through the rooms on the left first, feeling my usual rush of hurt and shame when my torch glanced off the hummingbird cabinet, and then I crossed the hall to the rooms on the right. The first room was just as I had left it the evening before, but in the second there was a shape on the floor, a slumped pile of sacking and rope that had come loose – or been removed? – from a collection of birds of paradise and, turning on the spot, I saw that a cabinet containing fragile birds' nests had been unwrapped too.

A sound of dismay escaped my throat and then I saw movement from the corner of my eye and whipped my torch round, catching the flash of something fleeing from the room.

I ran, racing through the rooms, my slippers slapping on the floor, my torch jolting in front of me, illuminating the brief vision of a figure dressed in white, which disappeared the moment the beam shifted. I fled into the hallway and then dashed through the corridor and back into the main house, pursuing the intruder.

But once there, I lost my trail, and there was no sign of movement, no sound other than the creaks of the house and the soft hush of the snow outside. I swung my torch around slowly, the other hand curling into a fist, legs trembling at more than the cold.

There. I pointed my torch towards the entrance hall. Two eyes glinted back, a white snout with a mouse caught between its jaws, the panting red sides of a fox – and then it turned and was gone, back into the dark.

Had the figure I had seen, the intruder in the long gallery, been the fox? But how could a fox look as tall as a person? Perhaps it was only my own reflection, I told myself, as the beam of my torch shook on the ground before me, as my ears rang and my body locked with panic. The sacking that had been untied, the birds—

Was there someone here, someone hiding in the dark?

I turned back round and blundered into something large and warm, something that grabbed me with its large claws and swore as I shrieked with fear.

'Jesus *Christ*,' the Major said, squinting as I pulled away from him and shone my torch on his face. 'Put that bloody thing down; do you want to blind me?' he bellowed. 'What the hell are you doing wandering about down here?' he demanded then, shining his own torch towards me. 'And wearing that,' he added furiously. 'Where did you get that? Did you steal it?'

'Lucy brought the coats down for us to wear,' I said, voice still shaking from the shock.

'She did, did she?' he said as if he did not believe it.

This was his wife's coat, I thought, feeling ashamed, *and here I am prancing around the house in it.*

'The rooms I gave you and your museum are not enough for you now, you desire to be clothed in the finest Russian furs too, hmm?' he said silkily.

'I'm sorry,' I said, feeling close to tears.

'What are you doing wandering about in the dark, Miss Cartwright; have you gone quite mad?' he asked, moving closer.

His breath smelled sour, his body of exertion, and his eyes were shadowed.

'I was checking on my animals.'

'In case they've shifted about while you're not looking?' he asked slyly. 'Or run away?'

My words seemed trapped in my throat; I felt like some miscreant being reprimanded for breaking into a locked wardrobe, for dressing in my mother's fine clothes.

'You're a very curious girl, aren't you?' he said.

Woman, I thought, gritting my teeth, *lady, anything but* girl.

'I knew from the very first day you arrived; your beady eyes, your greedy looks. Curiosity can be dangerous, *Miss* Cartwright, digging into secrets, opening locked doors. You should take more care wandering around in the dark.'

He shouldered me aside and walked towards the stairs. 'Get to bed, Miss Cartwright,' he called back, 'and stop using my hallways like a cross-country route.'

'Damn him,' I muttered once he had gone and I returned to the long gallery, breath hitching from adrenalin and anger. I checked the rooms there carefully, trying not to notice how the beam of my torch shook, and swathed the cabinet and birds back in their sacking. The servants must have been too slapdash with their wrapping, I decided, and a cold draught had done the rest, that was all.

It would be madness to think anything else, to believe that what I saw was anything but a cloud of breath, my reflection, or maybe the shadow of the fox elongated by my torch – but shadows are black, not white, are they not, and I had never asked myself to disbelieve the evidence of my own eyes before.

As I locked the door to the corridor, I finally took off the coat and folded its bulk over my arm.

'Have the animals vanished into the night then?' Paul asked when I returned to the kitchen, and I noticed that a bottle of rum had now been opened on the table.

'Some of the sacking had slipped off two specimens in the long gallery,' I replied, not in the mood for further mockery.

'Oh,' he said, deflated, brow creasing. 'Did I not tie it right this afternoon?'

'Evidently,' I said, still standing there under the eager gaze of the revellers, as Lucy got up from her seat by the range. 'And I saw a fox.'

'Inside?' Dorothy asked, leaning forward. Her cheeks were flushed with warmth, or rum. 'That's an omen, that is, mark my words.'

'In case you hadn't noticed, there's a blizzard outside,' the tweeny drawled.

Dorothy gave her a withering look. 'Weren't you the one who came knocking on my door last night after seeing the ghost?'

'It was nothing,' the tweeny, who had the wide-set eyes of a tamandua, said, crossing her arms. 'It was only a nightmare.'

Dorothy raised an eyebrow. 'Well let's hope you don't have one tonight, my dear, your elbows are uncommonly bony.'

The tweeny brushed a hand sharply through her hair.

'I'm off to bed now, if you're heading in that direction,' Lucy murmured, coming to my side.

'Yes,' I said, giving her a small smile. 'What should I do with your coat?' I held it out.

'Oh, you can borrow it for tomorrow too. Keep it until the snows stop,' she said and it felt too impolite to say *no, I'd rather not have it anywhere near me*. 'That goes for all of you,' she added.

'But not when you're working,' the housekeeper added tightly. 'I'll not run a house where my staff wear furs.'

The new laundress giggled and then ducked her head when the housekeeper glared at her.

'She would have killed us for borrowing her furs, the last Lady Lockwood,' Dorothy whispered to Joyce, who was dozing on her hand. 'I can picture her now, flying at you with those mad eyes of hers—'

I hoped that Lucy had not heard her words, but I knew by her stillness that she had.

The housekeeper stood up and clapped her hands. 'To bed, the lot of you, after you've checked on the fires and done your work. I'll have no more of this slovenly mayhem. And take off the coat, Dorothy,' she said icily. 'Goodnight, my lady,' she said to Lucy, and we left to the sound of chairs scraping and cups clattering in the sink, to a hum of disgruntled voices and laughter.

Chapter Twenty-Three

I was so busy talking to Lucy, nervously, quickly, trying to paper over the cruel talk of her mother in the kitchens by rambling on about coat camouflage in the polar circle, that I did not realize I was following her up to her own rooms before I entered the door behind her.

She set down her torch and took out a large box of matches, and I watched the quick, practised motion of her hand, the flaring match and the splutter of the first candle she lit before moving to the next and the one after that. The embers of her fireplace were warm and there were candles scattered over every surface – desk, chair, tables, mantelpiece.

'It's quite a lot of candles, isn't it,' she said bashfully, noticing my stare. 'I've always been deathly afraid of the dark, you see, so I have my own stores just in case.'

'That's very wise,' I said, picking up the spare box of matches. 'Let me help.' And with every match I lit, every flame that hissed into being, I felt an ease settle into my body.

'They were right, you know,' she said ruefully, as she stood on tiptoes to reach a candle on a high shelf. 'My mother would have gone crazy if we had borrowed her furs. She was possessive about her belongings, and paranoid. She thought that if someone had a lock of her hair, they could make spells against her. She was so worried that something would happen to her, that she was in danger here.' Lucy rocked back on her heels and lit a fresh match. 'And yet when death found her, she was elsewhere.'

'How did the accident happen?'

'They said she saw something, someone on the road, that she swerved and the car hit a tree. But if there was someone there that day, they never came forward.' Her sigh made the flames on the mantelpiece flicker.

'I can't imagine how terrible it must have been; I'm so sorry,' I said.

She put a hand on my shoulder in passing and sat down on the end of her bed, pulling the remaining pins from her hair so that it sprang free and curled around her neck and shoulders.

I finished lighting the last few candles and sat down opposite her on the gold pouffe.

'We haven't spoken much recently, you and I, have we?' she said, one hand plucking at the silk of her bedspread.

'You've been . . . busy,' I said, not knowing how else to put it.

She laughed wryly. 'I've cocooned myself away, you mean. I think that I've been embarrassed, about my nerves, about the nightmares you must have heard. At my age.' She shook her head. 'I've suffered from nightmares since I was about eight or so, terrible ones, but they slowly lessened over the years, as any childhood affliction might, and yet my mother's death has stirred them up again. I would understand if they frightened you, though, if *I* frightened you.'

'Nothing of the sort,' I said. 'The only thing I felt when I heard you cry out was concern.'

'Thank you, Hetty.'

'The museum has missed you.' I've missed you, I also meant.

'And I have missed the museum. As is evident from my nightly excursions,' she said wryly. 'You've not noticed anything moved since that night, have you? I gave the keys to the housekeeper so I wouldn't know where they were.'

'No, nothing,' I said. I rubbed at my neck where it still itched from the fur. 'If you wanted to, you could continue your work – if that wouldn't upset you – or I could give you something else to do, if you wanted, there's no need of course, maybe answering the letters, we get some very strange letters—'

'I'd like that, it's good to keep busy.'

'Yes,' I nodded quickly. 'I've always thought so myself.'

'Tell me, I haven't been at breakfast or dinner – Dorothy has been bringing me sandwiches – is cook feeding you well enough?'

'Oh yes,' I said, 'no complaints.'

'It's just with the rationing starting . . .'

'I wager that a Lockwood sandwich would be far superior to anything I prepared for myself in my lodging house in London,' I said, and then blurted out, 'One reads and hears advice to housewives about how to feed their menfolk great feasts of meat and dripping and it feels like another world, for truthfully I would be quite happy to eat only vegetable soup and some toast, maybe a square of chocolate now and then.'

'Chocolate, you say.' Lucy got up to rummage in her bedside table.

'Oh, no, I didn't mean—'

She came over to my side, pressing a warm hand to my hip as she passed me the chocolate bar. 'Please, I insist,' she said, and I broke off a piece and let it melt on my tongue as she sat back on the bed and crossed her legs, licking her own chocolate from her fingertips. 'I know what you mean. When

I was younger, I had this figure of a future husband in my mind, and when I learned to sew I would think, this is how I will darn his socks, or when cook showed me how to bake a cake, I would think of how pleased he might be to have a slice of my cake after a long day's shooting. And more intimate thoughts than that,' she added, 'how he would like my clothes, my hair, my underthings, how I would stand, how I would kiss him.' She laughed. 'My grandmother used to begin sentences with, *When you have a husband . . .*' She spread her hands and then shifted them behind her so that she could lean back.

'I had a little of that,' I said, pleased to be able to talk about thoughts that had long languished unspoken, 'but I was also oblivious in a way that infuriated my mother, blithely chattering away to her about the zoological facts I had learned and my plans for university, all the while she was worrying about my disinterest in stepping out with anyone. I think I can count the number of dates I've had on one hand.' Or less than that, I thought, but was too embarrassed to admit.

'I've had dalliances here and there,' Lucy said, shifting her posture on the bed.

I could feel the warmth of the fire on my side, see the flames of the candles dip and bob at the corners of my vision as I looked at her.

'But nothing that's stuck, nothing that would tempt me to give up my solitude,' she continued – a little wistfully, I thought. 'And I hardly ever think of that anonymous husband now,' she added. 'It's my mother looming over me instead, judging me. I suppose daughters always disappoint their mothers.'

'I know that I have disappointed mine dearly. I don't know if I would have disappointed my real mother, the one who passed away, but I like to think not, I like to think— I'm sorry,' I said, rubbing my eye with a knuckle, feeling the sudden prickle of tears, the remnant of tonight's shock finding a new tributary to flow through. 'I never really talk of it—'

'Oh no, Hetty,' she said, voice rich with sympathy as she came to kneel beside me, 'I'm sorry. Here I am talking about mothers, all the while knowing that you were adopted.'

'It's not a competition,' I said drolly, a lone tear trickling down one cheek, 'and besides, you lost your mother only last year.'

'And now I've made you cry,' she said and hugged me, and I found myself hugging her tightly back, feeling her ribcage move beneath my hands, surrounded by a cloud of her perfume.

'No, please, I did that all myself,' I said and then pulled away, wiping my eyes with my scarf. She smiled hopefully at me, the warmth of the room lending a sheen to her skin.

'Now, I've given you sustenance, but nothing to drink, poor hostess that I am. What do you say to some crème de menthe, for old time's sake?'

An ember cracked in the fire, spitting sparks. 'I had better get back,' I said, even though I felt reluctant to leave. It was only that this room, with its cosy glow, felt like some kind of intimate haven. I did not wish to overstay my welcome, to overtax her.

'Oh, I've made a mess of things, haven't I, embarrassing you.'

'No, please,' I said, clutching her hand. 'I'm not embarrassed. I loved talking with you, I always do; it's so wonderful to have a friend here. You will come back to the museum now, won't you, when you feel up to it? Please say you shall.'

She squeezed my hand. 'I shall indeed. Thank you, Hetty.'

When I returned to my cold, dark room, I thought what a fool I was not to have lingered longer up in that turret room with Lucy, in the warmth of her fire and company both, instead of scurrying back here – especially as she had insisted I take the mink coat with me and now it lay in a pale heap over my chair, as if there was something crouching there, and even in the dampening cold I could smell it: the must of animal's pelt, of mothballs and champagne and long-forgotten revelries.

Chapter Twenty-Four

It did not matter how busy I made my days, how tired I was by the end of them – each night, as I tried to fall asleep with the lights in my room left blazing, my eyes would open, almost of their own accord, to stare fearfully at the door and the blackout windows, and in my mind, I would be walking down the spiral staircase outside my bedroom and along the corridors of Lockwood, through room after room after room, pretending I was simply counting them and not searching for something lost, hunting for other horrors. I was still waking from those dreams of the leveret, still haunted, still thinking I might open my eyes to find myself back in the dark of the blue room again.

My insomnia, my crazed dreams, my jangling nerves – were these my lot in life or were they a ripple from my mother's death, a wave that would lessen with time? Had her own madness kept mine at bay in a strange sympathetic magic? The thought of ever leaving Lockwood, of the life I had been planning before that motor-car accident – of London, and parties, and a job somewhere, a little flat to call my own – seemed unfathomable. If I couldn't sleep without the lights on, if I was terrified of closed doors and curtained windows, if I had to flee to my bed every other day with sudden terrors, then how would I fare living independently?

I had slept in the nursery on the first floor of the house for the first few years of my life, before my mother had moved me to my rooms in the west turret.

'I would have died for a room like this when I was a girl,' she told me, 'a fairy-tale tower of my own; you don't know how lucky you are, protected here. Back home I used to wake to birds in my room, to the shutters banging open in a storm, to rats scurrying about the floor. Our house was wooden but this one is good stone,' she said, pressing a small hand against the wall of my bedroom. 'Nothing can get through this.' She spoke as if she was trying to convince herself.

There were three rooms in the tower: my bedroom and, above it, the blue room that was bricked up when I was still a child, and my playroom, which was converted into a private bathroom as an eighteenth birthday present while I was on a rare trip away from Lockwood, touring the south of France with my grandmother; a trip I returned to again and again in my mind as a glimpse of life far from here. The warm, sandy beaches; the hills with their winding roads leading to villages teetering at the top; the endless fields of lavender and the way my clothes still smelled of it when I came home; and the dresses, the glamour, of the Frenchwomen and the visitors to the Côte d'Azur.

As a young child I liked that my bedroom was situated above my parents' because I found the murmurs that I heard through the floor, the opening and closing of wardrobe doors, the rush of water as my mother ran a bath to be comforting. But as I grew older and realized that my parents' marriage was not something from a fairy tale, that my mother's jealousy and paranoia and my father's brusque obstinacy meant that they were often at odds with one another, I overheard many an argument that made my stomach ache with worry, and further kept me from sleep.

Later, when I was a young woman, and Lockwood had fewer

guests on account of my mother's growing madness, she abandoned the room she shared with my father and took to sleeping in other, vacant rooms. She would sleep in one room, the yellow bedroom, or the twin room perhaps (though never the purple, because she was convinced it was haunted by the woman in white) for a month and then work her way through the others, one a night, before settling on a new space – my old nurse's room, or the rose room, or the yellow bedroom again – which meant that I would never quite know where she slept or where to find her as she dozed the morning away, or napped after lunch; would never know where to lead her to when she was having one of her fits in the evening. It certainly gave the poor servants more work to do, but at least they could confer with one another in the servants' wing about which door they shouldn't knock on, or where exactly to deliver her ladyship's breakfast. I felt embarrassed to ask them where I might find her, as if it reflected poorly on me, and my grandmother was little help either, indifferent as ever to the travails of her daughter-in-law.

It felt like some cruel echo of our games of hide and seek. She never again locked me in a room, but now here she was shutting herself in different rooms and here I was trying to find her. It seemed as if she believed that if only she chose the right room, she might fix her frantic thoughts, make the world become solid again.

There's too many rooms, she would mutter angrily. I can't stand it, I can't hold them all, I can't remember.

For me, back then, it was as if my mother was in every bedroom, all at once, that each door I crept past for fear of waking her was the door she slept behind. The way she treated me – loving one moment, irrational the next; kind, and then frightened; utterly mad, followed by moments of startling lucidity – was discombobulating enough, but now that had expanded to fill the whole house, as if it were a maze and she stood at each corner for me to find.

It had not been a year yet since she died, and still her presence seemed to linger. Still I thought I might find her behind any number of doors: drowsing on the bed with her black hair tangled on the pillow; sitting upright on a chair, waiting to tell me off for startling her; peering out of the window, spying on the gardeners; or, the sight that had always disturbed me the most, weeping into her hands, her voice small and young, as if she were only a mirror of me, as if her fate was mine, as if what the house had done to her would be done to me just the same.

She's here, she would say, her cheeks flushed with tears. She's found me. And I would turn round, my heart kicking, as if expecting there to be a figure waiting behind me, ghostly, hungry, wild.

Chapter Twenty-Five

'There's someone been thieving the sugar,' the cook was saying, one day that spring. 'It's hard enough with the rationing and now I can't scrounge up any cakes.'

I was in the parlour and could hear her in the servants' sitting room, the smell of tea and cigarettes seeping through the wall.

'The *sugar*? Someone's taken my hat,' Dorothy said. 'It'll be one of those new maids, the ones that don't last a week, thinking that they're above it all, cheeky buggers, going on and on about their army sweethearts who are going to marry them and set them up in a home. Fat chance of that!'

'You're worrying about hats, I'm worrying about the Germans—'

'If I see someone wearing it, I'll scratch their eyes out—'

'There's too many bloody rooms,' another maid butted in, putting something heavy down on the floor. 'Christ, all these bedrooms, just close them up for god's sake, who are they waiting for?'

'The Germans?' the cook offered sardonically as the other two laughed.

'If her ladyship, the Major's mother, was still alive you know she'd be inviting them to tea the minute they invaded, nasty bitch.'

'*Dorothy.*'

'Well she was, wasn't she? And good riddance to her.'

'You might change your tune when we get a new Lady Lockwood, when the Major remarries; the new one might be worse than the others.'

'As if that man will marry again, he's having far too much fun,' Dorothy laughed.

'Ah, but he'll have to – didn't you hear him shouting at his money man on the telephone the other week?'

'What's this,' the cook said sardonically, 'gossip that Dorothy doesn't already know? Are you slacking in your snooping, dear?'

'Shut up, will you?' Dorothy replied crossly.

The mood in the house was fractious. There had been a flood of servants leaving for the war effort and the housekeeper was struggling to find anyone to permanently replace them. The duties for those remaining – Paul, the cook, Dorothy and Joyce, the housekeeper herself – were overwhelming. Dust was accumulating in corners of the house; fingerprints blazed on streaked windows in the yellow spring light; muddy footsteps lingered for days; and the floors of the bathrooms were slick and mildewed.

Nature herself was pressing in on Lockwood too, ivy crawling up the walls of the house, rose bushes shouldering further towards its windows, moss creeping inside its doors, the odd leafy plant growing through cracks in window frames, muscling into empty rooms. When the cherry tree bloomed, its sodden petals were soon tracked inside or blown by the wind even upstairs. I told Joyce one day, as I saw her struggling with brush and pan, that I would sweep them up and save her the work, but it seemed like a futile task when they stuck to the floor or to my hands, when they rotted to the carpets and refused to be shifted by brush or cloth and left their sour-sweet note of decay in the air.

I was worried about the animals with every news report from mainland Europe, with every bad dream, checking and rechecking where the stirrup pump was, circling the outside of the house each dusk to see that the blackout curtains were firmly in place.

'We are waking up from a childish dream of peace,' the white-haired groundskeeper, who was too old to be conscripted, said to me one day as he stood listening to the wireless reports drifting out of the drawing room window, 'to find the monsters at our door, having learnt nothing at all from the Great War except how to breed another one.'

Germany had by now invaded Belgium, France, and the Netherlands; our war of nerves was suddenly over and with British troops beaten back towards the coast of France, the tide was turning against us. How soon would it be until Britain stood alone, we worried, until we were ourselves invaded?

And then we received the first news of Dunkirk and I learnt that two of the museum's assistants had been lost there on the beaches, two men that I had taken tea with and discussed theories and specimens and research with; who I had blithely said good morning and goodnight to as if they were a permanent fixture of the world.

I did not cry when I got the letter from the museum's director: the news felt too horrible to induce something as easy as tears. Instead, I spent a Sunday wandering lost through the gardens, my breath short and my head so light I thought I would tip back and fall to the ground. Then I wrote a letter to my mother. I swallowed my pride and told her I was sorry for disappointing her, that I hoped we might be able to reconcile, that I wanted to be a better daughter. I cried finally as I signed it, imagining how she might sigh wearily and write me an answer, how a crack might open in the wall between us, how after all this was over I might just have a mother again. After I posted it I felt foolish that I had let myself be so emotional but I did not wholly regret sending it yet – I might still, though, once I received her reply, or if I never did.

Elsewhere in the country, I knew that people were having sleepless nights waiting for the invasion of the Luftwaffe who, by late June, were beginning to make small-scale raids into Britain, dropping bombs that were like the first few drops of rain before a downpour. But at certain hours of the night when I lay awake at Lockwood, I found myself listening closely – not for sirens and planes and bombs but for the sound of footsteps, the drag of fabric sweeping along the carpet. It was a different kind of incursion I anticipated in those small hours that seemed to stretch time to woozy proportions, a different damage I awaited – and I did not have to wait long, for the day after France officially surrendered, Lockwood was attacked by someone far closer to home than the Germans.

I was taking an early breakfast, struggling with the previous day's crossword, when a high-pitched scream sounded from a different part of the house, making my body jolt with alarm, and I dashed out of the room to find the cause.

'They've phoned the police and Jenkins has run off to see if he can catch them,' Dorothy declared, standing in the entrance hall holding a mop and staring towards the back door.

The door was open and a pale child's figure, oddly still, was silhouetted in the low morning light behind it, like an image summoned from one of my nightmares. I let out a high sound in my throat; my gut felt hollow as if I was walking across a high, narrow ledge. There was something dark on its face, something horrifying, like a gas mask fused to the skin; and white fluff surrounding it in a haze.

A cloud passed over the sun.

No, the figure was not a child, or a living creature; it was made of paper and stuffing.

It was the museum's ancient mounted juvenile bear, but it was missing its fur. Coming closer, I saw that it had been roughly skinned, leaving the dark false muzzle hanging on the remains of the face, with loose packing lying at its feet. I did not think of my animals as living creatures – I was not so far gone in the madness that had gripped me here at Lockwood – and yet I did feel pity, a twang of sorrow, looking at what remained, along with fury at the mutilation of one of the museum's specimens.

The bear had come from the collection in the drawing room and I checked that the other occupants were unharmed before hurrying frantically through all the other rooms, hands shaking as I unlocked each door, awaiting further horrors, snarling beasts or hunched crones, but finding nothing except the usual throng of bones and mounted animals.

Relieved, though hardly reassured, I returned to the bear mount which I had left at the back door, as if by doing so the fur would be called back to it, as if I would return and find it restored.

Last night's guard was there too, trouser leg already rolled up in preparation for cycling home.

'Did you not hear anything last night?' I asked him, my voice tight with anger and shock.

'Nothing, miss,' he said, and I did my best not to give in to the urge to shout at him. How on earth had he not heard a smash? Was he asleep? What was the point of night guards if they did not bloody *guard*?

'Ah, Miss Cartwright, there you are.' The Major appeared from the direction of his office. 'Terrible business,' he said, resting a hand on my shoulder that I immediately wanted to buck off. He took his hand back to open his cigarette case. 'Terrible business. What women will do for fur, eh?' he mumbled around the cigarette.

'Pardon?'

'They'll have stolen the fur of the bear for a coat or trimmings,' the Major said, waving his cigarette about.

'That fur has been treated with formaldehyde and arsenical soap,' I said, touching the stuffing of the naked beast. 'They can't use it for *clothes*.'

Had they really been stealing the fur? And if so, why leave what remained here like this, in the hall? Had they been trying to steal the whole thing but decided it was too heavy? No, I felt certain that it was left thus as a taunt, to frighten and perturb us – or rather me.

'The police are sending someone round but not for some time I'm afraid; they're busy,' the Major said. 'War seems to have turned half the country into criminals.' There was something self-satisfied about the way he blew the smoke from his mouth.

'How the hell did no one hear this happen?' I asked, coming back to myself now.

'There's no need for language like that, Miss Cartwright,' he said, eyes narrowing, motioning towards me with the cigarette in his hand, which I found ruder than any use of profanity could possibly be to a man who I had heard use the word *fuck* quite liberally through the walls of my office. 'And I might ask where *you* were? You're in charge of this fine collection, as you've so often reminded us.'

'It's not my job to guard the collection from thieves,' I said, thinking of the jaguar that had been lost on the first day here at Lockwood, and of the hummingbirds that had been hidden away in a room upstairs. I should have taken both incidents for a sign. I should have insisted that the museum be housed elsewhere.

'It's your museum that has drawn thieves here like magpies—'

'We never had any trouble with thieves in London, Lord Lockwood.'

'I find that very hard to believe,' he said sardonically, blowing a stream of smoke close enough to me that I wanted to hit him.

'Are you calling me a liar?'

We stood only a few feet apart. The light through the back door cast shadows on his face, making him look even more brutish than normal.

'Well, let me know if anything else is missing,' he remarked finally, and walked outside to join Jenkins, who had evidently given up his search for the culprit and had his rifle over his shoulder, as usual.

I searched the museum rooms again, since I had no one else to corroborate with and I did not trust myself not to have missed something in the frenzy. When I returned to the hall, Dorothy and Josephine, the new French maid, were crowding around the back door, the naked bear ignored.

'What's going on?' I asked, pushing past them.

Striding up the back gardens in the blinding mid-morning light was the Major, another cigarette in hand, and Jenkins next to him, cradling some dead beast in his arms. They had found the missing bear skin.

'There, you see, all's well that ends well,' the Major said as he came to the door, and the maids dispersed, back to their work. 'Looks like the thief had second thoughts. If it even was a thief; I think it might have just been one of the evacuated boys on a dare. They're running around like savages at the moment,' he said blithely, as Jenkins held out the pelt towards me distastefully, dropping it a foot away from my arms so it almost slithered through them before I grabbed hold of it. The skin smelt of chemicals and the loamy outdoors and had pieces of grass poking between the hairs.

'Thank you,' I said pointedly, as if I could, out of politeness, encourage Jenkins to be the same.

'Good luck putting that poor fellow back together,' the Major remarked, nodding towards the bear as he left me there, holding its fur in my arms, my heart heavy.

I carried the sorry shedding mount and the skin back into my office and sat at my desk, fingers rifling through the bristles of the fur as if it might yet reveal the mystery of who took it, and waited for the police to arrive. When I called the station a little later to hurry them along, they told me that someone at Lockwood had informed them that the pelt had been found. They had no time for dealing with professional squabbles or practical jokes, they said, and were quite curt when I tried to argue my case.

The person who had skinned the bear had to have had a key, or else been let in by someone with a key. Was it the same person who took the hummingbirds, who stole the jaguar? Was it an intruder, or someone who I passed by every day? A thief would hardly have left it out there in the gardens, but then why else commit such a crime?

I lingered over a cup of tea, aware of the unpleasant nature of my next task, and then ate a large chunk of the chocolate

I had been rationing, for fortification, sucking at my teeth in front of the mirror in the bathroom to remove any stains. *As if he will be inclined to treat me any better whether or not food is smeared around my mouth*, I thought acerbically.

The Major seemed ready and waiting for my arrival. 'Terrible news, terrible news,' he repeated, folding up the sleeves of his crisp white shirt as I took a seat before his desk.

'The locks of the museum rooms must be changed,' I stated firmly.

'You can't be serious,' he said with a snort. 'Many of these doors and their fittings are original to the house.'

'If you do not have the locks changed, the museum will be forced to find another home. Furthermore,' I added quickly, before he could interrupt, 'higher branches of the government will have to be informed of the reason for a second move.'

'Is that a threat? They will blame the museum for letting their specimens be stolen, not my household.'

Letting – he was determined to place the blame anywhere but on himself. 'I think you might be surprised at where the sympathy of the government officials will lie,' I said, even though I suspected those in positions of power would be likely to side with the Major, to think this all a little squabble and not a definitive threat to the museum's mammal collection.

'Fine,' he said, pressing his hands against the top of his desk and then reaching for a cigarette. 'Locksmiths will be called out tomorrow.' He waved his hand lazily. 'And don't think about bothering the police with it; they have far better things to do than deal with some jape.'

'The museum is, as ever, indebted to you and your generosity, Major Lord Lockwood,' I said in the sweetest voice I could summon, and stood up.

He raised his eyebrows at my cheek. 'It's good that the

museum has someone as single-minded as you to guard over it, *Miss* Cartwright. Frankly, it's admirable how dedicated you are to your animals, although one might caution against becoming *obsessive*, at the cost of other, more important, things in life. A husband, perhaps, children, that kind of thing,' he said pleasantly, blowing a stream of smoke towards me as I smiled thinly and left, shutting the door behind me.

I swore under my breath as I strode through the corridor to the long gallery. There was no one I could go and commiserate with. Lucy had a blind spot for her father, and the servants would be suspicious of my motives, believing that I was trying to trap them into badmouthing their employer; they might even think it was me who did it, just as Joyce had blamed me for the squirrel monkey outside my room.

There's only you lot to comfort me, I thought as I came to the first room of mute animals, *and what's the use in talking to creatures who won't talk back?*

Chapter Twenty-Six

Late that evening, sometime after dinner, I was sitting in the drawing room, the skinned bear having been moved to my office for fixing and leaving a dusty gap in its place. I had a flask of tea on the low table in front of me, two cups, two sandwiches on a plate, a novel to read, and my unfinished crossword. There were two torches on the seat beside me, and three blankets draped over the arm of the sofa.

There would be three night guards on duty tonight but I refused to put the safety of the museum in their apparently incompetent hands, so had decided to spend a night in the drawing room myself, where the okapi, one of the museum's rarest specimens, was kept, before the locks could be changed tomorrow and the doors properly secured. I was aware that I looked half-mad doing thus, but no longer cared. It was no less than what those in London were doing, the caretakers of galleries and museums and factories and offices and houses, preparing for the long night of glancing at the sky, waiting for the Luftwaffe.

I was trying out different cushions as backrests when I heard Lucy's voice in the hallway.

'What are you doing with all that bedding, my dove?' the

Major asked, his evening shoes clipping along the floor of the hall.

Over the past few months, I had waited for the Major to upbraid me again for 'allowing' Lucy to work for the museum, but he had seemed busier than ever, shut inside his office at all hours, dashing off to meetings in his motor car with Jenkins. Lucy said he was having trouble with one of his factories, that it was something to do with the war effort and that was why he had a greater petrol allowance. In the evenings, he was occupied with various female visitors who were whisked in and out of Lockwood so quickly and who all dressed so similarly that it almost appeared as if it were the same woman each time. I tentatively asked Lucy her feelings about her father's lurid love life, but she only shrugged and looked awkward. *He's not a man that does well alone*, she'd repeated.

Do you do well alone? I wanted to ask, but something held me back. Why don't you have a beau, a bevy of visitors, or even a husband? Is it just your nerves, or is it something else?

I did not ask her because she could easily have turned the question round on me and what would I have said? That I was shy of others; that I was lonely, and yet used to it? That I seemed to lack some vital element that other women had which made it easy for them to love and be loved in return?

'Miss Cartwright is going to spend the night in the drawing room,' she said now, in response to his question, 'in case the thief returns tonight, and I'm going to join her.'

He let out a disbelieving *ha!* sound that made me roll my eyes. 'My dear Lucy, I don't care if that woman builds herself a hut like a savage in there, you are not joining her in her madness. I forbid it. Do you not remember the state you got into last time you were involved with the animals?'

A pause.

'Now take your blankets back upstairs, my dove, and forget all this nonsense,' he said.

I heard the muted noise of footsteps ascending the stairs, followed by the Major calling to Jenkins to start the car, and the front door slamming as he left the house.

He was heading to a party hosted by his latest girlfriend, Lucy had told me earlier – she had come to my office to commiserate with me about the bear – and I had told her my plan, whereupon she had said straight away that she was going to join me, that it was the least she could do. I did not put any effort into dissuading her; I had come to know how stubborn she could be and, besides, I welcomed the company, and I could not think of anyone I would have liked to spend a night's watch with more than her.

Why then was I feeling an odd bubble of nerves in my stomach, separate from the curdle of anxiety over the threats to the museum? Why did my heart jolt in my chest when I heard the sound of soft footsteps approaching and recognized them for hers?

'Good evening, Hetty,' she said conspiratorially, as she swept into the room carrying a great mound of blankets and quilts and pillows, and I smiled at her, immediately feeling the kind of warm happiness that she seemed to bring with her whenever she entered a room, a calming of my frantic thoughts.

She settled on the couch next to me and put a flask of her own down next to the tea. 'Crème de menthe,' she said, 'our favourite.' Her eyes searched my face as I looked back.

She was wearing pyjamas and the pink silk dressing gown she had worn when I had caught her sleepwalking, her hair in a plait that failed to tame the curls that were coming loose and framing her face.

We were silent for a moment.

'If my mother could see me right now,' I blurted out with a short laugh. 'It's everything she feared,' I explained, as Lucy looked at me, 'that I would put my career ahead of everything else, that my interest in natural history was obsessive. *You can't marry a stuffed panther, you know*, she would say.' I shook my head. 'Except she wouldn't, that would be too whimsical a thing for her to say.'

'My mother,' Lucy began, smoothing her hands down her thighs and then tipping her head back, 'my mother would have forbidden me, like my father, or she might have joined us here for our watch. Or locked the door.' She sighed and her mouth quirked up as if she was trying to smile. She seemed restless suddenly, and stood and walked along the row of animals. She was working her way up to saying something, I thought, and I was quiet, hoping to encourage her.

She stopped at the panther, bending low to meet its glass gaze. 'I don't know how you get any work done, Hetty. If I was employed by the museum I'd get fired within a week for spending all my time staring at the animals.' She moved to the polar bear, which stood on its hind legs, far taller than her. She brushed a hand down its belly and I did not stop her.

She turned round. 'That blue room, that attic room next to my bathroom that I was frightened of – my mother used to lock me in that room in the dark; she said she was trying to protect me,' she confessed.

'My god, how *horrible*,' I said, aghast.

She nodded, her chin dimpling. I went to her and put my arms around her, and she hugged me tightly in return. I could feel a few of her tears dampen my shoulder and had the queer thought that maybe the salt in them, the tears, would stay even once the stain dried, like when the roads are salted against snow and one gets tide lines on shoes that cannot be scrubbed off.

'My mother could be cruel, but she would never do something quite so beyond the pale,' I said.

Her ribs pulled in a heavy breath, her chest brushing against mine. 'She was mad, you see, some of the time, most of the time. Her moods entirely capricious, her temper volatile. Do you think it's true, Hetty, that daughters always become their mothers?'

'Not at all,' I said quite firmly. 'And you're not volatile, you have nightmares, you get nervous. But –' I tried to gather my thoughts – 'those are inward-acting things, aren't they? You don't lash out at other people, it's all focused in on yourself.'

'I hadn't thought of it like that. Although I have acted out on your poor animals,' she said, pulling back.

'Nonsense,' I said. 'There wasn't a patch of damage on any of the things you moved around. That was what used to irritate me so,' I added wryly. 'It was like a ghost, though I don't believe in those.'

'You don't?' she said, settling down on the couch once more.

I shook my head. What was I doing bringing up ghosts, I reprimanded myself silently, thinking of the figure – sometimes a beast, sometimes a woman – who haunted my nights. I crossed to the record player that was normally overlooked for the wireless and the grim news that flowed forth from it.

'Do you think if we listened to music quietly, it wouldn't keep anyone else awake?' I asked.

She closed her eyes and tilted her head back. 'I don't think any occupied rooms are above this one, so we should be fine,' she said. She noticed me watching her. 'Sometimes I try and picture all the rooms of the house, the floorplans, when I have trouble sleeping,' she explained. 'It helps, but it also gives me strange dreams where I am wandering through the rooms. Perhaps that's when my sleepwalking started,' she said with a slight shrug. 'I used to find myself in the blue room in my nightmares, but I thought I had only imagined it – I had utterly forgotten that part of my childhood, I can't understand it.'

'The mind is a strange thing,' I reasoned, 'what it chooses to remember, to notice.' She nodded thoughtfully.

I put on a record and the murmur of music filled the room as I sat back on the sofa and smoothed my pyjama trousers, subconsciously – I realized later – copying one of Lucy's habitual gestures. I did not know why I felt nervous, pressured, as if I was the compere of the evening and she my guest.

'Do you ever name the animals?' she asked, staring at the polar bear. 'Not their proper classifications, but silly human names?'

'Only very rarely,' I said. 'That black panther over there –' I motioned to my favourite beast – 'that was at the museum when I first started visiting with my nurse as a child. I've never told anyone this, but I named it Bastet. I had a book about ancient Egypt at the time.'

'Bastet, how lovely.' She nodded to the polar bear. 'And if that fellow had a name, what do you think it should be?'

'Hmm,' I considered it thoughtfully. 'Pierre?' I suggested.

We spent a good hour arguing about the names the animals should have, with lengthy anecdotes for certain names that belonged to school bullies or favourite actresses, and with much laughter, aided by the crème de menthe Lucy had opened halfway through and which we drank to the dregs.

I could almost forget the events of the day, that we were supposed to catch a thief, that the mystery of the person stalking Lockwood had yet to be solved. It felt as if, when we had closed the door, we had shut out the world and all its horrors and it was just the two of us left; that all that existed was this room.

'One Day When We Were Young' came on the record player and Lucy tugged me over to dance with her, twirling us slowly around the room; past the polar bear, the okapi, the panther, the Sumatran tiger, the wolf and the foxes; a strange audience for a strange pair, I thought. Our high mood hushed as the song continued, our movements grew smaller, until we were barely turning at all. I had one hand holding hers and the other around her waist just as hers was around mine. I turned my head to the side, feeling too exposed, and then our cheeks were almost touching, my chin brushing against her taller shoulder. She smelt of soap and powder and when I sighed she shivered at the brush of air across her ear. I moved back as the song came to its end and looked at her. The side of her mouth tweaked into a smile as her eyes met mine.

'My feet are tired,' I said, breaking the odd mood.

'Let's make a nest for the two of us,' she said, and then formed a neat pile of blankets and quilts. 'There,' she said proudly.

I turned off the record player and two of the lamps, leaving the last small lamp burning, remembering Lucy's fear of the dark, and then joined her, sliding awkwardly under the covers and turning to face her. We were so close I could smell the mint on her breath, although perhaps it was mine instead. Her eyes were dark glints and the planes of her face were illuminated in the faint wash of warm yellow light.

'Your hair looks white when you're in shadow,' she whispered, bringing up a hand to touch a strand that had fallen on my cheek. She tucked it behind my ear and I felt my body shiver.

'It's cold,' I said, and tugged the quilt up to my chin. The curve of her cheek looked soft, and I thought about what it would be like to stroke it with the back of my hand.

'This is a little like the term I spent at boarding school,' she whispered, her breath warm across my face, 'or one of the pyjama parties I had with friends. Did you have those?'

'No,' I said, and shook my head.

'The silly things we got up to, the games and tricks. We put on shows for each other sometimes, sang and danced, and we gave dares and –' somehow I already knew what she was going to say next – 'we practised kissing, pretending we were each other's boyfriends.' She reached a shaking finger to brush against my chin, to find my mouth in the dim light, and then rub the pad of it gently across my lips, which had parted under the pressure. I was holding my breath, I felt hot and my stomach trembled.

She took her hand back and yawned. 'Drink makes me sleepy,' she said, and blinked slowly. Her head sank onto the pillow but she was still looking at me drowsily. 'You mustn't let me fall asleep, Hetty. You won't, will you?' she murmured. 'We need to stay up for the animals, protect them . . .' She trailed off, closing her eyes.

I did not sleep one wink that night, though my mind still spun strange half-dreams in which guarding the animals from the intruder became guarding Lucy from the animals, the glint of their eyes watching us, the fur on their necks bristling, their mouths open with silent snarls. Other, shapeless thoughts nudged at my mind too, as I watched the shadows of her face and felt the heat of her beside me.

Chapter Twenty-Seven

If I had children, would I have minded the house getting quieter, servants and guests leaving? Would I feel a consolation in their company, or would they only increase my anxieties? It was a moot point, for I did not have children and, though I had never spoken this aloud to anyone, I was not sure I wanted them either. Children meant a husband, meant sharing my bed with some great oaf of a man, a stranger who would be curt at breakfast and particular about his office, a man who might start to think of Lockwood as his alone and me as the interloper, the intruder.

'Will I always live here?' I remembered asking my mother as she sat in the sun on the terrace one day, eyes closed like a cat. I was sitting near her, playing with a doll, dressing it up in one outfit after another, my fingers clumsy on the buttons that were giant in comparison to the doll's frame.

'You shall,' she had replied without opening her eyes. 'You, and your husband.'

'My husband?' I said with bafflement. 'Who is he?' I asked, as if some man had already been set aside for me.

She laughed. 'You haven't met him yet,' she said.

'But why? Can't I live here just by myself?'

'You'll be lonely.'

'Not with the servants I won't.'

'You're such a funny child,' she said, propping herself up, looking at me in the way that I hated, as if I was a being with no relation to her at all, as if I were a stray animal that had crawled into the house and prostrated itself at her feet. 'It doesn't matter what you think now, you'll fall in love one day,' she said, 'and then you'll be stuck with him.' She laughed again, but it wasn't a happy laugh.

I spent a term at a boarding school when I was thirteen or so, and husbands were a hot topic of conversation there too. There were twelve of us jammed into a room, each trying to outdo the other in how womanly we were – how many lipsticks we owned, and how red the shades; how perfect the waves were in our hair; how many dances we had been to, and how many different boys we had danced with; and the exact height of the stack of cards in our pigeonholes on Valentine's day. I joined them with wanting to look pretty, with wanting to be admired and grown-up, but I felt an uneasiness too, a reserve I couldn't explain.

I was there for Halloween and we played two particular games for finding out more about our future husbands. We peeled apples with the blunt knives we used to spread butter on our supper-time toast, creating long strips of peel that we threw over our left shoulders, and then we all gathered around the fallen peel to decipher the initial that had been created and call out men's names. My peel had fallen in an 'A', it had been decided, and as the other girls suggested names – Arthur, Alan, Anthony, Alexander, Albert, Alfred – I roundly rejected them all, picturing a line of blank-faced men shuffling past. I was picky, the other girls said, the kind to have more than one husband; the kind, one girl called Ann said, to have an affair. This caused much consternation, for we were still of that prudish age where it was one thing to fantasize about a crowd of different men but another to have relations with any of them.

The second game was not quite so fun for a girl like me, with a febrile imagination, who was scared of the dark. We would light a candle each and stare into a mirror at midnight exactly and the figure of our husbands would appear behind us. The other girls had jostled me out of the bathroom where the long mirror above the sinks was occupied by six girls side by side (wouldn't they be confused, I remember thinking snidely, if a figure appeared between them: how would they know that they had seen the right husband?), the three mirrors in the dormitory were occupied too, and another girl was using a large hand-mirror that she had brought in her trunk. I was left with the mottled mirror in the long dark hall outside our dormitories.

Ann was the one who had counted down to midnight, her voice hushed so that we would not wake the housemistress, and as I stared at my reflection, candle fluttering with my nervous breath, I thought how terrifying it was to look at oneself, to see the movement of one's face as if it was the face of a stranger. I should not have played this game, I knew that even then, standing there as the clock was ticking. I should have pretended, or shut my eyes tightly at midnight.

But I did play. I stared into the dark of my reflection at midnight and I saw someone else there with me.

I was told later that my screams brought the housemistress running with her head bare of her scarf, her robe half on her shoulders, that it took a girl throwing a bucket of water over me to bring me out of my fit, but I did not remember.

I was taken home the very next day and did not return to boarding school; the experiment at my living elsewhere from Lockwood ended, and I was devastated. I had loved the school, not for its building, which was colder and more ramshackle than

*my home, but for the company, for the other girls, mean though
they could sometimes be. I loved chatting with them and laughing
with them after lights-out as the moonlight streamed through the
thin curtains; or when we got into each other's beds and cuddled
up against the cold; how if I woke afraid from a nightmare, there
might be another girl awake too to talk to or, if not, there would
at least be the sounds of eleven peaceful sleepers, their snores
and breaths and shuffling under the covers like talismans against
any fears.*

*They were all married now, of course, and most of them had
children of their own. How did their lives compare to the ones
they had dreamed of; how did their husbands compare to the
ones they saw in the mirrors or conjured up from a piece of apple
peel?*

*I knew that they thought me strange, to still be unmarried, to
have no fiancé or even a scandalous married lover. I often thought
that it would be easier if I had been wed briefly to a man who'd
had a tragic accident, that I would be quite suited to being a
widow, haunting this house alone, appearing at breakfast with
dark shadows bred from loss instead of madness.*

*But this was my lot, to remain here at Lockwood unpartnered,
and I was lucky, I was not so foolish as to not know that. How
could I bemoan a life of luxury in a manor house like this,
servants at my beck and call? My class gave me allowance to
never marry, for I would inherit all my father's wealth; it meant
idleness would not result in my being starving and penniless, and
that I would be known as an eccentric heiress to be pitied and
spoken of as a warning to those girls who did not want to do
what everyone else does, to tie themselves to the first man who
asked for their hand.*

*Sometimes I pondered whether I might put the house to some
other use when my father was gone, as it was now for the museum*

– a collection of art perhaps, a convalescent home or even a school. But then it would not be right to invite other vulnerable people here, when it had been living here that had turned my mother and me mad; when I was sure that something still lurked here inside these walls, something hidden, something – someone – malevolent and wrong.

Chapter Twenty-Eight

I regretfully woke a deep-slumbering Lucy just after dawn, and we gathered up the detritus of our night and emerged from the drawing room. Lucy took the back stairs up to her room, and I took the main stairs to my own room, nodding at the night guard sitting by the front door. I went straight to sleep the moment I crawled into my cold bed and woke up too late for both breakfast and the arrival of the locksmiths.

Having made myself presentable, I came downstairs to the sound of tools on metal and wood, the heavy clunk of hammers being set down on the floor, and the click of new keys being checked in locks. I peered into the rooms and felt an instant sense of relief when I noted the shining new brass of the locks that had already been changed. These particular locks, one of the workers explained to me once I had introduced myself, were almost impossible to pick.

But the noise of the locksmiths, the thud of work boots on wooden floors and the continued clatter of tools was an unwelcome addition to my already whirling mind. I shut myself in my office and tried to do some work but every clang and thump rang loudly in my ears and made me clutch at the edge of my desk.

I was thinking about that man in the hotel again. Thinking

that I had felt more desire from Lucy's hand on my waist, from her breath across my mouth, than I did having sex with him, more pleasure from resting my chin on her shoulder as we danced, from the soft touch of her finger rubbing against my lip.

My body heated as I remembered last night, and that afternoon last year when I had tried on dresses in her room, the feeling of her hands on my bare sides, moving me by my hips; the brush of her lips against my cheek when she greeted me out on the terrace at the ball.

I felt fevered. I could still smell her perfume from the bedding we had shared, and my hand kept lifting to my lips to touch the place where her hand had touched.

'This is madness,' I said under my breath. 'Pull yourself together.'

That women could be with women was something I knew very vaguely, hypothetically – but surely in those cases one or both of the women were mannish, with queer habits and manners of dress, not ordinary like Lucy and me?

I picked up my to-do list, trying to clear my mind of impossible thoughts.

Even if – if – Lucy felt the same for me, she would surely never act on it, just as I should not either.

And yet last night, with her talk of kissing; and yet every time she had looked at me; and yet this strange tension that had bloomed between us.

What was I to do? My life had been barren of anything resembling love, or companionship, or desire returned. Could I be happy living thirty more years knowing that there was a chance I could find that – love – here and now; could I live with myself if I did not take the chance?

I spent the rest of the day cloistered in my office, barely giving a thought to the museum, doing mindless work, copying notes and answering letters by rote. I vacillated from embarrassment;

from the certainty that this was all in my head, that I had allowed strange fancies to sway my thoughts in an unnatural direction, to hope, to a surety that Lucy *did* feel the same, that she wanted me as I wanted her, that we would hurt no one but ourselves by not being true to these feelings, that it – that I – was not wrong; and back again. I thought I might die when I saw Lucy again, and that I might very well die if I never saw her again too – these were the crazed thoughts in my mind that afternoon.

It became clear to me that I could not wait until dinner, I could not sit there opposite her with this maelstrom of thoughts still whirling, I had to know, this had to reach some apex, some end, even if it was my utter embarrassment and shame. And so, once my working day was done, I headed straight for her room, and the higher I climbed in the house, the more desperate I felt, until I had to wait in the empty hallway outside to gather myself together as best I could.

I knocked on her door. 'Lucy?' I called, my voice breaking with tension.

'Come in!' she called back. I could hear the smile in her voice and it fortified me.

'What's wrong?' she asked as I entered. She was standing by her dressing table, putting on earrings – and even that little motion, the intimacy of watching her do her toilette, seemed to floor me.

I shut the door behind me but kept a hand on the doorknob, squeezing it painfully.

'There's something between us, isn't there?' I said to her, before my bravery could abandon me, every word shaking. 'Or am I just a fool, embarrassing myself?'

She shook her head, and every inch of me hung on that very movement. 'You're not a fool, Hetty. Or if you are, then I am too,' she said, with a tremulous smile.

'I want—' I bit my lip and swallowed the words I could not say. 'I want—' I said again, and she walked over to me, and my breath suddenly caught in my lungs. She was close now, a look of sympathy and hope on her face, close enough to fill my vision with only her. I glanced between her lips and her eyes as our faces inched towards each other, almost but not quite meeting, and then I kissed her, and her lips were soft and damp, and she twined a hand in my hair and kissed me back, the both of us gasping, making small animal noises into each other's mouths.

It was as if I were kindling that had been lit by her touch and she had joined me in the flames, we could not slow down, we could not stop as I tugged off her blouse and she pulled off mine. My hands fumbled on the catch of her skirt as she kissed me and smeared her lips across to my neck, sucking at the skin as her own hands scrabbled at my trousers, and then we were falling down on the silk quilt of the bed, plucking off our stockings and socks, shifting camisoles and knickers out of place, kissing breathlessly, laughing into each other's mouths as we wove our bodies together.

I touched her then as I had always wished to be touched, with lips and tongue and hands and fingers, and she touched me back. We whispered secrets to one another, we looked at each other in shared amazement, and then I tucked my face into the curve of her neck as we brought each other to climax, our bodies wedged together, wet and warm and shivering.

'Is it mad of me to say that I think I've loved you since the first time I saw you, standing in your travelling clothes in the middle of the drawing room?' she asked, several hours after we should have been at dinner. We were sharing some of the chocolate she had hidden away in her room, licking and nipping at each other's fingers.

'I don't think so. I remember the first time I saw you too, how beautiful I thought you were, how singular,' I replied, my head propped up on her stomach. I could not believe how natural this felt with her, lying naked with one another. Perhaps it was because we were both women, that her body was only a mirror to mine.

'You know,' she said, 'no matter what the war brings, I am happy that it brought me you.'

I turned my head so that my ear was pressed against her skin and I could hear all the noises of her insides, the echo of her heart thrumming away. I wanted to believe in what she said, but I knew nothing of what war was really like, what horrors might ensue, and I did not trust this house to leave us unscathed. 'We'll be safe here at Lockwood, safe together,' I said, and tried not to notice that it sounded less like a promise and more like a plea.

Chapter Twenty-Nine

'What a funny-looking monkey,' one of the new maids said, squinting at the spotted cuscus posed on top of a cabinet of elephant bones, with its folded hands and patterned woolly coat.

She was the second new starter that July, and was more schoolgirl than maid. I did not wager she would last long at Lockwood, partly for her dreaminess and partly because of the way she spent so long in the museum's rooms gazing at the animals – a habit that I certainly could not begrudge her.

'It's actually a marsupial, not a monkey,' I said. 'It was caught in northern Australia. They're nocturnal, and you can tell this one is male because of the colours of its coat.'

'It almost looks like sheepskin, the coat,' she said, nodding towards the animal and its beady black eyes.

'It's a little softer than that,' I said, but did not encourage her to touch it as I would have if Lucy had asked the question instead.

The maid was perfectly pleasant but she was not the company I wanted for these few precious free hours before dinner. I glanced across the billiards room at Lucy, and she and I shared a sympathetic look. Our thoughts were as attuned as our bodies were now – we needed only a glance, the twitch of a smile or a raised eyebrow, to say myriad things – a fortunate turn of affairs because there seemed to be so many hours of the day we had to share with others, when we had to content ourselves with these looks and smiles, with a few carefully chosen words concealed in polite conversations, rather than the freedom we had when we were finally alone together, in those few hours we could steal when the rest of the house was asleep.

'I'm glad they're safe here,' the maid said with a nod towards the large-spotted genet in his cabinet. 'I wouldn't rate their chances in London; my mother says the city is going to be levelled, that there won't be a building standing.'

'I'm sure it won't be as bad as that,' Lucy said.

The new locks on the museum doors seemed to have done the trick, for no intruder had made their way in, and every morning when I opened the doors, I found not a hair out of place on any animal. But it did not stop my worry, the fear that still kept me awake on those nights I was apart from Lucy, or the nightmares I suffered when I finally snatched an hour or two of sleep.

Over the last month, I had prepared my excuses were I to be found on the way to or from Lucy's room. I might be returning a book, or a borrowed pair of earrings, or I might simply be coming to talk to her – for close female friends could talk at any hour of the day, surely? There was no real reason for Lucy and me to hide, and there was nothing about our public countenances that might reveal we were anything but good friends. But this was a new world and I did not know its rules, the way things were done – what did other women like us do to hide their relationship, to keep it safe? *Were* there other women exactly like us? It did not feel as though there could be; we seemed to be in our own singular world apart, discovering a new-found land together.

Lucy needed to see the cook and so she and I made our silent goodbyes in the hallway, as if we were heading for separate parts of the country and not different corners of the house, our hands meeting with a feather-light touch before she strode off, and even that slight brush of skin on skin inflamed me. I thought about the previous night, when we had tumbled down on her bed and pulled the covers around us, burrowing into a hot den with only our hands to guide the way.

Lately, the only time I felt solid, real, was when I was with Lucy, and when I was not with her, every other concern and fear came pressing in, the walls of the house seeming to narrow, my jaw tightening with anxiety. It was my nightly journey back from her room to mine, alone, that I hated most of all – descending the spiral staircase to the first floor of the west wing in the pitch-black and then traversing the long, hushed corridor to the lonely east wing and my room, with the meagre light from the entrance hall downstairs to guide my way. I hated it because it seemed a symbol of my solitary future, of the day I would have to leave Lucy for good, but also because I could not shake the feeling that there was someone watching me, following me along the corridor, their eyes glinting in the dark, their footsteps silent. Each time when I reached my bedroom door and looked back, I expected to see a flicker of movement in the gloom at the other end of the corridor, a figure slipping out of sight, and each time I saw only darkness. It was my own mind that was haunting me now, not a ghost or an intruder.

After the rains of July ended, a blue-skied hot August arrived which – when accompanied by the grim news that spilled forth every evening from the wireless – had the effect of making everyone want to live in the now, to take pleasure where we could. This could be the last summer, the last heat on our skin, the last sip of water warmed by the sun, the last crunch of dry grass underneath our toes, the last warm night, the last warm day. I took any excuse to spend time outside away from the house, staring with tired eyes at the blue of the sky or the lush green of the garden foliage, trying to ignore the grey towers of Lockwood looming at the corners of my vision.

One week, the Major was away again and the housekeeper was visiting her sister, and there was a holiday atmosphere in the house. The wireless and the record player hummed loudly throughout the day, the new French maid Josephine (whose long lashes reminded me of the stripes on a chipmunk's face) sunbathed for an hour after lunch, and Paul was found kissing a village girl in the pantry and scolded laughingly by Dorothy, who pushed the rumpled girl out of the house with her broom.

I ranged the gardens with Lucy, watching her freckles bloom, noticing that the tips of her hair had lightened ever so slightly; lying in the shade of trees, having picnics out on the grass. We swam in the lake too, lying on our backs gazing heavenward while the lip of the water danced across our skin. We picked flowers and tried weaving them into crowns, and when the sun had set and the gardens emptied of every other human soul, we crept out now and then under the dark of blackout, unseen by all but the animals – the prancing foxes, the cats, the nocturnal birds – and kissed in the walled garden, loved one another under the willow tree and lay on the grass staring at the stars, holding each other's hand and squeezing at odd intervals as if to say, *Here I am, with you.*

One night I asked her if she was scared of being outside at night without a torch but she said that even with a new moon it was lighter outside than a dark room ever was, that the stars were always there to light the way.

'There are no walls here,' she said, sweeping one arm out, 'just wind and grass and life going on forever. Perhaps I wouldn't have nightmares if I never had to go inside,' she mused, then cut her eyes to mine ruefully, 'but there are some things that are probably best done in one's bedroom.'

Since her turret bedroom was so high, and the grounds of Lockwood vast, it was impossible for us to be seen as long as we did not stand directly in front of the windows, and there was something thrilling about leaving the curtains open in the bright summer evenings, pushing the blankets back from the bed as we made love, the flowers we had brought inside turning the room into an indolent hothouse. And when dusk arrived and I saw her face draw tight with nerves, I would quickly close the blackout curtains and then usher her upstairs to her bathroom with its crystal lamps, where we shared the large bath and I saw her tension ease in the warmth of the water as the walls of the room perspired with steam, our fingers pruning as we dozed off and then woke with a start, chilled and stuck to one another's skin, before clambering down the metal staircase to her bedroom and the silken sheets and soft pillows that awaited us as I tried to prolong those blissful hours.

'If we lived in our own house, our own little flat, then we wouldn't have to duck and hide from servants –' from your father, I thought, but did not say – 'we could have breakfast in bed together and frolic about the house as we liked,' I said to her at three o'clock one morning, my voice thick with tiredness.

Lucy only smiled a little sadly in response to my daydreaming aloud. We did not speak much of the future, and in that regard I suppose we were like many of the couples that had come together in wartime, determined to grab happiness where we could without thinking of what might be ahead, but we had the added complication of our shared sex, of it being quite impossible to marry or buy a house together or do any of the things ordinary couples might aspire to do once peace reigned again.

In the meantime, the war was as easy to forget as a background hum, a kind of odd season, something I could do nothing about, until the day we saw our first German plane roaring across the sky, its sleek sides splitting the world into before and after just as it sliced through the air like some apex predator; perfectly, lethally, adapted to its environment.

Lucy and I were together in her bedroom listening to her record player, which she had retrieved from the drawing room, talking about *Gone with the Wind* which we had chanced a visit to see, when we heard the strange tinny echo of the air-raid siren in the village and then, moments later, the whining roar of Lockwood's own siren kicking in. As we panicked and fumbled about, we glanced out the window and saw the plane, its engine noise a rumbling bass underneath the siren, and we scrambled down and down the stairs until we finally found our way to the basement, where every other member of the Lockwood household was huddling.

'Did you see it?' Paul asked. 'The plane?'

'I did,' I said.

'So did I,' Lucy said, clutching the torch she had brought with her between her hands, glancing at the old-fashioned wall lights that lit the basement.

'We don't have any anti-aircraft guns in the village, do we?' Dorothy said morbidly. 'We're sitting ducks.'

'I'm sure he's just passing through, looking for a more interesting target than an old country house,' Paul said. We tried not to think about the damage, the loss of life, that might ensue at someplace that was *more interesting* to the Germans.

'There's an RAF station forty miles away, they'll be heading for that, or the ports on the coast,' the housekeeper said, as if the rest of us were very foolish.

The all-clear sounded and we emerged from the gloom into a bright summer afternoon that looked for a moment like some kind of large theatre backdrop, until we rearranged our minds to make space for the new experience of daytime air raids.

The siren sounded once more that day and once again at night, but no other plane was seen. We learned the next day of the massive raids across the country on the airfields and RAF bases – the Luftwaffe numbering a thousand planes, like some ravenous migrating flock – and of the bravery of our own men fighting against them in the air.

Thus began the new normal of air raids, increasingly confined to the long hours of night which seemed to become ever longer with the anxiety, as the Germans graduated from attacking airfields to factories, from ports to cities and towns. And then the Blitz in London began, and as I lay awake in bed, my body trembling with fear that I knew had little to do with the war, I thought of the millions there and I would tell myself to buck up, to get this madness under control, that I had no right to true terror, given I was living in such luxury, so far from a major metropolis.

The basement shelter was a great equalizer, holding as it did the servants, the lady of the house, the assistant keeper of the museum, the farmer and his wife, the gardeners, and even passing tradesmen. The only person who did not join us was Lord Lockwood himself – or any women he had visiting

him. On one occasion we emerged from our subterranean lair
to the sound of the wireless blazing and feminine laughter and
masculine merriment, as if the Major had forgotten that other
people lived in the house with him, so long had we been
underground.

It was a woman called Sylvia who seemed to receive the
most invitations now, and who Lucy seemed at best lukewarm
about. She was dark, like the photos I had seen of Lucy's
mother, and only twenty-two, and I decided that her face
reminded me of that of a harp seal, despite the fact she obviously did not have whiskers.

'Is it awkward for you, having Sylvia staying here?' I asked
one Sunday afternoon as we sat on the terrace in the sun,
watching as Sylvia walked the gardens arm in arm with the
Major, her face turned upwards to look at him as if he was
some wondrous painted ceiling in a church and not just a
middle-aged bore of a man.

'A little, but I'm thankful at least that it isn't Mary,' she said,
blowing cigarette smoke from the corner of her mouth. 'It was
too odd to have a childhood playmate move in as my father's
companion.'

'Quite,' I said, as she passed me a cigarette and our fingers
met with a fizz of sensation.

The Major looked over at us then and I took my hand back
quickly and fumbled with the lighter.

I used to hate him because of how tyrannical he was, how
he mocked me, but now there was a note of fear too when I
crossed his path, as if he might look at me and know what I
was doing with his daughter, as if he might write to tell the
museum that I was a degenerate who had taken advantage of
his hospitality in the most sordid of ways.

Although Lucy seemed resigned to the Major's parade of

younger women, she was not so sanguine about his refusal to take shelter with the rest of us, and I could tell sometimes by the quiet pain on her face that she brooded on it often. She had arguments with him that the rest of us pretended not to hear, embarrassed by the naked fear in her voice when set against the easy nonchalance of his.

'He is so stubborn,' she told me one evening, biting her nails. 'He will get himself killed, and all for hubris. All because he says he survived the last war and so the Germans aren't going to kill him here at home, as if *daring* them to.'

I tried to console her but my heart was not quite in it – not that I wanted him to die, I was not that craven, but I did not see the point in trying to argue with him or to sway him from his foolish actions. And anyway, if a bomb did drop straight on us, would it not be possible that all of us in the basement would die too? This was a notion I tried desperately to forget, to brush away like a spot of smut on the fabric of my mind.

Every hour spent in the basement I would sit there, on one of the sofas that had been moved down for our comfort, and stare at Lucy's hand next to me, the shadow of it, half wishing that we might hear a plane and then I would be allowed to touch it, to clutch her to me, because intimacy was allowed in moments of great fear when all the barriers of propriety broke down.

The other half of my mind was upstairs with my animals, slipping down the long gallery, nudging into rooms, past cabinets and boxes, my chest fluttering in anticipation. It was indeed likely that we would survive down here in the cellars, as long as someone came to dig us out, but the animals would be destroyed by a direct hit – all those many years of work at the tender hands of museum workers, blown to pieces, all those rare specimens that could not be found again. And then what would historians and scientists discover in the future on this very spot, I found myself thinking – bones of lions and bears and whales; skins of tigers, wolves and giraffes; fish scales, feathers, ostrich eggs; but no human skeletons. It would be as if this house had been populated by the wildest of animals, an ark of the rarest creatures left to drift alone, while all the people had long since fled, leaving them to their sorry fates.

It was not just air-raid sirens that woke the house, for inevitably the increase in general terror levels had brought a return of Lucy's nightmares too; nightmares that I did my best to soothe but could not stop. Nightmares which, with their occasional hysterical force, threatened to reveal our secret relationship, when the housekeeper or a servant came running and found me already in her rooms, woken up from an evening doze with the scream of the woman I loved beside me, and which eventually forced me to retreat to my cold bedroom the moment Lucy started to yawn – not wishing to keep her awake nor for the both of us to fall asleep accidentally. Our nighttime hours together became smaller and smaller, more precious and precarious.

Chapter Thirty

If only Lockwood could be untethered from the world, set loose to float somewhere safe, if only all the terrors of the war could be swept away. If only Hetty did not have to leave one day, when the museum did.

I was used to any moments of happiness, any months of contentment, being dashed by nerves and nightmares, and so I tried to remind myself to savour every minute with Hetty, basking in the warmth of her love, our little cocoon of joy and pleasure.

I revelled in getting to know another body just as well as I knew my own – the soft hollow of her belly when she lay down; the angle of her hip bones, like pottery shards; the whorl of the grain of hair between her thighs; a scar on her shin with dots where a doctor had made his stitches; her lopsided ribcage. She had moles that speckled her body like decorations from some absent-minded god – one on her left breast, five on her stomach, a row down her left calf, one on her backside and two on the nape of her neck. When I was studying her body, when she was studying mine, and making me gasp and shake, there was no room in my head for worries and fears.

I had tried to teach myself to ignore things that might not be real, to rationalize huddled shapes that I saw in the corners of a dark room or the whisper of the wind that sounded like dragging *footsteps in the hall, to tell myself that dreams were just dreams, so is it any wonder that I had been trying to push down my true feelings for Hetty, trying to tell myself that any romantic love, desire, that I thought hummed between us was just another phantom? And just as that hidden attic room had been revealed as truth, so had Hetty's feelings for me – except one was a gut-wrenching, painful truth and the other was luminous, thrilling, revelatory, heavenly. Was this why every husband I had tried to imagine had been as shadowy as a spirit and as unsatisfactory as a puppet?*

I thought that I had ruined everything that night we slept in the drawing room, that I had made her uncomfortable with my advances. But then to have her turn up at my door, trembling and so very brave; to think of how the stars had to be aligned for the director of the museum collection evacuated to Lockwood to also be the woman I fell in love with, who fell in love with me in return, astonished me.

Was I too happy now? Would this all come crumbling down? Would my bad nerves get too much for her, my nightmares?

The air-raid sirens were like a knife slicing through our pleasant afternoons, our bucolic evenings; the rudest interruption of the outside world; a horrid reminder that I had responsibilities beyond Hetty – responsibilities to the house and its inhabitants. Each time the siren blared it seemed to demand an accounting from me, like the roar of some wailing beast rattling against the walls of the house. How was I going to keep them safe; how was I going to protect Lockwood?

Or was the noise of the siren, I sometimes wondered – as I woke panting from a nightmare, convinced that I had heard the same sound blaring through my dreams – the roar of a beast inside the house braying to get out? Some monstrous creature trapped in another hidden room, its hackles bristling with hot fur, its teeth bared. For the siren blared within the walls of Lockwood itself, did it not? As if the true danger was inside those same walls, and not from the planes gliding through the sky so high above us.

And when I emerged from sheltering in the basement, fleeing towards the light of the day, I could not shake the notion that someone had been in the upper levels of the house, stalking through the corridors, rifling through the rooms, while we were hidden underground. I could not help but notice each time that certain things in my bedroom – clothes, trinkets, books – seemed out of place from where I had left them, and that one day when I had looked in the mirror over my mantelpiece that I knew had been cleaned just before the siren screamed, I saw, in the bright light of the September afternoon, the ghostly outline of a hand-print that did not match mine.

Chapter Thirty-One

'Is this too much, us together, right now? Does it only add to your worry?' I asked Lucy one night as we lay next to one another on top of her bed, sweltering in the heat of a warm September.

'No, you are a comfort, a haven in the middle of the storm of my mind,' she said, eyes roaming my face, palm curving around my neck.

Was I selfish for believing her, or was I simply trusting in her ability to decide for herself?

'I might ask you the same,' she said. 'Am I not a burden to you? Can you love a mad thing like me?'

'You are not mad; nightmares and bad nerves are not madness,' I said, squeezing her shoulder, feeling the sharp edges of the bones underneath. If I called her mad might I not have to call myself the same?

She turned onto her back. 'Every time I think I have escaped the nightmares, they come back, scampering after me, hunting me.'

'Is it memories of your mother?'

'Sometimes,' she said. 'Sometimes it's other things, odd images and scenes, strange sensations. Sometimes I have the normal kind of dream where one is being chased by some great four-legged beast, but then the beast catches me before I can wake, and I am surrounded by it, smothered by it, like I'm drowning in its fur, trapped there. I know it sounds so silly when I say it out loud but the timbre of the dream, the terror I feel . . .' She exhaled a long, shaky breath.

My heart was tripping in my chest, but then dreams of being hunted by a beast, and being caught, were common dreams, were they not? 'But the museum,' I said, propping myself up on my elbows, 'and the animals, they don't trigger your nightmares or make them worse, you're *sure*?'

'I am sure, Hetty, they're not new nightmares. I'm not a martyr, I would go and stay somewhere else for the duration of the war if I was distressed by your collection. God knows we have the money to rent out a series of lovely homes for me.'

What she was saying might be true – for she had never looked at my animals with terror or fear, only wonder and fascination – but I knew that even if it were not, it was exceedingly unlikely that she *would* leave Lockwood, for Lucy's world was getting smaller as her nerves were getting worse.

First it was that she did not want to venture further than the grounds of Lockwood, to traipse through the sunny fields or walk up to the village; and then that she only wanted to walk in those parts of the gardens which had a clear view of the entirety of the house – the front lawn, the orchard, the walled garden, the rose garden, and the flowerbeds around the little pond; and finally, that she did not even want to leave the house. The progression of this was not quite linear, there might still be days now and then when I could coax her out to the gardens, but I feared what the end to this was – how soon would it be until she could not leave her room, her bed? I hoped that I was only being alarmist and tried my best to help her, not to push her too insistently, but to encourage her, even as each air-raid siren seemed to undo both her and my hard work. What effort could counteract the might of an entire army; where could she hide from the war itself? Would she have to wait until the damned thing was over to find any true peace again?

I observed and catalogued the signs of her anxiety, as if this could bring me answers, and – a cynical part of me thought – as a way of not thinking about my own troubled nights. The way she trembled when I tried to persuade her to sit on the terrace, getting all the way down the stairs before she clutched at the end of the banisters as if she were being swept out to sea and whispered, *No, no*, as though unfathomable horrors awaited her. The way she tapped her fingertips on tabletops or on her thigh, hands as quick as hummingbirds, if I *had* managed to get her outside. The way she apologized over and over again for being ridiculous. The way that tears might spill from her eyes if she was particularly distressed, as she muffled quiet high-pitched keens into a cushion, while I tried to soothe her, rubbing my hand along her back ineffectually, as if I was trying to calm an animal that knew it was being sent to slaughter.

'Is it that you don't feel safe away from the house, or that you worry that the house isn't safe without you there?' I asked her one evening as she sat in her bath and I bathed her gently with a sponge – not because she was an invalid that could not do such a task for herself, she was not helpless or feeble, but because I liked to care for her. I liked that what we were together, who we were to one another, seemed such a myriad of things: friend, lover, mother, daughter, kin.

'It's both,' she said with a weary sigh.

I did not say that there was a cruel irony in her anxiety

causing her to stay inside, confining her behind walls and doors, in her ever-narrowing sphere of safety. For she was still afraid of the dark, still afraid of being locked inside, even as some part of her wished to shut herself away from the world.

Once, I was too scared to even close my eyes, she had told me, speaking of the blue room and its after-effects, *even with the lights on, as if my eyelids were doors themselves that might trap me in the dark. The sedatives helped with that but they also trapped me in my dreams, made me woozy, made the real world seem unreal, like I had never woken up at all.*

There was no peace for her to be found anywhere, and the comfort I could give her was not absolute, for one person could not stand against the might of Lockwood and its memories, its hidden rooms and ghostly traumas.

The doctors, when she allowed them to visit, had said that rest, and certain pills, would help, that she should take to her bed, but she refused the drugs and tried her best to potter about the house instead of hiding under her blankets, fought against being cloistered even as some forceful part of herself wished so desperately to be.

I had left the site of my unhappy childhood but her nerves, and circumstances, had kept her here, walking down the same corridors, waking in the same room, while the horrors of her past lay behind locked doors and bricked-up walls. Even without her memories, this house was not a welcoming home – the unsettling number of empty rooms with their sheeted furniture that made you think *you* were the ghost, haunting a shut-up house; the rows of blacked-out windows, the creaks and murmurs of old floors and walls – it was certainly working its brooding effect on me. Surely a charming little cottage somewhere, a fresh start, a house with no uninhabited wings for the mind to wander through and get lost in, would be the trick – although I never mentioned this to her because it sounded foolish, and because I feared it would give away my own desire for us to live somewhere small and humble by ourselves, away from here.

My mind was searching for my own escape route, and not only from my continued nightmares, because when I was not with Lucy, I was with the museum, where I was fighting a terrible invasion of my own, of beetles and moths, pests that threatened the entire collection of skins and taxidermy, and it was a battle I was losing.

The environment inside Lockwood Manor was not an ideal location for the specimens I had helped to evacuate from London, but it was the best that could be done when the other option was the utter devastation of the Blitz, which by now had already irrevocably damaged smaller museums and collections that had not been able to leave. The long gallery was difficult to keep warm during winter and to cool during summer; the roofs, walls, and windows of the manor were tired and patchworked, their cracks letting in all manner of beasts, foxes and cats and birds, that had to be shooed away. The fluctuations of temperature and humidity wore at the furs and organic materials of the collection and aged the wood of the cabinets and crates. Bones could swell and shrink and split with changes in the environment. On one cold day which followed an unseasonably warm day, I had heard, from a cabinet in the long gallery, the snap of a bone, so loud, so clearly *bone* snapping right through, that I cried out as if it had been one of my own breaking. And yet all this was somewhat manageable, expected, compared to the influx of insects.

It started when I saw a pile of dust underneath the mounted oxen and, when I studied it with a magnifying glass, I found frass, the droppings of insect larvae, and casts, the skin the insects shed as they grew from larvae. Then it was a race against time to prevent the insects spreading. I cleaned and vacuumed and dusted down on my hands and knees with a bright lamp to search for eggs in creases and folds, covering my face with a mask as I sprayed insecticides and potions on the mounted animals that ranged up and down that long gallery and its rooms. I ordered more mothballs and hid them around the rooms like a macabre treasure hunt, spread sticky insect traps in all corners and used my magnifying glass to search for tiny chinks and holes in floorboards and wooden skirting boards for so long that when I stood up the world seemed gigantic and strange.

I had catalogued four different pests and counting in quick succession: carpet beetles, hide beetles, carpet moths and casemaking clothes moths. Most of the cabinets were safe – and within them the slides and eggs and shells and study skins which were not mounted – but not all, because even wood could contract and expand, as if it remembered being alive, cracks opening up in its side, as if it were in conspiracy with the insects.

I had to open up some of the specimens to clean them and I trawled through the detritus of past taxidermists, discovering the secrets of these animals and their particular insides – for every taxidermist has their own favourite tools, their own methods of mounting and combinations of sawdust, clay, wood, cloth, newspapers. Little scraps of newspaper could tell me the very day that an animal was being brought back into a half-life from its previous flat existence, teased into three dimensions. The careful work that the scientists, hunters, and taxidermists had done was under threat; nature appeared to have had enough and wanted to reclaim these trophies, with the insects as its infantrymen.

It was enough to make one paranoid. I would walk along the long gallery and pause, believing that I had heard the scurrying of tiny feet, the susurration of miniature jaws gnawing on my charges; fearing that if I turned my back, a great plague of insects would appear, a flood of them. It was as if someone was conducting them, waving a baton, a wand, ushering them in waves of attack, I thought wildly, my eyes dry with lack of sleep, my heart sprinting like an animal whipped, my body starting at every creak even if I was the one who had made it by walking across the floorboards.

And in the course of opening up cabinets and crates and drawers that had not been touched for months, I discovered something else; a large crate that had contained a collection of elephant ivory on its arrival at Lockwood was now bare of all but sawdust and empty sacking.

When I discovered it, I knelt slack-jawed by the crate, trying to remember the last time I, or one of the movers perhaps, had crow-barred open the lid, and then I started to cry, silently, tiredly, thinking that this was surely it, the last nail in the coffin of my continued employment.

But if I told no one about it, I thought frantically, and entirely unprofessionally, an hour later, hammering the lid back into place, then no one would know about it, not until the collection was back in London and even a few weeks after that, as the boxes and crates were slowly opened – and by then the blame could not possibly be solely placed on my shoulders. But even with the crate closed, its missing contents still leached their way into my dreams as a beast made from bones, with four bristling tusks, bucked and rattled down the corridors of Lockwood after me.

And then there were the letters from soldiers abroad, sent on from London, looking for advice about exotic pests and vermin – and how could I be an authority on that, when I could barely keep my own animals safe?

What if I cannot do this? I had begun to think. *What if I cannot save the museum; what if everything I* do *is only making things worse?* Work had always been my salvation, but now it seemed only a curse. I could not seem to save my animals, or Lucy; I could not bloody *sleep,* or quieten my hysterical fears.

After school restarted in September, Lucy invited the local evacuated children for a trip to the museum, eager to do her bit to cheer them up, if only for an afternoon, for we had all heard about those poor souls that had been lost in London and knew that their parents were still living through the horrors of the Blitz. She asked the cook to make animal-shaped biscuits with sugar saved from our fortnightly rations and was hunting for an atlas that she could use to show them where each animal had come from.

'I want a proper big map for them to look at,' she was saying, as she perched on the top rung of the ladder in the library, finger running down the spines of heavy books, while I watched from the carpet below.

'If I was better at drawing, I could make a large map on some wallpaper and pin it up,' I said.

'Oh, I am terrible at drawing too,' she said, clambering down, forehead creasing delicately.

I glanced behind us to check the door was still closed and then stepped forward to kiss her. She startled and then kissed me back, clutching my face in her hands.

'What was that about?' she asked afterwards, with a smile, fingers touching her lips. She had stopped wearing her red lipsticks so often since we started kissing, and when I saw her around the house with her lips a natural peach, I sometimes felt a jolt of electricity, a warm proprietary glow.

'You looked darling, standing there, with your little frown,' I said.

'What a silly thing to say,' she said, pretending to be angry, and then kissed me again. 'Wait –' she mumbled into my mouth, her body stilling – 'a globe, that's what we need.' She pulled away.

I needed a moment to remember our last conversation. 'Do you have one?' I asked.

'No, but my father does. Come with me,' she said, dragging me out of the library and across the hall to his office. She tried the door but it was locked, and with Lord Lockwood away I thought our very short-lived quest was at an end. 'Stay here, I'll get the key,' she said.

I stood, staring at the door that I had looked at before every awful encounter with her father, feeling the shiver of a transgressive thrill.

'Got it.' She reappeared, holding up two keys, and unlocked the door. I followed her inside.

There was a lingering masculine smell in her father's office – tobacco, leather, sweat – and the furnishings were as uninspired as ever, dull and dark and lacking any feminine flourish.

'It'll be through here – I haven't been in here for years,' she was saying, bypassing the huge mahogany desk to unlock the second door behind it, the door to his personal library, which I had not even seen from the windows, since it looked out onto a private courtyard in between the ballroom and the long gallery.

The door swung open with a creak and she fumbled for the

light switch. I entered the illuminated room in a daze, walking into a nightmarish vision.

There were vast shelves of books in the double-storey space – leather-bound and old, and protected behind glass with brass lock and key – but it was what else he had hidden away in here that had shocked me.

The floor was covered with half a dozen animal skins – zebra, lion with head and mane, polar bear, tiger with its tail, leopard, wolf.

There was a mounted North American brown bear, rearing up on its hind legs, by one wall, opposite a polar bear doing just the same; an Asiatic lion and a Bengal tiger bracketing the sofas.

There was a stuffed panther and a stuffed wolf, the same ones Lucy had mentioned that she had not seen for many years, and a whole wall of mounted hunting trophies – stag, antelope, bison, lion, boar – alongside rifles and spears and swords.

And there, next to the working fireplace, was my missing jaguar.

And there, propped up against a wall of bookshelves, was my missing ivory.

I turned round to face a startled-looking Lucy. 'Did you know?' I demanded. 'Did you know he had all this here, that he had stolen the jaguar and my ivory?'

'I didn't, I swear it,' she said, shaking her head, moving towards the towering brown bear as if she was being pulled to it, reaching out a hand to it before recoiling. 'I haven't been in here for years; no one has. I think the housekeeper is the only one he lets clean his rooms.'

The same housekeeper who had listened to my woes about the damned jaguar and said she would do her best to help find it.

'I found the globe,' Lucy said in a small voice, standing next to it, her body tucked behind the polar bear.

I was still circling the room, noticing more and more of the Major's treasures – ivory figurines dotted around on shelves, fur cushions, a fox-fur stole draped over a sofa as if left behind by the last female visitor, antlers used as a hat stand, snakeskin curiosities, a goblet made from a ram's horn. The sense of ownership, the *arrogance* of taking museum items for his own collection, as if no one would notice them missing, or more likely, not caring if they did, infuriated me.

'How can you stand him, your father?' I implored. I felt teary-eyed at the scene before me, impotent in the face of it. 'He's a liar, a thief. He's a tyrant.' I swore.

She was tracing the continents on the globe. I studied her face for reminders of his but found none. 'He's set in his ways,' she said, looking at me pleadingly.

'He's rude and cruel. He wouldn't understand this –' I motioned between us – '*us*. You know that, don't you?'

'He's my father, Hetty,' she said. 'I don't know what you want me to say. I know he's not the nicest of men but beggars can't be choosers, and he's all I've got left now.'

'You've got *me*,' I said.

But what about when the war ended? What about when I left Lockwood? Those were the questions I could see on her face.

I turned away, throat thick with sorrow and anger, covering my mouth with the back of my hand.

This room was everything I disliked about natural history collections – the emphasis on the hunter; the animals posed as threats when they were the ones killed, often with a single shot from behind; the hoarding of all this natural wonder behind a locked door for the benefit of a single rich man. If a man's office, his private rooms, can be said to resemble his soul, then Major Lord Lockwood was a brutish huntsman at heart.

'I'm going to get Paul. We need to carry the ivory and the jaguar back to their proper places,' I said, leaving her there, a girl surrounded by snarling beasts.

Naturally, when the Major returned to the house from his travels a few days later, it was he who came storming into my office to accuse me of trespassing where I did not belong.

'What the hell do you think you're doing? My office and library are off limits, that was explicit in the contract I signed with the museum,' he said furiously, almost shouting, looming over the desk I sat behind.

'And where in the contract did it say you could purloin what you wanted for your own private collection, that you could steal from us?' I asked, voice shaking with anger.

'*Steal*,' he jeered. 'Once again you lose control of your wits, Miss Cartwright. There is no need to be hysterical,' he said, when he was the one who had entered the room like a crazed bull.

'I can take out the copies of letters if you like, the ones I sent to London and the other evacuated departments, asking about the jaguar that had gone missing,' I offered.

'You needn't bother,' he said, leaning back from the desk, hiding his beastliness under a cool sneer again. 'That would only prove you *believed* it was missing.'

'It *was* missing; you stole it and hid it in your private, locked room.'

'Yes, a *locked* room. It was safe as houses in there, unlike some of your other animals.'

'It's your house; if things have been going missing, it's *your* fault,' I said, standing up.

'You never reported the ivory missing,' he said, fingering the vole skull on my desk distastefully. 'That doesn't reflect well on you.' His eyes cut to mine. 'And I doubt the museum director will be keen on you braying about missing things when you've found them again. What a waste of paper those angry letters would be. Come, come, now, Miss Cartwright.'

'You won't accept any blame for this?'

'Blame for what? Your specimens are inside the house and they are safe.' He shrugged meanly and neatened his dark tie that stood out from the blinding white of his crisp shirt. 'But if I find out you've trespassed in my locked rooms again, I'll have you fired, and that's a promise. No one will hire you again. I'm very thorough in my dealings, Miss Cartwright, unlike some people.'

And with that threat made, he swept out of the room.

Chapter Thirty-Two

My father was particular about his belongings, his trophies, his paintings, his silver, his taxidermy.

As a child, he told me off for trying to ride his panther, and he wouldn't let me touch it, but I was allowed sometimes to visit his office and look at it, while he scratched his pen across letters and talked brusquely on the telephone.

'I wish they would come back to life, I wish I could hear it purr,' I said one afternoon sitting cross-legged in front of it, nose to nose, my tongue furred by the toffee my father had slipped me from his desk drawer.

'Hear it growl more like, as it hunted you. You're a brave girl but a beast like this would eat you for dinner,' he said, and then reached over to tickle my neck.

'Don't you wish you could see it alive?'

'I have, my doll,' he said with a wave of his particular brand of cigarette, whose scent lingered in rooms he had left hours ago. 'I've seen all the great beasts in the jungles and on the savanna; I've hunted them. But if you're wanting a magic spell to bring this creature back to life, you'll have to ask your mother,' he said, his voice changing, turning silky, so that I knew she had just entered the room. 'She's the witch in this house.'

A frisson passed between the two of them, a language I didn't understand – my mother at the door, wearing a satin dress and with her hair loose around her shoulders, her lips red as cherries; my father in his smart suit, his shining leather shoes that creaked with every shift of his feet as he lounged in his office chair. Sometimes when they were together it was as if no one else existed and I was so jealous I ached.

'Tell me the story of how you met Mother, please, Father,' I begged, knowing that otherwise he would call for my nurse at any moment to have me ushered out of his office so my mother and he could do whatever they did behind locked doors.

He hummed. 'I found her in the jungle. Didn't I, my love? Running through the trees with mud on her knees and an impish smile that made me fall in love with her on first sight. Her parents warned me off her. She's too wild, they said, but I wanted what I wanted.'

My mother had her arms crossed, her head resting against the doorframe. 'My husband's a liar,' she said. 'It was my mother who warned me against him. Never trust an Englishman, she said.'

'The same mother who lied to me about your age?' my father replied with a snort. 'Oh, yes.'

My mother ran a hand across her collarbone. 'We met at a ball, don't you remember, darling? I wasn't even out properly yet, and you couldn't keep your eyes off me. You begged me for a dance and I refused and so you watched me and you followed me and scowled at all the men I danced with and then you turned up on the steps of my house the next morning and begged me to marry you.'

'A lie,' he said and leaned back in his seat. 'I never begged.'

She raised an eyebrow and wound her way towards him.

'Your mother tells tall tales,' he pronounced, staring at her unblinkingly and stubbing his cigarette out in his ivory ashtray, and then he called for my nurse as I knew he would and I was whisked away to my nursery.

It was a phrase he used again, over the years, in unhappier times when my mother was ill in bed, when she had been dosed with sleeping tonics to stop her from raving about spirits and strange beasts haunting her. *Your mother tells tall tales,* he would say to me carefully, *and people love gossip. Words are powerful things, my dove, you must remember that.*

My mother's stories changed from day to day, from hour to hour. I would question her on something she had said – about an acrobat troupe that was to attend a ball at Lockwood, or the pet parrot she told me she taught tricks to as a child – and she would deny any knowledge of the conversation. *Don't be silly, she would say,* I never said anything of the sort.

If I had asked her afterwards about locking me in the blue room she would have denied it. *I never did that,* she would have said with a nervous flick of her hair, *what an imagination you've got.*

But sometimes, the things she said were more urgent; sometimes when she told me them she begged me to remember them, as if knowing she would forget.

'Remember that she's here,' she had said several years before her death, clutching my hands when I found her in the library staring at the flowers on the mantelpiece, 'that she's waiting. You won't forget, will you?' she asked, shivering, face creasing into childish pain.

'I won't forget,' I said.

Another time, not long before she died, she was adamant that she wouldn't live to see old age. 'Remember,' she begged, 'if anything happens to me, that I predicted it, that I knew it would happen.'

Not half an hour later she was in the kitchens, tasting the

cook's new desserts with a frown of concentration and I knew that if I asked her about our earlier conversation she would brush me off with a laugh and lean across the table to pass me the cake tin so that I could have a slice.

Were there different versions of my mother, did she walk into a room one person, and walk out another? Were there a hundred different mothers here, each in their own room? Did she know that other her – or hers, plural? Was there more than one of her inside her own body?

Was that my fate too, I wondered as Hetty dozed beside me after our lovemaking; would I forget things that I had done, would another me be cruel and mad, while I was helpless to stop it?

I stared at her sleeping, her eyelashes pale as a moth's wing, her hand lying open as if waiting for my own hand.

'Cross my heart and hope to die,' I whispered, and took her hand, squeezing her fingers gently and wishing she was awake too and could squeeze mine back.

Chapter Thirty-Three

After a day of three separate air raids, with the mood inside the basement shelter best described as almost belligerent, Lucy pleaded with me for something productive she could do to help calm her whirring mind. I put her to work in my office, organizing letters into different trays. It was a pleasingly domestic scene, me at a writing desk answering the letters while Lucy spread out on my main desk sorting them, calling out a choice word or an interesting passage, while the sun tracked across the room, the light warming and then dipping towards dusk. And yet it was also an oddly transgressive scene, for I knew that her father had forbidden her from any involvement in the museum. How could he begrudge her doing secretarial work like this? Could he not see the way it enlivened her, being useful, learning and setting her mind to things other than the house and her past?

In moments like this I could not help but think I could have it all – the museum *and* Lucy – that I could put into play the plan that I had yet to tell even Lucy about, that of her coming to London and working for the museum. She was independently wealthy and thus could volunteer with the great number who already did, without the need to worry about a wage, although of course I would fight for her to be properly employed just as I fought for the other women. We might live near one another in the city, and visit regularly, or even take rooms together somewhere; and in London, the night was never truly dark, the city's gleaming lamps and advertisements and bars and theatres lent the air a glow that sneaked through any closed curtain.

Of course, how to remove her from a house she did not want to leave at any cost was the great sticking point, along with her father's prohibition. But I would not abandon her here, alone, when the war was over – if it was ever over – I vowed that I would try to save her, that when the trucks came to collect the animals and transport them to their rightful home, she would come too, that I would whisk her away, out from under her father's nose and from this horrid house.

Not for the first time, I thought that all this would be easier if I were only a man. I could marry her then, and she would be under my protection, not her father's, and we could legitimately get our own house, have our own family.

Be sensible, Henrietta, I heard the memory of my mother say, her favourite phrase.

Did the Major's manner rub me the wrong way because his disdain was so close to my mother's; or would it have affected a different Hetty – a Hetty who grew up with a loving, tender parent – just the same? I had yet to receive a reply to the emotional letter I had sent her and she had given me no word about where she might now be residing. I knew that she would not stay in London during the Blitz – not because she might die, but because of the general upheaval to her routines and the social order, because of her fear of change. I imagined she was in a house similar to this one, except smaller, I thought spitefully, and less grand.

'This man,' Lucy declared, reading out a letter, 'says that he has discovered a new amphibious mammal and he humbly puts forward his own name for consideration for its nomen-clature.'

I put my elbow on the desk and rested my cheek on my hand, listening to her read the animal description aloud – *larger than a pine marten and yet smaller than a dog, slimy, with a distinct tang of iron in the air once it had vanished, a white patch of fur between its eyes* – her mouth curled in sardonic appreciation, her eyes bright and large. I let myself picture some halcyon future; let myself ignore the horde of beetles gnawing their way through the long gallery; the planes across the Channel being fuelled, bombs loaded in their bellies; the great crowd of stuffed animals who waited for the wars of men to be over, hoping that there would still be a museum left in London for them to return to; and the ghost, the intruder, that continued to haunt both my dreams and the house itself.

Autumn had returned by the time the evacuated children came to visit the animals, and when they clattered inside the front door they brought with them a swirl of leaves scorched yellow and a blustering wind that made the chandelier above them sway and groan.

I had never been in charge of child visitors to the museum in London, but in our correspondence, their teacher, a Miss Forbes, said that I should treat them as I would the adult visitors and that they would be too overawed by the house to get into mischief.

Seeing them walk past the animals open-mouthed, almost reverent, grabbing silently at each other in excitement, reminded me of my secret thrill of watching visitors to the museum in London and I felt a pang that we had shut the mammal collection away here at Lockwood, just as so many other museums and art galleries had fled the capital, leaving its remaining occupants bereft of their culture just when they might need it most to get through the barbarous bombardment of the Luftwaffe.

I gave the children a brief introduction to the collection, a simplified explanation of the various families and genera Lockwood held, and then a quiz about the classification of mammals, which Miss Forbes said she had discussed with them in advance.

Lucy had insisted on being my assistant and she was the one to kneel down by a girl who raised her hand with a question but was too shy to ask it, who accompanied a boy at the back to the bathrooms when she saw him wriggling about, and who listened patiently to the whispered tale of one girl who had a graze on her chin.

'You're a natural with them,' I said to her later, once I had sent the children on a sedate hunt to find their very favourite animal amongst the collection. We were standing in the corridor where we might by necessity stand closer than we would in one of the rooms, close enough to smell each note of the other's perfume but not to touch.

She smiled as she lifted a hand to fix a curl that had escaped from her pinned roll, but it was a sadder smile than she had used in the room.

'Do you think—' I began and paused, studying her face, the way the low afternoon light revealed the freckles on her chin. 'Will you have children one day?' I asked, feeling a painful ache in my chest.

'I don't think so,' she said slowly, carefully. 'I'd have to find a husband for that.'

I licked my lips. We did so well not to talk of the future,

but the temptation was always there, the knowledge that what we had was, by any logical understanding, temporary.

'I didn't have the best role model for it,' she said.

'Me neither,' I said as the laughter of a group of children in the library made me turn to look down the corridor.

'But if I don't have children then this house will be awfully empty in the future.'

'You'll stay here then,' I said, hating myself for only summoning the bravery for this conversation right now, when there were children wandering hither and thither and servants carting brushes and mops and linen between us as we shrank towards opposite walls.

'I don't think I'll ever leave Lockwood,' she stated sadly. 'I would worry too much about it if I were anywhere else. I feel responsible. I bear its name after all.'

'It bears *your* name.'

She tilted her head. 'It's strange, I always think of it in the opposite way. That the house has stood for generations while we come and go, that it owns us and not the other way round.'

It doesn't own you, I wanted to say. *It doesn't, you can do anything, you can live anywhere, don't you see how brilliant you are, how you'd be wasted here?*

'I should close my office door,' I said instead, my voice thick.

'Good idea,' Lucy replied hollowly, stepping back so that her feet were not crushed by children racing past. She strode towards the drawing room. 'Be careful where you run, children!' she called.

When I pulled the stiff door of my office towards me, key in hand, I noticed something that had not been there a few hours ago, before the children arrived; a hummock of fur, an animal shape, on my desk.

As I approached, I thought it might be someone's fur muff

– but these children would surely be too poor for that – or that it was one of our animals, or a dried skin that had been pulled out of a cabinet and mislaid. But it was not flat enough to be a skin, and nor did it resemble any of the stuffed animals in our collection.

It was a rabbit, its ears draped softly above its head. It was cold when I touched it, and it had not been skinned, for I could feel the bulging shape of flesh inside. By the smear of blood I found underneath as I lifted it, and the blood that painted my fingers as I searched through its fur for a pulse, I knew that it had been killed only today.

'Miss Cartwright—' Dorothy asked at the door, and when I turned round she saw the red of my hands. 'My goodness, are you hurt?'

'No,' I said, as Lucy came up to the door behind her. I held a hand on the rabbit's back, as if trying to protect it from further harm. 'I found this on my desk,' I said, feeling my heart tremble in my chest, and then I looked to Lucy, who was frozen to the spot, the pupils of her eyes ringed with white.

'Where did that come from? Is it real, alive, I mean?' Dorothy asked, coming closer. She touched its fur with a finger. 'But what was it doing here?' she said to me with an eager intensity in her eyes.

'I don't know,' I said and looked again to Lucy, who was still in the doorway, her chin now dimpling as if she were going to cry.

'I shall see if the teacher knows where it came from,' Lucy said, her voice strange, one of her hands rising to cover her mouth. The heel of her shoe caught on the floor as she left and I started towards her as if I could catch her from all the way across the room, but she righted herself and continued out of sight.

'I don't like this at all,' Dorothy said, stealing the words from my throat as we stared at a line of blood seeping from the carcass towards the edge of the desk.

I locked my office door until the children's visit was at an end, leaving the grisly gift where it lay for fear of one of them catching me ferrying it through to the gardens, and when I opened it again Dorothy was at my heel, ostensibly to help clean but really, I thought, because she wanted to wallow in the grim excitement.

'It's an omen, it is, mark my words.' She hoisted the rabbit by its ears into a bucket and slopped soapy water onto my desk while I hurriedly removed my papers and books to safer ground. 'Or a threat,' she said pointedly, turning to consider me with narrowed eyes.

'It's not one of the kitchen's rabbits?' I asked, as other servants peered into the room in passing.

'We might be overworked,' she sniffed, 'but we won't have mislaid a carcass on your desk, miss. Anyway, it's not a rabbit from the farm – the groundskeeper breaks the neck of those, he doesn't garrotte them,' she said, savouring her words as I clasped my hands together tightly and tried to settle myself, tried to appear as if I was yet unruffled by such a clearly personal attack.

Who had done this? Jenkins, who was often seen with a dead fox in his fist after catching them in his traps, and seemed to scowl at me every time we crossed paths? One of the groundskeepers? Dorothy herself, out of some twisted desire for excitement? Paul, as a poor joke? Another servant who was resentful of any extra work the museum had brought? The housekeeper? Was it the same person who had stolen the hummingbirds and skinned the bear and had they been here all this time, watching me?

'It would have been a barn cat, or a dog, or one of the children playing a trick,' the housekeeper said when I went to find her, talking slowly as if to an imbecile. 'Or some well-meaning villager who thought you might be looking for fresh specimens. There are many possible explanations before you might start blaming my staff,' she added as I stood there feeling sick.

'I wasn't going to blame anyone,' I said, unconvincingly. How had she turned this against me, why did I feel at fault?

'Frankly, Miss Cartwright, none of this nonsense happened before you and your animals arrived. And it's you who always seems to be the centre of these things, wandering about the house at all hours and then complaining that someone's been stealing your animals, giving us more work to do. If there is indeed a mischief-maker in our midst, I have half a mind that it's *you*,' she declared furiously, moving so close to me that I could see the pale hairs on her cheek, the angry spittle in the corners of her mouth. 'I think you put the rabbit there yourself. I know your type; I think you like the attention,' she sneered, and as she stalked off I cursed myself for standing there mute under her onslaught.

I was barely composed by the time dinner arrived. I sat there feeling hollow and shaken, glancing at Lucy's empty chair and wishing I was with her instead of being ushered into the dining room by her father when he caught me ascending the stairs towards her and told me he wouldn't have dinner delayed tonight, that he had far more important things to do than sit and wait for me to dawdle as his food went cold.

'I don't get involved in servant business, I leave that to the housekeeper,' he was saying, cutting into his meat, his mouth stained red with wine, 'but when my staff are dropping like flies, when the government keeps stealing them from me, and then you baselessly accuse them of nonsense crimes, frankly, it's beyond the pale.'

'I didn't accuse anyone,' I said, my teeth clenched, my plate of food uneaten. 'I just want to find out who is responsible.'

'You do make a fuss about things, don't you, Miss Cartwright? The children who you invited into my home were evacuated from some of the roughest parts of London, they've been running wild around the countryside, and no doubt they've taken up poaching too, little beasts.'

I sat there silently, breathing tightly, biting my lip so the pain might stop me from crying. When he was finished and rudely pushed his plate away he stood up with a yawn. 'I'll be writing a report for your employers; I'm sure they'll be eager to hear of your disruptiveness. I might have agreed to house the museum here, my dear, but I didn't agree to open my doors to someone like you.'

Chapter Thirty-Four

'Do you think there's something about Lockwood,' Lucy remarked tiredly a week later, as we lay side by side on her bed while her radiators clicked and a pipe clanged somewhere in a wall, 'that makes our dreams leak out into the day, that brings them to life?'

She was speaking of the leveret, the hare, that she told me she hunted through the house each night in her dreams, that she woke grasping at.

'No,' I said, because I had never been someone prone to whimsy, to superstition; I was not the type to wake from her own dreams – of beasts and hunts and wild women with teeth sharp as knives and claws that could pluck the eyes from your skull, the tongue from your mouth – and stare around the room clutching at the bedclothes, fearing what I would find there in the dark. My fears were human, rational ones, I told myself – of professional sabotage, of disgruntled servants and petty vendettas – not of ghosts and spirits and hauntings.

I could not sleep, and neither could Lucy, though I lied to her that I could because I did not want her to feel somehow responsible. When I read letters or books the words swam before my eyes, when I picked up specimens to clean and dust my hands shook alarmingly and I would enter rooms without ever remembering why I had visited them, or find my legs shaking when I tried to stand up after kneeling to check animals for infestation – and I had slipped just the day before while getting out of the bath and almost knocked myself out on the rim.

My only saving grace was that the Major had left the morning after the mess with the rabbit and without, I assumed, sending a letter to the directors of the museum in London. But what was my job worth if I could not do it properly? What if I dropped another specimen and it shattered on the floor; what if I used the wrong powder to clean a fur and ruined it forever? What was my job worth if I could not keep the animals safe both from others, and from my own mistakes?

In early November, I was woken in my own bedroom in the small hours, not by the usual sound of the air-raid siren, nor by that night's gale thundering against the walls, but by the loud smash of glass.

When I staggered downstairs from my bedroom in my dressing gown, I found the housekeeper similarly attired, with a fine silk scarf knotted around her pinned hair, and Paul and Dorothy hastily dressed, the group of them huddling by the drawing room next to a night guard shining his torch inside. A terrific wind was roaring through the open door towards us.

'What's going on?' I called frantically, my voice croaky with tiredness, having only snatched an hour or so of sleep in the past two days.

'It's the drawing room,' the guard said. 'The windows have been smashed.'

'Was it the storm? Has anything been taken?'

I pushed my way into the darkened room where I could see

the second guard leaning his head carefully out of the left window frame, its glass edges a barbed halo.

Were the windows smashed from inside or outside, I wondered, my mind still half taken up with the nightmare I had awoken from, of a beast on the rampage through the rooms, still lingering in my shaky limbs, my teeth chattering.

'Was the door locked when you got here?' I asked the night guard.

'Yes.'

But what if someone had been inside the room, hiding, when I had locked it last night? 'Hiding where?' I muttered to myself hysterically beneath the sound of the storm. 'Underneath the panther?' The guard next to me looked at me strangely.

'Give me your torch,' I said, and swung it round the room, looking for anything missing, the broken glass glittering in the beam of light, the wind whipping the blackout curtains towards me, cloaking the polar bear by the window, while I gasped for breath as if the wind was stealing it.

'Careful of the glass on the floor,' Paul called, and beneath the barrage of the storm I heard the crunch underneath my slippers, and then my foot kicked against something hard and I screamed at the unexpected pain and then fumbled for an explanation as the others turned to me. 'I found the brick they threw,' I said, and then repeated it when my voice gave out halfway through the sentence, shining the shaking light of my torch on it so that everyone could see the reason why I had made such a noise.

Pull yourself together, Hetty, I thought. 'Are they out there? The thieves?' I asked, pulling my dressing gown around me with one hand, holding the other in front of my face against the elements and so that no one would be able to see how frightened I was.

'I'm going to go out and look!' Paul called. 'Let me have the key to the gun room,' he told the guard by the door.

'Be careful!' Dorothy said. 'You don't know how many are out there. Oh, I wish Lord Lockwood were here, he would know what to do now. I thought it was the Germans, I really did,' she moaned, clasping a hand to her chest as Josephine patted her on the shoulder ineffectually. Dorothy grabbed my arm as I walked past and I jumped and stifled a yelp. 'They did warn us about parachutists, you don't think—'

'It won't be the Germans,' I said, angered by my reaction. 'It'll be the same thieves as last time.'

'I suppose the police should be called,' the housekeeper said, though she sounded half-hearted.

'Yes,' I called, voice breaking as the wind picked up to a high wail, screeching its way past the jagged edges of the windows. 'And have you got a spare blackout curtain or some board? This one has been torn,' I said, trying to bat it away while dodging the stuffed wolf by my side, feeling close to tears at the noise and mayhem, at the attack on the museum that felt like an attack on me too. 'And we need to turn the light on in here to see what the hell has happened.' I turned to the guard who was still near the window, leaning forward against the force of the storm. 'Have they taken anything? Did you see them?'

'I didn't see anything,' he said, wiping his face of rain, his white hair plastered to his forehead. He put out a hand to steady himself on the head of the Sumatran tiger and then took it back when he remembered who I was. 'We came running the moment we heard the smash,' he said. 'We thought it was the storm. God help anyone who's out there in it, there'll be trees coming down tonight.'

Josephine and the housekeeper came into the room with

two boards and I helped prop them against the windows with arms that felt weak and trembling. We pinned the curtains as best we could, and pushed the crowding animals out of the way with groans of effort that were echoed by the howls of the wind. Then someone switched on the lights and I blinked painfully as the dark, heaving shadows of the room, the hidden audience of animals that had watched us mutely, came into focus.

There was nothing missing: the thieves had not clambered inside, if that was indeed their intention, and if it was thieves at all. The brick they had thrown was on the floor in front of the left window but something else, an unfamiliar shape wrapped in newspaper, had been thrown through the window on the right. I bent over it and covered my hands in the folds of my dressing gown to brush away the shards of glass, and started to unwrap it, heart in my throat though I knew not why.

'Stand back!' the guard called out, dashing forward, 'It could be an explosive—' He stopped abruptly when the newspaper came free and, startled by the object I was holding, I dropped the uncovered projectile on the floor.

It was a worn porcelain doll, dressed for winter in a white fur cloak almost as pale as its blonde hair. I had felt the tightly curled hair and the fur of the cloak in my hands and been spooked by the thought that what I held was warm and alive. Now she lay at my feet on her back, her blue eyes staring up at me, and it felt as if my voice had been stolen from my throat, the edges of my vision prickling with dark spots.

Josephine had screamed when she saw the doll, further adding to my terror, but now she was tutting and repeating some choice French swear words underneath her breath.

'How perfectly horrid,' Dorothy exclaimed with a whimper

and then crouched down next to it as the winds picked up again. She nudged it with her finger. 'What a ghastly, spooky thing.'

'Is it one of Lucy's?' I asked, unable to make sense of the object in front of me, of the room and the people and the attack. Was I still asleep, I wondered, blinking and shaking my head.

'I shouldn't think so,' the housekeeper remarked. 'Lady Lucy got rid of all of those long ago.'

Paul eventually returned from outside, soaked to the skin and failing to hide his grin at his adventure, having caught no sight of our intruder. He and the guards nailed the boards properly against the smashed windows, sealing up the room from the storm, while Josephine swept away the glass and Dorothy wandered the room, ostensibly setting things to rights but mostly lingering amongst all the excitement, returning to the doll at intervals, shaking her head and sucking her teeth as if the doll meant something other than an attempt to frighten us; to frighten me.

I checked the specimens again, hands fumbling and feet tripping over air, blinking my eyes as if I could make this all go away and find myself waking from a good night's sleep instead. Nothing was missing but it felt as though something was, and the wind battering against the new boards outside seemed to jeer at me, while the presence of everyone in the room felt overwhelming, claustrophobic, as if they were all crowding around me, looking at me. I wanted everyone gone, and the storm stopped, and for the collection to be safe again, for these violations to *end*.

'From now on, every ground-floor window of all the museum rooms must be boarded up from the inside,' I announced, pleased at how confident and rational my voice suddenly sounded. But it *was* the rational thing to do, I thought: the museum was under attack and its collection must be saved from those who wished it harm. 'Can you find more boards from somewhere?' I asked Paul, bypassing the housekeeper who had just arrived back from telephoning the police, and looked horrendously unimpressed by my words.

'Lord Lockwood will not be happy about this when he returns, he won't agree with it,' she said, with the sort of tone that implied she would enjoy watching him upbraid me.

'He can take it up with me,' I said firmly, growing in confidence as my plan was formalized.

There was a pause, and then she announced to the rest of the room, 'Tonight's excitement is over now, everyone. The police won't be here until midday at the earliest, and we need to leave some evidence for them to sift through.' Her eyes were glued to me. 'You can start the day's work if you're looking for something to keep you busy, else back to bed with you lot.'

The room emptied quickly, leaving her and me standing there, the boards on the windows rattling in the wind.

'Has this happened before, the house being attacked like this?' I asked her, ignoring the fact she had blamed me for the rabbit; the animals were the important thing, not my bruised pride or whatever strange grudge she held against me.

'As I said before, nothing of the sort has ever happened here, not until you arrived.'

'Ever? What about before you started working here?' I said, lifting my chin.

She smiled thinly. 'I've been here a long time, since I was a girl, and my family have worked for the Lockwoods for longer.'

We left the room and I let her lock the door and then, after she had walked away, I tested it by pressing against it with my full body weight. I returned to my bedroom to wash quickly and get dressed and then spent the rest of the early hours acting as a sentinel downstairs, rambling blearily along the corridors, checking the doors with increasingly feeble pushes of my cold hands, listening to the gale trying to crash its way into the house as I shivered and kept an ear out for any more smashed glass, my mouth dry like bark. The night guards were taking their role seriously for once, patrolling carefully around the house, torches in hand, rifles over their shoulders, which should have reassured me but actually made me nervous lest they confuse me for an intruder.

After the house woke, Paul and the groundskeepers worked to ferry in boards and sheeting to barricade the windows from the inside. I felt sorrowful as I watched the first room being shuttered; there was so little light at the beginning of winter anyway, it felt wrong to darken the house even further. But it could not be helped; the safety of the museum was paramount.

Lucy was the only person who had not been woken by the storm and the attack, and I had not wished to wake her – better that she stay safe asleep, her dreams hopefully untroubled.

She found me in the dining room, where I was helping myself to the last of lunch, my stomach grumbling noisily and my mind in that persecuted state of tiredness where everything about the world is too loud and bright, where the very air seems to abrade your eyes, and it feels as if you might never sleep again.

'What's this about boarding up every downstairs window? A joke, surely?' she said, pouring herself a coffee.

I put the serving spoon down and turned to her. 'No, it isn't a joke,' I said. 'I'm sorry, Lucy, I know that it will make down-stairs gloomy and dark, and I'm sorry too if it upsets you,' I added, sincerely, loathing myself yet feeling that there was no other option, 'but the museum's collection must be protected.'

My job and future prospects must be protected too, I added silently, not wanting to allude to the day I would have to leave this house and her.

She put her coffee cup down with a clatter. 'Not *all* the windows?'

'I'm afraid so.'

'That's *mad*, you do see that?' she said, slowly. 'We can't barricade ourselves in here. Father will get a whole team of guards, and the Home Guard will help out too. There's no need to overreact.'

I felt my face folding into a grimace of disbelief. 'You think I'm being *mad*?'

'I didn't say that,' she said, but she was not backing down. 'I only meant that you should get some perspective. You're getting *obsessed* with this,' she said, swinging her hand out in a wide sweep. Were her words coming from her nerves, a gut reaction to the idea of being boarded up inside the house? Right then, in the state I was in, I did not care.

'*I* am mad?' I repeated, in angry incredulity, while the sun shone brightly into the dining room through one of the few bare windows left, and the silver service gleamed before us; while her chin began to tremble. 'You're saying that *I* am mad?'

I knew that I was hurting her, but what she had said was everything I feared, everything I suspected; that I *was* mad. And the way the light was hitting the angles of her face – she had looked just like him, and sounded like him too, as she stood there just like him, judging me, and it gutted me to the quick. I felt betrayed, my heart bruised, and so I lashed out viciously, like a cornered animal.

'I'm doing my job,' I said, voice quivering. A job that was precarious, that had been reluctantly assigned to me by those who sought to boot me back to the room of female volunteers.

I had no great fortune like Lucy, no home, nothing beyond my employment, for I knew now that there would be no husband on the horizon to support me. 'I'm trying to protect the work of hundreds of people, trying to protect specimens vital to science and our understanding of the natural world.'

'And I am – what? – a layabout? Worthless?' she said, tears dripping down the cheeks I had kissed just yesterday afternoon. 'The mad woman locked upstairs?'

I was silent. She bit her lip and shook her head. We stared at one another, and then she walked out of the room, letting out a sob that brought a lump to my throat as I turned back to the lunch I had lost all appetite for, my hands shaking as I set aside my plate and tasted the salt of the tears that caught in the corners of my mouth instead. I had let her down, I knew that, but what else could I do? Why must I be forced to choose between my duties to the animals and my love for her?

Chapter Thirty-Five

Alone again, I felt the walls of my bedroom, of any room I stood inside, crowding me, felt the horrors of my nightmares rising up in my chest, darkening the edges of my vision.

I took to walking the corridors of the house by night, torch in each trembling hand, as if testing my fears, my eyes wide and open, watching and listening and waiting.

Was I hoping to find the woman in white on my nightly wanderings, or to become her, in my pale dressing gown? Was I already, always, her; had I done all those things?

Whether or not I was, I knew that I alone had been the one to break my heart, that it had been no shadowy second self who had said those things to Hetty. I had called her mad, when the truth was that I worried she could not really love a mad thing like me.

I had been foolish to think we could ever remain together, that there was a happy future waiting for me – what had I thought, that she would agree to stay here when the war was over? Hetty had imagined a future for us in London, I know she had, but how could I leave this house? I felt panicked at the thought, thin as if I were made of chiffon and would blow away with the wind the minute I stepped out of the front door.

I would remain here, would live here until I died, like my

mother and grandmother. And all that would remain of Hetty – of our relationship – would be the initials we carved one giddy afternoon in the wardrobe of my room, and a few stray hairs fallen from the animals, faded patches where the great beasts once stood.

I hated the idea of the animals being trapped in their rooms downstairs by the boards on the windows, in the dark alone. Did I think I was one of them – frozen, dusty, untouched, unloved? My actions had certainly made me so. I did not feel betrayed by Hetty; it was not that I thought she was locking me in, and I understood how worried she was. This house could not seem to keep her animals safe just as I had been unable to keep my mother safe.

On my nightly patrols, greeting the snoring guards who startled to see me, smiling nervously, forgiving my actions as those of the mad aristocracy, I would pause outside the museum rooms listening for noises, holding my breath. But the only movement I caught, the only intruders, were the living animals – the cats and the mice and the foxes I spied hurrying down corridors and slipping inside darkened doorways.

I slept in the daytime now, once my room was bright with winter sunlight and all its corners and shapes had become familiar again.

But when I dreamed, it was always dark.

And in my dreams, I was hunting that lost leveret again. I was racing down the corridors and the stairs, stumbling, falling; I was throwing my hands out against the walls, bruising my palms and scraping my knees. And when I stood up, sobbing, to run again, I realized that I wasn't hunting the leveret at all, but that something was hunting me; something larger than a hare, something wilder, stronger, stalking me through the house. And I would wake in my bright bedroom and know that I could not escape, that Lockwood and all its inhabitants were in the gravest of danger, and that there was nothing I could do to save them.

Chapter Thirty-Six

Lucy and I were now estranged from one another, with neither of us making the first move to apologize, and the both of us knowing how much our words had wounded the other; and my heart was broken.

Sometimes, during the aching loneliness of all those years I had spent a spinster, the years spent living alone in one room at boarding houses and tired lodgings, I would have moments where I would realize how long it had been since anyone had touched me – even a handshake, or a hand placed on my forearm, a simple hug – and my body would ache, my soul would feel so heavy I would have to go out with shaking legs for a walk no matter what the weather was, because I feared that if I curled up on my bed like I so dearly wished to, I might remain there and never get up again. If humans are animals, I would think, then do we not require touch as well as food and water and air and a roof over our heads in order to live, to survive? It was a histrionic state of mind, these sudden funks, I knew that, but I could not escape them. And now, now that I knew what it was like to share my bed with another, to have a lover there to touch and hold and be held in return, now that I knew the true pleasures of sex, or how it felt for your jaw to ache from too much kissing, the rub of skin against skin that left a burn, the tight clasp of a hand in your hand, this estrangement felt even worse. I was marooned, adrift with no sight of land, for where or how would I ever meet someone like Lucy again, someone that could love me?

Although I had prepared to face the Major's wrath for boarding up his home, when he returned from his trip he did not mention the windows at all, not even in a veiled aside. Paul said that he had narrowly escaped a direct bomb hit while in the north, so perhaps he had had a change of heart where matters of security were concerned, and yet he still did not join us in our nights in the basement during air raids, preferring to stay tucked up in bed with Sylvia, the heiress, who Dorothy had said he might ask to marry him soon. Her throaty laugh had become a common sound in the hall outside the Major's office, but unfortunately for the rest of us they did not confine themselves to his office and private library – where I pictured her reclining on the skins on the floor, her pale skin a pleasing contrast – nor his suite of rooms upstairs, but made good use of the museum rooms to dawdle in and do heavens knows what else. He had his own set of keys to open up the rooms and then to lock them when they were finished, and he was irritatingly catholic about doing so, so I had no excuse for confronting him about putting the animals at risk.

'I'm being careful with the locks, Miss Cartwright,' he called out one day, when I left my office at the same time as he left the long gallery, as he bent to turn the key in the door, with lipstick on his cheek, and Sylvia leaned languidly against the wall, a loop of loose hair falling down her neck like a tail.

He patted the lock once he was done, tilted his head to me with a sardonic smile, and walked off, Sylvia following in his wake.

I grimaced as I stared at the long gallery door, trying not to imagine what he had been up to in there with only my animals for an audience, trying not to think of him tainting my work-spaces with his lusts, his seedy trysts.

The museum rooms had once felt like a safe haven for Lucy and me, our own little hideaway from the rest of the house, and the fact that he was now intruding on them made me feel even more wretched.

My work was the only thing I had to keep me company those winter months, but there was little consolation to be found. I lost a striped owl to a moth infestation and nothing I could do would save it at its advanced stage of decay, so I sealed it up in its cabinet where it would die a slow second death as I watched through the glass. A sacrifice so that the moths that feasted on its viscera would not jump ship to a new host once they were finished. My fingers stank of glue and poison, my arms burned from sweeping and vacuuming, and my eyes were strained from peering into corners, searching for tiny, wriggling things that I could never see.

Meanwhile, the animals stood and waited and watched me, with their silent eyes and fading fur, with feathers so dry and stiff they would not flutter in the strongest of winter winds, with the floor creaking and shifting in the cold beneath them. And whenever I finally slept – on those occasions when exhaustion or loneliness claimed me – I would toss and turn, my dreams monstrous and terrible, and then startle awake, my ears pricked ready for sounds: the engines of bombers muscling their way through the sky; the first dampened note of the siren before the wailing crescendo; Lucy's whimpering cries as she woke from another nightmare – and should I hear that, would I go to comfort her, I wondered, or would I be the last person she wished to see?; the shrieks of foxes in the gardens come to join their brethren already hiding inside; the muted smash of another window being broken and the silence afterwards when the interloper realized they had been boarded; or the sound that I seemed to fear the most, an everyday sound that would be transmogrified by the darkness, by the quiet of the east wing which was empty of all living souls but for myself – the sound of footsteps padding along the hall towards me. For I was more convinced than ever that whoever had been attacking the museum was not an intruder at all but came from inside the house itself, and that they had fixed their sights on me.

In late November, the Major announced he would be having a grand Christmas dinner party at Lockwood on 18 December, and that he had chosen for his setting not the dining room, nor the ballroom, but the long gallery itself.

'I want to showcase the specimens at their best. A couple of my guests have expressed interest in donating quite large sums to the museum,' the Major told me over breakfast. It was just the two of us, for Lucy hardly ever came down for it now.

'What room were you thinking of putting the table in?' I asked.

'Oh, the corridor itself. I am going to have some of the larger, more impressive mounted animals from the museum collection brought out there, and surround the table with them, put the paintings back on the walls, and generally return the place to its former glory.'

He was, was he? Nice of him to tell me what he was planning on doing with my animals.

He set down his knife and wiped his mouth with one of the fine linen napkins that came as standard here at Lockwood. 'No thoughts?' he said sarcastically, and I pursed my mouth.

'You can't object to my plan, surely, Miss Cartwright? For we will be watching the animals beadily; there can be no theft from right under our noses.' He tapped his nose mockingly as he said this. 'Or are you nervous about my guests being rowdy with them?'

I was, after seeing the behaviour of the officers who had come to the one and only ball I had attended here. 'How many guests will you be having?' I asked.

'Oh, about twenty or so. We shall just about fit on the two dining tables pushed together. It's a select group coming; old friends, army officials, a couple of politicians, a sprinkling of artist types for colour, you know. I suppose you'll be invited too, as a representative of the museum,' he said, glancing at me over the rim of his coffee cup.

As a director *of the museum*, I thought, and wiped my own mouth with a napkin, using it to hide my scowl.

'Sylvia thinks that candlelight will add marvellously to the atmosphere; she's got all sorts of ideas,' he said, twiddling his hand in the air in lieu of a more detailed description.

'The notion of having candles so close to the specimens does give me pause, Lord Lockwood.'

'Oh, come now, we're not using them as candlesticks. They'll be a good few yards from the table. We need to have room to sit at it after all. I'm not going to all this trouble just to feed the animals.' He gave a short laugh. 'I tell you, it'll be quite the coup, Miss Cartwright, for Lockwood and the museum,' he said, cutting into his sausage.

What could I do? I had no useful argument except that I did not want them damaged. I felt too tired to argue with him, my hands shaking around my cup of coffee, my thoughts treacle-slow.

'You shall of course be on hand to supervise their being moved there, the creatures from the main house,' he said. 'We can't have the nose of the polar bear being bashed against the wall on its journey before people get to see it, now, can we?'

'Quite,' I said and, leaving half my meal uneaten, made my excuses and left the room.

The next Sunday, I came back from a short blustery walk in the bare gardens, looking to read a book and warm my chilled toes in the parlour, thinking that I might pretend I was simply on holiday in a grand house and that I was not in charge of a collection crumbling at the seams from my own incompetence. But when I reached the door of the parlour, Lucy looked up from her seat by the electric fire.

I felt my heart lift at the sight of her, like a trained animal, and then fall when I remembered we were not sweethearts any more.

'Good afternoon, Hetty. Do you need the room?' she asked, fiddling with the buttons of her cardigan.

I catalogued her, drinking her in. Curly dark brown hair teased into waves, perfect red lipstick, bruises under her eyes, a hand fluttering at her side that I longed to catch in my own.

'No, I was just wandering about. You stay there, keep warm by the fire.'

She smiled but it had a pleading note, as if my presence was painful for her. *Yours is painful for me too*, I wanted to say. 'Good afternoon, Lucy,' I said instead, and left, my tongue aching with words unspoken.

I took the stairs two at a time back up to the first floor and then paused, hearing the clang of something dropping all the way down a different flight of stairs, followed by a groaned *damn it*. I went in search of the sound and found Paul at the foot of the stairs at the other end of the corridor, bending over a silver candlestick.

'Can I help you, Paul?' I asked.

'I'm fine,' he said, standing back up. 'Just retrieving some things from the attic for his lordship, for the dinner.' He held the candlestick in his hand. 'They're slippery buggers,' he said, 'and I'm all fingers and thumbs today. One week, miss, one week until I'm suited and booted and off for training.'

'You've enlisted?'

He nodded enthusiastically. 'I turned seventeen and three months recently, *finally*, and the army have taken me. I can't wait to actually *do* something, instead of sitting here like . . .' He trailed off – was he going to say like a woman, or like a duck?

I took pity on him. 'Well, I wish you the best luck in the world, Paul. They'll be lucky to have you. Let me help you carry some things down; I'm at a loose end today.'

'Much obliged,' he said, and then motioned up the stairs. 'There's a whole pile of things we're fetching down by the door of the store room; you can't miss them.'

I climbed the stairs to the second floor – the floor I thought of as Lucy's – and then continued on to the store room, almost tripping over the cluster of candlesticks that were, as Paul said, just by the door.

But I did not pick them up straight away; instead I crossed the length of the store room and opened the door to the attic itself, turning on the light to diffuse the fusty darkness. I felt the cold from outside creeping in through a crack somewhere, and brushed a hanging cobweb out of my face as I ventured further in, towards Lucy's secret room; separated by only a bricked-up door from the bathroom where I had bathed with her, and laughed with her, and been loved by her.

It was the same as it had been when we opened it up, blue and empty – except that was not quite true, because there was something there, lying on the dusty floorboards in the corner. A pigeon; a larger, more prosaic version of the dove that Lucy had stepped on all those years ago.

How could a dead pigeon, with no signs of violence on its body, frighten me, make my teeth clench together as I crouched closer and touched its dry corpse with the top of one shaking finger, jerking quickly back at the feel of it? If I did not pull myself together, I told myself, I would be unable to work for the museum at all. How could I be frightened of dead animals when I had spent the last decade of my life surrounded by them?

My clothes were now coated in dust, so after I had brought down the candlesticks and other things for Paul, I took them to the laundry room straight away. I had given up asking the servants for help with any additional task, for fear of being looked at askance by them, judged and gossiped about, and also because I did not want to give them more work.

In the laundry room, as my fingers chafed at the cold water in the tub, I heard someone at the back door, and then the clink of a cup being set down on stone, and laughter that I did not recognize.

When I took my damp load out to pin on the clothesline, whoever had been there had scurried off, leaving no trace beyond the stub of a cigarette on the doorstep, winding a thin trail of smoke into the air.

That night, and the following night, and the night after that, I had the worst nightmares yet. I dreamed that I had woken up to find a bloodied rabbit in my bed, too late to save it, that the bed itself was made entirely of freshly skinned rabbits, cold and wet with blood. That the museum's animals had moved to my room while I slept and when I woke they were crowding around me and I could not escape as they pressed towards me with their claws and paws and teeth. That there was a ghoulish woman leaning over my bed, her breath ruffling my hair, her icy fingers reaching for my face.

Ten days before Christmas, and three days before the dinner, I woke from one of these dreams, on a calm night so bitter I was convinced that it had snowed as I shivered in my bed. I twitched open my blackout curtains and peered out into the night, condensation clouding the glass before me.

There was no snow, but there was something else, there on the lawn by the kitchen vegetable plot.

The museum's Indian bison, its shape unmistakable.

I unlocked the window with a sleep-weak hand and leaned out, teeth chattering. Was it skinned too? It was too dark to see. I blinked as if the scene might vanish, like the after-image of a dream, but it was still there.

I fumbled into my clothes, tugging a jumper over my pyjama shirt, pulling on socks and boots, and then I locked up my room and ran, clattering, down the stairs.

The night guard was on his feet when I reached the bottom, alarmed by the noise.

'What's happened?' he asked, holding up his torch. The policemen had told the Major that the guards should not wear rifles, in case they accidentally shot someone, in case the intruders were only truant children.

I ran to the front door. 'The museum's bison, it's on the front lawn,' I said, my voice a frightened warble.

'My god,' the guard said, 'are you sure?'

I swung the heavy door open and pointed to the lawn.

'The entrance light, the blackout!' he urged, and I scrabbled for the light switch.

'There, do you see it?' I said, pushing the door further open now that we were in the dark, realizing that I did not trust my own eyes, that I needed him to say he saw it and that it was not just a figment of my imagination.

'I see it,' he said. 'Stay here,' he called to the other guard, who had appeared in the entrance hall. He jammed on his cap and followed me as I ran down the steps, over the driveway, and set out across the lawn wet with mist, my heart roaring in my ears.

You see, I imagined myself telling Lucy, *I'm not mad*, and I sprinted towards the figure that grew clearer in silhouette, its large rectangular side like a slab carved from the night, head down towards the ground.

It would be too heavy to carry between the two of us; we would need to ask the other guard for help and another man besides. How many had dragged it here in the first place? Was the skin still there? I could not tell.

We had just reached the beginning of the vegetable garden, a row of stakes ready for the spring's green beans, when the bison lifted its head.

I screamed and the guard jolted to a stop behind me.

The beast huffed and put its head back down.

'It's a cow,' I said. I coughed and then repeated it louder, in an ordinary voice to brush away the terror of dead beasts that could come back to life. But my teeth were still chattering.

The cow looked up at us again, its jaw working slowly on its pilfered dinner.

'I should have checked the museum room first,' I said, heart juddering. 'Indian bison have horns and a ridge, a hump, through the shoulders. Our bison isn't even posed with its head down, like the cow was. What on *earth* I was thinking?' The two bovines looked nothing alike; Indian bison of both sexes had horns, for god's sake.

The guard let out a breath. 'Well, I'm relieved,' he said. 'I couldn't imagine how it had got out on my watch, the dead one, I mean,' he qualified. 'We'd better get this fugitive back to the farm.' I let him circle the cow, crooning softly, and grab its rope: I was too scared to get close to it, as if the night might transform it into some other beast again. 'Hefty buggers up close, aren't they?' he said. 'I can take it from here; no need for the both of us to traipse through the mud.'

I glanced down at my boots, at the dark splatters on my linen trousers. 'If you're sure,' I said, my voice thick.

'I'm sure,' he said, kindly, as if he was trying to treat me carefully, as if he knew all the wild thoughts that whirled in my mind. He clucked his tongue and led the cow away, its footsteps oddly stumbling in the way of bovines, its bulk swaying from side to side.

I tipped my head up and stared at the stars in the sky as a sob caught in my throat, and then I trudged back towards the pitch-black house.

There was no more sleep that night for me, and the next day, after another morning of roaming up and down the long gallery hunting down infestation, jumping at the shapes of mounted animals and cabinets even though they were in the same positions as they had been for over a year now, biting my lip on tears that threatened to fall, I decided that I had had enough.

The museum would not, could not, remain here for the rest of the war: the infestation alone – never mind the intruders who were likely plotting more mischief – had made our position here untenable. More to the point, though, *I* would not, could not, remain here; the experience would turn me utterly mad, would destroy the last shreds of my professional dignity and the last threads of my sanity too.

I did not want to leave Lucy, I felt heartsick at the thought – and only now that I had loved, did I know what heartsick felt like. A life without her in it, even if all we shared currently were silent breakfasts and awkward passings-by in the corridors of the house, was a life devoid of joy. Now that I knew what it felt to love and be loved in return, even if only for a few months, I knew that my loneliness would be more acute, might very well swallow me whole. And yet we were not together any more, I had ruined all that, and thus all I had was the museum and my employment. I would lose my position as assistant keeper for calling for another evacuation, for confessing the full extent of the damage and the loss to the specimens under my watch at Lockwood, but I would fight to be kept on in a lesser role, would give it everything I had.

As I was called out of my office to help supervise the movement of the mounted animals from the main house to the long gallery (members of the new local Home Guard had been conscripted to help with the heavier items for the dinner), I drafted in my head the letter I would write to London; the evidence that I would lay out, in black and white, on the page; the culpability I would admit to for not requesting a second evacuation sooner.

The morning of the Major's damned Christmas party, after a night with no sleep at all, and as the humans in the house scurried to and fro, industrious as I had never seen them, I posted the letter.

And as I dusted and cleaned my animals in their temporary

home in the long gallery – the Sumatran tiger, the polar bear, the spotted hyena, the black panther, the giant pangolin, the juvenile elephant, the grey wolf, the wallaby, the wolverine, the southern muriqui, the white-tailed mongoose, the blesbok, the large-spotted genet, the lar gibbon, the southern African lion, the capybara, the giant golden-crowned flying fox, the jaguar, and others – ready for their audience, I imagined the postman carrying my letter to the railway station; it being hoisted in a large sack onto the night train and sorted by men in a lurching carriage. I pictured the postman in London picking up his sack in the morning and heading out early to deliver his load; my letter being put in the pile on the director's secretary's desk as she yawned from a night spent in an air-raid shelter. I pictured it being passed to the director himself to read, as he puffed on his pipe, and the choice words he would have to say about my behaviour. He would agree that another evacuation was needed, I was sure of it, and would have the secretary start drafting letters, and organize a meeting with the Ministry of Works and Buildings, and then the mammal collection would move.

The animals would be safe again, and I would be gone from here, the both of us rescued – from the tyranny of Lord Lockwood, from the hungry beetles and moths, from covetous thieves, from the elements, from the house and all the strange things that seemed to stalk its rooms nightly.

Chapter Thirty-Seven

The tableau for the dinner party that the housekeeper and other servants had created, under orders from Sylvia and the Major, was like something from a play, decadent and astonishing and, to my eye, more than a little grotesque. When I expressed my amazement at the spectacle to Dorothy, as she took a break from polishing the parquet floor in the main entrance hall that afternoon, she said that this was small fare compared to some of the parties she had seen back when Lord Lockwood's wife and mother were alive, let alone the kind of thing the Victorian inhabitants of Lockwood were said to have got up to – masquerades where the jewelled masks and costumes worn by each guest would have been enough to purchase a small house each; Indian-themed summer balls complete with wild animals who were paraded through the house on silver leads; extravagant party games that lasted the whole weekend with specially made rulebooks printed on paper embossed with gold; nightingale-listening parties, where the birds were drowned out by the chorus of champagne corks from a regiment's worth of butlers. Even a regular Christmas during the time when the manor had housed thirty-five servants or more, and half as many guests, was a sight to behold, she said.

The main house itself – the entrance hall, the library where pre-dinner drinks would be held, the billiards room for coffee and after-dinner liqueurs – was decked out in exotic flowers that spread their rich scents throughout the rooms, and every surface had been buffed to a gleaming, almost disorientating, sheen, but the true pageant began at the door next to the Major's office that led towards the long gallery. The door had been propped open and a blood-red velvet curtain hung in its place. Beyond the curtain was the short corridor, where dark, glittering cloth was suspended in oily folds from the ceiling, and the Major's collection of snarling mounted heads had been placed on the walls to either side, with men's and ladies' hats balanced on their horns and muzzles. The long gallery itself was lit by candles, in chandeliers far apart enough to create dips of thick darkness, and in candlesticks on the dinner table and on the occasional tables surrounding it. But before one reached the table, the parade of the museum's animals began, as if they too were making their way to dinner. First came the spotted hyena, with its mouth open in a growl and the hair on its neck raised in warning; and a few steps after that, a table draped in black cloth on which stood the juvenile Brazilian tapir, with a drooping snout and its reddish-brown coat patterned with dizzying white stripes and dashes; and then, to the left, the blesbok, a type of antelope with a white forehead and great ringed horns that tapered to a sharp point; followed by an orang-utan to the right, looking half human in the gloom; then the spotted cuscus on another platform; the giant pangolin, armoured with scales, and balanced by a long tail; and finally the hefty bulk of the Indian bison – the real one this time, not a beast I had conjured in my mind.

As one neared the table, the decorations started to include flora as well as fauna, with potted plants from the greenhouse bringing with them the scent of close, loamy days; vases of hothouse flowers that perfumed the air; houseplants purloined from other rooms, their waxy green leaves dark and tropical in the dim light; holly wreaths with beady ruby-red berries; and sheaves of cane and twigs potted and painted gold, gleaming in the candlelight. The vegetation continued around the table, wherever a spare space could be found in between the congregation of animals that would surround our feast – the Sumatran tiger at one end, the juvenile elephant at another, and in between them: the polar bear; the grey wolf; the jaguar; the black panther; the southern African lion; the zebra; the wallaby; and the wolverine, southern muriqui, the white-tailed mongoose, the large-spotted genet, the lar gibbon, the capybara, and the giant golden-crowned flying fox, all on occasional tables.

The freshly polished teak walls, where they could be seen behind such a crowd, held some of Lockwood's collection of portraits – great men and women, plump with wealth and indolence, peering lazily out from between beeswax candles in gilded brackets. (I had assumed that the Major would put his own portrait up, but apparently even he was not so gauche as that.)

The heavy antique table and matching chairs were standing on a carpet of animal skins borrowed from the floor of the Major's private library – and I had studied them carefully to check that he had not pilfered skins from a locked cabinet belonging to the museum, that we would not be resting our feet on type specimens and rare species. I was immensely uncomfortable with his choice of carpet – heads and tails and claws positioned carefully so that they could be seen – but not wishing to start any argument with the Major when I was so close to finally leaving this hellhole behind, I refrained from expressing my opinion.

The dining table itself was very modest compared to its surroundings – containing as it did the silver candlesticks that I had helped to retrieve from the store room, creeping ivy and sharp holly branches, a stark white tablecloth so weighty it took both maids to carry it after they had spent hours ironing it, and, in pride of place, the immaculate silver formal tableware.

And the servants themselves, the reason this dinner could actually take place? They would be standing, hands at their backs, in the shadows (there was a Japanese lacquer screen too, which also hid a trolley) surrounding the table, waiting to squeeze in between the animals and the diners to fill up water glasses and pour champagne and wines. They would be ferrying in the food from the other end of the corridor – since the entrance from the house, with its walls of mounted heads, was now too narrow to manoeuvre plates and trolleys through – and would have to walk a frigid path across the gardens from the kitchen to the long gallery in the dark, their way lit only by the moon.

Supplementary servants had been drafted from the village and further afield, black and white uniforms brought out, and even an aged butler unearthed from somewhere, who would be greeting people in the entrance hall and directing them to the cloakroom and the library for drinks and, later, to the billiards room for coffee and cigars – although he had no other tasks, for he was quite doddering despite his immaculate bearing. In addition, the door would be guarded at all times by two night guards, I had been told, who would prevent our erstwhile intruders from gaining access and pilfering specimens while we feasted the hours away.

The way my animals were posed, as if they were a private menagerie owned by the select few who would sit at the table, discomforted me immensely, and that they were turned with their faces and snouts and noses towards the dishes and plates, the food we would be eating, lent an unnerving atmosphere to the corridor, as did the flickering candlelight. The candles themselves were far enough away from the animals that they would not be in danger – I had checked carefully myself – but still they did not feel quite safe here, and neither, I suspected, would the diners, with the gloom of the long gallery at our backs like a dark fog threatening to swallow the scene whole.

And yet, I thought sardonically, despite my distaste for it, this extravagant dinner tableau would be a fine send-off for the museum's collection. The Major had unwittingly created a farewell party for both them and myself, and we would soon leave his greed and brutish behaviour, and all the dangers and nightmares of Lockwood, behind.

Of course, I would also be leaving Lucy behind, but I tried very hard not to think about that. If she and I were still together – and if I were staying – we might have gossiped about Sylvia's arrangements, about the guests and the ridiculous pageantry of it all. If she and I were together, I might have been getting ready in her room, sipping on crème de menthe and slipping into one of her dresses, feeling the soft touch of silk – silk that had once adorned her body – against my skin. Instead, I was peering into the small mirror in my bedroom, dabbing layers of powder beneath my eyes, using the last dregs of perfume in a bottle I would be unable to replace under rationing, smoothing down the dull frock I had brought with me to Lockwood for formal events and which looked like a very poor cousin indeed to any item in Lucy's wardrobe.

Lucy, and the Major, would be the only dinner guests I knew, and I did not imagine I would have much in common with the rest. Still, it was true what the Major said, that I would be there as a representative of the museum, and if they wanted to donate money, to have a room or indeed a wing named after them, then I would do my best to encourage that, with my animals looming like Mafiosi over their shoulders doing most of the work for me.

The nervousness I felt leaving my room and making my way along the hall and down the stairs, into the reservoir of air thick with beeswax and pollen, with base notes of rich cooking, was solely about facing Lucy – in the library for drinks, and across the table at dinner – for I did not care one fig what anyone else but she thought of me. I did not want her to look at me with pity, for her to notice the distance between me and the other, glamorous, women in attendance and find me wanting; I was vain when it came to her. I wanted her to want me, to care for me – I, who had hurt her so grievously; I, who had done nothing to make amends.

The heels of my shoes stuttered on the floor of the corridor as I prepared myself to enter the library, for there she was, her black gown sweeping to the floor, its silk so light it rippled around her legs, her lipstick red as blood, her soft hair piled over one shoulder, a mink fur over the other, and a jewelled evening bag in her hand. Had this wondrous creature ever really loved me, I thought, me with my sallow skin and hands rough from museum work? An unfair thought to have, for had we not shared our innermost thoughts with one another, did I not know that a glamorous mien could hide all manner of emotions, from love to pain?

She smiled sadly when I finally met her gaze and tilted her head minutely. *Hullo*, I mouthed, and then the gossamer moment was dashed away by the appearance of a cocktail at my elbow, and Sylvia, who had waived her right to a fashionably late arrival, bustling over to introduce me to one of her guests.

I put on my professional hat and espoused the wonders of the museum, drawing attention to the specimens posed in the library as conversation pieces, and sipped gingerly on the cocktails handed to me, grazing on the canapés – caviar, salmon pastries, rolled toast with foie gras, and cheese puffs – sparingly, trying not to remember the guests at the ball who asserted that I was *intense* and hopeless at casual conversation, hoping that no one could tell I was shaking from anxiety that had nothing to do with tonight. The museum was the most important thing, I reminded myself as I left the room for the bathroom. It did not matter if the other guests thought me poor and plain – they could hardly expect someone stylish as a museum worker – or if they seemed surprised that a woman was in charge of the mammal department – *but then women are doing lots of things nowadays*, one army man, whose portly bearings reminded me of a wallaby, had said to me dubiously, peering at the décolletage of a female guest walking past us.

'Excuse me,' a woman's voice said, and then a hand clutched my arm quite tightly, making me jump.

It was Mary. She was wearing a glittering sheath of a dress with a white fox fur stole almost as pale as her bleached hair, which was teased into dramatic wings and set off by the shimmer of diamonds on her earlobes and at her throat. Had the Major invited her too? Was there some kind of seedy *ménage à trois* occurring tonight?

'Can I help you, Mary?' I asked, trying not to snatch my arm out of her grip, to make a scene.

'Are you enjoying living here?' she asked me with a sharp smile that did not quite reach her eyes.

'The museum is happy to have such a wonderful home during the war,' I replied by rote. *We shall be out of your hair soon, never you fear*, I wanted to say. *You're welcome to it – to Lockwood and life under that tyrant.*

'Your hair is so pale,' she said, reaching out to touch one of the pinned waves I had tried to form with little success. 'Is it natural? I used to have hair as white as this when I was a child. It takes so much work now,' she said, as if that was my fault.

'Yes, but it's straight as a pin,' I said. There was something feral about her, something beyond the easy cattiness of her words, that made me want to treat her like a wild animal, soothing and careful. 'I could never hope to tease it up like yours,' I added and she smiled triumphantly and finally let go of my arm, sauntering away as I stood there unsettled and baffled.

When I returned to the library, after staring, horrified, at my tired reflection in the bathroom mirror and muttering to myself to keep it together, it was to a full house – a sea of men in regimental dress or sharp black tie and women in sequins and chiffons and silks, satin and velvet, nearly all of them wearing furs atop their gowns that I catalogued as I passed by, searching for a quiet spot near the okapi cabinet: mink, ermine, white fox – in the form of capelets, stoles and scarves – many still bearing claws and heads and tails. I could not help but find this gruesome: I, whose work was spent putting animals back together, preserving them in the nearest semblance of life, preferred it when furs were almost anonymous in their shape, as if they had come from one large amorphous beast, an entirely hypocritical preference.

'Ah, Miss Cartwright, just the woman I was looking for.' The Major's voice cut across the buzz of conversation as I waved away the offer of another canapé. 'Come and tell these fine folk about the animals in this room.'

'I'd be glad to,' I said, without looking at him, and then coughed, trying to clear my throat of the senseless, fearful sob that had seemed trapped there for months. I gave my best introduction to the specimens in the room – the okapi, whose unfamiliar form seemed to fascinate the guests; the giant otter shrew; the mastodon skull; the cabinet of big cat skulls; the Arabian oryx; the Norway lemming; the platypus; the cabinet of red pandas, their shrew interlopers long gone; and finally the collection of foxes, which set off a spirited conversation about hunting to which I could add very little.

'It's this damn war,' one man was saying, holding a cigar in his fist. 'The army have requisitioned my forest, you see. Not that you fellows aren't putting it to good use, I'm sure,' he added to the one man in uniform listening to him speak, 'but if I don't get in there and shoot my pheasants, then the poachers'll have 'em. I never thought the day would come when the poachers would increase in number again. They say it's rationing but I can't believe that.'

'Oh, it's been too long since I've been shooting,' the Major said, one arm around Sylvia, who was gazing up at him in adoration, her pink lips folded into a pleased little smile. 'I've been too busy with work. Perhaps in the new year I'll arrange a drive.'

'Oh, you must,' another man said.

Thankfully, this dull conversation, which I was trapped next to and could not escape from, was interrupted by the *dong* of a dinner gong being rung by the poor old butler (who resembled nothing if not a domesticated goat), the ringing sound of which set my teeth on edge, and we dutifully made our way out of the library towards the long gallery, with most of the women taking the arm of the men they had accompanied tonight, while I watched Lucy's dark head a few paces ahead of me, a diamond pin coaxing her curls into place, glinting at me like a faraway lamp. She was walking alongside an actress who had a stunning heart-shaped face and a familiar profile, a pale pink dress fashioned so simply that I knew it was extraordinarily expensive, but I could not hear what they were talking about. The sex ratio tonight was exact, with some poor sod, perhaps the artist who walked behind me and was trying to explain his avant-garde work to a rather dowdy older lady, being matched to me.

I could hear the delighted gasps of wonder and amazement as the guests in front of me reached the little corridor and made their way into the long gallery itself. And I did feel pleased at the way people slowed to gawp at the animals they passed, murmuring excited comments at each new creature that appeared out of the shadows. The animals had been lacking their usual crush of eager visitors in London, so it was only right that they received a good share of the attention tonight, I thought. A small smile twitched at my mouth as we reached the table itself, where the diners looked awestruck, with those who had sat down already craning back to peer at whichever animal had been chosen to stand behind them, or tugging at the clothing of the person next to them to point out a particular creature in the crowd. *Marvellous*, people said, *astonishing, simply outstanding*, and I clung to those words and tried not to hear the backslaps and hearty congratulations given to Lord Lockwood for *outdoing himself*. They were the museum's animals, I wanted to say, not his.

Champagne was poured once everyone was settled, and I peered at the specially printed menu as if I had not already read it, the text appearing to dance before me as I tried to calm my thumping heart and keep my eyes from sliding towards Lucy, who was sitting at a diagonal from me, next to the artist directly opposite my seat.

I had been expecting a whole boar's head with apple in mouth, some pheasants shot in the Major's own forest by his own hand, or perhaps a large turkey, taken apart to be roasted and then stuffed with all manner of things so that it would sit upright in the centre of the table, but the Major's tastes were more cosmopolitan that that.

First we would be having a clear consommé – an extravagance when one knew quite how much meat went into producing such a flavour – with delicate garnishes and a splash of sherry; and to follow, lobster Thermidor with green beans; and then a meat course of veal noisettes, with new potatoes and perfect asparagus tips. A salad next, with a rich dressing, and then a croquembouche, its tower glazed with threads of caramel, followed by praline ices and exquisite petits fours, with a cheese course to finish.

It was clear that a good portion of this had been smuggled in against regulations, that it cost vast amounts of money – and with all the servants' gossip about his funds, was it really wise, I thought, to be spending so much on one fleeting meal? But, expensive though it may be, it tasted of very little to me as I did my best to focus on the too-quiet voice of the lemur-like businessman next to me (who kept asking me whether certain animals were mammals or not, even though I had already given him a general description of the mammalian class that the children who had visited the museum had grasped quickly) while ignoring both the lord sitting on my other side, whose body seemed strangely rigid in his seat and who kept sniffing loudly, and my beloved Lucy, who looked painfully beautiful and – equally painfully – remote.

How many days, hours, would I have left at Lockwood, would I have left in her presence, I thought, as my hand brushed against the dry ivy leaves on the table. Perhaps I could be like some desert plant, and these months together could be the rarest of summer rainstorms, could be all the water I would ever need to survive, to live on – but I knew that could not be true, for I was a creature of flesh and blood.

Chapter Thirty-Eight

My mother would have loved a dinner like this, *I thought,* *as I sipped on my wine, hoping in vain that the alcohol* *might help soothe my frantic nerves, my fears that the trembling* *of my heart was a portent, an omen of terrible things to come.*

She would have been glittering and luminous, she would have *had the men hanging off her every word, the women squirming* *with envy and not a little awe – at least until the evening curdled,* *and my father provoked her drunken jealousy, so that she and he* *would fling barbs like silver knives across the table.*

He liked to bring up her island beginnings in company, as if *it were a trump card, mockingly naming her a savage, describing* *how he had found her in some whitewashed shack with no elec-* *tricity or running water – despite everyone knowing that she had* *grown up in a grand plantation house – or running along the* *beach, a wild little thing with no corset or shoes.*

I hated it. I hated it too when they continued their arguments *in the room underneath mine after the guests had all gone home,* *his voice scornful, hers desperate, and then the way the sounds* *would change to grunts and moans and the bed shifting on its* *legs.*

My hothouse flower, *he would call her,* my Eve in the jungle, my innocent, my wild beauty.

My name is Heloise, *she would reply.* Use my name, you coward.

Coward, me? To take such a wild wife as you? *he would say and then I would hear her slap him and him laugh and say,* See? See?

You've cursed me, you witch, *my father liked to declare – fondly or hatefully, depending on his mood – as the two of them sparred with words in the drawing room, or the dining room, or in the ballroom with the doors flung open as the summer sun heated the world to blazing.*

No, *my mother would spit back,* it's you who has cursed me, who has trapped me here in this awful house. Why not just kill me? *she would say, holding her arms out wide.* Why not stuff me like one of your exotic animals and be done with it, place me in some forgotten room, silent and dutiful and forever young?

What a mad thing to say, *he would drawl in response, and she would either fly at him with her nails or run from him, fleeing along the corridors, up the stairs, in and out of rooms, looking for somewhere safe to hide; looking, I thought now, for the door that would lead her back home, back to a time before she married my father, before she had me, before she ever stepped foot over the threshold of Lockwood Manor.*

Chapter Thirty-Nine

Just after the lobster course, our cocoon of gluttony was interrupted by the arrival of an uninvited guest.

'What's that?' a woman said, with a startled tone of voice. 'Just look over there; the eyes . . .'

We craned our necks to follow her pointed finger and saw the reflective glint of a pair of eyes in the dark of the corridor, there one moment, and then vanished the next.

'It's a fox,' I said, pleased that my voice did not shake.

'What, a real one?' the businessman beside me said.

'Yes.'

'Speaking of a hunt,' the man with the thick moustache (a manatee) said to the Major, and rubbed his hands together. 'Shall we get the guns out now, and do some shooting in between courses?'

There were hearty guffaws from the table, but I felt a nervous pang in my stomach that seemed to be shared by Lucy who, across from me, was frowning. I put my napkin on the table and murmured an *excuse me*, but as I made to stand up, the Major halted me. 'You can check afterwards, Miss Cartwright, otherwise it will disrupt the serving of the next course.'

Every person there was staring at me now, and under the

weight of their gaze, I sat back down. 'Miss Cartwright is not used to these old houses and their wild interlopers,' the Major said to the others, leaning back a little in his seat. If only he would lean so far back that he might jam his head in the jaws of the grey wolf behind him, I thought. 'Foxes, cats, swallows; we have visits from them all,' he said, as several other people mentioned animal sightings at their own estates and manor houses. 'Even tiny little scurrying *mice*,' he added, tickling Sylvia beneath her chin and causing her to shriek delightedly and at such a high pitch it made the hairs on my arms stand up. The Major kissed her cheek in repentance and stared baldly at me, his eyes half lidded, like a lioness feigning nonchalance.

Just a few more days, I told myself, trying to picture his face turning red with outrage when he learned that the museum was to be moved, imagining what it would be like to be safe and far from here, to be myself again.

As the veal was taken away, its richness weighing sickly in my stomach, the officer sitting in front of the southern African lion was passed a message from one of the servants; apparently there had been a telephone call for him and, making his apologies, he went to return it. Mary, who had been sitting next to him, immediately stood up and made a beeline for the Major. We watched as she draped her arms around his shoulders, her red nails like talons on his black suit.

'I miss you,' she said, ignoring Sylvia sitting next to him, who was doing her best not to look furious.

The Major patted her forearms much as one might pat a small dog, but when she kissed him on the neck, he gripped them tightly. 'You said you were going to behave tonight, darling.'

'You like it when I *don't* behave,' she said, as a woman near me sucked in a breath between her teeth and another man coughed. I had a sudden vision of how parties must have been when Lucy's mother was alive: the extravagant festivities that could turn from harmless enjoyment to uncomfortable spectacle in the blink of an eye.

'Go and powder your nose, Mary,' the Major said tightly, twisting in his seat. He released her arms and instead held her chin, his knuckles white with the force of his grip, before pushing her away. She stumbled and righted herself with a hand on the table where the spotted cuscus crouched. 'A little too much champagne tonight,' he declared and the table tittered, pleased to break the tension. Mary walked away towards the west wing of the house, her white furs like a gleaming banner in the dark.

'Poor form of Malcolm to bring another man's ex-girlfriend to dinner at his own house,' the Major drawled, gesturing towards the two empty spaces at the table, making the officer closest to me snort and an older woman frown daintily. 'You wouldn't go crazy like that if we broke up, would you, darling?' he asked Sylvia.

'I think having to say goodbye to you would turn anyone crazy, darling,' she gasped theatrically, and the Major kissed her on the cheek.

'Women's hearts are such sensitive things,' he said, and she hit him lightly on the arm, 'like little fluttering birds.' He stroked her neck and she giggled.

I hid my distaste with a sip of water. I felt for Lucy. Having to sit at dinner and see your father fawn over a girl younger than you, with an audience watching, must be terrible. Let alone having his last girlfriend make a scene too.

The salad arrived next, ferried by the servants in their

immaculate uniforms, bringing with them the cold, fresh smell of the outdoors as if the walls at the darkened end of the corridor were melting away and the night was creeping in. Josephine served me and I thanked her awkwardly.

The artist opposite me was looking over his shoulder at the polar bear behind him, or perhaps the painting of one of the lords of Lockwood behind the bear.

'Such an interesting setting,' the woman sitting in front of the zebra said.

I glanced at Mary's still-empty seat and the dark eyes of the large-spotted genet that peered back at me from behind it, its bushy tail curled around the table it sat upon.

'Well, at least that ghastly Priestley is off the BBC,' the officer with the southern muriqui peeking over his shoulder was saying. 'They did the right thing there, booting him off, he would have stirred the country to revolution if he got his way—'

'I have it on good authority that the order came from the very top,' another man said, leaning forward conspiratorially, but the officer was not done yet.

'—all this talk about *after the war, after the war*,' he said, 'about housing and social justice and *fairness* – we have to win the bloody war first. All these factory workers dreaming about their new prefabricated homes should be putting their minds to the task at hand.'

'Hear-hear. Don't get Lord Lockwood started on unions,' said one of the two politicians, his cheeks flushed from the strong red wine that had been served with the veal course.

The Major shook his finger and clicked his tongue.

'Here, you're not a Bolshie, are you, Lillian?' one man asked the red-headed singer next to him, the one who had offered to perform for us later.

'God, no,' she said, with a little flick of the tail of her fur over one shoulder, but her eyes met mine and I was not sure she was telling the truth.

After the plates were all taken away, and as thoughts turned to the sticky delights of dessert, the Major stood up and rang his knife against his glass.

'Now, I did have an ulterior motive for inviting you here tonight, I'm afraid, an announcement I want to make.' He paused. 'I am delighted to announce that the museum, whose fine animals you see around us now, has asked me to host some of their collection permanently at Lockwood once the war is over.'

My heart kicked and blood drained from my face, as the table congratulated him and told him what a marvellous idea that was.

'I'm sorry, Major Lockwood, but that simply cannot be true,' I said, my voice shaking with fury now, not fear. What the hell was going on? He could not be serious, surely?

'I beg your pardon, *Miss* Cartwright; are you calling me a liar?' he asked with a smile.

'The remit of our museum is education. Your hosting a separate collection here will prevent researchers, and the public, from accessing it,' I said, rather than *yes*. My mind was whirling and the blank accusing faces of the mounted animals around the table seemed to press in towards me.

'Oh, I'm not going to put them away under lock and key, Miss Cartwright,' he said with a little laugh. 'Naturally, we shall be open for visitors.'

This was why he was looking for funds then; not for our museum but for *his*.

'What a fine setting for them,' the man to his left said.

'I'm sorry, but this is unfathomable, the museum's mammal

collection cannot be split between two locations,' I said, standing up, unable to sit placidly, listening to this rubbish.

'It can, it *will*,' he said, as people shifted in their seats and looked at me disapprovingly.

I grasped at any argument that he might understand, beyond the fact that he could not do this, that he was lying and that the museum would *never* have agreed to this. 'The cost of hosting the specimens here in an environment appropriate to their conservation—'

'Cost, you say,' he said, and rubbed his finger across his mouth. 'If you are so concerned about cost, Miss Cartwright, then perhaps you as a museum attendant' – attendant, as though I were nothing more than a caretaker! – 'should not have caused so much damage to my property. Damage caused by changing original antique locks and hammering nails through original window frames to board up windows in some fit of paranoia. The museum actually owes me funds, Miss Cartwright—'

'Father,' Lucy cut in, 'perhaps we could wait until after dinner—'

'It's all right, my dove, just some healthy tussling over particulars. Miss Cartwright is embarrassed that the museum directors saw fit to keep her out of the loop.'

'Lord Lockwood—' I exclaimed, but the wail of the air-raid siren interrupted me.

'Ah, saved by the bell,' he said, smiling lazily. He clapped his hands together. 'Now, I have a very comfortable basement should any of you like to lurk there, but if not, feel free to remain in your seats. Our ARP warden is a bit keen, I'm afraid.'

I stood there, the siren an echo of my own rage, my toes curled tightly in my shoes, my chin shaking, as the Major started pontificating proudly about *his* new collection. I was confident he had fabricated the museum's agreement; that he thought if he presented it to me, and them, as a fait accompli, then they would be too embarrassed to correct him. But the museum had experience dealing with rich collectors, with wealthy visitors who demanded to buy our specimens, and we would not be cowed by one ridiculous man. Perhaps I could throw one of his silver knives at him, I thought, staring at the knife handle, my fingers aching to reach for it.

In the end, of course, I did nothing of the sort; I simply turned away to join the handful of guests, mostly women, who were heading for the basement, my hands clenched into fists and an angry sweat prickling underneath my dress. As I left, I glanced back at the crowd of stuffed animals who could not choose whether or not to shelter in the basement, as ever worried that while I might survive, they might not.

Well, perhaps if a bomb fell on the long gallery the Major might get knocked out by a piece of flying shrapnel, I thought darkly, and then tapped my fingers on the side of my head as if I could remove that thought. I was not someone who believed in jinxes, but equally it did not seem like a good time to start tempting fate. That was what the house had done to me, ripping away my rationality, leaving me using terms like *fate*.

Lucy was walking ahead of me again, chattering brightly to the lord next to her, the same man to whom the Major had called across the table – while the diners close by looked knowing, and Lucy's face froze in a polite grin – *doesn't my daughter look a jewel tonight?*

The Major could not force her to marry someone, I thought wildly, as we squeezed our way past the mounted heads, one of our number stealing a hat from a snarling tiger and placing it on their own head to much laughter. We were not in the eighteenth century; he could not make her walk down the aisle and say yes. If he did, I'd fight him, I decided. I could not protect my animals with brute force but I could and would for her.

Because Lucy did not want a boyfriend or a husband, I knew that. It was more likely that when Lockwood was requisitioned for some other war task once the museum was gone, she might fall in love with a nurse, or a brave spy, a schoolmistress charmingly frazzled by her charges. I could find another woman of course, back in London where there was sure to be at least some of my ilk hiding somewhere but, I thought, as I took my seat on the sofa in the basement, and Lucy took the space next to me, as her perfume and the warm smell of her skin enveloped me, as my hand trembled in its attempt not to reach for hers, I knew that I would love no other woman but her.

The servants had taken one side of the basement, and the guests the other. In the big hotels in London, one woman said, there were fully stocked underground bars and dance floors, singers for entertainment, and then, realizing that the daughter of Lord Lockwood was sitting near her, nervously added that she was not complaining, not at all, only gossiping. And so began a spirited sharing of air-raid stories, even the servants chipping in with gruesome tales they had heard from relatives working in factories in northern towns.

'I can't believe your father lying like that,' I said softly, looking at Lucy's hands clasping her clutch with the heavy torch inside.

'I've heard nothing about it, nothing at all,' she said, shaking her head so that her hair brushed against my shoulder, 'and it was terrible of him to bring it up at dinner like that without warning you. He's done this before with other things, ridden roughshod over people to get things done the way he wants. It's how he does business.'

'Are you all right?' I murmured, as her body quivered. I had been so wrapped up in my outrage that I had not thought about Lucy's nerves, her fear of the enclosed space of the basement. 'I can find you some wine, or something. I'm sure the all-clear will sound at any moment.'

'I'm fine, Hetty,' she said, and pressed a hot hand to my thigh, and now I was the one to shiver. 'Thank you for asking, though.'

'Of course,' I said.

I should apologize to her now, hang my pride. I should tell her about the letter I sent this morning too, but I was a coward who feared my news would hurt her further, who did not want to hear her say that she did not accept my apology.

The all-clear sounded faintly and the guests stood up, shaking the dust from their clothes, glad to be heading back up to the warmth and light of the house, back to a dinner setting that seemed to be of another time, back when the waters between Britain and the rest of the world did their job, and war was fought elsewhere, and did not batter its cities and towns and villages, its defenceless people.

We made our way through the corridor into the long gallery and I paused by the blesbok, the candlelight making the table ahead of me seem like some painted backdrop.

'Are you not coming back to the table for dessert?' Lucy asked, touching my elbow.

'In a moment. I shall have a walk through the museum rooms first, burn off my anger so I don't throw my petits fours at your father,' I said, trying to make light of my vicious hatred, of the blaring sense of alarm that the siren had engendered inside of me. *I should go to bed now*, I thought. I should retreat, knowing that I had the upper hand, that the letter was already making its way on the train to London. But I was not someone who backed down, who ran away, I told myself – all the while knowing that, in a sense, I was doing precisely that in requesting that the museum be evacuated a second time.

I opened the door to the first room to the left of the corridor and shut it behind me, switching on the floor lamp in the corner. I touched the edges of cabinets and crates and jars, cataloguing them under my shaking breath as I passed by: skins of manakin birds from the Amazon Basin, marsupial skeletons, the double-headed lamb foetus floating grotesquely in its spirit jar, gazelle skins from the country that had been British Somaliland before it was conquered by the Italians a few months ago, rodent skulls from South America, walrus ivory, Asian black bear skulls. I moved into the connecting room with the ambient light of the first room to guide me, and circled its collection, and then made my way to the third room, which was even darker than the last.

My eyes were still adjusting to the gloom when I noticed a small shape lying in the middle of the floor. I moved closer and reached out a hand that dwarfed the object. I felt dry feathers against my palm.

A hummingbird.

There was another one a few steps away, and then another after that. A trail of them, leading onwards into the blackness of the night.

Chapter Forty

I *didn't want my father to marry Sylvia, to have my mother replaced, for Sylvia to be mistress of Lockwood and my mother's presence here, all the years she had spent in these rooms, forgotten. But could I begrudge my father happiness, when it was hardly right that he should be as lonely as I now was?*

Would another woman, another wife, do better here than my mother did, I wondered, watching Sylvia check her make-up with a hand-mirror, frowning at her reflection as my father turned away to talk to another guest; or would she be haunted just the same, would Lockwood work its witchery on her too?

Six months before my mother died, I found her wandering in the gardens soaked to her skin and hurried her inside. I placed her by the fire in the morning room and patted her hair dry with a towel, peeled off her sodden sweater and wrapped her in two blankets, as if I were the mother and she my wayward child.

'What were you doing out there?' I asked.

'Walking my gardens,' she said, her voice tired, but a petulant set to her chin.

'You should take an umbrella next time, you'll catch your death of cold.'

'I wouldn't if he hadn't lied to me,' she said, plucking a thread from one blanket and staring into the fire.

'Who?' I asked, knowing that the only 'he' she ever talked about was my father.

'My husband,' she said primly. 'He promised me he'd build me an orangery, a palm house, a proper hothouse for my flowers. He lied. Look,' she said, hand reaching out for a photo frame on the mantelpiece that I retrieved for her. 'Here I am. Do you see me?' she asked, fumbling the frame into my hand.

I stared at the faded photograph, at a pale girl in a froth of white petticoats from neck to ankle, shod in shining black boots and with her ringlets in ribbons, a faint scowl on her blurred face. She was standing on a tightly groomed lawn next to a soaring white house with the forest some way behind her, dark and over-grown. 'I see you,' I said, seeing myself too in that little girl.

'That girl wanted everything, she wanted the world. A palace, a palm house, a prince to sweep her off her feet and take her away from the heat and the noise and the backwater of her home.' My mother gave a short, mirthless laugh, resettling the blankets around her shoulders. 'That girl knew nothing.'

My knees were aching from crouching beside her but I didn't want to move yet, for I sensed a rare glimmer of sanity in her that I wanted to savour.

'I, she –' she poked the glass of the photograph – 'used to dream, terrible dreams about la diablesse.'

'Who was she?' I asked, even though I had been told many times before.

'The woman in white, my nurse called her. She was human once but became a demon. She put spells on men; she used to wait for them in the forest and then run away and let her beasts eat them. She wore a large white dress with many petticoats that hid her single cloven foot, and a hat or a veil to cover her monstrous face.' My mother's hand touched her cheek. 'I used to dream of her, waiting for me in the forest, hunting me. I thought that if I left my home, I might leave her too, but I got it wrong, don't you see?'

'How did you get it wrong?' I asked, suddenly desperate to hear what she might say.

'She was trying to warn me; the dreams were her gift,' she said. 'That day when I arrived at Lockwood, my wedding day, my husband took me on a tour of my new home, room after room, all his, all mine, until we came to one room, a bedroom with purple wallpaper, with a sloping floor and a window that rattled in the wind, and I turned round and there she was, waiting for me. Don't you see?' my mother said again, turning to clutch my hands. 'It was the mirror, I saw my reflection, I saw her inside the mirror, the woman in white, it was me all along.'

Chapter Forty-One

I walked forward as if in a trance, following the trail of hummingbirds lying still on the ground as if they had dropped dead while fleeing from something awful, their faded colours dulled by the darkness to smudges of black.

The light shifted into greasy shades of yellow as I waded through the blackout, the glow of a candle appearing ahead of me as I came to the very last room, where the hummingbird cabinet was situated.

The birds were strewn like a carpet there, as if thrown by a child having a fit.

And standing by the cabinet, a candlestick at her feet, was Mary, her furs discarded in a pale heap behind her, like the hump of some unidentifiable creature. The sequins of her dress glimmered like sparks in the flickering light.

'What are you doing?' I cried.

She reached into the cabinet again – she had prised off the wooden board that had replaced the broken glass last year – and flung out another bird, its body so insubstantial that it did not make a sound when it fell onto the floor.

'Stop!' I called, and she turned to face me. 'Leave the hummingbirds alone.'

'I was a child when he first had me, do you know that?' she

said, her voice breaking with pain, the whites of her eyes glinting. 'I got lost during a game of hide and seek and found him waiting for me in his office. I was just a little thing. *Little bird*, he called me all the times when we were together, *little angel, little rabbit, little beast, little doll*. He used to have me wear his wife's furs with nothing underneath; he used to have me run away from him and then chase me down.'

My knees shook, and the hairs on the back of my neck stood on end.

Her face was a picture of agony, her gaze blank, as though she were looking back to some monstrous past.

'*My little rabbit*, he called me, when he had me. Other times he called me a bird, or an angel, because of the whiteness of my hair and the dresses I used to wear,' her hand floated towards her head, as if her limb had been untethered, 'and he said he'd buy me lace wings like an angel from a play. But even when we were together last year, it wasn't the same. He fucked me but he didn't love me.' Tears spilled from her wide eyes, gleaming gold in the light. 'He didn't – doesn't – want me like he did back then; he doesn't even speak of it, it's as if that girl, that child, that little doll of his, was someone else, someone he doesn't remember, but *I* remember. I remember. *My little secret*, he called me, but how many of those did he have?' She gave a sob, and seized another hummingbird.

'I don't know what you're talking about,' I said weakly, my eyes fixed on her as though she was something dear of mine that had been ignited into some terrible inferno.

'You know *who* I'm talking about. The Major. Lord Lockwood. He doesn't want you either, even with your pale hair. He wants Sylvia; he's going to marry her instead of me.'

'He hurt you, when you were a child?'

'He *loved* me when I was a child.'

I wanted to cry.

'He liked to beat me too, said I was a naughty little savage, but I didn't mind that; he would be so gentle afterwards. It was a game.' She smiled. 'He used to have me right under his wife's nose, in a different room each time. He used to kiss me and love me while his wife ran around the house looking for him. Once, he had me hide in a wardrobe and when she came into the room asking who he had been talking to, he told her she was mad.'

'Stop,' I said, raising my hands as if I could push the horrific images away. Mary's story was terrible, but somehow I knew she was not lying. Pain like this could not be feigned.

'Even when his wife was dead, he wouldn't marry me. He promised me he'd buy me furs of my very own but he never did, I had to wear his wife's, his mistresses', his daughter's.'

She looked at the hummingbird she still held in her hands, then threw it, its body skidding into the wall.

'Please stop!' I begged. 'You'll damage the birds.'

'The birds . . .' she repeated, turning to face the cabinet, the dark shadows of the hummingbirds on the branches looking almost like one great winged creature crouching inside. 'The birds, and the bear, and the rabbits, and the foxes,' she said, as if it were a line from a nursery song. 'He thinks he can own everything. He thinks he can take us and discard us as he wishes. I wanted to make him pay. He *will* pay.'

'You were the one who stole the birds, who skinned the bear,' I said, trying to follow her strange logic. 'The porcelain doll, was that yours too?'

'Oh, he liked to give me dolls. I wasn't old enough to be given my own furs, but he could give me dolls. My mother was very impressed with them,' she said, smoothing her hair back from her face with an open palm. 'She thought he might sponsor a place for me at some nice school, that he might help me get work when I was older. But he got bored of me.'

The night's rich banquet curdled in my gut and I wanted to vomit. I had known that the Major was cruel but I did not know that he was a monster too. Had he hurt other girls, other children?

'The rabbit, was that you too, and the thief, the woman in white haunting the house?' I found myself asking, as I stared at a woman so raw it hurt to look at her.

She laughed. 'The rabbit was my brother's idea; he poaches them from the Major's woods. I was hoping to make you leave so that I could come back – because it was your arrival that caused the Major to throw me out in the first place,' she said.

I remembered seeing her the very first time I arrived at the manor; her tear-stained face and the look of loathing she gave me as I entered and she left. 'But how did you get inside?'

She laughed again and the sound made me flinch. 'Oh, there's so much happening here, so much you don't know. You're as blind as his poor wife. It was the housekeeper who let me in.'

'Why?' I asked, my voice thin.

'Because I know all about her, and she's worried I'll tell someone, she's worried about someone finding out,' Mary said, leaning forward with a mad conspiratorial glint in her eyes, even though her teeth were chattering. 'She's greedy, she is, don't look at her plain dresses and think otherwise, she has an Aladdin's cave in her rooms. She does very well for herself, doesn't she, doing Lord Lockwood's bidding. The pretty ones, he wants, the young ones just out of school. And it's her job to hire them, to be so strict with them they wouldn't dare tell anyone about him slipping into their rooms in the dark, and it's her job too to drop them back with their families afterwards and tell them their daughters are flighty and foolish and *liars*.'

'The maids, he preys on them?' I thought of the steady stream of fresh-faced girls during my time at Lockwood and I wanted to wail; the ones who left so quickly, the ones whose work ethic *the housekeeper* complained about. 'Then he's the ghost,' I said, with horrifying certainty, thinking of the rumours of strange cries in the night, of figures gliding behind you in the dark and reaching out to touch you. I thought of how many young women, how many girls, had passed through this house as servants and guests and friends of his *daughter*. I thought of all those rooms, all those opportunities to corner someone, alone. I had been entrusted with the task of keeping my animals safe but what about them, the girls, who was in charge of *their* safety? Who would watch them and tend to them and keep guard at their door?

'There's no room he doesn't have the key for, no door he can't open,' Mary was saying, 'nothing he wants that he doesn't get.' She sounded almost triumphant but her chin was trembling, she was swaying on her feet. 'He said I might be his mistress, but he wouldn't marry me because I wasn't rich enough, that the house needed funds or else it would crumble. *I married my first wife for love and look how that turned out*, he said.' Her face crumpled. 'I put the rabbit there during the children's visit so that they would be scared away and never return. I *tried*,' she said. She plucked another hummingbird from the cabinet and held it in cupped palms as I watched, mesmerized and horrified. 'His wife was mad, everyone knew that,' she said, and then she crushed the bird in her fist and we both cried out. 'She thought I was haunting her, don't you see? And when he told me to step in front of her car dressed all in white like a bride, to get rid of her so that we could be together forever, she looked like she'd seen a ghost.' A keen escaped her mouth, her teeth clattered and her whole body shook. 'But even when she was gone, he wouldn't marry me,' she sobbed.

'Mary—' I said, holding out my hands as if I sought to tame her.

'He's going to pay,' she said again, voice harder, and then, squaring her thin shoulders, she marched past me, into the corridor, her dress like a thousand tiny eyes glinting. As the door slammed behind her, the candle was extinguished. I cried out at the shock, at the horror of everything she had said.

The room was black, its features invisible although my eyes invented shadowy forms and shapes in the darkness. Not wanting to crush the thick carpet of birds beneath my feet before I could find the light switch, I knelt on hands and knees, brushing away the stray bodies with gentle sweeps of my hands as I made my way to the furthest room and its lamp. I was weeping.

My little beast, my little bird, my little dove.

Heloise and her fears about what might occur behind locked doors; Lucy and her nightmares about something stalking through the house, about searching for a wounded leveret; Mary, and the maids, and the Major's beastly collection of animals and girls—

There was shouting as I came into the corridor, brushing my clothes free of dust, my face of tears.

Mary was face to face with *him*, screaming accusations at him – the things he'd done to her; to others – while a group of servants whispered by the door that led to the opposite row of rooms. The other guests had already left – for cigars and coffee in the billiards room, if I remembered the plan for the evening correctly – but Lucy was standing by the table still, frozen as she watched her father grapple with Mary, who seemed to be trying to claw his eyes out. I stepped forward just as Mary spat at him and then broke free of his grasp, one hand flying out in a slap.

Lucy grabbed my arm. 'Come outside,' she said, pulling me with her.

We stumbled past the animals – who seemed to be crowding closer to the grisly scene – Lucy squeezing between the table and the beasts, her fur stole dragging an array of things from the table that fell, clattering, onto the floor, while I manoeuvred myself past the paintings on the wall, bruising my shoulder against their frames. And then we broke into a run, shoes skidding and sliding, and Lucy flung the garden door open with a crash, startling the guards waiting there.

I turned back to look down the long corridor and saw a flicker of light, as if the pale polar bear were somehow haloed for a moment, and then I followed Lucy outside.

'Everything all right?' one of the guards called.

'Just coming out for some air,' Lucy replied as we moved further into the dark, past the overgrown knot garden and along the banks of dead roses.

We stopped, panting, by a copse of trees, our breath clouding in the frigid air.

'You're cold,' she said, and draped her fur stole around us, but when I flinched at the once-familiar sensation of fur against my skin, she dropped it and replaced it with her arms around my neck.

I hid my face in her shoulder, breathing in the comforting smell of her perfume, my body shaking.

'Did you hear what she said, what Mary said?' I asked. Mary had not yet confessed to her part in Heloise's death before we left the long gallery, but what she had shared would be horrifying enough to any daughter.

'I did,' Lucy said, and dug her hands into my shoulders.

'I found her in one of the rooms off the corridor, tearing the hummingbirds out of their cabinet, flinging them on the floor. The things she was saying—'

'I think they're true,' Lucy said in a small voice.

We held each other as the cold of the night pressed in and a breeze whistled through the bare branches of the trees, rustling the last remaining leaves, making the bushes surrounding us shuffle in the gloom. There was a waning gibbous moon that cast shadows in the garden, and touched our skin with its silver.

'I should never have said those things to you. I was cruel, forgive me,' I begged tearfully.

'Only if you forgive me for calling you mad,' she said.

'I *was* mad, this house has turned me mad.'

She stepped back and held my face in her hands. 'No, you're not mad.'

'Neither are you,' I said. 'It's Lockwood, it's your mother, your father—'

She shook her head.

'Come with me,' I pleaded, kissing her cheek. 'The mammals are going to be moved somewhere else; it's too dangerous here.' Although I now knew who the culprit was, it was still not safe for *any* creature here, living or dead – even if the latter at least could not be hurt by the Major and his monstrous desires. 'Come with me, we can live together, *be* together.'

She closed her eyes, the soft skin between her eyebrows creasing into a frown, and then she kissed me feverishly as if she could meld the both of us together, and I could taste her tears, the sweetness of her mouth, her sour breath.

'I love you; come with me,' I said, needing to hear her say the word, to hear her say *yes*.

But it was another voice that rang out, coming from the direction of the house.

'Fire!' someone screamed. 'There's a fire!'

Chapter Forty-Two

We had been too wrapped up in each other to notice that the light in the sky had changed, that a warm glow bled from the long gallery of Lockwood; brightest in the cracks around the boarded-up windows halfway down the wing, near where the table was. The table with my animals arranged around it.

The museum's mammal collection, the crates, and boxes, and cabinets, and jars—

Oh god.

'The stirrup pump!' I called, racing towards the door of the gallery wing, where the night guards and servants huddled.

'Where is my father?' Lucy shouted, sprinting after me.

As we reached the building, Mary came running out, a hot rush of air behind her like a sweltering summer's day. We could see the fire now through the open door – the table and the animals around it both ablaze, flames licking towards the ceiling and walls, but it was still manageable, I thought, not yet out of control. We could save almost all of the other animals, I was sure of it.

'My father?' Lucy asked, grabbing Mary, whose hair was hanging loose from its pins, her face flushed and smudged with soot.

'He went back inside,' she panted, her expression wild, 'he's trapped by the fire—'

Lucy pushed past her and entered the long gallery.

'The stirrup pump!' I called again, my hand on the doorframe, torn: wanting to follow Lucy, not wanting her to put herself in danger, but also knowing I needed to save the museum. I saw two temporary servants, women from the village, carrying the pump towards us across the dark grass. 'Shovels and sand and water,' I ordered, looking around wildly. 'Quick!' I told the guards.

'It's no use,' the guard nearest to me said. 'The fire's too large already.'

'We have to try,' I said, following the women with the pump into the corridor, eyes fixed to the silhouette of Lucy ahead of me.

The flames were climbing up the walls on both sides of the table, filling the entire width of the long gallery, and the air was hot and sharp in my throat as I tried to see whether they had reached the rooms at either side – the ones with boarded-up windows. The windows *I'd* had boarded up. Oh god, if my actions had made the fire worse, if they turned the whole wing into a furnace, oh god—

'We need more water, more buckets!' I called, and one of the women ran back to fetch some.

Lucy was right at the edge of the flames, arm held across her face against the heat, screaming, *Papa, papa!* I crouched to the right of her, pumping the water that was being aimed towards the base of the blaze by the other servant, trying not to notice how all three of us were having to inch backwards as the fire strengthened and pushed out towards us. The water was gone in moments, useless.

My eyes were stinging; my skin felt flayed. 'Lucy!' I tugged her back as something in the inferno exploded. My animals, all that work; we were about to lose it all.

'We need to leave,' the villager holding the hose said, her eyes wild with fear. 'The whole place is going to go up.'

The fire was travelling towards us like a predator who knew its prey was already weakened. It was feeding itself with the teak of the walls and all the wood of the crates and boxes in the rooms to either side, gorging on each hummingbird body left like kindling on the floor; it was growing taller, louder, hotter. The long gallery was crackling and groaning and roaring. The museum was on fire.

The animals were burning in their cases, boiling behind shattering glass, their feathers and fur igniting like candles, their newspaper bodies sparking into flame, clay mounts melting, eyes rolling onto the floor and turning back to stare at their own destruction.

The ceiling shrieked loudly and a large beam fell a few feet away, shaking the ground, sending up sparks that burned our skin. Lucy turned and broke into a sudden run. 'He might have made it through to the house, I'm going to check his office!' she shouted.

'Back!' the woman was saying, pulling me, and I picked up the stirrup pump and fled outside with her.

'Is that everyone?' the guard called when we rushed through the door. 'Lord Lockwood?'

'We couldn't see him. Is the fire brigade here yet?' I asked, but before he could answer me I was racing across the grass towards the back door of the main house, passing two more people with buckets.

Maybe if we cut off the fire before it spread to the main house? We could still save some of the collection then.

'Dorothy!' I called, barrelling into her in the entrance hall, steadying myself with my hands on her shoulders. 'The fire brigade?'

'They're on their way,' she said. 'You need to wait out at the front with everyone else!'

'I can't! My animals!' I looked around. 'Where's Lucy?'

Dorothy glanced towards the west wing of the house.

'We need to get a stirrup pump here now, and stop the fire spreading!' I skidded across the floor towards the other entrance to the long gallery, next to the Major's office. If we kept the door closed, if we sealed the fire in—

The door was open, heat and smoke already coming through.

I could hear a cough as I slipped through the narrow corridor, my dress snagging on the teeth of a mounted lion's head that had fallen off the wall.

'Lucy!'

'Papa!' she was crying, her form barely distinguishable in the haze.

'We need to keep the door closed!' I shouted, grabbing her.

'He wasn't in his office or his library; I checked,' she sobbed.

'He won't be here either! He's not here! He'll have gone to the front of the house with everyone else.' I had forgotten to ask Dorothy if she had seen him. But I didn't need to, I already knew the answer: she wouldn't have seen him because he was somewhere in the fire, dead, and Mary was somehow responsible.

'He's not here,' I said again, pulling Lucy along and out of the corridor, turning our backs on the inferno as we scraped past snouts and jaws and noses and antlers, past faces posed as placid prey or ferocious predator, their dark eyes flickering with reflections of the fire that stalked towards them, a final hunter they could not escape from, far fiercer than the man with the rifle, the dog, the arrow, that had killed them first.

Lucy rushed through the house towards the front door as I slammed the door to the long gallery shut, holding my hands against its warming surface as if I could hold the fire back myself. The collection, the work of thousands, the rare specimens, *everything* –

The kitchen errand boy and one of the guests, still wearing black tie, hurried towards me, carrying another stirrup pump and bucket of water. It wasn't going to be enough. This fire needed a flood to put it out, a biblical downpour.

The water from the pump turned almost instantly to steam, the smoke curled its way through the tiny cracks between door and doorframe, and the roaring heat of the fire seemed to mock our paltry efforts against its hunger.

'Miss Lucy!' I heard someone call, and turned my head. Dorothy came running through the haze. 'She's gone upstairs,' she panted, grasping my elbow. 'I can't get her to come back. It's not safe in here. We all need to leave.'

She gestured to me to look up. Up, where the ceiling was smouldering, the plaster burning. The fire had leaped from the long gallery to the first floor of the main house.

'We need to save the other museum rooms,' I said, staring at the ceiling, but I wasn't thinking about the museum, about the animals ablaze, I was thinking only of a girl, a woman, with dark eyes and a tremulous smile.

I ran back down the corridor, my hands slamming hard into the wall as I took a tight corner.

Lucy.

Chapter Forty-Three

I was searching frantically for my father, for his familiar form somewhere amongst the chaos of smoke and fire. My father —

The things Mary had said.

Little doll, little bird, little rabbit.

The creature who hunted me in my dreams. The lost leveret I tried to save. The beast, the ghost, stalking the corridors of Lockwood —

Was I dreaming? Was this some nightmare I couldn't escape from? My hands grasped at walls, at doorways, my feet tripped on the carpet, the dry air made me choke as I clambered on. But as I continued through the house, my hunt, my search, changed without conscious thought, just as in my dreams, and it wasn't my father I was looking for any more, but my mother, it was always my mother.

How could I leave her alone here to wander these halls, trapped inside with no way out, crying and wailing? How?

Mother, are you here in the flames? Is that your voice underneath the roar of the fire? Are you waiting for me?

The house was groaning, the inferno like thunder, like the end of everything.

If each room of Lockwood Manor held one of my memories,

held another secret yet to be excavated, then how could I leave it? If it burned down then wouldn't I forget everything; wouldn't I go mad? How could I survive outside of it?

Chapter Forty-Four

I raced up the stairs, the skin of my palm burning from the friction of my hand on the banister, the toes of my shoes scraping against the carpet.

'Lucy!' I shouted.

Where was she? I sprinted down the corridor towards her father's rooms, passing smoke escaping from the doors to my left where the fire had spread, a wall of heat pressing in on me. I burst through the door. 'Lucy!'

I could just make out a figure next to the bulk of the wardrobe. I scrabbled for a light switch and the lamp illuminated a room with dark wallpaper and heavy mahogany furniture, a row of mounted heads opposite the large bed.

'She's not here,' Lucy said, and looked at me with haunted eyes.

'No,' I said, 'she isn't.' I grabbed her hand and pulled her from the room, back towards the stairs, past the flames that were now devouring the right side of the corridor, spreading up towards the ceiling with such heat I cried out and shut my eyes, fearing they were singed.

But when we reached the top of the stairs, Lucy pulled her hand from my damp grasp and headed up, not down.

'No! Lucy!' I cried, clambering after her. All thoughts of my animals, of trying to rescue the last of them, were gone. They were my life's work but she was living, she was my heart, and I would do anything to save her.

She had reached the second floor; the smoke was thicker here, brown like mud, and rolled up from the warm floorboards.

I stopped a few steps below her and glanced back at the glow of the first floor. We had to leave *now* or we would get caught here and die.

'Lucy! Come with me!' I begged.

I saw her shake her head. Her face was pale and terrified, and I realized she was that little girl again, haunted by dreams and the living nightmares of her life here.

'I can't leave it, I can't leave Lockwood!' she sobbed. 'I can't do it.'

'You can,' I said, and held out my hand. 'I'll help you, take my hand. You *can.*'

There was a screeching groan of metal twisting and falling, and then the muffled thud of a ceiling crashing to the ground.

Lucy screamed as if the noise had broken through her terror, and reached for my hand.

We ran down the stairs, she leading me now, both of us stumbling, almost falling, as we made our way through the smoke and heat, clutching so tightly to each other's hands that I could feel the bones grind together, blundering past walls and rooms and furniture rendered unfamiliar by smoke and panic.

The fire thundered to our left and bellowed at our backs as we dashed through the entrance hall and burst into the clean air of the night.

We were out, we were safe and, once we reached the front lawn, I fell to my knees and was violently sick, hands clutching at the grass in front of me.

Chapter Forty-Five

'Did everyone get out?' Lucy asked. She was sitting beside me on the grass, shoulder against mine. I could feel tremors working their way through her body but she was no longer crying.

'We think everyone but your father. Miss Lucy, I'm so sorry,' Dorothy said, having walked towards us from the huddle of servants and guests who were staring up at the house. Her face was smeared with soot, her voice cracked from the smoke, and the white of her collar had turned grey.

The housekeeper was standing a little way away from the rest of them, trembling. When she had recovered, I would tell Lucy about her and what she had done; what a monster she was. No wonder she had hated my arrival at Lockwood, my curiosity, my poking about in shut-up rooms. I might have felt a hollow glee at her being so devastated if the museum had not been lost as well.

'The fire brigade will be here soon.' Dorothy shivered, her arms wrapped around herself. 'If the Luftwaffe don't find us first,' she continued, staring at the clear sky. 'We're like sitting ducks here, we've made a beacon to guide their way.' She waved a hand towards the house.

'Dorothy,' the cook admonished and motioned with her head towards Lucy.

At that moment, something inside of the house fell with a boom and a roaring crunch, sending a plume of smoke and flames up to the heavens. I let out a single bark of hysterical laughter.

The fire had taken the whole of Lockwood, silhouetting it against the night – as if the real world were made of flames, and the dark of the night covering it had been cut open to reveal the inferno inside. Any windows we could still see were now white with heat, a mirror of their blackout selves, the glass exploding as we watched, as if the house were expanding, muscling its way out into the grounds of the estate.

'Your animals,' Lucy cried, and clutched my hand.

My animals. I had called them that in my head and out loud to other people, my animals, *mine*. Had I been covetous of them in my own way, just as the Major was? Had my selfish hubris been their downfall? They were not mine, they were the museum's, the nation's. They never belonged to me at all; I was only supposed to safeguard them for the next generation, the better generation, the ones who would not start wars and raze cities to ash and cinder, and murder millions.

'How did the fire start?' Dorothy asked us, the last vestige of formality towards her lady going up in smoke with the manor. 'You were in the long gallery, weren't you, did you see it?'

I glanced towards the cluster of guests. Most of the women were crying; Sylvia was in the arms of one of the officers, her face a rictus of pain.

'I didn't see it,' I said. 'There was an argument and when we left Lord Lockwood was still by the dinner table.'

'An argument with who?'

'With Mary,' Josephine said, joining our group. 'That was her name, his ex-girlfriend, the one with white hair, yes?'

'Where is she?' the cook asked.

Josephine shrugged. 'Gone,' she said. 'She and her man, they left in their car. The artist and the singer too.'

Had Mary set one of the animals on fire, or the tablecloth, or a fur someone had left behind? Had she done it accidentally, or on purpose? If the latter, did she even know what she was doing?

Or was someone else to blame?

I remembered Lucy squeezing past the dinner table as we left; her fur stole knocking things onto the floor – ivy wreaths, cutlery, *candlesticks*. I knew the sound of a candlestick clattering onto wooden floorboards; I had heard it when Paul had dropped one down the stairs just a week or so ago. I remembered too that the polar bear had seemed to glow when I stopped on the threshold of the long gallery and looked back – was that the first flames of the fire Lucy had unwittingly lit?

I would never tell her my suspicions. I would not make her feel responsible for destroying her home, as I was responsible for destroying the mammal collection of the museum.

For I had no one else to blame, no one but myself.

I should not have let the Major host a candlelit dinner; I had had the power to refuse him, to call in help from the director in London to support me. I should not have had the windows of the long gallery and the ground floor of the main house boarded up, turning the inside of the house into a heat trap. I should have demanded that the mammal collection was moved the moment the infestation got out of control, the moment the thefts began. I should have never been arrogant enough to presume that I could keep them safe, that I alone could be their brave protector. I had been trying to save face, selfishly trying to prove that the fossil I had smashed had been an anomaly, that I was up to the task.

How wrong I was, how foolish.

The fire gorged itself on Lockwood, on its rich woods and fine wallpapers, its oriental carpets and Turkish rugs, its silks and velvets and linens, its wardrobes bursting with dresses and suits and furs, its shelves of books, its brass fittings and crystal chandeliers, its silverware and copper kitchenware, its porcelain and glass, its marble and flagstone, slate and tile, its feather mattresses and plush sofas, embroidered cushions and oil paintings. It devoured skins and furs and mounted animals, cabinets and cases and crates, jars and drawers, skulls and bones and teeth, pickled flesh and dry feathers, hides and tails and hooves.

There was a woman in there too, I imagined, my mind fire-drunk and hysterical; ablaze and white-hot, she strolled down corridors, sparks like petals flung from her hands, burning beasts at her heel; and she crooned as she bent over the body of a man whose bones were reduced to cinders, while the walls of the flaming house screeched and hummed a chorus.

Could everything be blamed on Mary, on the Major and the housekeeper? All those sightings of a ghostly figure, the handprints on mirrors, the wild animals drawn to the house, the feverish scent of orchids that lingered even after the dried flowers had crumbled – could everything that had happened within the walls of Lockwood be explained?

Soon, the front lawn was crowded with people, a great host of villagers come to see the end of the big house whose foundations had been here longer than the village itself. Voices calling and crying, and sirens and shouts; the shattering and falling of the last beams and walls; the crackling of the fire that was still burning despite the efforts of the fire brigade, who had finally arrived, and all the people who ferried hoses and buckets along from the lake.

Go back to your homes, find shelter, the ARP wardens told us. *The fire could draw the enemy; they might think it's a target – a factory or an aerodrome.* But we could not leave, we could not look away; Lockwood seemed to demand our vigil, one final service from all of us, whether or not we had worn the livery of its servants.

By now, everyone had heard that the lord of the manor had died inside, surrounded by his great wealth, his possessions. I could hear people sharing stories about him – most mythologizing him, a few cursing his memory, all the old gossip about the Lockwoods spilling forth, talk of curses and bad luck, of the inheritance of madness, as they tried to catch a glimpse of Lucy. I was sheltering her with a blanket given to me by the ambulance, the both of us propped against the great trunk of the oak tree opposite the house, whose bare branches, tipped with the reflection of the fire, reached out into the lightening sky.

For a time after dawn, the glow of the fire surpassed the light of the sun itself and then as the day lengthened and the flames retreated, with no more fuel to burn, with water from the lake sprayed on the lawns and gardens about the house so it would not spread, the sun won out and we began to shiver in the late December cold. It was winter, we remembered suddenly, the heat of the fire's false summer disappearing. The villagers returned to their homes, the guests gave statements to the police and drove off, packed into the cars that had not been damaged by falling masonry.

But the inhabitants of Lockwood – the surviving servants; the mammal keeper who had lost her mammals; the daughter of the dead lord, the inheritor of this burned-out shell of a grand manor house – remained behind, shivering still and looking at the pile of rubble and debris and blackened stone, the glow of the last embers, the smoke sending its unintelligible trails into the sky.

A monstrous bonfire, a funeral pyre for a monstrous man who had got his wish – for the mammals would remain here now, surrounding his corpse.

Somewhere inside that building were the ashes of the museum's mammal collection: the jaguar, the stoats and weasels, the foxes, the polar bear, the shells and feathers and butterflies and beetles, the black panther, the platypus, the mastodon skull, the weasel, the okapi, the hummingbirds' nests, the infested owl, the tiger, the wolf, the lion, the lynx, the elephant.

An ark had been dispatched to safety but had burned inside the four walls meant to protect it. The years of work by hundreds, maybe even thousands of people who strove to preserve the past, to dissect the world of animals and understand them, classify them, to mount and preserve them – all gone, in one night, as nature took her children back to the earth from whence we had taken them or dug them up; from where they had been felled by a hunter's shot or a trap or a net; from where they had been stolen before they could be buried and mourned and turned into fodder for new life.

What would grow from the ashes here; what plants would feed on animals that had never stalked this land, never taken a breath here, but instead been dragged, dead, to stand in its dusty halls? In days and months to come, mice and insects would nibble on exotic leathers and charred, unfamiliar bones; and, as months became years, worms and fungi and bacteria in the soil that would creep its way into the house would have a rare feast indeed.

Meanwhile, the echoing building in London would forever bear a hollow where my collection should have been; a void that would only be more obvious when the other evacuated

collections – the reptiles, the birds, the butterflies, the inver-
tebrates, the rocks and fossils – returned to mark the absence
of their fellow beasts who had not returned from war.

I had lost the collection and with it my future employment
and career. I would find no other job in my speciality – what
job was there for me when most of the mammal collection of
the museum had been destroyed? And who would hire someone
whose own negligence had caused their priceless charges to
go up in flames?

But what was one destroyed house compared to all the
others in London, or on the coasts, in the Midlands and in
the north? What was one building in comparison to the cities
and towns that had been razed across Europe, to the people
who had been stolen from their homes and interned in camps?
Lockwood was but a speck of dust in the rubble of Europe.
Even the museum's mammals were only a small part of the
horde of historical and scientific collections under threat from
bombs and tanks and guns and men starting fires.

I might have lost the mammal collection, and my livelihood.
But Lucy had lost everything. Everything, except her life.

'What will you do now?' I asked her as we staggered up the
frosty road towards the village in our heels and sooty finery,
blankets around our shoulders, towards beds made up by kind
villagers, warm baths and borrowed clothes, maybe even a bowl
of soup by the hearth. 'Will you rebuild the house?' Was it
hers now, or did the Major have a long-lost brother that would
swoop in and steal the empty piece of land she had left?

'What will you do?' she replied, her voice hoarse from the
smoke. 'Will you go back to London?'

'I don't know. There's nothing there for me. I might be found negligent and put in jail, although at least that would solve my worry over finding future lodgings,' I said with a bitter laugh, as she took my hand.

'You won't go to jail. You can use my family lawyers, or I'll pay for others. You're not responsible for what happened. If anyone is, it is – was – my father.'

'Oh, Lucy,' I said, and felt tears threatening to spill down my cheeks. 'I'm so sorry. If the museum had never come, he would have never hosted such a dinner party, the long gallery would have still been empty, not – not filled with flammable matter, and the fire would have been put out before it reached the main house.'

'You don't know that,' she countered, as we passed the village church and its wooden archway, the sign pointing towards the shelter in the crypt and the noticeboard of organizations looking for volunteers – the WI, Land Army, the ARP – and posters warning us against gossip, about ears that heard everything and eyes that saw all. 'If the museum had not come to Lockwood, then you would not have, either. I'm not saying that you're worth Lockwood being destroyed.' She paused. 'Or perhaps I am,' she added in a small voice, and with trembling lips.

In the bright winter sunlight, she looked worn, with dark shadows under her eyes, soot smeared across one side of her face, her bottom lip bleeding where she had cut it on her teeth, a scratch across her nose, her hair full of ash and dust, and I could not wait until we were alone behind a closed door and I could take her in my arms and hold her tightly to me.

Chapter Forty-Six

My *dream is always the same. I am running down a corridor whose walls are made of flames. I am running away from that little blue room at the very top of the house which is filled to bursting with white lace and dresses, with animal skins and furs and heads and skulls and bones, a menagerie squeezed within its narrow walls. There is a roar behind me, of fire, of animals and birds and monsters, their voices a howling chorus. My feet are bare and cold on the slippery wooden floor as I bolt down that endless corridor, the flames singeing my hair, plucking at my dress, grasping for my toes, straining to catch my hands. And there is a beast in the inferno behind me that pads after me, its stride three times as long as mine; it stalks me, with white-hot eyes, with fur made of flickering flames and paws of embers, a tail that whips out like a lash of lightning. And when I finally reach the end of the corridor, when I burst into gardens white with ice, it follows me across the grass, treading sparks into the ground, turning the air around it into steam and smoke, its light casting a shadow of myself before me. And then I come to the end of the garden, and my feet will not run any more, and I am trapped, chest panting, limbs trembling, crying as the beast moves closer, stretching open its mouth to show the fire in its gullet.*

But when it reaches me, it does not devour me, it falls on the ground with a huff, sending up a shimmer of sparks towards me, and then it curls around my feet, warming my frigid toes but not burning them, its great purr thrumming through my body as I stretch down to touch its gleaming sides, but before I can, before my fingers reach those first flickers of fur, I wake from my dream with a jolt. I wake up, and there is a large living creature curled around me in bed, a hand thrown over my stomach, a very human face on my shoulder, and pale hair tickling my cheek.

'Hetty,' I whisper, and if she is dozing she will answer, and if she is not, she won't. 'Hetty, I had that dream again,' I'll say, and she'll reply with some nonsensical hum that means, I'm here, you're safe, and wrap her hot little feet around my legs.

When we left the ruins of Lockwood behind, we took the train down to London. We passed barren winter fields, sleepy villages, bustling towns and factories whose chimneys poured out trails of smoke that I craned out of the window to follow. We passed bomb craters in fields and the wrecks of buildings; stations with no names, their platforms stacked with sandbags and crowded with soldiers in uniform, with ordinary folk wearing hats and gas masks in boxes around their necks, getting on with their days as usual; we passed bare trees waiting patiently for spring; snowmen with scarves and stick arms marooned in the middle of muddy gardens where children played; and Land Girls, their hair tucked inside colourful scarves, winding along lanes back to their farms.

There were Land Girls moving into Lockwood's farm which had, through some miracle, not caught alight, the fields and gardens still there to be worked and put to service for the country. The farmer and his wife had offered the farm to me but I did not want it; cosy and well-loved though it was, it was theirs, not mine. Besides, I couldn't stay there with the wreck of Lockwood Manor looming over my every waking hour, working its way into my dreams. So I corresponded with other estates to find the remaining servants employment in other grand homes if they wanted it – although most had decided to take other war work – and I made sure that the housekeeper would never find employment in any home again, nor be able to ruin the lives of other poor girls. And then I travelled with Hetty to London.

London was a shock of colour and life and activity; of holes in roads where bombs had taken buildings and lives; the glitter of shards of glass too fine to sweep from the streets; the smell of dust and charred wood and stone, and of chestnuts roasting, and the steamy insides of pubs and bars spilling out onto pavements, and hot chocolate and good tobacco. Hetty and I stayed in a hotel at first, after she had put up a cursory fight against using my money to pay for the both of us. There were offices to visit and official forms to sign, queues to wait in, and interviews to be had, administration to sort out to get us on our feet again. We went together as much as possible, trying to remember that we couldn't hold each other's hand as we walked along the streets, but that we might take each other's arm and pretend we were just good friends instead.

I accompanied Hetty to the museum and waited on a rickety chair opposite the secretary as Hetty sat through the ordeal of her first interview, my fingers clutching at the seat tightly when I heard shouts and Hetty's tearful voice. She was not jailed, as she had feared, but there was an investigation by the museum, the government, and the insurers. Lockwood had not been properly insured, we came to learn, so I gave a large chunk of my fortune to pay the shortfall of compensation. I didn't need all that money, I told Hetty, and I did not want it.

Mary, meanwhile, was never convicted, there being no evidence *that she had started the fire, no witness to the aftermath of her confrontation with my father.*

My father—

My mother. Had she, in her madness, been trying to save me, to protect me? To lock me away from what might hurt me? I thought she was the monster who haunted Lockwood, and though it is true that what she did could never be justified by any measure of sanity, there had been a greater threat stalking the house, a predator lurking in plain sight.

I do not think about my father much these days, nor my mother, which is strange since my thoughts were almost consumed by the both of them during my time at Lockwood. While I was living there, in their house, I had been like a child, even when I was years past the schoolroom, and when I left, when it burned down, I relinquished that protracted childhood too.

Hetty and I lived in London for two weeks, spending most of our nights in the opulent basement of the hotel during air raids, while I trembled and cried and tried not to look too pathetic amongst the crowd of worldly-wise Londoners, and then we moved into rooms further out of the city and took the train in for meetings and interviews. We tried to find a bar or a club for women like us, to dance there together, but our search was futile, for we did not know who to ask or where to look, even though we sometimes passed women in the street who looked the right sort, their clothing mannish or their eyes glancing across other women in a familiar way.

And when our business in London was at an end, when I had instructed my solicitor to sell the Lockwood estate for me and present me with the papers to sign when they had done so, we fled north, past the Midlands and the whole of northern England, all the way to Scotland, which I had visited once on a happy holiday with an aunt, and where I bought a small cottage in a village outside Edinburgh for us both.

It has two bedrooms with large windows, one which we keep dressed for appearance's sake, and the other where we sleep in one double bed, our limbs tangled together underneath blankets and thick quilts and, more recently, the purring forms of two tortoiseshell house cats. I have become a housewife with my new leisure time, and with the exemption from service that came with my bad nerves, although I do my best to volunteer now and then for the local WI, to help out with its collections for soldiers and its stalls, with donating to help evacuated families who have lost everything just as I did. I hope that if I am well enough in the future I might use the money from the sale of the estate to become a teacher or organize a charity for women in service, as a small way of making amends for the horrors that occurred under my roof without my noticing.

Hetty got a clerking job with the government in the city and takes regular fire-watching shifts locally for the ARP. Although she likes to say that I lost everything, ignoring the fact that we are both now orphans, it's she who seems to struggle the most to adapt to our new life. She had given all of herself to her work, to the museum, and feels that she has nothing to show for it, that her years of study are now wasted.

'Who am I, without my work?' she asks sometimes, standing in the garden at night, smoking, the familiar planes of her face lit up by the moonlight, her head lolling back on her neck. 'What was it for, all that work, what use am I to anyone?'

And, depending on her mood, I either tease her, tell her to get over herself in order to make her laugh, commiserate with her, remind her that she is worth something to me, that she is doing important work now for the government even if she says it's the *kind of work that anyone with half a brain could do, or suggest that she might find another job after the war where she can use her zoological knowledge.*

Despite the idyllic nature of our new surroundings – our cottage with its neat kitchen garden and banks of rosebushes, the comfortable velvet couch in front of the parlour fire, our shelves of books that grow almost daily; my weekly attempts at baking vegetable cakes that never taste as good as regular cakes, and the bracing walks I take through the fields around our home; the late nights loving one another to exhaustion in all the rooms of the house, dozing together in the bath afterwards – my own anxieties have not vanished completely. Hetty had to hold my hand a lot in those first months, squeezing it tightly until my mind returned from its horrors, until I could right myself. The air raids have not got any easier to bear either, for they still feed into my old fear of being trapped.

Walls can crumble, but the destruction of one's prison or cage – which was also one's Eden, one's home – does not fix nerves that have been delicate since birth. Yet it did give me my freedom; it gave me a path to somewhere, to a future where my happiness would outweigh my sadness and anxiety, a future that I could decide for myself.

A future that we can decide together, I muse, as today's morning light sneaks its way underneath the blackout curtains; as we share a pot of weak tea in bed, lazily planning a trip to the seaside, listening to the wireless tell us that the end is in sight, that the war will be over in but a few months; as a house cat pads across the quilt above our legs and then yawns, showing off its teeth, and burrows its head in the hollow between our legs to doze, while its tail twitches happily in the air.

Acknowledgements

Thank you to Anna Hogarty for taking a chance on me and for that vital first edit. Thank you to Madeleine Milburn, Alice Sutherland-Hawes, Liane-Louise Smith and everyone at the Madeleine Milburn Literary Agency for your tireless energy and ambition.

Thank you to Hayley Steed for being the best agent a girl could wish for – shrewd, brilliant, compassionate, ambitious and driven – I owe so much to you, and I can't wait to watch you continue to blaze a path through the publishing world.

Thank you to Sam Humphreys for your vision and your kindness, and for making the editing process both revelatory and enjoyable, I knew from our first meeting that you were the editor of my dreams. Thank you also to Alice Gray, Natalie Young, Ellis Keene, Ellie Bailey, Neil Lang, Lara Borlenghi, and everyone at Mantle and Pan Macmillan, I'm sure I'm only aware of the smallest part of the work you've done for this novel.

Thank you to Helen Atsma for your keen eyes and your enthusiasm, I'm beyond thrilled and grateful to have you as my North American editor. Thank you also to Jenny Xu, Michelle Triant, Elizabeth Anderson, Martha Kennedy, and everyone at Houghton Mifflin Harcourt.

Thank you to Tom Avery for being the best first reader I

could hope for and for encouraging me to finish my manuscript and send it out to agents, and thank you to the Penguin Random House WriteNow programme for connecting us and for such an inspiring scheme.

Thank you to Josh Henkin and the Brooklyn MFA programme and my fellow cohort of writers for pushing me to write something new (or something old, in the case of historical fiction). Thank you to the short-story competition judges and journal editors who championed my stories and encouraged me to keep writing.

Thank you to all my teachers and professors of English literature who taught me how to read, and how to write. Thank you to my creative writing teachers, especially Viccy Adams, Darcey Steinke and Irina Reyn, each hour I spent in your classrooms has been multiplied a hundred times in the inspiration I have taken with me.

Thank you to everyone in publishing and bookselling who has and will support this book after the arbitrary deadline of writing these acknowledgements.

Thank you to my friends who never once told me that wanting to be a writer was a foolish thing, especially Iza Vermesi for their enthusiasm and Aude Claret for her fierce support.

Thank you to my sisters Katherine Harding and Sally Brammall for all the love.

Thank you to Andy and Madeline for your encouragement and for the late-night laughter in the kitchen, I'm so glad I got to share a house with you two wonderful weirdos.

And last, but by no means least, thank you to my parents, for letting me live in their attic while I wrote this novel and, more importantly, for gifting me with a lifelong love of story in any and all forms – art, books, film, journalism, theatre, dance, TV – and for always championing me, I will be forever grateful.